THE
BODY
IN THE
BOAT

Also by A. J. MacKenzie

The Body on the Doorstep
The Body in the Ice

THE
BODY
IN THE
BOAT

A. J. MACKENZIE

ZAFFRE

First published in Great Britain in 2018 by
ZAFFRE PUBLISHING
80–81 Wimpole St, London W1G 9RE
www.zaffrebooks.co.uk

A CIP catalogue record for this book is
available from the British Library.

ISBN: 978–1–78576–126–3

also available as an ebook

1 3 5 7 9 10 8 6 4 2

Typeset by IDSUK (Data Connection) Ltd
Printed and bound in Great Britain by Clays Ltd, Elcograf S.p.A.

Zaffre Publishing is an imprint of Bonnier Zaffre,
part of Bonnier Books UK
www.bonnierzaffre.co.uk
www.bonnierbooks.co.uk

To Heather and Mike, with thanks for their unstinting help and support

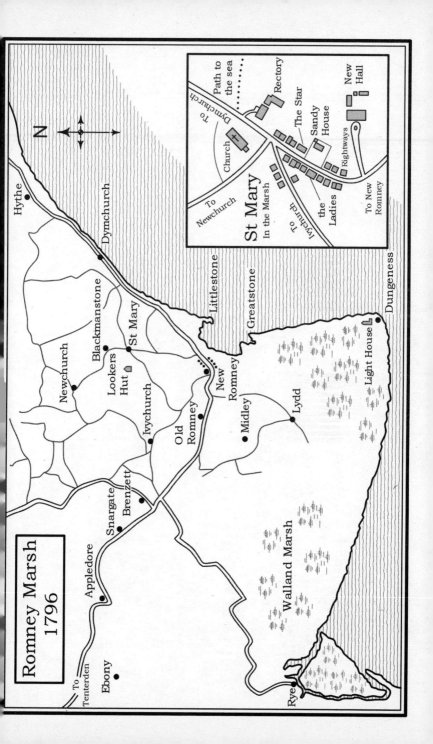

1

Ships in the Night

On a moonless night in high summer, a small boat lay drifting in the English Channel, rising and falling slowly on the long, low swells. A single man sat on the rowing bench, hands resting on the oars. The boat, its oarlocks stuffed with rags to stifle their sound, was almost silent as it glided over the black water. Every so often he dug the oars into the water and rowed a few strokes, keeping the boat on station against the current. Mostly, though, the man simply sat, and waited.

The night sky was clear and beautiful. Stars flamed in their thousands, flickering against the deep blue of midnight. In their midst the Milky Way glowed like the vault of heaven, arching from horizon to horizon. There was no other light save for the faint spark of Dungeness lighthouse, shining four miles to the south. A light wind blew gently from the north, rippling the surface of the water.

The man in the boat paid no attention to the stars. He sat staring east, listening and watching, his attention focused on the dark sea. *They must come soon*, he thought. In a few hours, dawn would arrive, and the cloak of night that hid him and his boat would be dispelled.

In the shadows to the east there was a flicker of movement. The man stirred. He pulled a small spyglass from his coat pocket, raised it to his eye and focused. There, black against the blackness, was a small ship, a cutter creeping along under a single jib. The man puffed out his cheeks and exhaled with relief. *About bloody time*, he thought.

The cutter drew closer. The man in the boat cupped his hands and gave a soft hail. 'Finny! Say voo?'

A moment, and then a voice sounded low over the water from the ship. '*C'est moi, bien sûr. Où êtes-vous?*'

'Heave to. I'll come to you.' He dug in the oars again. A few minutes later the smaller boat was alongside the cutter, hulls bumping together in the long swells.

'Yorkshire Tom,' said a shadowy figure in the cutter. He spoke good English, though with a rasping north French accent. 'It is good to see you, my friend. All is well?'

'All quiet, Finny. Are we on?'

'As agreed, in two days' time. We'll come a little before high tide, as usual. Here are the manifests.'

An oilcloth packet was passed over. Inside it, the man called Yorkshire Tom knew, were lists of the consignments that would be smuggled across the Channel: tubs of gin, casks and bottles of brandy, bolts of silk and lace, chests of tobacco – comforts and luxuries that were heavily taxed in England.

'You have the downpayment, of course,' Finny added.

Yorkshire Tom reached into the boat and pulled out a heavy canvas bag that clinked a little. 'Twenty per cent,' he said, handing the bag across to the cutter, where eager hands grasped it. 'Rest to follow on receipt of the goods.'

'*Bon.* I will inform Le Passeur. The location is the same? St Mary's Bay?'

'Yes. Look for the usual signals.'

'And the Preventive men?'

'The revenue cruiser went down the Channel yesterday. She'll be down Brighton way until next week. We've arranged a distraction for the land guard, but if they do come near us, Clubber will have enough men to deal with them.'

'Then all is well.'

Yorkshire Tom nodded in the dark. 'Le Passeur will be in charge of the boats. What about Bertrand? Will he be there?'

The man called Finny chuckled. 'Bertrand does not want to see you. Does he still owe you the money?'

'He does,' said Yorkshire Tom.

Finny chuckled again. All the smuggling communities on both sides of the Channel knew that Bertrand owed this debt, and why.

'I saw Bertrand's lugger this evening,' said Finny, conversationally. 'He set out from Wimereux just after sunset, shaping a course west. On that heading, I reckon he was making for Dungeness.'

Yorkshire Tom swore. 'What's that blasted lubber up to now?'

'I have no idea. We do not see each other socially.' Finny was from Ambleteuse, while Bertrand was from Wimereux; the French smugglers, just like the English ones, had their local rivalries.

'I must go,' said the Frenchman. 'It will be light soon. *Au revoir*, Tom.'

The man in the boat waved and dug in his oars, pulling away from the cutter. Dim in the darkness he saw her mainsail run up, and then another jib, before she turned, gathering speed, and vanished into the night.

Yorkshire Tom, who also answered to the name of Joshua Stemp, rested on his oars for a moment, thinking about the man called Bertrand. Six months ago, he had helped the Frenchman escape from an English gaol and recover his ship. The price for this had been clearly agreed; but since then, Bertrand had been elusive.

'Dungeness,' Stemp muttered to himself. 'What would that daft French bugger be doing down at Dungeness?' If Bertrand had a new English business partner, Stemp wanted to know who it was. He dug in the oars again and bent his back, turning the boat south and rowing steadily across the quiet, rolling sea.

High above, the stars shimmered in their cold, distant glory. The coast of Romney Marsh lay low to his left; he could just make out the tall tower of New Romney church, dark against the starlight. From time to time he stopped and turned to scan the sea ahead through his spyglass.

An hour passed. The gleam of Dungeness lighthouse was brighter now. Dawn must not be far away. Stemp drew in his oars and turned to look ahead once more, letting the boat drift on the gentle sea. Through the glass he could see a shadow against the stars; a dark rectangle, the lugsail of a ship perhaps half a mile away, crawling over the sea in the light breeze. He stared hard at the sail.

That was not Bertrand's ship. In fact, he was quite certain he had never seen that particular rig before.

Even as he watched, a light flashed from the ship's deck, a lantern briefly uncovered and then covered again. The signal was repeated. Stemp strained his eyes looking for an answering signal from the shore; he saw none. But the ship's captain must have been satisfied, for the sail came down. The lugger drifted on the current now, her bare masts and yards dark lines against the faint sky. Cautiously, Stemp dipped his oars and rowed a little closer.

A new sound came to his ears; the creak and splash of oars from another boat, rowing out from shore. Again Stemp peered through the spyglass, watching a silhouette emerge from the night. He studied the other boat, and then went still. All the boats along this coast were of the same design, with high thwarts and pointed prows, but every one was built by hand and each had its own unique character.

This particular boat belonged to man called Noakes, a boat-man from Hythe. Like Stemp himself, Noakes was a smuggler; but even in that unruly fraternity, he was regarded as a violent and dangerous man. Stemp suspected him of killing at least three men. He focused his spyglass on the man at the oars. *There: that bulky shape, driving the boat over the water with powerful strokes; that surely is Noakes himself.* Instinctively, like a man trying to ward off danger, Stemp crouched lower in the darkness.

The boat moved up alongside the lugger. Voices called quiet greetings. Stemp continued to study the ship. She was broad in the beam, and judging by the way she rolled on the swells, of shallow draught. From the rake of her masts and the angle of her yards, he was certain she was not French. *Dutch, perhaps?* he wondered. He had seen ships out of Rotterdam in the past, and they looked a little like this.

He looked again. There were gaps in her bulwarks too; gun ports. This ship carried cannon.

Something was lowered carefully into Noakes's boat, something long and apparently heavy. In the darkness, Stemp could not see clearly what it was. He watched the silhouettes of the men on deck, talking and gesturing to Noakes. Then the lugger hoisted her sails and turned away east, sailing close to the light wind. Noakes watched her go for a moment, and then began to row again, heading straight back to shore.

Cautiously, keeping to a parallel course, Stemp followed. They were not far from Dungeness now, no more than half a mile, the lighthouse a stone finger rising from the empty wastes around it. And now the night was fading. In the east, pink streaks began to flush the sky, the waves below reflecting patterns of rippling pale and shadow.

Fog began to rise feather-white from the water. In minutes the sunrise and the coast were both out of sight. The lighthouse vanished. Visibility fell to perhaps twenty or thirty yards. Cold and clammy, the fog settled on Stemp. Sweating though he was from his exertions, he still felt the chill bite into him. A gull mewed, its cry muffled in the thick air.

Up ahead more gulls were wailing. Something had disturbed them; Noakes, perhaps, landing his boat. Stemp turned towards the direction of the sound and rowed on, slowly, straining his ears. Now he could hear the sea against the invisible shore, waves breaking with a soft thump, foam hissing on the beach, then the rattle of stones as the receding waves dragged the shingle after them.

Ta-whoom ... sheeeee ... ratta-ratta-ratta-ratta-ratta
Ta-whoom ... sheeeee ... ratta-ratta-ratta-ratta

The beach loomed out of the mist, a steep bank of shingle in front of him. Stemp ran his boat ashore with a grate of keel on stones and climbed out, dragging the boat up onto the beach. His boots crunched with every step. The fog hung like a grey cloak, hiding everything. Still the sea hissed and rattled.

Ta-whoom ... sheeeee ... ratta-ratta-ratta-ratta

Ee-ow! Ow! Ow! Ow! Something hurtled, shrieking, out of the mist and nearly hit Stemp's head before veering off sharply, still wailing in alarm. Stemp started violently, reaching for his knife, before realising it was a gull, lost in the fog like himself. He cursed, then stood working out what to do next.

He thought Noakes might have landed a little way to his left. Slowly, with deliberate steps, he set off down the beach. The wind rose at his back and sent ghostly shapes of fog spinning around him, clutching at him. His heart thudded hard in his chest. He was sweating and cold. The fog reeked of the sea, filling his nostrils. The clumps of sea kale that grew out of the shingle were black in the dull light. *Crunch, crunch, crunch* went his boots, and the sea continued its hissing rhythm, sinister in the fog.

Ta-whoom . . . sheeeee . . . ratta-ratta-ratta-ratta-ratta

A dark shape in the fog ahead, a low lump on the beach. Stemp crouched down, drawing his knife. A gull cried mournfully overhead, setting his stretched nerves still further on edge. He wiped the water from his face and moved forward, crunching. The outlines of the dark shape hardened and he saw Noakes's boat, deserted. Indentations in the shingle showed that the boat's owner had climbed the beach and disappeared inland. Stemp waited for several minutes, listening for any sound of Noakes's return, but beyond the sea and the nerve-shredding cries of the gulls, all was silent.

He walked forward to the boat. He listened again for a moment, then stooped and drew back the canvas cover.

Lying in the bottom of the boat was a coffin.

Tingling with tension, Stemp studied it. The coffin was plain, of dark wood with carrying handles on either side. The lid was securely nailed down, either to protect the body inside or, more likely, to prevent the smells of corruption from escaping. It had been a little damaged; splinters had been knocked out of one corner. *Whose body was inside?* he wondered. *Where did it come from?*

Stemp was not a superstitious man, and the proximity of a corpse would not normally concern him. He had seen the dead before, many times. But here on this lonely fogbound beach, with the sea hissing and rattling and the dark sea kale glowing like devil's eyes against the pale shingle, the hair stood up on the nape of his neck. He drew the cover back over the boat, concealing the coffin, and backed away. His hands were shaking. He no longer cared who the body in the boat was. He only wanted to get away from this place before he was spotted.

Too late. *Crunch, crunch, crunch* came to his ears. Invisible overhead, a gull screamed a warning.

Panicked, Stemp turned and ran back towards his boat; but the thing pursuing him ran faster still, drawing closer and closer, the rattle of shingle louder and louder. Cornered, he wheeled, knife in hand, and out of the fog came an immense shape, its size magnified by the dim light, bounding on four legs across the shingle. It was a mastiff, a huge one, black fur matted with damp, jaws dripping long strings of slaver. When it saw him it skidded to a halt and then stalked forward slowly, hackles raised, eyes mad with violence, growling deep in its throat. Then the dog threw up its head and barked loudly, twice.

Stemp cursed. He stepped backwards, still facing the dog, waiting for it to attack. One leap and it would throw him backwards and pin him, then rip out his throat. More running steps; the dog's master coming in response to its call. Stemp continued to back away, his eyes never leaving the dog, until he bumped against his own boat.

Crunch, crunch, crunch. The running footsteps were only a few yards away. Still watching the dog, Stemp heaved his boat into the water, then scrambled in over the thwarts. The mastiff rushed after him, teeth bared and ready for the kill. Stemp stood up in the boat, an oar in his hand. He flailed at the dog, then pushed the oar against the shingle to drive the boat into deeper water. Balked, the mastiff raged at him, dancing up and down the line of the water, snarling and barking. After him out of the drifting fog came a big man with lank, greasy, dark hair, carrying a knife of his own. His seamed face and broken nose were dark with rage.

'*Yorkshire Tom!* Get back here, you bastard!'

'Go to hell, Noakes,' said Stemp, breathing hard.

Noakes roared at him, baring yellow, gapped teeth. 'What're you doing down here? This ain't your patch!'

'No more is it yours.' Stemp sat down on the bench, slammed the oars into their locks and dug into the water, pulling hard.

'Get back here, I say! Get back here!' The boat was carried further from the beach and Noakes snarled. 'Nah, that's it! Run away, you bloody coward!'

Stemp gritted his teeth and pulled on the oars again.

'I'm coming after you, Tom!' Noakes shouted, slashing the air with his knife. 'I'll finish you, by God I will! I'll cut your heart out, you son of a whore!'

'Go bugger yourself,' said Stemp. It was not the most original insult, but it was all he had energy for. Then the fog swirled again and the beach was hidden from view, and all he could hear was the complaint of the gulls and the mad snarl of the dog. Weary with relief, he turned the boat north towards home.

2

Magpie Court

Clouds scudded across the sky, flinging the odd splatter of showery rain against the windows of the rectory of St Mary in the Marsh. Between the showers, the sun shone brightly off the bridle of the horse waiting patiently outside the door. Inside, much less patiently, the Reverend Marcus Aurelius Hardcastle, rector of St Mary, shouted once more for his sister to come downstairs – as quickly as may be, if you please! – so they could finally depart.

At last Calpurnia Vane came wafting down the stairs, smelling of violets, dressed as if for a London salon and trailing scarves. 'You had best take a coat,' the rector said. 'Those scarves won't keep out the rain when it comes. And it will.'

'Oh, Marcus, don't be such a bear.' A widow, Calpurnia had moved into the rectory last year, ostensibly to find a more congenial atmosphere in which to write, but in reality, the rector believed, to annoy him.

'You will enjoy the party once you are there,' she said firmly. 'You know you love music. No, no, Rodolpho, you cannot come with us.'

This last remark was aimed at a very large, very shaggy wolfhound who was making ready to jump into the dog cart. Hardcastle thought seriously of offering up his place to the dog, then with weary resignation, handed his sister up to the seat and climbed up beside her, taking the reins.

They travelled the ten miles from St Mary up to Shadoxhurst, above Romney Marsh in the rolling woodlands near Ashford. Hardcastle drove as quickly as the horse and his own skills would allow, trying to block out the sound of Calpurnia's voice as she discussed the private lives of most of those coming to the party, before turning to how she would work them into the plot of her next novel. Just before reaching the village, they turned onto a short avenue and came finally to their destination.

Magpie Court had been built five centuries ago, and added to progressively ever since. As a result, the house was a cheerful jumble of stone, brick and half-timber, with spiral chimneys and tall windows. A range of barns ran to one side, balanced by a walled garden on the other. A big, solidly built man with a pleasant smiling face in a blue coat, fawn breeches and a flamboyant red and gold brocade waistcoat came out of the house and bowed in greeting.

'Reverend, how very good of you to come. And Mrs Vane, what a pleasure it is to welcome you.'

'The pleasure is entirely ours, Mr Munro,' said Hardcastle. Annoyingly, Calpurnia was right; he was starting to look forward to this evening. The owner of Magpie Court, Frederick Maudsley, the local justice of the peace, was an old friend; most years, Hardcastle came to stay for a few days in winter for the shooting. Hector Munro was his son-in-law. 'And how is the birthday girl?'

Before Munro could answer, there came the sound of hooves and wheels travelling fast, and an elegant little gig came racing up the drive towards the house. Hardcastle did not need to look at the gig to know that the driver was a woman, or that the groom sitting on the bench beside her was white-faced and clinging on for dear life.

The gig pulled up beside them, the house grooms coming to take both horses and rigs. 'Welcome, Mrs Chaytor,' said Munro to the driver. 'I say, that's a splendid little mare you have there. Does she run?'

'No,' said Mrs Chaytor, the driver of the gig, smiling and patting the horse on the flank. 'She flies. She is called Asia; I bought her last month in Tenterden. I am very proud of her.'

'And you are now more likely than ever to break your neck in a driving accident,' the rector said to her. He and Mrs Chaytor were near neighbours in St Mary, and friends. She smiled at him, and then took the arm Munro offered as they passed into the house. Hardcastle and Calpurnia followed, he ignoring the meaningful looks cast at him by his sister.

'I must thank you again for all your help in arranging the music for my dear wife's birthday,' said Munro to his companion.

'It was nothing,' said Mrs Chaytor. 'The summer season always brings the best musicians out of London to escape the heat. I knew Mr Salomon and his orchestra were in Kent, and Mrs Mara too, and it was a simple matter to write to them. And it is good to do something for Cecilia, after all her kindnesses to me.'

'And here she is,' said Munro. 'Now, not a word, any of you, about the music. It is a surprise.'

A small, pretty woman with a fine-featured face, plumply pregnant in a long, loose-flowing robe, came up and took Mrs Chaytor's hands. 'Oh, my dear Amelia! How simply splendid to see you! And Reverend Hardcastle, and Mrs Vane! My darling Hector has invited all of my dearest friends! Oh, I am quite over-whelmed.'

'Happy birthday, my dear,' said Hardcastle, smiling. He was very fond of Cecilia Munro; everyone was. Her husband watched her proudly. Hardcastle did not know him well, but approved of what he knew. Like his father-in-law, Maudsley, Munro was a partner in the local East Weald and Ashford Bank, and seemed solid and reliable. There was no doubt that he adored his wife.

They passed into the hall, already crowded with people. One of the oldest parts of the building, it was normally rather gloomy, but today it was bright with garlands and bunting and masses of late-blooming flowers. Frederick Maudsley came through the press, bluff and cheerful as ever, bowing to the ladies and clapping Hardcastle on the shoulder. 'How are you, old fellow? Capital to see you, as always. Come and have a drink.'

'A small glass,' said Hardcastle.

Maudsley turned to look for a servant. Calpurnia had already been swallowed up by a little group of women, and Hardcastle could hear her talking about her latest book. He looked at Mrs Chaytor. 'It was good of you to come,' he said.

She seldom accepted social invitations of any kind, especially formal ones. 'I could not refuse her invitation,' said Mrs Chaytor. 'I spoke truly about her kindnesses. Why did you come?'

'Calpurnia insisted. It was a case of anything for a quiet life.'

She smiled. 'Hector has worked very hard,' she said. 'Most of the district seems to have turned out. Indeed, there is Edward Austen.'

'Austen?' The rector peered across the room. 'I've not seen him for ages.'

'That is unsurprising. He has a young family, an estate to run and his duties as a captain of Volunteers; I do not expect he has much time to call his own. The lady with him must be his wife. If you will forgive me, I must go and be introduced to her.'

'I don't expect she gets out much either,' the rector said.

She was right about the turnout; there were fifty people or more in the hall and drawing room, a fine testament to the regard people had for Cecilia Munro. The rain was clearing away now, and the tall windows had been opened to take advantage of the afternoon sunshine. Let us hope they remain open during the performance, Hardcastle thought; otherwise the players may have to overcome the sounds of snoring from some of the audience. Not all the company looked as if they appreciated fine music as much as their hostess did.

A servant brought him a glass of punch. Freddie Woodford, rector of Ashford and an old friend, hailed him. 'Hardcastle, old fellow! Come and join us. Gentlemen, this old reprobate you see before you is the Reverend Marcus Hardcastle, rector of St Mary and a justice of the peace in Romney Marsh.'

'Temporary justice of the peace,' Hardcastle corrected. 'I took on the post as a favour for Lord Clavertye after Fanscombe's . . . untimely departure last summer. I'm still waiting for him to find a permanent replacement.'

'You may be waiting a while,' said Woodford. 'Too good at your job, old fellow, that's the problem. Do you know everyone here? This is Cranthorpe, our solicitor in Ashford, and this young dandy is Ricardo, down from London.'

'I imagine that between the smugglers and the French spies, being a JP on Romney Marsh is a busy occupation,' said Ricardo. He was hardly a dandy; his dress was sober, though expensive.

'At present, the spies seem to be more numerous than the smugglers,' said Hardcastle. 'Much of my time over the past year has been spent chasing spies and rumours of spies. I fear our proximity to the French shore makes them overly bold. As for the smugglers, I leave them alone and they leave me alone.'

They all turned as Hector Munro joined them. 'Ah, here he is,' said Cranthorpe. He was a big, bluff man in his early forties, both face and paunch showing signs of high living. 'The very model of uxoriousness! Surely now, Munro, you have made a rod for the back of every husband in the district. We shall all have to work very hard to impress our own wives in future.'

The others agreed. 'Aye, that's your lookout,' said Munro in his soft Edinburgh accent. 'There's no man alive will prevent me from spoiling my dear wife if I choose. So, gentlemen, what is the news? Has anything more been heard from Lille?'

The entire county, indeed the entire country, was hanging on events in Lille across the water in France, where the British

diplomat Lord Malmesbury was meeting with French negoti-
ators, hoping to bring the four-year war to an end. 'Do any of
us think his lordship will meet with much luck in Lille?' asked
Hardcastle. 'I certainly hope so. I for one should like to be able
to gaze out to sea without expecting to see a French armada on
the horizon.'

The stockbroker, Ricardo, responded with a wry laugh. 'Even
if he returns with peace treaty in hand, the government will have
to hope that the French also cease stirring up trouble in Ireland,
if we are to see any real peace. The Irish and other troublemakers
with revolutionary sympathies were certainly behind the muti-
nies in the navy last spring, at Spithead and the Nore. And all
this uncertainty about French intentions is making for jitters in
the market.'

'Ah, but uncertainty also makes for good profits in the market,
does it not?' asked Munro, smiling. 'A financial genius such as
yourself should look on these events as an opportunity.'

Ricardo bowed. 'Those who have the right contacts and
sources of news will do well, perhaps,' he said, smiling in return.
'But what of the banks? They don't like uncertainty either. They
are so rattled they are issuing paper £1 banknotes instead of gold
sovereigns. Is it true that your own bank has begun to do so,
Munro?'

'Small-value paper money is more convenient than coin,'
said Munro. 'The banks will get used to it, and so will the country. And now, Ricardo, let us stop boring my guests with talk of
banking. Is anyone going to the races at Canterbury next week?'

'Austen. Very good to see you. And you too, Mrs Austen.' Tall
and aristocratic, wigged and elegant in a fashionably cut coat
and breeches, the speaker bowed.

'Mr Faversham,' said Edward Austen. He was a tall man in
his late twenties, with a cheerful face and an air of reliability.

His voice was not exactly full of enthusiasm. The three of them, Austen, his wife Elizabeth and Mrs Chaytor, had been having a cosy chat about the time, years ago, when Austen had called on Mrs Chaytor and her husband in Paris. Mrs Chaytor had been recounting some of his exploits that summer, to the amusement of his wife.

'May I present Mrs Chaytor, from St Mary in the Marsh?' said Austen.

'Charles Faversham,' said the other man, bowing again. He had an affected voice of a kind Mrs Chaytor knew well, and disliked; his name came out as *Chawles Fevashem*. 'An honour to meet you, ma'am. May I present my wife, Anne? My son Grebell; my daughter Charlotte. And this is Mr Stone, from London.'

'And what do you do in London, Mr Stone?' asked Mrs Austen.

'I am a banker, ma'am, with Martin, Stone and Foote,' said Stone. He was young and keen, very smartly dressed. The same could not be said for Grebell Faversham; he had red hair and slightly protuberant brown eyes, and wore a purple brocade coat that Mrs Chaytor thought one of the most vulgar things she had seen in some time.

'I very much fear, ladies, that you have fallen among bankers,' said Faversham, smiling. 'I too am in the profession, as is my son.'

'I would expect little else in Mr Maudsley's house, when both he and his son-in-law are also bankers,' said Mrs Chaytor, smiling in return. 'And on the subject of money, how is the Restriction Act affecting your business?'

There was a short silence as the men reacted to her question. Charles Faversham blinked; his son simply stared at her. George Stone recovered first.

'We are managing to work within the confines of the new laws,' he said. 'We trust that the restriction will not be of prolonged duration.'

'For your sake, gentlemen, I hope so. The currency is no longer backed by gold. This must be affecting confidence, in the markets and among the populace.'

'Oh, indeed, ma'am,' said Charles Faversham. 'But these little ups and downs are all part of the everyday world of business for we men of money. The modern bank is designed to withstand such vagaries. You may be assured that the banks will weather this storm, as they have weathered many others.'

'Truly it is remarkable to find a lady such as yourself interested in business and banking,' said Grebell. He was still staring at her. He was in his mid-twenties, only a half-dozen years her junior, but he seemed younger.

'Perhaps your husband or father was in banking?' he asked.

'No,' Mrs Chaytor said. 'But I do think it desirable to understand the institutions who control our money. You hold the future prosperity of your clients in your hands.'

Grebell looked at her even more intently. His father had turned away and was talking to Austen; his mother was chatting with Mrs Austen about her latest baby. 'You are right,' the young man said. 'Ma'am, I feel sure that your opinions on such matters would be valuable to a man of business such as myself. Would you be so kind as to allow me—'

He got no further before he was interrupted by his sister, an effervescent young woman with red hair and sparkling eyes and what seemed to be an extraordinary number of teeth. Mrs Chaytor got the impression that she was used to interrupting her older brother. 'Oh, ma'am, you come from St Mary in the Marsh; do you know the famous authoress, Cordelia Hartbourne?'

This was Calpurnia Vane's nom de plume. 'I know her very well,' said Mrs Chaytor. 'Indeed, she is here tonight.'

'Oh, Mrs Chaytor! I simply adore her books. I would be so honoured if you felt able to introduce me to her.'

Mrs Chaytor smiled. 'I should be delighted to do so. But perhaps at the interval? I see the musicians are coming in.'

The musicians were indeed coming in, a dozen of them led by Johann Peter Salomon, the doyen of orchestral conductors in London, and with them a tall woman in a dark gown and headdress of swan's feathers, the renowned German soprano Elisabeth Mara. Silence fell around the room. Cecilia Munro sat in a chair, her eyes enormous and round with astonishment, one hand resting on her belly, the other clapped to her open mouth.

Hector Munro came to stand beside her, smiling down at her. 'My dear wife is aptly named,' he said. 'Cecilia, the patron saint of music, has clearly touched her, for music is her great love . . . though I very much hope that I can at least claim second place in her affections,' he added, to laughter in the room. 'As you know, in her condition she cannot travel to hear the music she loves. So, with the aid of a few affectionate friends,' and his eye fell on Mrs Chaytor, 'we have brought the music to her.'

Applause, and Salomon lifted his baton and the music began. They played Handel and Purcell and Arne, the music flowing like a soft river through the room, sweeping them all along. Hardcastle's fears were unfounded; country solicitors and clerks and yeomen and their wives the guests might mostly be, but they sat straight in their chairs and listened, absorbed. And when Elisabeth Mara sang, in a voice of pure liquid gold, holding each note and letting it sigh into the flower-scented air, they held their breath. The applause at the interval was rapturous.

Outside the light was dimming a little; the servants were lighting candles, and little sparkling points of flame blossomed among the flowers around the room. Nervous and excited, Miss Charlotte Faversham was duly introduced to her heroine.

Mrs Chaytor left Charlotte and Calpurnia to talk of the delights of the Gothic novel, and moved to join Hardcastle beside the terrace doors.

There was another man with him. 'Mrs Chaytor, may I present to you Mr Ricardo, from London?'

'Your servant, ma'am.' Ricardo bowed gracefully. He was a likeable young man, immensely self-possessed in a way that young Mr Faversham could only dream of, she thought. *This one has confidence; the other merely has bumptiousness.*

'And how was London when you left, Mr Ricardo?'

'Hot and humid, ma'am. My wife and I were grateful for the excuse to leave.'

'Are you staying with Mr Maudsley?' asked Hardcastle.

'No; with relations of my wife, who have a house near Canterbury. And yourself, Mrs Chaytor?'

'I live close by, in Romney Marsh. I am one of Reverend Hardcastle's parishioners. What is your connection with the Munros, Mr Ricardo?'

'I've known Mr Munro for some time, since before he came down from Edinburgh. And the East Weald and Ashford Bank have recently become one of my clients. Thanks to Mr Munro, I have been appointed the bank's stockbroker.'

'Oh,' said Mrs Chaytor. She peered at him. 'You don't much look like a stockbroker.'

'You mean, I don't have port wine cheeks and a chequered waistcoat?' said Ricardo, smiling. 'Perhaps with time these things will come to me, but I am relatively new to the business.'

'Then you must have considerable skill,' observed Hardcastle. 'The bank is unlikely to have entrusted you with its affairs, unless it was certain of your abilities.'

Ricardo bowed. 'You are kind, sir. I have some years of experience working with my father; I meant to say that I have only recently struck out on my own. But I am sure neither of you is remotely interested in talking about finance.'

'You would be surprised to learn what interests Reverend Hardcastle,' said Mrs Chaytor. 'And how do you find the East Weald and Ashford Bank? Are they not a little provincial, after the excitement and hurly-burly of the City?'

'I don't mind provincial things,' said Ricardo. 'I actually quite like the quiet life.' He paused for a moment. 'Tell me, if you will. Are either of you clients of the East Weald and Ashford?'

'No, not I,' said Hardcastle. 'I bank with Hoare's.'

'So do we all,' said Mrs Chaytor, 'but very few of us ever realise it.'

Both men looked at her. She smiled benignly back. 'My affairs also are in London. Why do you ask, Mr Ricardo?'

'It is of no great matter,' said Ricardo, still looking at her wryly. 'I was merely curious to meet some clients of my clients, if you take my meaning. It is of no account. What do you make of the music? I must say, Madame Mara is in fine voice this evening.'

Dr Mackay, physician of New Romney, made his way through the press of people looking for interval refreshment. Conversation and laughter washed around him in the candlelight. He scanned the crowd, looking for the one person who mattered to him.

He found her, for once on her own, by the windows where the soft evening air flowed in from the terrace. 'Good evening to you, Mrs Vane,' he said in his soft Scots accent, bowing.

'Why, good evening, doctor! I have been having such a delightful talk with young Miss Faversham. So wonderful to meet one's readers, and know that one has touched their lives. This is a very pleasant soirée, is it not? Such a fine house, and such distinguished company.'

'And the music is splendid,' said the doctor.

'Oh, it is simply heavenly. Mr Salomon's orchestra is reputed to be the finest in London.'

'They are living up to their reputation,' agreed the doctor. He hesitated for a moment. 'May I be so bold as to congratulate you, ma'am, on the success of your latest novel? I am told *The Lighthouse of Vavassal* has become the most talked-about book in Town.'

Calpurnia beamed at him. 'Dear doctor, you are too kind. My little tale has been fortunate to enjoy some modest success. It has not quite achieved the fame of my first book, *Rodolpho, A Tale of Love and Liberty*, but nevertheless, I am pleased. Have you read it?'

Mackay flushed. 'I . . . I confess I have not. I'm not really a—'

'Then I shall send you a copy as soon as I return home. Inscribed to you personally, of course. And you must tell me what you think of it.'

The doctor bowed. 'And are you writing another novel, ma'am?'

'Why, yes. It is to be called *The Cardinal's Jewels*. It is a tale of lust, greed and revenge, set in Rome. There is a great deal of popery in it, but I trust my readers will understand that with any story set in Rome, popery is something of a necessity.' She launched at once into a description of the plot. The doctor listened, his face a mixture of admiration and mild horror.

'It sounds . . . fascinating,' he said at the end. 'You are clever, ma'am, to think of such stories.'

'Oh, stories come naturally to me. I am a teller of tales, Dr Mackay; I am a spinner of dreams, a weaver of mysteries.' Her hands made motions vaguely akin to spinning and weaving in the air. 'We are alike in some ways, doctor. You deal with the physical realm, while I work in the realm of the mind; you heal the sick and make their bodies healthy and whole once again, while I elevate their senses and stir their imaginations. But our purpose is the same.'

'You have the advantage of me, ma'am,' said the doctor after a while.

'We both make people happy, doctor,' she said, beaming at him. 'Don't you see?'

He did not see; but for the sake of that smile, he was prepared to pretend. He bowed again.

On the far side of the room, Mrs Chaytor turned to see Grebell Faversham approaching. Her heart sank. 'Good evening once more, Mrs Chaytor,' said Grebell. 'I am sure that to your sophisticated eyes our little country parties must seem simple and homely. You must be used to much greater events than this.'

'On the contrary, Mr Faversham, the music this evening has been of the highest quality. And unlike London, the room has been comfortable for all, and not so stuffy as many London soirées can be.'

'To be sure, to be sure,' said Grebell. 'I myself often find the press of people in London to be overwhelming.' He paused, his face going pink. 'But you must find Romney Marsh very empty, after London and Paris and Rome.'

He had clearly been making enquiries about her during the evening, she thought with displeasure. 'But the Marsh appears to agree with you,' he said.

'Thank you. Yes, Romney air is very wholesome. So far this year, only a few people have died of marsh fever.'

'Ah. Ah . . . yes. We are blessed in Rye. Up on our hill, we are safe from the marsh miasma. Rye is quite a delightful place. Do you know it well?'

'I know it a little.'

'You must call on us, next time you are there,' he said, his blush deepening. 'I know that my mother would be delighted to receive you.'

'Thank you, sir. You are kind.'

'You are most welcome. Meanwhile, Mrs Chaytor, I wonder . . .'

His voice trailed off. 'Wonder what, Mr Faversham?' she prompted.

'I wonder if I might be permitted to advance a small hope? Should there be dancing after, would you be willing to partner me?'

She turned her head then and looked directly at him. He is nowhere near as handsome as he would like to think he is, she thought.

'I do not dance,' she said.

'Really? I cannot imagine why a lady of such grace and elegance as yourself does not dance.'

'I have not danced since my husband died,' she said. 'Forgive me, sir, but I must go and thank our host and hostess for the wonderful music.'

To the rector's relief, the music and supper had ended with no dancing. He had arranged with Mrs Chaytor to drive back together to St Mary in the Marsh, on condition that she kept Asia to an easy pace so he could keep up with her. While Mrs Chaytor and Calpurnia were making their goodbyes to Cecilia, he stepped outside to wait for the carriages to be brought round.

The long summer evening was clear, with a sky turning to deep blue. Long shadows stretched from the house across the garden. He stood still, and drank in the silence for a few moments.

The silence was broken by voices from inside the house. 'You are still determined to go?' he heard Maudsley ask.

'You know I must.' The second voice was that of Hector Munro. 'There's no choice.'

'I don't like this. I have never liked it, right from the beginning. There must be another way.'

'No, Frederick. We cannot carry on like this. We must find out what is happening.'

'Then send someone else. It need not be you.'

'We don't know who we can trust in this business. You know that too. If I thought I could trust anyone, I might approach Hardcastle . . . But no, I must attend to this myself.'

Unwilling to be an eavesdropper, the rector had been turning to go, but at the sound of his own name he stopped.

'I want to make sure this whole affair is kept absolutely quiet,' Munro was saying. 'And speaking of keeping things quiet, what is Stone doing here? I nearly jumped out of my skin when I saw him.'

'I invited him. It seemed the polite thing to do.'

'Are you mad? What if he learns something? My God, if the Grasshopper finds out what we're up to, there'll be hell to pay!'

'The Grasshopper won't find out. Stone is a good fellow, but he is not the most perspicacious of men. Hector, I beg you. Think of Cecilia.'

'I think of very little else.' There was a tender note in Munro's voice. 'Frederick, all will be well. Men make this journey all the time.'

'Then you are resolved,' said Maudsley. His voice had gone quiet. 'There is nothing I can say that will sway you?'

'Nothing whatever. Father-in-law, I understand your fears. Put them away. I'll not be gone for long.'

'When will you go?'

'There are a few things I must attend to first.' The two men moved away then, and their voices faded and became inaudible.

3

The Absence of Hope

Dawn broke over Romney Marsh. Church towers rose like stone fingers against the skyline. Light washed over the flat open fields, brilliant in the clear light. Sheep bleated softly in their pastures, watched by sleepy shepherds. Ducks quacked among the reeds that fringed the sewers, the network of drains holding back the waters that threatened to reclaim the Marsh. In the distance the green hills of Kent rose, a wall sealing off the Marsh from the rest of the world.

Out of the sunrise came a young man, running. He wore rough fishermen's clothes and a battered hat, and had long hair flowing down over his shoulders. His face was red and perspiring, for the morning was already warm, and his eyes were wide and shocked. Reaching the village of St Mary in the Marsh, a mile from the sea, he hastened down the village street. Finding the cottage he was looking for, he knocked hard at the door.

The knock brought Joshua Stemp awake in a moment. He sat up quickly in bed. Maisie, his wife, was still asleep beside him, and so were their two daughters. He slid out of bed and went through the little cottage to the door, picking up his fisherman's knife as he did so. Two weeks had passed since the encounter with Noakes and there had been no trouble, but Stemp was still uneasy.

'Who's there?' he hissed.

'It's Florian Tydde, Josh. You'd better come out. There's trouble down by the water.'

Relief, of sorts. 'I'll be out directly.' Stemp pulled on his clothes and tucked his knife into its sheath, then unbolted the door and stepped out into the bright, glowing morning. Seen in daylight, he was a short man with dark hair and cheeks scarred by smallpox. He stared at the fisherman, who was still breathing hard from his run. 'Well?'

'Sorry to disturb you, Josh. But you need to see this, you being parish constable and all.'

They started to walk towards the sea, the wind hissing over the flat fields around them. 'Tell me what's happened.'

'My brother Eb and I were out fishing last night. Come dawn, we saw a boat drifting. Then it got a little lighter and we could see more clearly, and Eb says, ain't that Jem Clay's boat? You know Jem. He lives nearby to us, in New Romney.'

'I know him well.' New Romney was only a couple of miles away; the fishermen and smugglers of New Romney and St Mary were often friends and allies.

'Well, we thought first he was out fishing like ourselves. But then we realised the boat was empty, or it seemed to be, so we reckoned it must have come loose from its moorings. And then Eb says, look at the gulls circling round. What do you reckon is drawing them?' Tydde swallowed. 'It's ugly, Josh.'

Stemp looked at him sharply. 'Is it Jem?'

'No. We've never seen this fellow before. He's dressed like a gent, too.'

They climbed the rear slope of the dunes that fronted the sea and then slithered down to the beach. It was a little past high tide. They walked out across the short, wet strand to the boat, beached in the gentle surf. Another man waited here, armed with an oar to ward off the gulls who were still intent on their feast. Ebenezer Tydde, more stoic than his brother, nodded to Stemp. 'Nasty, this.'

It was more than nasty. Joshua Stemp was a hard man, but when he looked into the boat, even he felt a little queasy. The body of a man lay sprawled on its back across the rowing bench. The eyes were gone, plucked out by the greedy birds, and the soft flesh of the cheeks had been ripped away, exposing bone and teeth. The birds had been at the man's throat, too, and the backs of his hands had been pecked to rags.

The floor of the boat was full, a reddish mixture of salt water and blood. The front of the man's waistcoat was soaked with blood, too, beginning to dry in the sun. In the middle of the waistcoat was a round hole, crusted with black.

'God damn,' said Joshua Stemp quietly, and the words might have been an invocation or they might have been a curse. He straightened and turned to the two fishermen. 'All right, Eb, Florian. Get the boat up onto dry ground and stand over it. Keep those bloody birds off him, and don't let anyone else come near. I'll fetch the rector.'

By the time Stemp returned with Hardcastle forty-five minutes later, the sun was well up. The gulls had settled down, resting on the water or stalking along the beach, eyeing the boat with single-minded determination and waiting for the men to leave so they could resume their meal. The Tydde brothers sat on the thwarts, smoking pipes, their backs to the body. They stood up as the rector approached.

'You're the men who found the boat?'

'Yes, reverend,' said Ebenezer.

'Tell me what happened.' They recounted their story again while he watched their faces. He knew them by sight only; they were Ebenezer and Florian Tydde, the sons of old George Tydde of New Romney.

'You've not touched the body?' asked the rector.

'No, reverend.' Florian shuddered a little. 'Didn't fancy handling him, not at all.'

The rector approached the boat and gazed at the ravaged body, bending down to inspect the wound more closely. The bloody hole was nearly an inch in diameter; the weapon must have been of large calibre, a heavy pistol or perhaps an army musket.

He straightened. 'While you were fishing last night, did you see any other ships or boats? Any other vessel at all?'

The Tyddes shook their heads. 'And did you hear anything? Any sound that might have been a gunshot?'

'No, reverend,' said Florian regretfully. He had the air of a man who wanted to be helpful, and was disappointed that he could not be so.

The rector nodded and bent over the corpse again. There was too little left of the face to allow for recognition. Carefully, he began to go through the pockets, beginning with the blood-stained waistcoat. Here he found a watch, glinting gold when he pulled it out and held it up to the light. It was a fine piece, with a London maker's name on the case. That was good news; the watchmaker could probably help him trace the owner.

In one outer coat pocket there was a small pistol, plain and unadorned with a proofmark engraved on the barrel; Hardcastle recognised the mark as that of a London gunsmith. He thumbed back the cover of the pan and saw the priming powder; the pistol had not been fired. An inside pocket yielded coins – several shillings and some small change – and a notecase containing six of the East Weald and Ashford Bank's new £1 banknotes.

The rector straightened, and as he did so a glint of metal in the bottom of the boat caught his eye. He reached down into the blood and brine and pulled out a coin, a bright gold guinea. How it had come to be there was impossible to say; fallen from the man's pocket when he was shot, perhaps? He laid the guinea down on the thwart beside the watch.

There was a small valise resting in the bow of the boat. The rector wiped the bloody water from his fingers, then lifted the valise out onto the grass and opened it. A couple of changes of clothes, a hairbrush and clothes brush, a small writing case; a man of affairs, perhaps?

The writing case had an engraved nameplate on the front. He picked it up and read the name, and stood suddenly very still.

HECTOR MUNRO, ESQ.

Slowly, Hardcastle turned to look at the body in the boat once more. The face had been obliterated, but he should have recognised that big, broad-shouldered figure. The watch would confirm the dead man's identity, of course; but he knew he was looking at the body of Hector Munro. Maudsley's son-in-law. Cecilia's husband, father of the child still in her womb.

He remembered the quiet confidence of that overheard voice. *Nothing will happen to me. Men make this journey all the time.* He closed his eyes and uttered a silent prayer, wishing God's protection for Hector Munro as he made his last journey of all.

'Bad news, reverend?' said Stemp.

'It could not be much worse,' said Hardcastle.

Dr Mackay arrived soon after from New Romney. The stocky middle-aged Scot had seen much worse than this in the course of his duties as assistant coroner; he clucked his tongue at the sight of the dead man's face, and then examined the body with brisk care. He looked shocked when Hardcastle told him who the dead man was.

'Aye, now you say it, I can see it's him. But what the devil was he doing here?'

'That is what I am asking myself. I assume the cause of death to be the gunshot wound?'

'I can see no sign of other injuries. Of course, I'll only know for certain when I get him on a table. Rigor mortis is not fully advanced; mind, last night was a cool one. If you're wanting a time of death, sometime between midnight and four in the morning would be my estimate.'

'By then the tide was coming in,' said Stemp. 'That would have carried the boat back in towards the beach. Good thing the boys found him when they did. The tide's been going back out since dawn. If the boat had drifted back out to sea and got caught in the mid-Channel current, we might not have found it 'til doomsday.'

Hardcastle nodded. 'Find Jem Clay. Ask if he knows how his boat came to be here. Ask around among the other fishermen too; they might have seen something. And check with Mrs Spicer at the Ship, and also the New Inn and the rooming houses. If he drove down from Shadoxhurst, he'll have left a horse and rig somewhere.'

The parish constable nodded. New Romney was outside his patch, but he knew the Romney constable well; they often worked together. 'What'll you do, reverend?'

'I must inform the family,' said Hardcastle.

'Do go gently with Mrs Munro,' warned the doctor. 'She is near her time. She is under my care, so I shall come up and see her when I am finished here.'

'Magpie Court is rather outside your usual area, is it not?' Hardcastle asked.

'Mrs Munro found the doctor in Ashford was not very sympathetic to women in her condition. Knowing that obstetrics is a particular interest of mine, she asked for me instead. Tell her I will be there as soon as I can.'

As soon as I have learned for certain how her husband died, was the unspoken thought. Hardcastle nodded, looked once more at the ravaged remains of Hector Munro and turned away towards the village.

Rumour on Romney Marsh sped faster than the wind. By the time Hardcastle returned to St Mary, the village was stirring. Heads turned as he walked down the street, and several people called to him, anxious, asking for news. He prevaricated: a body had been found; it was not known who it was, but it did not appear to be a local man. That reassured them; relief turned instead to curiosity.

He knocked at the door of Sandy House, Amelia Chaytor's home. Lucy the housekeeper admitted him and showed him into the morning room where Mrs Chaytor sat drinking strong, sweet black coffee. 'I am sorry to intrude on you so early,' he said, bowing.

'Not at all. Like you, I rise with the larks. What has happened?'

She could see most of it in his face; he told her the rest. 'This is a dreadful imposition, I know, but will you come with me? Cecilia Munro is the only woman in the house apart from the servants and her young sisters. I would like someone to be with her when we break the news.'

He meant *someone strong*. 'Of course. I shall go and change. Lucy! Call Joseph and tell him to harness Asia and bring the gig round at once.'

Ten minutes later they were away, the gig racing across the flat lands of the Marsh towards Newchurch, the green hills rising steeply beyond. They were silent, Mrs Chaytor concentrating on her driving, the rector holding on to his seat. The day was brilliant and clear, the sky a flawless blue, but the brightness of high summer was beginning to fade a little; today was the 11th of August, summer just beginning its long curve into autumn. *The 11th*, thought the rector. We were at Magpie Court only four days ago, listening to Elisabeth Mara sing. Hector was so happy, so proud of his little wife bubbling with expectant joy.

We don't know who we can trust in this business, Munro had said later. And then, *There's no choice. I must attend to this myself.*

They reached Ruckinge and slowed to walk up the long hill into the Weald. Trees closed in along the road, their branches intermingling overhead, dark and rustling. There were few trees on Romney Marsh, and after that wide, flat land open to the sky, this rolling wooded country felt enclosed, almost claustrophobic. It is odd, thought the rector, how in seven years the Marsh has begun to feel like home, and I am uncomfortable anywhere else. I must be getting old . . .

'Penny for your thoughts,' said Mrs Chaytor.

The rector shook himself out of his reverie. 'I imagine you can guess. How did Hector Munro end up in a boat in the Channel? And who killed him there, and why?'

'Did he die in the boat?' she asked. 'Or was he killed somewhere else, and his body put in the boat and left to drift?'

He thought about this. 'It's a good point. Stemp says that if the boat had been dragged back out by the tide, it might never have been seen again. Perhaps someone wanted Munro to disappear completely.'

'It is hard to know which is worse,' she said quietly.

'What do you mean?'

'For his wife and family. Which is worse: to know what has happened to one's loved one, or never to know, and always wonder if he will return? To have vain hope, or no hope at all?'

He was silent at this. A cuckoo called from the woods. 'Have you any ideas?' she asked.

'Some . . . By chance, when we were at Magpie Court the other evening, I overheard part of a conversation between Munro and Maudsley. Munro spoke of going away on business. Maudsley tried to dissuade him, saying it was too dangerous.'

'Ah. Any idea what that business might be?'

'None, I am afraid . . . No, that is not quite true. Munro mentioned the Grasshopper. If the Grasshopper finds out, he said, there will be hell to pay.'

'The Grasshopper? Meaning the bank?'

'I assume so.' For reasons that were lost in antiquity, the London merchant bank of Martin, Stone and Foote was universally known as the Grasshopper. 'I assume further that there is some sort of connection between that bank and the East Weald and Ashford, and that the latter are involved in something they do not wish the Grasshopper to know about.'

Mrs Chaytor thought for a moment. 'Mr Stone from the Grasshopper was at the soirée at Magpie Court, and seemed on good terms with Mr Faversham and Mr Munro. But I don't suppose that is terribly surprising. Banking is a shadowy business. I'm sure the Grasshopper has its secrets too.'

'That may be so. But there was an urgency to the conversation that made me think they were discussing more than just a straightforward business relationship.'

'Hmm,' said Mrs Chaytor. She paused for a moment. 'While we are speaking of the East Weald and Ashford Bank, may I raise another matter with you? Yesterday I had a rather odd conversation with Miss Godfrey and Miss Roper.'

'Does one have any other kind of conversation with them?'

'Tut-tut. They are your most loyal parishioners. No, they asked, in a most elliptical way, the same question Mr Ricardo asked; that is, whether I had any of my money with the East Weald and Ashford.'

'Don't tell me they too are thinking of taking up stockbroking.'

'I wouldn't put it past either of them. To be serious, they are rather concerned. You will recall that the husband of Miss Roper's niece is a senior clerk with the East India Company in London. The niece, in her last letter to Miss Roper, made an allusion to the health of country banks, such as the East Weald and Ashford. Miss Roper in particular was all aflutter. It transpires that they have virtually all their money with the bank. Should it go down, they would be destitute.'

They were trotting on towards Shadoxhurst now, the morning heat rising around them. The rector wiped his brow. 'If I understood correctly, Munro and Maudsley were discussing some sort of deal that had gone wrong. Whatever that is, I very much doubt the bank itself is at risk. The East Weald and Ashford is one of the largest and best-funded country banks in England; and they are partnered with the Grasshopper, the most powerful merchant bank in London. I cannot imagine the ladies have anything to fear.'

'It would be a kindness if you would tell them so. They trust you.'

'I know, and thank you for informing me. I shall try to find a way of reassuring them.' Ahead, the gatehouse of Magpie Court came into view. 'Amelia, thank you for coming. I know this will not be easy for you.'

'I am not the one who matters,' she said quietly. 'Not now.'

'Hardcastle, what a pleasant surprise! And Mrs Chaytor too, welcome, my dear. Capital to see you both. Sit down, sit down. Is it too early for a glass of madeira?'

Hardcastle sat, uncomfortably. Mrs Chaytor sat down too, straight-backed with her gloved hands clasped in her lap, silent. Outside the lead-paned windows of the library, the sun poured across the garden. The warmth and beauty of the scene mocked them. 'I am sorry, Maudsley,' the rector said. 'I must tell you that I am here in a professional capacity.'

He watched Maudsley's smile fade. 'Oh? As a clergyman, or as a justice of the peace?'

'Both, I fear.' Hardcastle reached into his pocket and pulled out the watch and handed it across. 'Do you recognise this?'

Maudsley went very still. 'That is Hector's watch.'

'Then that removes all doubt. It grieves me to tell you this, but Hector Munro's body was found near St Mary in the Marsh early this morning.'

He watched the blood drain from Maudsley's face. 'Oh, dear God,' he said faintly. He continued to stare at the watch for a few moments, and then forced himself to look up at Hardcastle. 'What happened?'

'I'll know for certain when the assistant coroner provides his report. But it would appear that he was shot dead. His body was found in a boat, floating in the Channel.'

Maudsley raised a hand to his face, covering his eyes. 'Dear God,' he said again. 'Dear God.'

'Believe me when I say how truly sorry I am,' said the rector. 'I met him several times, as you know. I formed an impression of a kind and generous man and a loving husband.'

'Oh, God. Poor Sissy. She must be told . . . I don't think I can do this alone. Will you . . . will you come with me, Hardcastle?'

Hardcastle inclined his head. 'Of course.'

'I will come also,' said Mrs Chaytor quietly. 'That is why I am here.'

'But before we go to her, there are a few things I must ask you,' said Hardcastle. Maudsley nodded dumbly. 'When did Hector depart?'

'Two days ago,' said Maudsley. Speaking was a visible effort. 'Wednesday morning, I think. Yes, that's right.'

Today was Friday. 'Was it bank business that took him away?'

'Oh, yes. It was ... some investment he was trying to put together. I don't know much about it, Hardcastle. I don't take much interest in the bank's affairs, as you know.'

'Do you know where he was going?'

'London, I believe,' said Maudsley. He had gone very pale. Hardcastle rose and crossed to the side cabinet, unstoppered a decanter of brandy and poured a stiff measure, handing it to Maudsley. Mrs Chaytor sat still as a statue.

Maudsley drank, and a little colour came back into his face. 'London,' he said again. 'I'm positive it was London he was going to. Oh, God ...' Maudsley broke down then, tears welling in his eyes, his throat tightening. 'Poor Hector,' he whispered. 'I loved that lad like my own son. He was such a good fellow ... Oh, poor little Sissy.'

'I think we must tell her now,' said Mrs Chaytor softly. 'Shall we go to her, Mr Maudsley?'

Cecilia Munro was in the drawing room, embroidering something that Hardcastle recognised vaguely as a baby's garment. She sat bathed in sunlight, her brown hair glowing. From outside came squeals of merriment, her younger sisters playing in the sun. She smiled at her father, and then she saw Hardcastle and Mrs Chaytor behind him.

'Father! You did not tell me we had guests.' She put her hands on the arms of the chair and pushed herself to her feet, standing with her hands under her round belly. 'Reverend, Mrs Chaytor, how delightful to see you!'

Then she took a closer look at their faces. 'What is wrong?' Prescience came to her and she said, 'Is it Hector?'

Mrs Chaytor walked forward and took the young woman's hands in hers. 'It is Hector,' she said softly. 'My dear, I am so sorry. It is the worst news there could be.'

'He is dead? My Hector is dead?' It was said quietly, almost without emotion. 'How can that be?'

'We don't yet know what happened,' Mrs Chaytor said in the same gentle voice. 'We shall find out.'

Cecilia Munro's knees gave way. Mrs Chaytor caught her, struggling to keep her from falling to the floor. The two men sprang forward to help, and between them they eased the unconscious young woman onto a settee. 'Oh, dear God!' said Maudsley in horror. 'Parrish! Parrish! Come quickly!' The butler hurried into the room, gasping when he saw Cecilia. 'Send for the doctor!' Maudsley cried. 'At once, do you hear?'

'Dr Mackay should already be on his way,' said Hardcastle. 'He said he would call as soon as he could.'

He looked down and saw that Cecilia's skirt was soaking wet. Mrs Chaytor saw it too and moved sharply, resting her hand on Cecilia's belly. 'Never mind the doctor,' she said. 'She needs a midwife.'

The young woman's eyes fluttered as she regained consciousness, and then she gasped and clutched at her belly. 'Lie still, my dear,' said Mrs Chaytor softly. 'Mr Maudsley. The midwife?'

'We have a month-nurse here,' said Maudsley, on the verge of panic. 'Hector insisted she be installed here in the house, in case something—'

'Then I pray you send for her without delay,' said Mrs Chaytor, her voice full of calm command. 'Do not fear, Mr Maudsley. All will be well.'

The nurse hurried in and knelt beside Mrs Chaytor, briskly taking charge. More servants arrived. Maudsley stood awkwardly, getting in the way, and Mrs Chaytor shot the rector a quick look. 'I think we should withdraw,' said the rector, laying a hand on Maudsley's shoulder. They walked back to the library, Maudsley moving like a man half-stunned. The rector made him drink the rest of the brandy and then poured another glass.

'What do I do now?' asked Maudsley after a while.

'I intend to say a prayer,' the rector said kindly. 'You may join me if you wish.'

There was a fine Turkey carpet on the floor. They knelt on this and prayed for the safety of Cecilia Munro and her child, and the rector said another quiet prayer for the soul of her husband. Then they waited, in silence at first, hearing the sounds of the house, and the wind in the trees and the birds singing in the meadow beyond. The rector knew he should be asking more questions about the murder – where Munro had been going, who he intended to meet – but he found he could not bring himself to do so. At this moment he was a clergyman first, a magistrate only a distant second. There would be time later to deal with the dead; here and now, it was the living who mattered most.

'Who else needs to be told?' he asked after a while.

'My son and the younger girls, of course. They will take it very hard. They're fond of him; were fond of him . . . Oh, God, poor Hector! Would you come with me while I tell them, Hardcastle? Please?'

'Of course. I shall do whatever I can. And Munro's own family? He was from Edinburgh, I believe.'

'His brothers run the family firm there. His mother is still alive also.'

'Should you like me to write to them on your behalf?'

'Hardcastle, we would be so grateful.' Maudsley stood up and walked, stumbling a little, across to his desk. After searching for a few minutes, he found the piece of paper he was looking for. 'Here is the address. Thank you, old fellow. I don't think I could bear it. Oh, God, I feel so weary . . .'

They lapsed into silence again. Parrish the butler entered the room quietly and asked if they desired further refreshment; both men shook their heads. Some time later, Maudsley stirred again. 'Who will investigate?'

'The incident happened in the Romney Marsh jurisdiction. I shall take the case myself. I'll inform the deputy lord-lieutenant.' The Lord-Lieutenant of Kent, the Duke of Dorset, rarely troubled himself with his duties; his deputy, Lord Clavertye, did most of the work. Clavertye was currently in London, attempting to further his political ambitions.

'Good,' said Maudsley vaguely. 'I am glad it will be you.' Silence fell once more.

They heard the rumble of iron-shod wheels on the drive; Dr Mackay, arriving as promised. Gently, Hardcastle reminded Maudsley of the other children. Like a man in a trance, Maudsley rose and walked slowly through the house, Hardcastle beside him. They found the three younger girls with their governess. The rector waited quietly while their father told them the news of their brother-in-law's death. They were shocked into silence. Maudsley kissed all three of them, silently, then rose to his feet and motioned to Hardcastle.

They found Maudsley's son in his room, sitting half-asleep in his bathchair, his crippled hands resting on its arms. The young man made a little movement when he heard the news of Munro's death; he murmured something indistinct, then closed his eyes. 'He's just had his dose, sir,' said the nurse who looked after him. She too looked upset.

'Laudanum,' said Maudsley to Hardcastle. 'For the pain, you know. It gives him some ease, for a while at least . . . I don't know if he understood what I said. Later, when he wakes, it will hit him hard. Poor boy, poor boy.' It was hard to know to whom he was referring: his own son, or the dead man he had so loved. Perhaps it was both.

They returned to the library. Half an hour later Amelia Chaytor joined them. She looked pale and tired, and there were fine lines at the corners of her blue eyes. 'She is doing well,' she said before either man could speak. 'She had fainted, but the doctor and midwife both concur that this was due to the shock of the news. She is strong, and she is in excellent hands.'

'And the child?' asked Maudsley.

'Soon. And before its time, of course, so we must hope it is strong enough to survive.' The younger children came to join them, all three with faces shocked and streaked with tears. Quietly, Hardcastle and Mrs Chaytor tried to comfort them. Maudsley sat still, slowly stroking the youngest girl's hair and looking out of the window, not speaking while the sun tracked across the sky.

It was early evening before Dr Mackay knocked and entered the library. 'Mr Maudsley, I know this has been a terrible blow to you and your family. I am glad now to be the bearer of more fortunate tidings. Your daughter has given birth to a son, and although he is small, both he and his mother are healthy and well.'

'I should go to her,' said Maudsley, standing up with an effort. The three children rose, too, their young faces pale in the sunlight. The doctor held up a hand. 'She is sleeping, in the care of the nurse. Wait until morning. You yourself should get some rest, sir, if I may say so.'

It was sound advice; Maudsley was white with shock and exhaustion. 'Then, with your permission, we shall take our leave,' said the rector. He and Mrs Chaytor could do no more for the moment; the family needed time now, time to grieve and time to heal. He put a hand on the other man's shoulder. 'Go and rest, my friend. We shall see ourselves out.'

Maudsley nodded. The rector and Mrs Chaytor walked out into the evening light, looking up at the trees swaying overhead. The wind was changing and strengthening; the fine weather was coming to an end. There would be a storm later.

Dr Mackay followed them. 'Will you stay?' Hardcastle asked him.

'For a while longer. Mrs Munro is in no danger, and neither is the child; but I want to assure myself that all is well.' Mackay too looked up at the trees and sky. 'From terrible death to new life,' he said. 'It has been an eventful day.'

'Yes,' said Mrs Chaytor. 'There may be more such days to come, before we get to the bottom of this.'

The two men looked at her, but said nothing. The groom brought the gig around, Asia stepping smartly in the traces. Hardcastle handed Mrs Chaytor up to the seat and climbed up beside her, and she took the reins. At the end of the drive they turned onto the road towards Ruckinge and back to the Marsh, picking up speed to a trot.

'I was wrong,' said Mrs Chaytor, watching the road.

'About what?'

'Whether it is better to hope in vain, or have no hope at all. To not know is always to wonder, what happened? Who is responsible? Could it have been prevented? The absence of hope at least means certainty. One may not be able to bear what has happened, but at least one *knows*.'

'What are you saying, my dear?'

'I am saying that Cecilia Munro and her child deserve the truth. We shall find out who killed her husband, and why.' She turned to look directly at him. 'Shall we not?'

He found that he could smile. 'Did you doubt it?' he said.

4

Taking Stock

THE RECTORY, ST MARY IN THE MARSH, KENT
12th of August, 1797

My lord,

I write to inform you of an incident that took place in my parish early yesterday morning. The body of Mr Hector Munro of Magpie Court, Shadoxhurst was found in a drifting boat and brought ashore by two local fishermen. The assistant coroner has now confirmed that the cause of death was a gunshot wound. The evidence suggests very strongly that Mr Munro was murdered.

Anticipating the verdict of the coroner's inquest, I have begun to make enquiries. I have also informed Mr Munro's family. Mr Munro, you may recall, is the son-in-law of Mr Frederick Maudsley JP, and is a partner in the East Weald and Ashford Bank.

It is likely that my investigation will take me beyond the bounds of Romney Marsh, and thus outside my present authority. I therefore humbly request that your lordship, in your capacity as deputy lord-lieutenant, gives me discretion to conduct this investigation wherever necessary.

Yr very obedient servant

HARDCASTLE

The Rectory, St Mary in the Marsh, Kent
12th of August, 1797

My dear Mr Munro,

Permit me to introduce myself; my name is Hardcastle. I am rector of St Mary in the Marsh and also a justice of the peace for Romney Marsh.

It is my sad duty to inform you that the body of your brother, Mr Hector Munro, was found in my parish early yesterday morning, in a boat drifting just offshore. Mr Munro's wife and father-in-law have been informed.

Needless to say, both are deeply grieved. Indeed, the shock of the news brought on Mrs Munro's labour, and she has been delivered of a son before her time. At the moment, both she and the child are recovering, but she is in no condition to write to you. I have volunteered to write on her behalf, so as to save her and her family from further distress.

I met Mr Munro on several occasions, and formed a very high opinion of him. Allow me to express my deepest condolences to you and your family for the loss of so fine a man.

I must also inform you that Mr Munro's death is the subject of a criminal investigation. As justice of the peace, I am investigating the circumstances of his death. I will endeavour to keep you abreast of events, and will certainly inform you once there are any significant developments.

Once again, sir, you have my deepest condolences.

Yr very obedient servant

Rev. M. A. Hardcastle, JP

Hardcastle folded the second letter, tipped a small blob of red wax onto the paper and sealed it. The letter would take three or four days to reach Edinburgh. It would be too late for any of Munro's family to attend the funeral, of course; given the summer heat, burial would have to take place as soon as the coroner had concluded his business.

The inquest was scheduled for Monday, the day after tomorrow. Doubtless it would not take long. Dr Mackay's autopsy report was on his desk; it contained some useful information, but no surprises.

The rector looked out the window. Last night had been wild, with wind and thunder followed by a sharp downpour. Now the last dregs of the rain were washing out of the clouds, a thin, sluggish drizzle falling through misty air. He watched the rain fall, his mind drifting away to the family at Shadoxhurst. How torn they must be; a joyous event, the birth of a son and grandson, quite overshadowed by the death of a beloved husband and father.

He heard a knock at the front door, and a moment later Mrs Kemp the housekeeper knocked and entered the study with her usual shuffling step. She was a woman of indeterminate age, with a face like a wrinkled apple and a soul pickled in vinegar. 'Joshua Stemp wishes to see you, reverend.'

'Show him in, please, Mrs Kemp. And ask Biddy to bring us some coffee.'

Stemp came into the study a moment later. 'Good morning, Joshua,' said the rector. 'Do sit down. What have you learned?'

'Not as much as I had hoped, reverend. I spoke to Jem Clay. It's his boat, all right, but he didn't lose it. He rented it out, to a fellow from Hythe, afternoon of the day before last.'

The day before the killing. 'Not to Munro?'

'No, reverend. I described Mr Munro – well, as best I could – and Jem was positive he'd never seen him.'

'This man from Hythe, what did he look like?'

'Jem wasn't sure. About average height, bit on the light side, brown hair. Dressed simple but spoke smart. That's all I could get out of him.'

'Why did Clay rent him the boat?'

The door opened again and Biddy, the little red-haired Irish maidservant, came in with coffee. Stemp waited until the girl had departed and said, 'Jem managed to gaff himself in the leg a couple of days ago, so he's laid up and can't go out fishing. He needed the money. He wouldn't say how much he got either. I reckon he was paid pretty well, on condition he asked no questions.'

'Why would a Hythe man come down here to rent a boat? There are plenty of boats in Hythe itself.'

'Hythe's a small town, reverend, same as New Romney. They all know each other's faces up there, and each other's business. If he wanted to hire a boat on the quiet, he'd have to come down here.'

Hardcastle nodded. 'I wish to speak to this man. Go back to Clay and put pressure on him. Get a better description if you can. And I'll ask Sawbridge, the Hythe magistrate, to make enquiries. If he can let us know of any Hythe men who have recently been down to New Romney, that might be a place to start. What of the other fishermen?'

'Saw nothing, heard nothing. Most of 'em were down south, fishing for cod. The Tydde boys were only up north because they were after bass.'

'And the Tyddes? Have they anything more to say?'

'No, same story as before. They took their boat out just before dawn and rowed north 'til they were opposite the Warren, and then put out their lines. An hour or so later they saw the other boat drifting, thought it was abandoned and went to retrieve it. When they saw the body, they towed the boat inshore and Florian came to fetch me. That's all they have to say.'

'Do you think they are telling the truth?'

Stemp considered this. 'I don't have a reason to think otherwise,' he said finally. 'They're pleasant enough fellows. Eb is the thinker; Florian does pretty much what his brother tells him to do. They're both idle as the devil's bones, cuz thanks to old George's money there's no need for 'em to work. They fish a little, and dabble in the free trade, but mostly they just sit around smoking pipes and daydreaming. They've never been involved in any trouble.'

'As a matter of interest, how did old George make his money?'

Stemp shrugged. 'There's no harm in telling now. He started out as a fisherman, but moved on to other things. Back in the day he was one of the biggest free traders on the coast. He made plenty of money, bought that big house in New Romney and settled down to live comfortable. He's been retired a good few years now. I haven't seen him in a long while. I hear he's none too well.'

'And his family live off his money,' said Hardcastle.

'That's right. Old George's money greases a few wheels around New Romney. That's how his daughter married that town councillor.'

'Very well. What of the inns, and the rooming houses?'

'Nothing, reverend. No one remembers seeing him. And there's no sign of any horse or rig. I thought he might have brought a groom with him, who drove the carriage away again. But if he did, no one saw it.'

There came another tap at the door and Biddy entered again. 'Mrs Chaytor to see you, reverend.'

'Ah, good.' He had been about to go and call on her when Stemp arrived. 'Joshua, be so good as to stay.'

Mrs Chaytor entered the room a few moments later, a breath of summer air coming into that severely masculine room. She took her seat as Biddy poured coffee, looking around at the neat rows of books packed tightly into bookcases, the mahogany cabinet where she knew the rector stored his smuggled brandy, the big desk where, she also knew, he kept a pistol in the second drawer on the right. 'Good morning, Joshua,' she said.

'Good morning, ma'am.' Stemp regarded Mrs Chaytor with the natural respect a man will have for a woman who had once pointed a gun at his head. 'What have we learned so far?' asked Mrs Chaytor directly.

The rector repeated what Stemp had said about Jem Clay's boat and the man from Hythe. 'Dr Mackay has also delivered his report. The conclusion is beyond doubt. Munro died of a gunshot wound to the belly.'

'An unpleasant death,' she said.

'Yes. The doctor thinks it may have taken him some while to die.'

All three were silent for a moment, all with the same thought: that Munro might still have been alive when the gulls came to feed on him.

'According to Maudsley, Hector Munro left home on Wednesday, the 9th' said Hardcastle. 'He was found dead on the morning of the 11th, yesterday. The first question, therefore, is: where did he go? And the second is: what did he do in the interim?'

'What did Mr Maudsley say, reverend?' asked Stemp.

'He thought Munro was going to London. But the more I think about it, the more unlikely that seems. Munro was killed less than forty-eight hours after leaving home. It is just feasible that, by riding post, he could have travelled from Ashford to London and then back to Romney Marsh in that time. But is it likely? I do not think so.'

'What of his valet?' Mrs Chaytor asked. 'Surely he would know where his master went? Assuming the valet went with him, of course. But it would be unusual for a gentleman such as Munro to travel without a servant.'

The rector pondered for a moment, staring out the window at the damp garden. 'I shall speak to the valet, of course. And I must also interview Maudsley in more detail. And Mrs Munro.'

'Let me talk to Cecilia,' said Mrs Chaytor. 'You would be gentle and kind, I know. But this is something I can do better than you.'

Hardcastle trusted her as he trusted few people in this world. 'Thank you. The next question is, what was Munro's purpose in making this journey?'

'Indeed,' said Mrs Chaytor. 'Most importantly, why would a banker from Ashford come to Romney Marsh? What was there to draw him here?' She paused for a moment, reflecting. 'There is, I suppose, one obvious possibility.'

'The free trade,' said the rector, nodding. He looked at Stemp for a moment, wondering whether to take this subject further. 'I have heard it rumoured that Maudsley is involved in smuggling,' he said finally.

'I've heard that too,' said Stemp, without blinking. 'It is said – just a story, mind you, there's no proof – that Mr Maudsley lets the lads from Dymchurch store run goods in his barns before they ship inland. And I've heard it said too that he sometimes puts in money to buy cargoes, and sells them on.'

'And Munro? Any rumours about him?'

Stemp shook his head. 'None that I've heard, reverend. Of course, he might have been working with his father-in-law, on the quiet.'

The rector pondered again. 'It is an interesting possibility. "We must find out what is happening", Munro said. I assumed he was talking about a business venture relating to the bank, but he could equally have been referring to a smuggling operation. If so, that could also explain why Maudsley was concerned that Munro was going into danger, and why Munro was so concerned with secrecy. "If the Grasshopper finds out, there will be hell to pay". Yes; an ancient and respectable City bank might not be too pleased to find that members of a partner bank were consorting with smugglers.'

'I don't imagine they would care that much,' said Mrs Chaytor sceptically, 'so long as Maudsley and Munro did not get caught. Profit is profit.'

'Perhaps, but Munro made it quite clear: they were concealing *something* from the Grasshopper. And then he said to Maudsley, "We must find out what is happening". Perhaps something had gone wrong with some smuggling venture, and Munro came down to the Marsh to investigate.'

'But in that case,' said Mrs Chaytor, 'why Mr Munro? Why not Mr Maudsley? He knows the free traders, and presumably they trust him and accept him. Mr Munro, on the other hand, has lived in Kent for little more than a year, and would have been an unknown quantity.'

'I don't know,' said the rector.

'And then another question,' said Mrs Chaytor. 'Why would the smugglers kill him? What motive might they have had?'

'It's rare for the free traders to turn against each other,' said Stemp. 'When they do, it's usually a matter of revenge; one side believes the other snitched on them to the Preventives. Or a breach of faith; someone takes money and doesn't pay it back, or takes part of a cargo that don't belong to them. That's the most likely reason. Sometimes there's rivalry between the gangs,' he added, thinking of Noakes, 'but that's rare.'

'I did not know Mr Munro well,' said Mrs Chaytor. 'But I struggle to imagine him as either a cheat or a snitch. Very well. What next?'

'Next, we wait to hear from Lord Clavertye. And of course, the inquest, and the funeral.'

They rose, and Mrs Chaytor took her leave. The rector gestured to Stemp to remain for a moment. 'I hope this investigation does not create difficulties for you,' he said. 'But if it does, you must tell me, and I will appoint a new constable. I intend to take the killer of Hector Munro, and nothing shall stand in my way.'

The two men looked at each other. The rector knew full well that Joshua Stemp the parish constable was also Yorkshire Tom, the leader of the local smuggling gang. Neither ever spoke of the matter, and until today Hardcastle had never asked questions about the free trade.

Smuggling was the lifeblood of the coastal villages. Most people were involved in it, one way or another. Men sailed the boats that brought the cargoes over from France, and unloaded them; women helped hide smuggled goods in barns and lofts and cellars; children served as lookouts, warning if the Preventive men came too near. To do his job, both as a clergyman and as a justice of the peace, Hardcastle needed the trust and cooperation of his parishioners; Stemp foremost among them. If he attempted to interfere in the free trade, the entire community would close ranks against him.

And so he turned a blind eye and a deaf ear. At this very moment, his church tower was full of run tobacco – he could smell it, when the wind was in the right direction – and another dozen bottles of finest old Hennessy cognac had arrived on his doorstep as a thank you for looking the other way. None of these things disturbed Hardcastle's conscience to the slightest degree.

There were two Preventive services, the Customs and the Excise, whose task it was to prevent smuggling. They could get on with it; he had other things to do.

But if Hector Munro had been killed by smugglers, then both he and Stemp would face a test of loyalties. He had told Stemp that he had made his choice. Now he waited for his parish constable to do the same. He hoped Stemp would not resign; he doubted very much whether he would ever find another man of Stemp's acuity.

Stemp nodded, pausing a little to choose his words. 'Reverend, I can think of no reason why any of the Gentlemen of the Coast would want to kill Mr Munro,' he said. 'But if it turns out they did, I'll not protect them. And you have my word on that.'

The following day was Sunday. The rector rose early as usual, dressed and drank a cup of coffee and then took his sister's dog for a ramble. Rodolpho, the wolfhound, needed plenty of exercise, and as Calpurnia rarely emerged from her bedroom before late morning, the rector usually took the dog with him on his morning walks. He did not mind; Rodolpho, immense and shaggy with a huge head, was a gentle soul and good company.

This morning there were sheep in the fields between the rectory and the sea, white-faced Romney ewes and their half-grown lambs, grazing peacefully. The sheep gazed at Rodolpho with disdain; they recognised him, and knew they had the whip hand. Despite his ferocious appearance, Rodolpho was terrified of sheep. The lead the rector slipped around the dog's neck was not for the protection of the sheep; it was to reassure the dog that *he* was safe from *them*.

They climbed up over the coastal dunes and scrambled down to the beach. Here the rector slipped the lead and Rodolpho raced down the strand trailing clouds of sand and water, barking happily at the gulls. The rector tramped after him, deep in thought. The air was warm but humid and thick, the clouds dark and threatening more rain.

Mrs Chaytor had wondered why Munro, rather than Maudsley, had come down to the Marsh. Hardcastle wondered that, too, but other things bothered him still more. The boat, for example. All the local smuggling gangs had their haunts on dry land; if Munro wanted to meet them, why would he need a boat? And why, after he was shot, was his body left in the boat? Stemp had suggested that the next tide might have carried the boat far out to sea, so the body would never be found; but it would have been equally effective simply to tip the body into the water, perhaps with some weights to carry it to the bottom.

Whoever shot Munro had abandoned the boat, and that too did not make sense. Good boats were expensive, and the Gentlemen of the Coast were thrifty men.

And what might have led Hector Munro to smuggling in the first place? Unlike the people of the Marsh, Hector had money; he did not need the income. Maudsley and others like him dabbled in the free trade for the fun of it; there was a certain guilty pleasure to be had from cocking a snook at the Customs, whom no one liked, and of course the cheap brandy was welcome too. But Munro had seemed a sensible, careful, level-headed young man, in no way given to adventurousness. He was about the last person one would expect to find mixed up in smuggling.

He whistled to Rodolpho, who came bounding back down the beach with ears and tail flapping, skidding to a halt and grinning up at the rector. His shaggy coat was matted with sand. 'You are a disgrace,' the rector told him, but his voice was gentle. The dog grinned again, and held up his head for the lead.

After a quick breakfast of ham and eggs, Hardcastle crossed the road to the church of St Mary the Virgin, the bells already tolling in the heavy air. He robed in the vestry and walked out into the church just as the bell-ringers departed, slamming the door behind them. His usual congregation waited for him: the deaf, white-haired verger; the churchwarden who had already settled himself comfortably into his pew and was nodding off; the two elderly spinsters, Miss Godfrey and Miss Roper, peering out from under their ancient bonnets; and the old man from Brenzett, about whom Hardcastle knew almost nothing save that he stank beyond belief. Over time, he had observed that the old man's odour changed with the seasons: in winter, the smell was a mixture of decaying fish and turnips, while in high summer, as now, there was a combination of raw dung and cheese, mixed with mustard.

Five parishioners only. It was the same, he knew, in many churches across England; people flocked to the chapels of the Unitarians and the Methodists, but the old churches were nearly empty. Some clergymen complained about this, ranting at what they saw as a lack of godliness among the people. The rector disagreed. His people had faith enough, and on the whole they did not need him to help them find it. If they wanted the church, they knew where it was; and they knew also that whenever they came to church, no matter how infrequently, they would find him waiting to welcome them. To Hardcastle, that was all that mattered.

He raised his arms and let his deep, rich voice fill the nave of the church. 'Dearly beloved brethren, the Scripture moveth us in sundry places to acknowledge our manifold sins and wickedness ... And although we ought at all times humbly to acknowledge our sins before God, yet ought we most chiefly so to do when we assemble and meet together, to render thanks for the great benefits that we have received at His hands.'

The service, as always, left him feeling clear-headed and refreshed. Afterwards he stood at the door of the church and thanked his little congregation. Miss Godfrey and Miss Roper were the last to leave. 'Ladies, thank you as always. God bless you.'

'And may He bless you too, reverend,' said Miss Godfrey firmly. 'Your sermons never fail to uplift me. I feel positively joyous after hearing you speak.'

He bowed. 'Thank you again. And I must apologise. I have been so busy of late that I have neglected my favourite parishioners.'

They took the hint at once. 'You must come for tea,' said Miss Godfrey. They settled on Thursday and the ladies took their leave. Quietly, Hardcastle hung up his robes in the vestry and then walked through the churchyard and over the road to the rectory. From the north came a grey curtain of rain, blotting out the hills beyond Hythe and sweeping steadily across the Marsh.

That afternoon Hardcastle dined with his sister, as usual barely hearing her chatter, grunting occasionally to signify assent to whatever she was saying. The dining room had once been a forbidding place, dark with wainscoting. Calpurnia had redecorated it last spring, with light curtains and some bright wallpaper of mock-Oriental pattern, freshening and lifting the room. The rector looked around and thought, as he did during every meal, how much he missed the old gloom.

Biddy brought in a platter of roast duck and the rector began to carve. Only when he was halfway through his task did he realise Calpurnia had asked him a direct question.

'Your pardon, sister, I was thinking of something else. What did you say?'

'Oh, Marcus, you are so inattentive. I *said*, what progress are you making on the case of Mr Munro? Dr Mackay is quite convinced that the poor man was murdered.'

The rector laid down his knife. 'When did you see Dr Mackay?'

'Yesterday morning, while you were out. He came in person to deliver the autopsy report.'

'He did? Whatever for?'

'He wanted to be certain you received it promptly. He arrived about eleven, having driven directly from New Romney.'

He looked at her, incredulous. 'Eleven? And you were out of bed?'

'Marcus, don't be vulgar. Of course I had risen by then, and as you were out, I received the doctor on your behalf. It was very kind to come all that way himself, don't you think? Instead of sending a messenger?'

'Very kind,' agreed the rector, considering. Was he imagining it, or had Dr Mackay begun in recent weeks to pay more than ordinary attention to his sister? They had been very thick together that evening at Magpie Court, for example. Hope leaped suddenly within him. Might Mackay have deeper intentions? Did he intend to ask for Cordelia's hand? Even better, might they be intending to elope; and for preference, very soon?

'Dr Mackay said it is a most perplexing case,' said Calpurnia. 'Why would anyone kill Mr Munro and set his body adrift at sea? he asked. It seemed most odd to him. But I think I may have the answer.'

'Oh, dear God.'

'In my books, bodies are either disposed of in highly devious ways so they will never be found; or else they are left artfully arranged in places where they are *sure* to be discovered. Sometimes the body is left as a warning.'

The rector was caught off guard. 'A warning? About what?'

'Take *The Ghost-Hunters of Mirador*, for example. When Cassini was killed by the Periculpi, his body was left in a prominent place so that the Incandeschi would be sure to see it and understand the message: stay away from us. Whoever killed Mr Munro could easily have hidden his body by disposing of it at sea. But *I* think they left the body in the boat quite deliberately, so it would be found.'

'And why do you think so?' Hardcastle asked heavily.

'Dr Mackay told me about the coin. Surely that is significant? Remember, the Periculpi left a single gold coin placed in the centre of Cassini's forehead. The coin was to pay his passage; you know, the fee for Charon, the boatman who ferries lost souls to Styx.'

'No, he doesn't ferry them *to* Styx, he ferries them *across* the River Styx, into the underworld.'

'I'm sure you are wrong. The underworld is called Styx, the river is called Lethe.'

'Of course,' said the rector sarcastically. 'What would I know? I merely have an MA from Cambridge.'

'Exactly,' said Calpurnia. 'Now, as I was saying, in *The Ghost-Hunters of Mirador*—'

'Calpurnia, I beg you, stop. These are stories, inventions of your own mind. I am attempting to deal with a real murder, in the real world.'

'—in *The Ghost-Hunters of Mirador* the murder turns out to be an illusion. Cassini is not actually dead. The Periculpi made him *appear* dead to warn off the Incandeschi.'

The rector clutched briefly at his forehead. 'What has this to do with *anything*?'

'The killers placed Mr Munro's body conspicuously in the open where it would be found, so his associates would take note. They were sending a message, don't you see? Just like the Periculpi did. They were saying, do not interfere with us, or you will suffer the same fate. I said as much to Dr Mackay, and he agreed with me.'

'I'm sure he did. It might interest you to know that Joshua Stemp thinks the body was abandoned in the boat so the currents would carry it out to sea, and it would never be found.'

'Then Mr Stemp is clearly wrong,' said Calpurnia. 'Now, as for the motivation behind the murder, Dr Mackay and I discussed that too. I think the novel I am writing now, *The Cardinal's Jewels*, holds the key. In *The Cardinal's Jewels*, the motive for the killing is greed. I am certain this case is the same. Mr Munro was a banker, was he not? Then surely money is at the heart of this matter.'

The rector had resumed carving the duck. Calpurnia looked at him suspiciously. 'You are saying nothing. What do you think?'

'I think,' said the rector, 'that in the morning I shall ask Amos to take the long ladder around to Dr Mackay – with my compliments – and beg him to make swift use of it.'

Later, in his study with a second glass of port at his elbow, the rector sat staring at the fire. Rain continued to hammer down outside, thumping against the windows behind the curtains.

A glint of metal caught Hardcastle's eye. He looked down at his desk and saw the gold guinea he had taken from the boat, from beneath Munro's body. It was of quite new minting, the image sharp and clear. On the one side was the royal coat of arms inside a shield, with a crown resting on top; on the other, a rather pudgy profile of the king, identified for those who might not recognise him as GEORGIUS III DEI GRATIA.

A coin for passage to the underworld. A banker, killed for his money, and his body left as a warning to others: this is what will happen if you meddle in things you should leave alone.

Dear God; could it be possible that his imbecile sister was actually *right*?

5

The Funeral

On Monday morning the rain had stopped and the Marsh was shrouded in a thin white mist, draped across the open fields and ditches. At a quarter to ten Hardcastle walked down to the Star, a whitewashed, two-storey building in the middle of the village. A rather handsome sign – a neat white star above a pattern of black and silver waves painted by a highly professional hand – hung from an iron bracket above the street.

Ducking under the low lintel of the door, the rector saw the common room was already largely full. Dr Stackpole the coroner had arrived with his secretary and was unpacking his bag. The jurymen were in their seats, talking in low voices; the spectators sat watching them, the men with mugs of beer and glasses of gin, the women clustered together and whispering behind their hands. Hardcastle saw Mrs Chaytor with Miss Godfrey and Miss Roper, the latter ladies bright-eyed with curiosity. His sister sat just behind them, her round face intent as she watched the scene.

He made his way to the bar and asked for small beer. Bessie Luckhurst, the landlord's daughter, a smart young woman of seventeen, served him. 'This is a bad business, reverend.'

When she said it in those tones, she sounded exactly like her father, now at the far end of the bar talking to Jack Hoad, one of the local fishermen. 'Such a tragedy,' she said. 'They say the poor fellow's wife has just given birth to a child who will never know its father.'

There was curiosity as well as sympathy in her pretty face. We are fascinated by tragedy, he thought. And why not? It is all around us. People die frequently, often without explanation. We are all closer to death, and to God, than we like to believe; these tragedies serve to remind us of this.'

Heads turned, and the rector looked up to see Frederick Maudsley entering the common room. He looked pale and tired, and there was a hesitation in his walk that Hardcastle had never seen before. He crossed the room quickly and laid a gentle hand on the other man's shoulder.

'You did not need to come,' he said. 'I would have informed you.'

'That is good of you. But I felt I must be here.'

They sat together, quietly, as the coroner opened proceedings. Dr Mackay was summoned to give evidence and took the stand, square-jawed and prepared to be pugnacious. He and the coroner did not like each other; Mackay had received his medical training in Edinburgh and the coroner, an Oxford man, was inclined to treat anyone not educated at Oxford as a charlatan.

'Thank you for your report, Dr Mackay,' said Stackpole. He was a long, thin man with a bony face. 'I found your conclusions clear for the most part. Scotchly ungrammatical in places, of course, but that is of no great matter. There are just a few points we need to clarify for the record. Your report indicates the cause of death as a gunshot wound followed by damage to the internal organs and bleeding. How in your view might this wound have been received?'

'It is quite clear that the weapon was fired by another hand,' said Mackay.

'I see. There is no possibility of suicide?'

'None whatever. A pistol fired at point-blank range would have left flecks of powder and smoke stains on the body. I found no sign of these. Also, the pistol in the deceased's pocket had not been discharged.'

'And I see further from your report that the weapon that killed him was of larger calibre than a pocket pistol. But the deceased may have carried a second weapon as well,' suggested Stackpole. 'A dragoon pistol or a musket. And perhaps, after discharging the fatal shot, he dropped this weapon into the sea.'

Mackay stared. 'Are you saying that a man might shoot himself, and then in his dying moments throw the weapon overboard? That rather passes belief, don't you think?'

'The weapon might have fallen into the sea by accident. Very well, very well, doctor, I am merely trying to eliminate the possibilities,' said the coroner testily. 'I assume that for the same reasons you are prepared to rule out an accidental discharge of the deceased's own firearm? A simple yes or no will do, thank you. Now, you further state that the weapon was apparently fired at a distance of a few yards. Can you explain your reasoning, briefly?'

'I found the projectile lodged against the spinal column,' said Mackay, red in the face. 'As the weapon had been fired from in front, that meant the ball had very nearly passed through the entire body.' Beside Hardcastle, Maudsley gave a slow shudder. 'If the weapon had been fired from a distance, penetration would not have been so deep. Had it been fired at closer range, there would have been powder residue, as I have already mentioned. My estimate is that the fatal shot was fired at a range of no less than three yards and no more than ten.'

Meaning that, even in the dark, the killer was likely to have seen Munro's face. That made it even more likely that he knew who his victim was. This was a deliberate killing, not the random shooting of a stranger.

'One final point,' said the coroner. 'You note in your report that the ball, after entering the victim's body, travelled downward at an angle of about sixty degrees from the vertical; that is, the angle between the entry wound and the point where the ball was recovered from the cadaver. What do you take this to mean?'

'The man with the weapon was standing on a higher elevation, above the deceased. If, for example, he was three yards away, he would have been three to four feet above the deceased. At ten yards' distance, the height might have been as much as twelve feet.'

'Thank you, doctor. That is all we require from you; you may step down.'

Ebenezer Tydde was summoned and repeated his story of how he found the body; his brother Florian corroborated his evidence almost word for word. The parish constable, Joshua Stemp, confirmed the position of the body when he first saw it. The coroner instructed the jury, who took less than two minutes to bring in a verdict of unlawful killing. Dr Stackpole nodded at Hardcastle. 'The matter now rests with the judiciary. This inquest is closed.'

Out in the street, Maudsley's coach waited. Hardcastle walked him to the carriage door. 'How is Cecilia?'

Around them the mist was clearing, a pale sun breaking through. 'Not well. She is recovering from the birth . . . She is very quiet, Hardcastle. She hardly speaks at all.'

'That is unsurprising. Her body and mind have suffered severe shocks. She needs to rest and recruit her strength. When is the funeral to be?'

'Tomorrow. The undertakers are there today, making ready. Hardcastle . . . Our vicar also has the living of Goudhurst, and spends most of his time there. And the curate is a weedy little man. Hector never liked him much. I thought of asking Woodford, but . . .' Maudsley hesitated.

'You need say no more,' said Hardcastle. 'I should be honoured to conduct the funeral service.'

'Thank you,' said Maudsley, and then his voice choked and fell to a whisper. 'Thank you so much.' There were tears in his eyes when he stepped into the coach and was driven away.

The first thing the rector saw when he arrived at Magpie Court the following day was Mrs Chaytor's gig, parked with other carriages and rigs beside the stable block. Parrish the butler greeted him quietly at the door and showed him to a room where he could robe.

The drawing room where Hector Munro lay waiting for burial was elegant and sombre. As well as the local undertakers, Maudsley had engaged a London funeral finisher to come down and arrange the details. The room was hung with black crepe flecked with silver, a hint of the celestial firmament to give a little starlight glint of hope among the colours of mourning. Black candles rested in silver candlesticks, glowing with light. The coffin, covered in black velvet tacked down with gilded nails, rested in the centre of the room, surrounded by silver baskets and sprigs of rosemary, whose sharp scent cut through the air and lifted the senses. The coffin, of course, was closed.

The mourners stood in little groups. Hardcastle moved among them, talking quietly to friends and neighbours and tenants, offering what condolence he could. In nearly every face he saw the same shocked expression. Only a few days ago Hector Munro had been among them, young and strong, smiling and full of life. Now he was dead, and they could not understand why. He found Ricardo talking quietly with Edward Austen from Godmersham.

'I understand you are investigating Munro's death, reverend,' said Austen.

'That is so.'

'He was a good man. I find his murder very troubling. You will let me know if there is anything I can do. Anything at all.'

'And myself also,' said Ricardo. 'I am returning to London in three days' time, but you may write to me there if you need my services.'

He thanked them and moved on. Charles Faversham was there, tall and aristocratic as ever, in a beautifully cut black coat and breeches, his grey wig perfectly brushed. 'Thank you for coming to take the service, reverend,' he said, his usual drawl a little muted. 'It means a great deal to Maudsley to have his friends around him on this unhappy day.'

'There is nowhere I would rather be,' the rector said gently. 'I see your son is here also. It is good of you both to come.'

'Munro was our partner. We owe it to him to pay our last respects. Poor fellow,' Faversham added.

'He is with God now, Mr Faversham. We have that to comfort us.'

'Indeed.'

Beyond Faversham was Mrs Chaytor, talking with a quiet, black-haired woman, both clad in mourning. 'I did not know you would be here,' he said to the former.

'I felt someone should be with Cecilia during the funeral. Mrs Redcliffe had the same thought. Reverend Hardcastle, may I present Mrs Martha Redcliffe to you? She is also a partner in the East Weald and Ashford bank.'

Hardcastle bowed; the other woman curtsyed without speaking. The clock in the hall chimed. 'It is time,' he said, and bowed again. 'I must go.'

On the edge of Shadoxhurst village he waited outside the lychgate, the little church of Sts Peter and Paul behind him. The wind stirred. White clouds drifted over the sun. Rooks cawed, distant in the trees beyond the village. From the church tower the funeral bell tolled, sad and slow.

Down the road the procession came. Two black Belgian horses drew the hearse, their harness topped with black ostrich plumes. Behind came the mourners, led by Maudsley and some of his tenants. The hearse halted, and the pallbearers lifted the coffin onto their shoulders and bore it forward, followed by the mourners. As they reached the lychgate the rector raised his hands and intoned in his deep voice, and around him the world fell silent save for the tolling of the bell.

'I am the resurrection and the life, saith the Lord; he that believeth in me, though he were dead, yet shall he live; and whomsoever liveth and believeth in me, shall never die.

I know that my Redeemer liveth, and that He shall stand at the latter day upon the earth; and though this body be destroyed, yet shall I see God, whom I shall see for myself and mine eyes behold, and not as a stranger.'

In her bright, pretty bedroom, Cecilia Munro lay propped against bolsters and pillows, gazing out at the garden. She wore a black bedjacket. Her brown hair had been brushed by her maid, but her face was still sunken and there were dark shadows under her eyes. The fingers of her right hand toyed with the gold wedding band on her left.

'You must tell us if you wish us to go,' said Mrs Chaytor.

'No. No, it is comforting to have you here. It stops me from thinking.'

'That is the hardest part,' said Martha Redcliffe, sitting on the far side of the bed. Her face seemed stretched tight over the architecture of bone beneath; her skin had a sallow quality about it. It was hard to tell how old she was.

'The mind goes over and over the past, wondering,' said Mrs Redcliffe. 'And, of course, we women have an inbred tendency to blame ourselves for our losses.'

'Oh, and I do blame myself. I could have stopped Hector from going, or at least tried. But I believed his assurances. It will only be a for a little while, he said, and he would be quite safe. I asked if he would return before the baby was born. He said no power on earth could keep him away. I believed him, and so I did not hinder his going.'

There was a catch in her voice, a half-sob, but she was not weeping. She is cried out, thought Amelia. I recognise the signs all too well. The body can only hold so many tears.

'He assured you he would be safe?' said Mrs Redcliffe. 'Did he think he was going into danger?'

'I asked him that too. He said, absolutely not. Then he called me his bonnie wee lassie. He knew that always made me laugh. It was his way of getting me to change the subject, I think.'

'Mrs Redcliffe is right,' said Amelia gently. 'You must not blame yourself for your loss. None of us should do that.'

The girl turned her head. 'Did you blame yourself when your husband died?'

Amelia smiled a little. 'Touché. Yes, I did, for a time. Then I blamed God, and the world, and everything under the sun. After some time I realised how futile this was.'

'Dr Mackay told me that time is a healer. Is it, do you think?'

'With time, the present becomes easier to bear,' said Mrs Redcliffe in a soft voice. 'I was widowed eleven years ago, and still each morning I feel the pain. But I give myself other things to do. For his sake, in his memory, I find reasons to live, to carry on, to work and build and dream. Life is supportable.'

'You are ahead of me,' said Mrs Chaytor quietly. 'I am still searching for those reasons.'

'I have had a long time to think about it, my dear. When did you lose your husband?'

'Nearly four years ago.'

'That is not long. Give it more time.' The older woman looked back at Cecilia. 'And you have something we do not have. You have a child to cherish. So long as you have your son, you have part of your husband as well.'

'I know,' said Cecilia. 'I think that is what keeps me from breaking entirely into little pieces.' She gave another half-sob, but soon mastered herself. 'You are right, Mrs Redcliffe. Our son is the reason why I must carry on.'

'You will find more reasons, as time goes by,' said Mrs Redcliffe, and she smiled a little. 'Are you to be one of your son's guardians?'

'Yes. According to Hector's will, Father and I are joint guardians.'

Something rang a small bell in Mrs Chaytor's mind. 'Did Hector have family of his own?'

'Three brothers, and a mother still living. They are all in Edinburgh.'

'Were they close?'

'Yes, I think so.' A ghost of a smile crossed the young woman's pale lips. 'Although, I gather his family did not entirely approve of Hector moving south and marrying a Sassenach.'

'More fools they,' said Mrs Chaytor. 'Did he visit them often?'

'No. He had not been north since we were married. He said we would go together once this business with the bank was settled, and have a proper honeymoon at last.'

Mrs Chaytor and Mrs Redcliffe looked at each other. 'Business with the bank?' the latter enquired. She saw Cecilia hesitating, and said, 'My dear, you can surely tell me. I was your husband's partner.' She laid a gentle, slightly trembling hand on Cecilia's arm. 'I promise to keep any secret quite safe.'

'I fear I know very little about it,' said Cecilia. 'There was some scheme that began not long after we were married, some big investment abroad, that Hector was much engaged in. He and Charles Faversham were both involved. Some complication had arisen, I think. Hector was going up to London to deal with it.'

'Oh?' said Mrs Redcliffe. 'Did he tell you so, my dear?'

'Yes. He told me last Tuesday, the day after my birthday.'

It felt heartless to ask these questions, but talking about Hector seemed oddly to give some comfort. A little colour had come back into Cecilia's cheeks. They talked for a while about her birthday, and the trouble Hector had gone to in making the arrangments for the music and the party. After a few minutes Mrs Redcliffe rose, excused herself and left the room. Cecilia looked at Mrs Chaytor. 'I am a terrible hostess. Are you certain you do not wish for any refreshment?'

'Rest easy, my dear. There will be food and drink when the others return.'

There was a little pause while Cecilia stared out the window again. 'I wish I knew more about the bank,' she said a little fretfully. 'Our son will inherit Hector's share, and I will be his guardian. I must be able to look after his inheritance, but at the moment I feel woefully ignorant.'

Come, this is better, Amelia thought. *She is taking an interest in the world already.* 'I am afraid I am a bit simple when it comes to such things,' she said artlessly. 'I don't understand banking at all.'

'Oh, it is quite simple,' said Cecilia. 'We take money on deposit at three per cent, and either loan it out or invest it in the City at five per cent; the difference is our profit. Martin, Stone and Foote are our City partners and invest in ventures for us, and we also acquire stocks through the good offices of Mr Ricardo. He was Hector's discovery, you know. Our old stockbroker was not much good, so Hector dismissed him and recruited Mr Ricardo. He is reputed to be something of a wizard on the markets.'

'I thought you said you were woefully ignorant? You sound very well informed to me.'

'But I do not know any of the details. In what do we invest? What stocks do we buy, and how long do we hold them? To whom have we lent money, and on what terms? And these foreign ventures, like the one Hector and Mr Faversham were engaged in, I know nothing of these. I think it is important that I start learning about these things, don't you?'

'In your place, I should certainly do so,' said Amelia. 'Did you and Hector ever talk about the bank and its affairs?'

'Sometimes. Not often enough . . . Oh, I must not give you the wrong impression. If I asked a question about the bank, he would answer it. But I always felt that he was just being patient with me, and he would really rather talk about other things. Me, the baby, the family, the estate. All the things he loved, and has left behind . . .'

Mrs Chaytor reached out and squeezed the young woman's hand, hard. The door opened and Mrs Redcliffe slipped quietly back into the room and resumed her seat with a rustle of black silk. The tremor in her hand had disappeared, and she was calm and composed. Her dark eyes were now quiet, her pupils a little contracted.

Cecilia turned her head. 'Do you know anything about this foreign venture, Mrs Redcliffe? The one Hector was working on with Mr Faversham?'

Martha Redcliffe shook her head. 'I too am in the dark,' she said. 'As it happens, I do not follow the bank's affairs in any great detail. I manage the commercial venture my late husband established, and I find that takes all of my time. The dividends the bank pays are welcome, but I fear I do not enquire too closely where they come from.'

She glanced over at Mrs Chaytor, and then looked back at Cecilia. 'Forgive me, but I overheard part of your conversation. If you are thinking of becoming more active in the bank's affairs, I would encourage you to do so. Charles Faversham will not like it, but I'm sure you won't let that stop you.'

'No . . . Hector did not always speak highly of Mr Faversham,' said Cecilia thoughtfully.

Martha Redcliffe's lips pursed in a little smile. 'Once you know Charles Faversham, you discover that he is like a fireworks display. He puts up a very good show and people admire him; there are lots of *oohs* and *aahs*. But when you look more deeply, you will find there is very little of substance behind the lights and smoke.'

A laugh escaped Cecilia's lips, the first since her husband had died. 'Thank you both,' she said, reaching out and taking their hands lightly in her weak grasp. 'You have made me feel better . . .' Then to their ears came the clip-clop, clip-clop of hooves, the hearse returning, and the sorrow came flooding back into her eyes.

Later, when the funeral meats were finished and the other guests had gone, the rector and Maudsley sat alone in the library, each with a glass of brandy to hand. 'Thank you, Hardcastle,' Maudsley said. 'It was a splendid service. We gave him a fitting send-off, don't you think?'

'He was a good man,' said Hardcastle. 'He deserved a memorable occasion.'

'Indeed, he was a good man, wasn't he?' Maudsley raised his glass. 'To Hector. God keep you close, my boy.'

They drank, and lapsed into silence. 'I don't suppose there is any news,' said Maudsley after a while.

'None yet. Maudsley, you do know that I will have to interview you.'

'I assumed as much.'

'When might be convenient?'

Maudsley roused a little. 'Why not now? I'm not in my cups, not yet. And I have no overwhelming desire to be alone.'

Hardcastle paused for a moment. He had not yet received Clavertye's authority to act outside Romney Marsh. On the other hand, Maudsley clearly wanted to talk. 'Are you certain?'

Maudsley nodded.

'The first thing I must establish is where Hector went after he left this house,' Hardcastle said. 'What time did he depart?'

'After breakfast last Wednesday. My God, is it really only six days . . .'

'What baggage did he take with him?'

Maudsley frowned, trying to remember. 'He carried a valise, I recall. I don't know if there were any other bags. I don't think so.'

'Was he accompanied? Did he take a servant with him?'

'No. He said there was no need; he would be looked after where he was going.'

'And how did he travel?'

'Billings drove him to Ashford in the dog cart. Billings is one of the grooms,' Maudsley explained.

'And Munro intended to travel to London by the mail coach? Why not take your own coach? It would have been more comfortable.'

'But not so quick. He was in a tearing hurry, you see. Wanted to make certain he was back before the baby arrived, in case Cecilia needed him.'

'And you are certain he was going to London? Can you tell me more about what he intended to do there?'

'There was some big thing in Baltic timber, I think. One of the Hamburg banks was promoting it, and Hector wanted a piece of it.'

'And the Grasshopper? Were they involved?'

Maudsley looked up sharply at the name. 'No, not at all. Hector was dealing directly with the Hamburg fellows.'

'Presumably he was meeting the Hamburg bank's agents in London. Do you know the name of this other bank?'

'Lossberg. Gossberg. Something like that.'

'Do you mean Berenberg & Gossler?'

Maudsley's eyes opened. 'Yes, I suppose I do. How do you know about them?'

'Even we country clergymen read newspapers from time to time,' said Hardcastle, smiling. 'Berenberg & Gossler are very important in the Baltic trade. Very well, Maudsley, this gives us a start. We can arrange to trace Munro's movements in London. What did he do in the days before his departure? Did he go anywhere, or meet anyone? Did he receive any callers?'

'Sunday and Monday he was here all day,' said Munro. 'He spent much of his time with Parrish and cook and the musicians, organising everything for Sissy's birthday. He was quite fussy, you know; liked to attend to details, and he wanted everything just right for the party. Then on Tuesday he went into Ashford.'

'Do you know what took him there?'

'Oh, bank affairs, I imagine. Tidying things up, you know, before going away.'

'He said nothing specific to you about his plans?'

'No. He knows I'm not much interested in the bank.'

'Yes, you often say so,' said Hardcastle. 'Who looked after the Ashford branch while Munro was away?'

'The chief clerk, Charles Batist, handles day-to-day business,' said Maudsley. He rose and went to the cabinet, where he poured himself another glass of brandy. 'You'll have another with me? You're sure? You're being very abstemious these days, old fellow. Not like you at all.'

'I am on a new regimen,' said Hardcastle.

'Oh? Doctor's orders?'

'No. Strictly self-imposed.'

Maudsley nodded and sat down heavily in his chair, raising his glass. 'Your health. Yes, I was talking about Batist. He's a splendid fellow. Been with us for nearly fifteen years, man and boy. Very hard-working, very enterprising fellow too. Before Hector came, he virtually ran the branch on his own. He referred to me occasionally if something came in that exceeded his authority, but in practice, he would tell me what he thought we should do and I agreed with him.'

What a lot of information, suddenly, Hardcastle thought. *He really is going out of his way to distance himself from the bank.*

Aloud, he said, 'Why did you think Munro was going into danger?'

Maudsley sat up a little, opening his eyes again. 'What?'

'By accident, I overheard part of a conversation between you the night of Cecilia's birthday. You were convinced he was going into danger, and tried to persuade him to send someone else.'

'Did I? I suppose I would have done. I didn't want him to go, certainly. I thought he should have sent Batist to handle the business. He's quite capable.'

'But Hector insisted he had to go himself.'

'Yes, well. I loved the lad, but when he dug his heels in, nothing could shake him. Scotch, you know.'

'I cannot imagine that buying and selling Baltic timber is particularly hazardous. I'll ask it again; why did you think Munro was going into danger?'

Maudsley rubbed his forehead. 'I wasn't thinking of any specific danger, I suppose.' He was silent for a moment. Hardcastle waited.

'I was probably just being an old woman,' Maudsley said finally. 'The truth is, I wanted him to stay here, to be by Sissy's side, and not go haring off on some business that Batist could have handled perfectly well. That's about it.'

'Do you think Batist knew where Munro was going? Or who he was meeting?'

'He might, I suppose. But Hector could be quite secretive when he wanted to be. Especially when he was trying to broker a big deal. He liked to do these things himself.'

'Is there anyone else in the bank who might know? Faversham?'

'Possibly. Although they weren't all that fond of each other.'

That confirmed what Faversham's demeanour at the funeral had suggested. 'But as senior partner in the bank, Faversham would need to be kept informed of any deals Hector was working on.'

'Yes,' said Maudsley vaguely. 'I suppose he would.'

In the hall the clock chimed seven. Quietly, the rector rose to his feet. Evening was coming on; he must go soon, if he were to reach St Mary in the Marsh by dark. He would have a word with Munro's valet before he departed, but it was clear that Munro had travelled alone and in haste. It was unlikely in the extreme that the man would know anything useful.

'Thank you,' he said. 'I know that cannot have been easy for you.'

Maudsley looked exhausted. 'No, no, Hardcastle. I'm glad to do what I can. Thank you again for today. It meant the world to me, to all of us, to hear the service so well conducted. Poor Hector. But we did give him a good send-off, didn't we?'

The sun set. To the east, darkness spread out over the rolling sea. Wave crests glimmered a little in the bright starlight; the moon had not yet risen.

Two boats met in mid-Channel, a cutter from Ambleteuse and a fishing boat from St Mary's Bay. Lantern signals were exchanged, sails came down and the boats drew alongside each other, rolling in the gentle swells.

'All quiet, Finny?'

'All is well. You have the order book?'

A canvas packet was passed over to the cutter. In it were lists of goods desired: so many tubs of gin, so many casks and bottles of brandy, so many yards of lace; orders from the English merchants and traders and negociants, the men who invested in the free trade. 'We'll meet as usual to hand over the downpayment,' said Yorkshire Tom.

'*C'est bon.*'

'Any more word on my old friend Bertrand?'

'I found out who he is working with. A *clique* from Hythe. Bad people to know, these ones, I think.'

'You mean Noakes?'

'*Oui*, I mean Noakes. It is a small operation, just a few men. They do not work with the other men from Wimereux, nor anyone else from Hythe. Just this one small gang, and the one ship.'

'What else have you heard?'

'I am not certain. I grow old; my memory plays me false.'

Coins clinked in the darkness, were examined briefly by lantern light and pocketed. 'And now I am young again,' said

Finny Jack cheerfully. 'If you want to know what Bertrand is doing, you may ask him yourself. He makes a run one week from tomorrow, and lands down near Dungeness.'

'Dungeness? Why not Hythe?'

'Perhaps they do not want the other men from Hythe to know what they are doing. Dungeness is a lonely place.'

Stemp remembered his last visit to Dungeness. He remembered too the ship he had seen, offloading a coffin into Noakes's boat. 'Finny, you ever seen a Dutch lugger in these waters? Bit broad in the beam? Rotterdam rig?'

'A Dutchman? In our waters?' The French smuggler was outraged. 'No, I have not. If I do, I shall sink him. This is our place.'

'Easy, Finny. He's bigger than you, and I reckon he carries metal. Go wary of him. But if you see him, let me know, will you?'

'With pleasure. Now, we must depart. The moon will rise in half an hour.'

Sails were hoisted. The cutter slipped away into the darkness towards France, and Stemp turned his own boat for home. Bertrand was landing in England in eight days' time. Good, he thought. I'll find out then what the bugger is up to; and with luck, what Noakes is up to as well. He remembered the coffin, and felt a little shiver of unease.

6

Theories and Rumours

Wednesday, bright and clear with a brisk east wind; in St Mary, they could smell the sea in the air. In the distance was a low, irregular murmur: incoming surf crashing against the Dymchurch Wall, the eastern sea defences of the Marsh. Amelia Chaytor sat in her drawing room playing the harpsichord, idly and without much concentration.

Yesterday she had been calm and collected while talking with Cecilia and Mrs Redcliffe. Outwardly, at least, she had still been tranquil when she set out from Magpie Court late in the afternoon. But once she was out of the Wealden hills and back on the low flats of Romney Marsh, she had raced for home, urging Asia to ever greater speed. She managed to hold herself together until she reached Sandy House, but as soon as she walked into the drawing room she broke down, collapsing onto the settee and sobbing helplessly.

She had been lucky. She had married for love, to a man who adored her and who was the light of her soul, and she had ten years of bliss with him; ten years which came crashing to an end in a few short weeks of illness and death. Even now she could not entirely believe that John was gone.

But he *was* gone, and his absence was a pain that never ceased. Mostly she could keep that pain at bay; but sometimes, like now, it washed over her in waves and dragged her under. She lay weeping for the love she had lost, and the unendurable prospect of years stretching into the distance, alone.

The storm of nerves lasted for several hours, and left her weak and shivering. Lucy, her maid and housekeeper – dear, understanding Lucy – helped her to bed, where she slept the clock round. Morning found her pale and drawn, refusing all nourishment save a little coffee. By afternoon she was mostly recovered, although her hands on the harpsichord keys still trembled a little. Perhaps I should take Martha Redcliffe's remedy, she thought; but she banished the idea as quickly as it came. The poppy disguised grief; it did not cure it.

She was vaguely aware of a carriage outside, and a knock at the door. Lucy entered the room carrying a silver salver with a card on it. The card had an ornate crest above the caller's name in flowing script: *Grebell Faversham, Esq*.

Her soul flinched. She did not want anyone's company, and she particularly did not want the company of the bumptious Grebell Faversham. But already her rational mind was re-asserting itself. Hardcastle, she knew, would speak to Faversham senior, but it was always possible that his son might know something useful as well. Anyone and anything connected to the bank must be of interest.

'Shall I say you are not at home, ma'am?' asked Lucy.

'No, show him in. And bring us tea, please. The inferior tea, the stuff you offer tradesmen.'

Lucy giggled. It was good to see her mistress on the mend. Grebell Faversham was shown into the drawing room, where he halted and made a flamboyant bow. His coat, waistcoat and breeches were all of a deep wine red, with gold buttons; not the best colour to go with ginger hair.

'Mrs Chaytor. How good it is to see you again.'

'Mr Faversham. To what do I owe the honour?'

'Why, my sister is visiting Mrs Vane over at the rectory, and I drove her up from Rye. It seemed an excellent moment to call on you, if you were at home.'

'It was kind of you to think of me.'

Grebell bowed again. 'I had been intending to call on you ever since we met at Magpie Court. We got along famously there, if you recall? I have been desirous of renewing your acquaintance ever since.'

'Desirous of renewing my acquaintance?' She raised her eyebrows. 'In that case, you had best sit down. Ah, here is Lucy with tea.'

They sat, he on the settee, she in a chair opposite, and they waited until Lucy had left the room. 'Poor Mr Munro,' she said before Grebell could speak. 'Such a tragedy for his poor wife, and for all of you at the bank as well.'

'Oh, indeed. He'll be sadly missed. And poor Cecilia. How sad to be widowed so young. My sister has taken it badly too; she was fond of Munro. I say, this is excellent tea.'

Silence fell. Grebell slurped his tea appreciatively. Mrs Chaytor fought down the impulse to run screaming from the room.

'Tell me a little about yourself, Mr Faversham,' she said. 'You are a partner in the bank, are you not? Along with your father?'

'Me? No, no, I'm not yet a partner. One day, I hope, but that is Father's decision to make.'

'If the partnership is in your father's gift, then surely that day cannot be too far off. I'm certain Mr Faversham must think very highly of your abilities.'

Grebell stared into his tea for a moment. 'Oh, well, yes, of course. It's not a question of ability, you see, more one of . . . making room. The bank has . . . Well, it *had* five partners: Father, Mr Maudsley, Mr Cotton, Mrs Redcliffe and poor Munro. Six would be, well, you know. Too many cooks spoiling the broth, and all that.'

'Yes, I see.' She watched him, growing interested. 'Then what is your role at the bank, if I may be so bold as to ask?'

'Why, I am manager of the Rye branch. That's the oldest branch, and the largest in terms of deposits taken. It's a very prestigious post,' he assured her.

'I am sure. How long have you held this post?'

'Six years now. I was made manager when I was only twenty,' he said proudly.

'Six years! Then I am even more surprised to find you are not already a partner.'

Grebell flushed. 'To tell the truth, when Father started to talk of expanding the partnership, I rather hoped he might include me. But then Mr Munro came along. The bank needed him, Father said, and so I made way.'

'That was good of you. To step aside in the best interests of the bank, I mean.'

'Well . . . One must think of others, not just oneself.'

'But why did the bank need Mr Munro?'

'We've been expanding, you see. We're the biggest bank in Kent now, by some distance. But we needed more capital to invest. Banks always need more capital, especially big, well-founded ones like ours. That's where Mr Munro came in.'

He has no idea what he's talking about, thought Mrs Chaytor. Capital, investment, expanding; these are all just words to him. Cecilia knows more about banking than he does, and would almost certainly make a better partner. 'But I'm sure you don't want to talk about the bank, Mrs Chaytor,' said Grebell. 'A lady of refinement and sensibility like yourself cannot possibly be interested in the mundane world of finance.'

Mrs Chaytor, who wanted very much to talk about the bank, gave an inward sigh. 'What other topics of conversation would you think suitable?' she asked.

'Well.' Grebell looked around, at a loss. Inspiration came in the form of the harpsichord. 'We could talk about music,' he offered.

They talked about music. She resisted, firmly, his suggestion that she should play for him. To her mild surprise he turned out to be quite knowledgeable, though she suspected this came from a hard-forced education rather than any genuine sympathy for the subject. The clock chimed the half hour. Grebell showed no sign of leaving.

'Will you excuse me?' she asked. 'I am a little tired. The last few days have been something of a strain.'

'My dear Mrs Chaytor, do forgive me. I have presumed far too much.' That seemed genuine; indeed, there was real concern in his eyes. 'I shall take my leave at once. It has been very kind of you to put yourself out, especially for Sissy; Cecilia, I mean. You have been a wonderfully good friend to her.'

'I am glad I was able to help. You've known her for long?'

'Oh, ten or twelve years, ever since our bank merged with Maudsley's. She and my sister Charlotte went to the same ladies' academy; they were inseparable when they were young. We've been friends for a long time.'

Mrs Chaytor smiled, a little mischief coming into her voice. 'I'm surprised no one thought of matching the pair of you. It would keep the bank in the family.'

Grebell blushed again. 'Well, you've hit the mark. Father and Mr Maudsley did talk of the idea, quite favourably too. We'd have made a good match, I reckon. But then along came Munro. Charlotte, my sister, quite fancied her chances with Munro at first, but he'd already met Sissy, and that was that.'

She smiled again. 'And so you both made way gracefully.'

'I don't think Charlotte minded, really. She was happy for her friend.' Grebell looked at her as they rose. 'Sissy said that when she met Munro, it was love at first sight. What do you think, Mrs Chaytor? Does such a thing really exist?'

'It exists,' she said, keeping her voice neutral. 'But like lightning, it never strikes twice.'

'Ah. Interesting.' He said no more as she walked him to the door, but on the step he turned. 'This has been delightful. And my apologies again for tiring you. Would you . . . would you permit me to call on you again?'

'Yes,' she said, her voice still carefully calm. 'Of course.'

After Grebell had gone, driving his smart gig with blue wheels away towards the rectory, Amelia sat for a while looking out at the garden. Lilies nodded in the breeze, and a few late-blooming roses glowed blood red. She was proud of those roses; she had worked hard to establish them and protect them from wind and salt. They reminded her of better days.

The last half hour had confirmed the impression she formed at Magpie Court: that Grebell Faversham was a shell covering a hollow centre. Beneath the bluster and fine clothing was a deep insecurity. His father, it was clear, doubted his abilities and had refused him promotion. She wondered if Grebell himself really believed he was fit material for a partnership.

Whatever the case, it was clear that he had not liked Hector Munro. He had pretended modest gallantry: *one must think of others, not just oneself.* But Munro had deprived him of the partnership which, as Faversham's heir, was rightfully his. Munro had taken the woman intended for him. Munro was the favoured one; Grebell still languished in the same post he had held for years, all chance of advancement denied . . . so long as Munro was alive.

But the death of Munro changed everything. There was a vacant partnership at the bank. And Cecilia, Sissy, was available once again; and this time, with the additional advantage of her late husband's fortune.

'Does Grebell Faversham have a motive for murder?' she asked herself aloud. 'Oh, yes. Oh, yes indeed.'

MIDDLE TEMPLE, LONDON
14th of August, 1797

My dear Hardcastle

Thank you for your letter of the 12th inst. You have my full authority to investigate the death of the late Mr Munro wherever necessary within the county of Kent. A warrant to this effect is enclosed, along with a letter instructing the Kent magistrates to give you their fullest cooperation.

Of course this does not apply in Sussex, so if you want to talk to that fellow Faversham in Rye, you will need a separate authority. Inform me if you think this is likely to be the case, and I will approach the attorney-general.

Do please keep me informed of events as they arise.

Yr very obedient servant

CLAVERTYE

The rector did want to talk to Faversham, and he did not want to wait for the attorney-general. He could not conduct a formal investigation in Sussex, but there was nothing to stop him paying a quiet private visit to the East Weald and Ashford Bank.

THE RECTORY, ST MARY IN THE MARSH, KENT
16th of August, 1797

My dear Mr Faversham,

I shall be passing through Rye tomorrow, later in the morning. Would it be convenient for me to call upon you then? There are some private matters that I wish to discuss. If it would not be agreeable for you to receive me, then of course I understand entirely.

Yr very obedient servant

REV. M. A. HARDCASTLE, JP

THE RECTORY, ST MARY IN THE MARSH, KENT
16th of August, 1797

My dear Miss Godfrey, my dear Miss Roper,

You have very kindly invited me to take tea with you tomorrow afternoon. I write to you now begging your forgiveness; a legal matter calls me away tomorrow morning, and I fear I shall be away for several days. Will you accept my heartfelt apologies?

And it would be my pleasure and my privilege to join you on another occasion. Would Wednesday, the 23rd, be convenient for you?

Once again, I most earnestly beg your forgiveness,

Yr very obedient servant

REV. M. A. HARDCASTLE

The Rectory, St Mary in the Marsh, Kent
16th of August, 1797

My dear Freddie,

A legal matter brings me up to Ashford and Canterbury
for a few days. Forgive me for the short notice, but might
I beg a bed for a couple of nights, Thursday and Friday?
    My warm regards to Martha.

Yr friend as always

M.A.H.

'Come in, Joshua,' said the rector. 'Sit down. Would you care for
refreshment?'

'Thank you, reverend, but no. Have you instructions for me?'

'Yes. We still need to learn for certain where Munro went
after he left Shadoxhurst. I spoke to the valet, but he knew
nothing. That leaves Billings, the groom who drove Munro to
Ashford. I was unable to speak to him as he was away from the
house. Talk to him and find out where Munro got down, then
follow the trail. And keep an eye out too for the man who hired
the boat.'

'Will do, reverend.'

'I'll be away until Saturday, but you can reach me at the rectory
in Ashford. And Joshua?'

'Yes, reverend?'

'Munro's connections with the smugglers, if they exist. Do
what you can.'

'I'll do my best, reverend.'

The door closed behind Stemp, and opened almost immediately to admit Calpurnia. The fact that she never knocked before

entering a room was one of the many things about her that irritated Hardcastle. 'Marcus, I shall require the dog cart tomorrow.'

'What is wrong with your own carriage?'

'One of the wheels has begun to wobble. Amos says it is not safe to drive.'

'How long has it been like this?'

'For a week or more now.'

'Then send for the wheelwright and have it mended.'

'But he'll not come before tomorrow!' Calpurnia complained. 'It is much too short notice.'

'He'll never come at all if you don't send for him,' said Hardcastle, his temper rising. 'I require the dog cart. I am going to Rye tomorrow, and then will be away until Saturday at least.'

'This is very remiss of you, Marcus. What am I meant to do here for three days, without any form of transportation?'

'I neither know nor care.'

Calpurnia stamped her foot. 'You are utterly thoughtless! You never think of me and what I might need ... Oh, who is that at the door? Why, it is Mrs Chaytor.' Her mood changed in a moment. She bent towards the rector and hissed, 'Have you given any further thought to making her a proposal?'

'No, I have not.'

'You must do so, Marcus, and without delay. She is young still, and very marriageable. If you do not move soon, someone else will snap her up; and where will you be then?'

'Alone, which is all I have ever desired to be. Now will you leave me in peace?'

'What was that about?' asked Mrs Chaytor, entering the study a moment later.

'That was Calpurnia, talking nonsense as ever.' The rector surveyed her with concern; she was very pale and looked utterly spent. 'My dear, what is wrong? Are you ill?'

'No; just the usual. Exposure to someone else's grief reawakened my own.'

'I should never have involved you. This was bound to be hard for you.'

'Yes, you should. No matter how hard it has been for me, it is a hundred times worse for that poor girl. Marcus; this is not your fault.'

She knew he hated his given name, and she only used it when she wished to make a point. 'Cecilia wanted to talk yesterday,' she went on. 'We spoke at some length about the bank. And she said one thing that puzzled me. According to Munro's will, she and Maudsley are the only guardians of her son.'

The rector raised his eyebrows. 'Only the two of them? No one from Munro's family?'

'No. In the normal way of things, one would expect one of Munro's male relatives to be a guardian. Munro has several brothers, but none were named in the will.'

'Was there a rift between Munro and his family?'

'If there was, it would seem to have healed. But I don't imagine the Munro family will be terribly pleased when they learn the terms of the will . . . Other than that, I discovered very little. Hector told her only that he was going to London. She thinks it was something to do with a venture that he and Charles Faversham had arranged.'

The rector nodded. 'Baltic timber,' he said. 'I heard the same from Maudsley.'

'Ah, you spoke to him. What else did he have to say?'

'Like Cecilia, very little. He told me several times that he has no interest in the bank, and knows nothing of its affairs.'

'Hmm. Mrs Redcliffe said much the same. The remaining partners, Faversham and Cotton, must be the only ones who know what is going on. Faversham certainly gave the impression of a man who likes to control affairs. Cotton, of course, is an unknown quantity. There is also Faversham's son, Grebell, but I saw no evidence that he knows anything about banking at all.'

'Yes. I must speak to Charles Faversham, and Cotton too . . . What did you make of Mrs Redcliffe? I know her name, but I had not encountered her before.'

'She is an interesting woman. Rather deeper than she appears, I suspect. She runs her late husband's business, which she says keeps her fully occupied.' Mrs Chaytor paused. 'She is also a very heavy user of laudanum, and I would say that she has been for some time.'

'How do you know?'

'Dull eyes, sallow skin, and she wears a wig to cover her own hair. With addicts, the hair becomes rather lifeless and lank. I've seen it before.'

Hardcastle pondered for a few moments. 'None of this gets us very far,' he said finally. 'I remain unconvinced that Hector Munro went to London, but one must keep an open mind. I have sent Stemp to follow Munro's trail.'

'And what will you do?'

'I am away tomorrow, to interview the other partners. I must also speak with Batist, who was Munro's chief clerk at Ashford. Maudsley says that Munro was in the bank the day before he went away. Batist may know what lay behind his departure.'

'The partners? You will include Mrs Redcliffe?'

'From what you say, she is unlikely to know much about Munro's doings.'

'I would interview her anyway. She is perceptive and acute, and she may well have noticed something that will be of value to us.'

Hardcastle smiled. 'I defer to your judgement. I shall interview the four of them, and I shall ask whether Munro was travelling on bank business when he was killed. And, I shall ask also whether they had heard any rumours that he might have been involved in smuggling. It will be interesting to see how they respond.'

'Shake the tree,' she said, 'and wait to see what falls out of it. You will ask them about Baltic timber?'

'Of course. It may turn out to be quite unimportant.'

'Perhaps, and perhaps not. There is a great deal of money in timber,' Mrs Chaytor pointed out. 'The Admiralty is in desperate need of timber to build and repair its warships; and the navy is our principal line of defence against France.'

'It is our *only* line of defence against France.'

She smiled a little; the lack of coastal defences and garrisons, in a place where the coast of France was plainly visible on a clear day, was a hobby horse the rector had ridden many times. 'I have another theory for you to consider. Grebell Faversham has paid me a call.'

She told him what Grebell had said. 'Jealousy is a good motive for murder. And Grebell also has much to gain by Munro's death, if he plays his cards right.'

'Yes.' The rector stroked his chin. 'But there is absolutely no evidence pointing to him.'

'Not yet. May I make a suggestion? Let me cultivate Grebell. If he *is* a murderer, then sooner or later he will give himself away to me.'

'Why so?'

'He desires my regard,' said Mrs Chaytor, 'and he is weak. He wishes to impress me, so he will not be able to resist giving away little hints about how clever he has been. I very much doubt he would make a full confession, but I may learn enough to determine whether he might be our murderer.'

Hardcastle watched her in mild alarm. 'If he *is* the murderer, and learns that you suspect him, you could be in danger.'

'Don't worry. I know how to handle men like Grebell Faversham.'

7

The Bank

'Good morning, reverend,' said Charles Faversham in his cultivated voice. He spoke in round tones from the front of his mouth, like an actor delivering his lines.

'Will you join me in some refreshment? Bring us coffee,' Faversham told the liveried servant. 'Now then, sir, how may I assist you? I assume your visit concerns poor Munro.'

They were seated in Faversham's office on the ground floor of East Weald and Ashford Bank's offices in Rye, a splendid building with elegant, rounded windows outlined in stone. The office was large, panelled in oak and designed to impress. Two enormous oil paintings in heavy gilt frames, one depicting East Indiamen in convoy on a stormy sea, the other a hunting scene, hung on opposite walls; a copy of Ramsay's portrait of King George hung above and behind the great oak desk. Faversham himself, grey-wigged in the old style and wearing a coat of immaculate royal-blue velvet, sat behind the desk, toying with a silver mounted pen.

'First, let me thank you for receiving me,' said the rector. 'You are quite right, this does concern the late Mr Munro. However, I must point out that this is not an official interview. As you doubtless know, I am a magistrate of Romney Marsh, and I have no authority here in Sussex. Therefore, Mr Faversham, there is no requirement for you to answer any of my questions.'

'My dear sir. You may ask any question you wish. I am as anxious as you to find out what happened to the poor fellow.'

'Thank you.' The coffee arrived; the servant departed, closing the door softly behind him. There were lines in Faversham's face, the rector saw; lines that had not been there when they first met at Magpie Court, nor even at the funeral. Beneath the *bonhomie*, he looked strained.

'As you know, Munro left home several days before he was killed,' said the rector. 'He told his wife and father-in-law that he was going away on bank business. I am trying to determine whether that business might be connected to his murder.'

Faversham raised his eyebrows. 'I confess that notion had not occurred to me,' he said. 'I assumed the poor devil was murdered by footpads.'

'Footpads, who placed his body in a boat and set it adrift in the Channel?' Hardcastle shook his head. 'As an explanation, sir, it simply will not do. There must be a connection between Munro's journey and his death. I was hoping you would be able to enlighten me as to the reasons for his journey.'

Faversham nodded. 'I will do what I can.'

'Thank you, sir. First of all, did you know Munro was going away last Wednesday?'

'I had no idea whatever. But then, Munro did not always tell me when he was travelling.'

'He told his family that he was working on a new investment in Baltic timber,' said Hardcastle. 'A deal that involved Berenberg & Gossler, the Hamburg bank. Did you know about this?'

'Oh, yes indeed. We bought a stake in a major shipment of timber from Russia, destined for the Royal Navy. Berenberg & Gossler were the dealmakers. But that deal was concluded over two weeks ago. I know, because I signed the papers myself.'

'Oh? Then it was you who arranged this deal?'

'Munro made the first contact with Berenberg & Gossler, but then I took over. I handled all the final negotiations. I went up to Town, met the Hamburg representatives and we signed and sealed the agreement. That was, let me see . . . The 2nd of August, a week before Munro disappeared.'

'And that was all? There were no further negotiations, no complications arising that might have needed dealing with?'

'None whatever. The Hamburg bankers are gentlemen; they keep their word. Whatever Munro was doing, reverend, you can be sure that it was nothing to do with the timber deal.'

Then why did he tell his family that it was? 'What other business might Munro have been involved in, do you know?'

'There was nothing special that I am aware of,' said Faversham. 'But to be certain, you would need to ask Batist, his chief clerk. There may have been small loans and investments in and around Ashford that had not yet come to my attention.'

'But if he had been working on another big investment, you would have known about it?'

'Most certainly. Our policy is quite strict; all major investments must be referred to the senior partner, which is myself.' Faversham paused. 'I must say, reverend, I am surprised to hear that Munro told his wife and Maudsley that he was travelling on bank business. I would be even more surprised if that turned out to be true.'

The rector looked sharply at Faversham. 'That is an interesting observation,' he said. 'I wonder if I might trouble you to explain it?'

'I'll be frank,' Faversham said. 'I respected Munro's acumen, and I admired his ability. But I never warmed to him as a man. There was always a slight sense of . . . superiority about him.'

Hardcastle waited. 'I'll give you an example,' said Faversham. 'We'd been using a stockbroker in London, same fellow for years, chap called Leeming. Offices in Change Alley, very well respected. Soon after Munro joined us, Leeming bought stock in a couple of poorly managed ventures. Both went smash, and we lost money. Munro blamed Leeming for the decision, and urged me to fire him and replace him with the new fellow, Ricardo.

'Now, Leeming was indeed to blame, and there's no denying Ricardo has been an absolute Tartar for us on the markets. But the manner in which Munro went about things concerned me. Leeming had been with us for years; I knew the fellow well. We owed him some loyalty, I thought. But Munro treated him like dirt. And he was pretty offhand with me too. You know, it was almost as if he blamed *me* for the failure.'

'That seems rather unreasonable,' the rector said politely. 'If I may ask, how does this relate to his disappearance?'

'The point I am making, reverend, is that Munro and I were not close. He was, if I am honest, quite secretive. He used to disappear for days at a time, never tell me where he was going, then just turn up again as if nothing had happened. I know one shouldn't speak ill of the dead. But I was beginning to have my doubts about his reliability.'

The rector nodded slowly. 'Why did you accept Munro as a partner in the first place?' he asked.

'That was down to Maudsley. Munro met Sissy Maudsley at some social event in London, and it was soon obvious that they would marry. Sissy was unwilling to leave her family and go to Edinburgh, and Munro was happy to settle here. He had enough capital to buy a partnership and, well, I needed someone like him, young and energetic.'

'Someone to share the burden of running the business,' said Hardcastle.

'Exactly, sir. I've been running this bank more or less on my own for the past sixteen, no, seventeen years, ever since my father retired. I took over Henry Maudsley's share of the Ashford Bank and went into partnership with Frederick, his son, but it was quite clear from the outset that Frederick had no interest in banking. Then I thought I had found a good partner in Andrew Redcliffe, but the poor fellow died six months after he came on board. As for his widow ... Well, you know. Women have no head for banking.'

The rector nodded without comment. 'What about Cotton?'

'Cotton is very good at what he does, which is country banking. He has useful links with the Church, too, even though he's a Quaker. But he doesn't see the larger picture. He lacks breadth.'

'One final question, if I may,' said Hardcastle. 'Have you ever heard that Mr Munro might have been involved in smuggling?'

'Smuggling!' Faversham stared at him. His face showed his alarm. 'Whatever do you mean?'

'The free trade, Mr Faversham. Munro would not have been the first gentleman of means to dabble in it. Do you know if he did so?'

Faversham spread his hands. 'Reverend Hardcastle, I don't know what Munro did in his private life. As I have indicated, we respected each other and worked together, but we were not close. *If* he had any connection with smuggling, well, I would deplore it, of course. I would also be more than a little angry that he would so recklessly endanger the reputation of this bank. If word of this had got out, or were to get out now ...'

He looked sharply at the rector. 'Why do you ask this question? Do *you* think he was smuggling?'

'I am exploring several possibilities,' said the rector. 'That is one of them.'

'If you learn anything further that might suggest this ... possibility, reverend, then I would be most grateful if you would let me know.'

'Of course.' They rose together. 'Thank you once again for receiving me,' the rector said as they walked to the door. 'You have been most generous with your time.'

'Please don't mention it. Munro was a respected colleague. I am happy to do what I can.'

In the antechamber another man was waiting, presumably Faversham's next appointment. He was a man worth looking at: past sixty but still tall and strongly built, with white hair brushed back and clubbed at the back of his neck. His skin was tanned and seamed like old leather; his dark eyes were set amidst a web of crow's feet wrinkles. He could only have been a sailor.

'Reverend,' said Faversham, 'allow me to introduce one of Rye's most worthy citizens; my client and good friend, Captain John Haddock of the Customs Service. The captain commands our local revenue cruiser, the *Stag*, of which I am sure you have heard.'

'Indeed,' said the rector, bowing, 'and the name of Captain Haddock is also known to me.'

'Captain, I present to you Reverend Hardcastle, justice of the peace and rector of St Mary in the Marsh.'

'A pleasure, reverend,' said the old captain, bowing in turn. 'St Mary, you say? I was up your way last week, cruising off Romney Marsh.'

'I hope my parishioners did not give you any trouble,' Hardcastle said politely. A memory clicked in his mind. 'When was this, captain, if I may ask?'

'Surely. We sailed up from Rye on Thursday evening, bound for Dover. We passed your way in the small hours of Friday morning.'

Hardcastle was fully alert now. 'During the night, did you happen to see a ship near New Romney or St Mary?'

The captain looked at him keenly. 'Now, sir, how did you know that? We did run across a ship, a Dutch lugger, standing inshore bold as brass. A curious thing, that was.'

'Why so, sir?'

'The moon was just past full. The smugglers usually wait for cloudy nights, or the dark. What was she doing out on a night like that?'

'What happened next?'

'We spotted her, but she saw us too and made off north-east, heading towards home. I gave chase, but she could sail closer to the wind than my *Stag*, and we couldn't get near her. I gave up the chase around dawn and brought my ship back to Dover. I've noted her, though. If she comes this way again, I'll be looking for her.'

'Can you be more precise about when you spotted this Dutchman?' Hardcastle asked.

Haddock frowned. 'During the middle watch. Four bells had just gone, so it would be a little after two in the morning. Is this important, sir?'

'It might be,' said the rector.

The captain nodded. 'When I'm back aboard, I'll check the log for you and send word.'

'And did you by chance also see a smaller boat, a fishing boat, anywhere nearby? Or did you hear anything such as a shot?'

The captain shook his head. 'Can't say I did. I was concentrating on the Dutchman. I'll ask my crew, see if any of them saw or heard anything.'

'Please do,' said the rector, bowing. 'Thank you, captain. You've been most helpful.'

Hardcastle drove the dog cart back across the Marsh, full of thought. Dr Mackay had estimated the time of Munro's death at between midnight and four in the morning; just when the *Stag* had sighted the Dutch lugger off St Mary.

The rector did not believe in coincidence. The Dutch ship must have some connection with Munro's death.

But what might the connection be? The Dutch were also involved in smuggling, of course; every year, hundreds of thousands of gallons of gin flowed out of Dutch distilleries and into English ports. Haddock assumed the Dutch ship was a free trader, and she might well be. But Hardcastle wondered, not for the first time, how Munro had managed to insinuate himself with any smugglers, Dutch or otherwise, in the short time he had lived in Kent. The Gentlemen were a cautious breed, and did not accept outsiders easily. It took time to win their trust.

It was well past midday, so he stopped at the Woolpack, south of Brookland, to rest his horse and dine on soles and beer. His mind continued to work on the problem. Of course, he thought, we do not know very much about Munro before he came south and married Sissy Maudsley. His family have a business concern in Edinburgh; what sort of business is it? Might it by chance have business contacts in the Netherlands, perhaps? Was Munro now using these, and would that explain the approach of the Dutch ship?

What sort of man was Munro, he wondered. Hardcastle had met him half a dozen times, and had formed an impression of a steady, pleasant, reliable man. But how well do we ever know our fellow creatures? Most people have secrets that they keep hidden, he thought. I know I do.

Certainly his own impressions of Munro were sharply at odds with the picture Charles Faversham had painted. And yet . . . did he believe Faversham? Was Munro really as devious, secretive and ruthless as Faversham implied? The rector stirred restlessly.

I didn't ask if Munro was unreliable, he thought; Faversham volunteered the information himself.

But why? Why, with the earth still new on Hector Munro's grave, should Faversham choose to blacken his character?

From the Woolpack, the rector drove north to Brenzett, crossing Hangman's Bridge and continuing on to Ham Street, where he paid his toll for the turnpike to Ashford. The road climbed up into the high, rolling country of the eastern Weald. The day was fine and the fields were busy with harvesters; the air smelled of the dust of threshing. He passed wagons drawn by teams of big, plodding horses, loaded with corn, on their way to the warehouses in Ashford.

As time passed the sun began to dip, turning orange in the dusty light. Dim in the sky was a streak of white light. The rector recalled the *Morning Post* a few days earlier, announcing the discovery of a new comet. In ancient times, the appearance of a comet in the sky was a matter for great wonder. These days, it seemed, they were two a penny; every time one opened the newspapers, Miss Herschel had discovered another one.

It was late when he reached Ashford, pulling his weary horse to a halt outside the rectory. Freddie Woodford, the rector, strolled out into the yard, wearing a dilapidated blue coat and breeches with a hole in one knee. 'Hail, traveller from afar. How was the journey?'

'Long,' said Hardcastle with feeling, stepping stiffly down from the box. 'I hope there is some beer in the house, Freddie, because I am parched.'

'Martha is pouring a glass even as we speak. Come inside.'

After a light supper, they reclined in chairs by the fire, Hardcastle still stretching his aching arms. It had been a very long time since he had driven so far. Mrs Chaytor, he reflected, would have thought a journey of thirty miles by carriage to be a pleasant day out.

'You're being very abstemious, old fellow,' said Woodford, looking at Hardcastle's half-full port glass.

'It is a habit I am trying to cultivate,' said the rector.

'Oh? What has brought this on? Have the quacks been nagging you about your liver?'

'No. But I find that I conduct my present duties better when I have a clear head.'

'A sober magistrate? Whoever heard of such a thing!'

'Freddie. That joke is even older than you are.'

Woodford laughed. 'Where do your investigations take you tomorrow?'

'I'm going up to Canterbury, but first I intend to call at the bank and talk to Batist, the head clerk. Do you know him?'

'Oh, yes. My personal affairs are handled in London, of course, but I also have an account at the East Weald and Ashford, for parish funds and the like. I usually deal with Batist when I'm there. He's a good fellow. His father's the 'pothecary here in town.'

'Is the family French? It occurred to me Batist might be a corruption of Baptiste.'

'Very well deduced. They are indeed French by origin.'

'Did they come over when the revolution began?'

'No, they've been here longer than that. Batist senior has been settled in Ashford with his family since I've been rector, which is getting on for fifteen years. Exactly when they came over from France, I couldn't say . . . By the way, forgive me for changing the subject, but we've had some very good news from France. A courier came through two days ago, from Lord Malmesbury's mission on his way to London. It seems his lordship is confident that the French are ready to settle. We could have peace by Christmas.'

'Oh, huzza. Let us pray it is so,' said the rector fervently. 'God knows, we're in no fit state to defend ourselves. We have no coastal defences, most of our army is deployed overseas and the navy is still half-mutinous. Peace is our only hope.'

'To peace,' said Woodford, and they raised their glasses and drank.

Ashford's high street bustled in the morning. The harvesters had started work at dawn, rushing to get their work done before the weather broke; by sunrise, the big corn wagons and their heavy teams were already thundering down the road, barging their way through the press of coaches and delivery drays. Dust hung thick in the air.

The East Weald and Ashford Bank, a handsome brick building at the far end of the high street, was busy too. Corn was big business in Ashford; the negociants from London were down to inspect the warehouses and buy consignments, and the bank was full of people. That was why the original Ashford Bank had been founded, of course, to facilitate this trade; Hardcastle recalled that Maudsley's father, old Henry, had been a prosperous corn chandler before going into banking.

Charles Batist, the chief clerk, was a slender man in his thirties, impeccably dressed with light brown hair tied back simply. His manners were as fine as his clothes, and his voice bore no trace of a French accent. 'Reverend Hardcastle, welcome, sir. May I thank you for the beautiful manner in which you conducted Mr Munro's funeral? It was a very moving and uplifting service.'

'Thank you, Mr Batist.' Hardcastle glanced around the bank, full of corn dealers and merchants. 'I have a few questions for you concerning Mr Munro, if I may? I see how busy you are, so I will be as brief as possible.'

'Of course. This way, reverend, if you please.'

Batist's office was like the man himself, neat and quiet; the furniture was plain, the oak panelling decorated only with monochrome prints of local scenes. 'I understand you worked closely with Mr Munro after he became a partner,' said Hardcastle as they sat down.

'It was my privilege to do so, sir. Mr Munro was, if I may say it, a very fine banker. His knowledge was thorough and his judgement excellent. He was also a very decent man; a gentleman.'

Munro and Batist were about the same age. 'Would you say he was your friend?'

Batist looked down at his desk for a moment, then back up at Hardcastle. 'I was honoured to have his friendship, yes.'

'I am sorry. I did not intend to distress you.' Batist made no response. 'As his friend and colleague, you must have been privy to his affairs,' the rector went on. 'Therefore, I am sure you can guess my next question. Where was Mr Munro going when he departed on the morning of the 9th?'

'I wish I knew, reverend. Truly I do.' Batist was tense in his chair, and the rector realised there were lines of strain in his face as well. 'But I am afraid he did not tell me.'

'Did Mr Munro often go away without telling you his plans?'

'Sometimes, sir, yes.'

'Mm. Do you know about this investment in Baltic timber that Munro and Faversham were arranging?'

'I know of the investment, sir, but not the details. I should explain that I am responsible for this branch of the bank only. What happens among the wider partnership is not always disclosed to me.' It was said as a simple statement, without rancour.

'Mr Munro told his wife and Mr Maudsley that he was going to London,' said Hardcastle. 'Could this timber investment have been the reason for his departure?'

'It is possible, sir, but I really could not say for certain.'

The rector changed course. 'I understand that Mr Munro came here to the bank on the Tuesday, the day before he departed. Is that correct?'

'Yes, sir. He spent the morning here. There were some papers that needed signing: letters of credit for the corn merchants, primarily. I can show you the papers, if you wish.'

'Thank you, but there is no need.' *I would not know what I was looking at. He could show me anything.* 'Did he spend all day at the office?'

'No, only an hour or so. As there were no other matters requiring his presence, he went to see his solicitor. After that, so far as I know, he drove straight home. Certainly he did not return here that day.'

Or ever, was the unspoken thought at the end of the last sentence. 'Who is his solicitor?'

'Mr Cranthorpe. His offices are close by in the high street.'

Hardcastle thought again of the Dutch ship, and asked the question that had nagged him all yesterday afternoon. 'Mr Batist, do you know if Munro, or any of the partners, ever had investments or ventures in the Netherlands?'

'I'm sorry, reverend, but I do not know. Once again, I have little knowledge of what happens in the bank outside this branch.'

'Given the state of war that exists between the Netherlands and Britain, would it even be possible for an English bank to do legitimate business in the Netherlands?'

'Yes, sir, I believe it would,' said Batist, surprisingly. 'One of the Scottish banks, Hope, had offices in both countries before the war, and still has large investments in Amsterdam. The government allows Hope to continue to trade with the Netherlands, despite the war. I believe that, in exchange, Hope also supplies intelligence to the Admiralty. There may well be other banks in the same position.'

Hmm, thought the rector. *It turns out he does know more than just the business of the Ashford branch.* Aloud he said, 'Do you think Mr Munro might have dabbled in smuggling?'

'Smuggling!' Batist stared. 'Whatever makes you say that?'

'It is one of the lines of enquiry I am following,' said the rector. He waited.

'I have to say, sir, that from what I knew of Mr Munro, he would be most reluctant to involve himself in anything illegal or criminal.'

'But you are not certain.'

'I am sorry, sir. I was Mr Munro's friend, but I was not always his confidant. What he did in his life outside the bank, I would not know.'

'And as his friend, do you know of any other reason why Mr Munro might have been killed? Was there anyone who bore a grudge against him? One of the other partners? A bank employee, or a client?'

Batist looked helpless. 'So far as I know, sir, Mr Munro had no enemies, within the bank or without. He was a good man, and as I say, a thoroughly decent one. I can think of no reason, absolutely none at all, why anyone would wish to kill him.'

8

A Woman of Substance

Hardcastle called at Cranthorpe's offices, where a clerk informed him that the solicitor was ill with jaundice and would not return to the office for some time. When questioned, the clerk recalled that Mr Munro had called on Mr Cranthorpe on the afternoon of the 8th of August, and the two of them had been closeted for over an hour. No, he did not know what they had discussed, and even if he did, the clerk added stiffly, he could not disclose it.

Retrieving his dog cart from the rectory, Hardcastle drove north to Canterbury, fifteen miles away. The road followed the valley of the Stour through the North Downs, the cornfields giving way to meadows studded with sheep. The sun was warm on his back, the wind gentle on his face.

Ashford had been a brash, bustling market town; Canterbury was a small city, ten thousand souls living in the shadow of the great cathedral. Hardcastle left his horse and rig at the Fountain Inn, tossing a coin to the groom. He was tempted to stop for a quick glass, but resisted. Cotton was a Quaker, and therefore probably an abstainer; it might be unwise to call on him with breath smelling of beer.

Sylvester Cotton received the rector in his office on the first floor of the bank's premises on the high street. He was in his mid-fifties, thin and ascetic-looking with sandy hair and a pinkish complexion with a few liver spots. Two fingers of his left hand were missing, a third bent and crooked.

Cotton saw the direction of Hardcastle's gaze. 'An old wound,' he said, holding up the hand. He had a slow, almost lazy voice, an East Kent accent softened by a good grammar school in his youth. 'There was an explosion in one of my powder mills. A piece of barrel hoop did that to me. I was lucky; my superintendent of works was killed beside me.'

'Gunpowder?' said the rector. 'You were a powder-maker, sir?'

'Still am. I have three mills out on the River Stour, working night and day. Powder is much in demand these days.' Cotton's light blue eyes stared at him. 'Now you're going to ask, why is a Quaker making gunpowder? Aren't they supposed to be peaceful people, against war and killing?'

'That has always been my experience,' said the rector.

'I make gunpowder; I don't use it. Other people fire the guns. If blood is spilled, it's them that has to live with the consequences. Me, I've never harmed another human being in my life. My conscience is clear.'

'I see.'

'You don't approve, do you? But you're a Church of England man; you should rejoice to see me serving my country. I provide the gunpowder so our sailors and soldiers can defend our shores from the perfidious French. By your lights, I should be assured of salvation.'

'It is not up to me to approve or disapprove,' said the rector, 'nor to judge your case for salvation. And I am not here in my clerical capacity. I *am* here as a justice of the peace, investigating the death of your late partner, Mr Hector Munro.'

'Well, then, you're off your turf. You're a Romney Marsh JP, ain't you? If that's so, then your writ don't run up here.'

'I have a warrant from the deputy lord-lieutenant authorising me to conduct my investigations anywhere in Kent. Do you wish to see it?'

Cotton waved the matter away as if it were of no account. 'Well, I can't help you, in any case. I barely knew Munro; I was not acquainted with his affairs, and I have no idea where he was travelling to when he left home. Which is the question you were about to ask, ain't it?'

'It is,' said the rector. 'You were not, for example, involved in this investment in Baltic timber?'

'I heard about it, but it was nothing to do with me. I'm a country banker in Canterbury. That's all I know about, or care about.'

'Were you on good terms with Munro?'

'Saw the fellow at partners' meetings, that's all.'

'Is that why you didn't attend his funeral?'

Cotton looked at him. 'I'm a Quaker. We are not welcome in your churches.'

The rector ignored this. 'In your estimation, is it possible that Munro may have become involved in smuggling?'

Cotton's face flushed, and he sat forward in his chair. 'What?'

'Smuggling,' said Hardcastle. 'The free trade, Mr Cotton. Is it possible that Munro was connected to it?'

'I don't believe it,' said Cotton. His voice had sharpened and he was speaking more quickly. 'A man of good standing in the community, a partner in our bank—'

'Many men of good standing dabble in smuggling,' the rector reminded him. 'Only last year, the Dean of Canterbury was forced to resign thanks to allegations that he had taken money from smugglers. I am sure you heard of it.'

'No partner in this bank would be involved in anything so heinous,' declared Cotton emphatically, and his face grew redder still. 'I am a God-fearing man, reverend, and I would not countenance any such activity by my partners. And now I think it is time to bring this interview to an end. I have already told you all I know.'

The Archdeacon of Canterbury was a very tall man who had been educated at Oxford, meaning that in terms of both height and dignity he looked down on the rector, who was a Cambridge man. 'To what do I owe this pleasure, Hardcastle? You do not often leave your lair down on Romney Marsh. I presume something serious has brought you here.'

'I am investigating a murder,' said the rector. They were seated in the archdeacon's office in the cathedral precinct. From a distance came singing, the sound of the choristers practising for evensong.

'Really? Oh, yes, of course, you are also an officer of the law. This appointment as a JP was supposed to be temporary. Is there any sign of it coming to an end?'

'You would have to ask Lord Clavertye about that,' said Hardcastle. 'I shall not detain you for long. I wish to ask you about Sylvester Cotton.'

'Cotton? That Quaker hypocrite, who prays for peace while making gunpowder?'

'And lends money to the Church,' said Hardcastle.

'We use his services, yes. His is the nearest bank. It is convenient.'

'Do you recall when Cotton's Bank was taken over by the East Weald and Ashford? What were the circumstances?'

The archdeacon wrinkled his nose as if a very bad smell had suddenly entered the room. 'Really, Hardcastle. You are asking me about matters of which I have very little knowledge, and even less interest.'

'You are a senior official of this diocese,' said Hardcastle. 'You must have some remembrance of the event.'

The archdeacon ruminated for a moment. 'Just after we went to war with France, a rumour began to circulate that Cotton's Bank was unsound. People began pulling out their deposits; I believe in banking parlance this is known as a "run". Like all these country banks, of course, Cotton had lent far more money than he had on deposit, and he had not enough cash in hand. He came to me in desperation, asking the Church for help.

I informed him there was nothing we could do, and sent him away. The next news I had was when Mr ... I don't recall his name – someone from the East Weald and Ashford wrote to inform me that he had taken over Cotton's Bank, and would be retaining Cotton as a partner.'

'And that stopped the run?'

'It would seem so. The East Weald and Ashford Bank is very large and well found; as they never cease to tell us,' the archdeacon added. 'Though I did hear a rumour that they borrowed heavily from the City in order to cover Cotton's losses.'

'Oh? Where did you hear that?'

'I really cannot remember,' said the archdeacon in a bored tone. Outside, the cathedral bells were ringing. 'And now, if you will forgive me, evensong is about to begin. I do not recommend you join us. We have been honoured by the archbishop's presence, and as you know, the very mention of your name causes him to turn purple. Should he see you, then I fear for the sanctity of the Third Commandment. Leave by the side entrance, if you please.'

Wearily, Hardcastle drove back to Ashford, where he spent a second night with the Woodfords. In the morning he bade them farewell. 'Thank you so much for offering a bed to a tired traveller. When this business is over I promise to return for a proper visit.'

'You owe us for an interrupted Christmas last year, don't forget,' said Martha Woodford. She was a bright, forceful woman of forty who enjoyed managing people. 'This time you shall come to us for a week, and nothing whatever will drag you back to your mouldy old Marsh. I shan't permit it.'

Hardcastle drove through another bright, hot morning down the turnpike to Hythe, giving thanks as he did so for the continued run of fine weather. He passed fields full of harvesters at work, stripping the crops to bright stubble. After about three hours the ground fell away sharply to the south and he looked out over Romney Marsh shimmering in the August heat, the thin spike of Dungeness lighthouse rising in the far distance. He felt a sudden uplift in his heart. He had come here as an exile, driven by his own excesses and a series of scandals out of the bosom of the Church and confronted with a stark choice: Romney Marsh, or a living in one of the remoter colonies. He had chosen the Marsh, and had never regretted it.

It was not Eden, nor anything like it. In autumn and winter the Channel storms roared over the flat fields without hindrance, drenching them with rain, biting with cold. Summer heat brought with it marsh fever, from which many people suffered; thus far he seemed to be immune, but his time would undoubtedly come. Fogs shrouded the flat fields in dripping gloom, often for days on end. And sometimes, like last winter, there were cold winds from the north that cut like a knife.

Then there were the people: silent, suspicious of strangers, disliking the uplanders from the rest of Kent who regarded them in turn as lower forms of life; moody, much taken with alcohol, occasionally inbred, periodically violent, and with both smuggling and a resentment of authority bred into the bone for generations far back in time. Cross-grained and incurably stubborn himself, the rector knew that like called to like. The Marsh had become his home.

Hythe lay at the bottom of the green slopes where the North Downs met the sea, on the very northern edge of Romney Marsh. The crumbling stones of Saltwood Castle, ruined by an earthquake two centuries earlier, frowned down from the slopes over the town. Like New Romney, Hythe had once been a busy seaport; again like New Romney, its harbour had now mostly silted up, and was home to nothing more than a few fishing vessels and coasters; and, of course, smugglers.

A woman of substance, Martha Redcliffe lived in a fine house near St Leonard's church, overlooking the town. The rector pulled up before the house, seeing broken windows in some of the buildings along the street, tiles missing from the roofs of others. A footman, hearing him arrive, looked out the door. 'Bring your rig around into the yard, sir. Don't leave it in the street, or someone will nab it as soon as your back's turned.'

It was good advice; there was a large and ugly man loitering not far away, smoking a pipe and spitting into the gutter, with a large and even uglier dog on a lead beside him. Hardcastle drove into the yard and stepped down, the footman coming to take the horse. He too was a big man; the blue tattoos on his cheeks suggested he was once a sailor. 'You here to see Mrs Redcliffe?'

Hardcastle handed over a visiting card. The big man took it and disappeared inside, coming back out in a moment. 'She'll see you now, reverend.'

Martha Redcliffe received him in the drawing room of the big house. Tall windows looked out over the town and the sea. To the right, a yellow strip of sand curved away south towards Dymchurch and New Romney. Far away, just on the edge of sight, the cliffs of France lurked like an enemy spy watching from the horizon.

'Will you take coffee, reverend? Or something stronger?'

'Coffee will be capital,' he said. She dispatched the big footman to the kitchen; he returned a few minutes later to serve the coffee from a silver pot. He had tattoos on his wrists, too, but he handled the china cups dexterously. Despite the sunlight pouring through the windows, the room was dark; the paper on the walls was night blue, unrelieved by any design. Martha Redcliffe herself wore a gown the colour of charcoal. The rector noticed her sallow skin and dull eyes.

'You are here, of course, to talk about Mr Munro,' she said. 'I fear I will almost certainly disappoint you. Since my husband's death I have largely been a silent partner. I know very little of the bank's day-to-day workings.'

The rector nodded. 'You have no knowledge of why Munro might have been killed? Did he have any enemies that you know of?'

The widow shook her head. 'Did you know about the timber investment that he and Faversham were making?' Hardcastle asked.

'No. I had never heard of it until this moment.' She pondered. 'I wonder if that was an entirely wise move. If Lord Malmesbury's mission succeeds, we shall have peace soon. The navy will be paying off ships, not building them.'

And there would be less demand for gunpowder too. Peace might not be altogether a good thing for the partners in the East Weald and Ashford Bank. The unease that had been stirring in his mind since the interview with Cotton made itself felt again. 'Allow me to ask another question,' Hardcastle said. 'What do you think of the bank and how it conducts its affairs? Are you satisfied with the way it is run?'

He had expected bland reassurance. Instead she stopped to consider the matter in silence, taking a sip of her coffee and then sitting with her head a little to one side.

'Things had improved after Mr Munro arrived,' Mrs Redcliffe said at last. 'I felt he had a good head for business. He made some economies, and dismissed the bank's old stockbroker, who had been cheating us for years. The appointment of Ricardo was a very good decision, I think, and we shall reap the benefits over time.'

'And before Munro came? Who governed the bank then? Cotton and Faversham?'

'Cotton is a provincial dullard, with no more vision than a mouse. Faversham made all the decisions. The problem, reverend, is that Faversham thinks he is far more clever than he actually is.'

'Oh?'

'He likes the grand gesture, the big coup. He has expanded the bank greatly from its old base in Rye, but at a cost. He borrowed heavily to buy out Henry Maudsley, and again to rescue Cotton. The smaller branches, in Tenterden and Cranbrook, have a number of bad loans. Overall our ratio of capital to debt is little short of catastrophic. The bank is overextended; though by how much, I am not entirely certain. Faversham keeps the books very close to his chest.'

She seemed quite calm. Was that the opium, Hardcastle wondered. 'Does this not concern you, ma'am?' he asked.

'It does,' Mrs Redcliffe said quietly. 'Not for my own sake; the money I have in the bank is an historic investment, made by my husband before he died. I have many other assets. If the bank fails, I will survive the loss. But the same cannot be said for the bank's many depositors: merchants, tradesmen, ordinary people. A bank failure would ruin them.'

'And do you think the bank is in danger of failing?'

'I don't know,' she said directly. 'You would have to ask Charles Faversham, although even if the bank is in difficulties, he might be unwilling to admit it. My impression is no, not yet. We have very large debts, but we also have other assets we can realise. One sensible decision Munro made was to use some of our reserve capital to buy gold. That will shore up our position and maintain confidence in our currency.'

The rector frowned. 'Even with the Restriction? Your notes can no longer be redeemed for gold. Whatever gold Mr Munro bought must still be sitting in your vaults.'

'The fact that we *have* gold is what matters. People know it is there, and that gives the impression that we are still well found. Perception is everything in business, reverend. If people *think* your business is sound, then it *is* sound. Lose their confidence, and all the strength in the world will not avail you. Your customers will ebb away, and your business with it.'

'May I ask one further question? I promise the answer will not leave this room. Your husband was a shipowner. Was he also involved in smuggling?'

'Of course,' she said coolly. 'So am I. Most of our business is legitimate cargo, but yes, we are also part of the free trade.'

'I see. And do you know whether Hector Munro might also have had connections with the trade?'

'Well, his father-in-law does, so it is quite possible. Maudsley's path never crosses mine; he is a backer, while I am in the carrying trade. We use different routes and employ different gangs. So I am in no position to know what Munro's involvement might have been.'

'You have no financial link with Maudsley or Munro, apart from the bank? Neither ever employed your services, or gave you instructions about smuggled consignments of goods?'

She smiled. 'I don't obey orders, reverend. I give them.'

The rector nodded, slowly.

'Am I the last of the partners to be interrogated?' she asked. 'I hope you also spoke to Mr Batist in Ashford. If anyone would know Munro's affairs, it would be him. Were I in your shoes, I would have begun my investigation with him.'

'Indeed I did speak to Mr Batist,' Hardcastle said. 'He was not very illuminating.'

She smiled a little. 'Batist is very good at being discreet,' she said. 'Well, it was a thought. I imagine Cotton and Maudsley were of no use at all.'

She was testing, he knew, to find out what he might have learned. He wondered why. He decided to trail his coat a little. 'That's not quite true,' he said. 'I think Cotton did know about Munro's smuggling. He pretended not to; he got onto his high horse and ranted about Christian morality, then more or less threw me out of his office. I'm still not quite sure why.' The rector looked at the woman. 'You know him better than I.'

'Cotton is a prig,' she said, 'who preaches sanctimony while making money out of death. But that is about all I know of him.' She looked at him. 'I warned you I would be of very little use.'

He smiled. 'Thank you, Mrs Redcliffe. May I call upon you again, should I have further questions?'

'You are always welcome,' she said. 'Kindly give my regards to your friend Mrs Chaytor. I enjoyed her company. I would welcome a call from her, if she so wishes it.'

Hardcastle had a brief, unsatisfactory conversation with Sawbridge the magistrate before taking the road home. He left Hythe without regrets. The crumbling town, the big man and his dog, the tattooed footman, the dark house had all unnerved him. He recalled Joshua Stemp once saying that the smugglers from Hythe were among the toughest and most villainous on the coast; even worse than the men from Deal, and that was saying something.

Out in the open lands of the Marsh, he tasted salt air on his lips and felt free once more. The afternoon sun glistened out of a brilliant sky. He flicked the reins and his tired horse picked up to a grudging trot. The high road followed the line of the shore to Dymchurch, where he turned off onto a country lane, a strip of grass distinguished from the surrounding fields only by the presence of a dilapidated fence down each side. Ahead, the tower of his church, St Mary the Virgin, rose into a periwinkle sky.

He turned into the rectory drive opposite the church and drove up to the house and stopped. Amos the groom came out to take the horse and cart round to the stables. Mrs Kemp greeted him in the hall. 'Mr Stemp was here earlier. He wants to see you.'

'Send Biddy around and ask him to call on me. I need a change of clothes and a drink.'

By the time Stemp arrived, the rector had washed the travel dust away and drunk a glass of cider, cool from the cellar, and was feeling like a new man. He offered a glass to the parish constable. 'I didn't expect to see you back so soon. I thought it would be at least Monday before you returned.'

'Happens I didn't have to go too far afield,' said Stemp. 'You were right, reverend, he never went near London. He came straight down to Romney Marsh and spent the whole time here, right up until he was killed.'

9

Gunpowder, Treason and Plot

'He took the post-coach from Ashford to Hythe,' said Stemp. 'He arrived in Hythe around midday. He went into the Swan, where he hired a private parlour and asked not to be disturbed. He was calling himself Mr Bradford, but the landlord recognised the description I gave and was sure he had a Scotch accent.'

Stemp had gone carefully in Hythe. He had not seen or heard any report of Noakes since the incident near Dungeness three weeks earlier, but he knew the threats made on the beach were not empty ones. If Noakes found Stemp had been on his 'patch', in Hythe, then the boatman would come looking for him. Fortunately, Manningham the landlord at the Swan was an old acquaintance and occasional ally in the free trade; he did not like Noakes either, and would be discreet.

'The landlord brought him food and drink and left him alone,' said Stemp. 'About an hour later another man came in and went straight into the parlour. The landlord didn't get a clear look at him, but thought he was a slightly built fellow, quietly dressed; that's all he could say. That's also how Jem Clay described the man who hired the boat,' Stemp added.

'Was he meeting Munro to receive instructions, or to give them? I wonder which. Go on.'

'The other fellow left, and then a few minutes later Mr Munro left, too, on foot and walking south. A couple of people saw him on the Dymchurch road, and another spotted him walking on towards New Romney. He was wearing the same coat as when we found him and carrying a small bag, so that's how I know it was him.'

'So, he went to New Romney on Wednesday,' said the rector. 'But he wasn't killed until Friday morning. Where did he spend the rest of the time? You checked the inns and the rooming houses.'

'I reckon he was trying to disappear. Perhaps he thought he was being followed, or people might be watching for him; maybe he didn't want to attract the notice of the Preventive men. He surely reckoned the inns and rooming houses would be the first places anyone'd look for him. So he knocked on the door of a private house and asked for a room for the night, offering to pay well. You'll never guess who took him in.'

'Surprise me,' said the rector.

'Ruth Tydde. Ebenezer and Florian's mother.'

Hardcastle sat bolt upright in his chair. 'Well, you've certainly succeeded. Why in the name of God did she not come forward when the body was discovered?'

'According to her, she didn't want to cause trouble for her boys after they found the body. She was sure that if it became known the stranger had been staying under her roof, they'd get blamed for the killing.'

'For God's sake! Concealing evidence in a murder investigation is a criminal offence!'

'I told her so, reverend. She got very uppity at that point. Said she hadn't concealed anything, cuz no one had ever asked her anything.'

'I don't suppose she knows anything useful?'

Stemp shook his head. 'She's dancing with the fairies most of the time. Reads novels like those ones your sister writes, and treats 'em like they're real. She thinks Munro's ghost is still haunting New Romney, and won't go away until justice is done. According to her, Munro kept to his room the whole time, never went out, didn't meet anyone. Then late on Thursday afternoon he thanked her and took his leave. She didn't see which way he went.'

The rector pondered for a moment. 'Can her sons confirm this?'

'I spoke to them again too. They were out fishing in the afternoon, then went straight to the Ship and had a late night, and slept most of the next day. They didn't even know their mother had taken in a lodger until I told them.'

'Mrs Tydde said nothing to them? Why?'

'I went back and asked her that same question. She said nothing to them that evening because she didn't think it worth mentioning. I get the impression they don't talk to each other that much. When she heard about the body next morning, she worked out pretty quick who it was.' Stemp grimaced. 'She said she didn't tell the boys because she didn't want to worry them.'

'Do you think she is hiding something?'

'Well, you can never be sure, reverend. But I honestly don't think so. She's no sort of murderer, and neither are the boys.'

The rector considered briefly whether to interview Mrs Tydde himself, then pushed the matter to the back of his mind. 'Something else happened that night that may be of importance,' he said.

He told Stemp about the chance meeting with Captain Haddock and the story of the Dutch lugger, and saw Stemp's face change. 'What is it? Do you know that ship?'

'I do,' said Stemp. 'I saw her a week or so before. Reverend, I'm afraid I have a confession to make.'

He told his own story, omitting mention of the French smuggler but describing Noakes's boat and the meeting with the Dutchman and his discovery of the coffin. 'I should have reported the matter, I know. But I wasn't at all sure of what I had seen, or what it meant. It's not illegal to bring a coffin ashore, is it? There's no duty on them.'

'No,' said the rector slowly, 'but to land one from a small boat on a deserted beach is certainly odd. You are convinced there was a body inside the coffin?'

'I didn't open it,' said Stemp, 'so of course I can't be certain. There was *something* inside that box, though. I watched them handling it, and there's no doubt it was heavy.' Stemp paused. 'This Dutchman. Do you think it was someone on that ship who killed Mr Munro?'

'A pound to a shilling says it is. Dr Mackay said he was shot from a close distance, though, not point-blank. Also, the man with the gun was standing at a higher elevation.'

'Like a man on the deck of a ship shooting down into a small boat,' said Stemp.

'Exactly. I wonder if the killing happened just before the *Stag* arrived on the scene. In their haste to get away, the crew of the Dutch ship abandoned the boat with Munro's body still in it. The *Stag*, intent on its quarry, failed to spot the smaller boat in the darkness.'

'So now we've a good idea how Mr Munro was killed,' said Stemp. 'What we don't know is why.'

'I asked several people whether they thought Munro might be involved in smuggling,' Hardcastle said. 'Most professed shock at the idea.' Mrs Redcliffe hadn't, but then it was difficult to imagine Mrs Redcliffe being shocked by anything. 'Have you learned anything further?'

'Manningham in Hythe deals with half the smugglers there, and knows about most of the rest. He had never heard of Munro, though he knew about Maudsley. Same goes for the boys in Dymchurch and New Romney. I'll ask in Lydd, but I suspect I'll get the same answer. There's only one other group I can think of.'

'What's that?'

'Noakes and his gang, also from Hythe. Manningham doesn't know what they're up to, but I heard a rumour they're working with one of the French captains, Bertrand. They might well be working with the Dutch as well. With your permission, reverend, I'd like to find out what they're doing. It don't seem likely that a villain like Noakes would work with a gent like Mr Munro, but you never know.'

'Very well. But Joshua, this man Noakes has threatened your life. Be wary of him, and take no unnecessary risks.'

'I'm not frightened of Noakes, reverend.' *That bloody dog is a different matter*, he thought. 'But I'll go careful.'

The next day was Sunday. The rector conducted the morning service as usual, and then went out to visit some of his more needy parishioners. The weather had turned, with a brisk south-westerly blowing ragged clouds up the Channel, and he dodged between rain showers as he went from house to house. At dinner, he was so quiet that his sister finally give up attempting to hold a conversation and lapsed into an uncharacteristic silence herself. After the meal Hardcastle retired to his study, still tired from travelling, drank a glass of port and fell asleep in his chair before the fire.

At midday on Monday he called on Mrs Chaytor. In the drawing room, over her excellent coffee, he told her about Stemp's journey, the revenue captain and his own travels and interviews. 'I feel we have spent the last few days chasing shadows,' he said. 'Maudsley and Cecilia were convinced that Munro went to London on business for the bank; Faversham was equally adamant that he did not. Batist could not be sure. Faversham and Cotton both denied knowing anything about smuggling, but I am certain Cotton was lying.'

'Then let me offer you a thought,' said Mrs Chaytor. 'Two of the partners of the East Weald and Ashford Bank are engaged in free trading; Maudsley by common report, Mrs Redcliffe by her own admission. Cotton knew about it, even though he denied it. Munro's journey to New Romney is highly suggestive. Munro; I said I couldn't imagine him as a smuggler, but perhaps I was wrong. That leaves only Faversham.'

'I do not understand.'

'Just like Cotton, Faversham may have been lying. What if both of them were involved, along with Munro? All three active partners in a scheme together? We must face the possibility, my dear, that the entire East Weald and Ashford bank could be implicated in smuggling.'

Hardcastle considered this. 'Why would the largest bank in Kent choose to risk its reputation in this way? What could be so important as to make that risk worthwhile?'

'Perhaps Mrs Redcliffe is right, and the bank is overstretched,' she said. 'The partners may have turned to smuggling as a way of earning money to repair the bank's fortunes. It is a course of desperation, to be sure; but perhaps things are indeed so bad that they felt they had no choice.'

'How would they do it?' the rector asked. 'There are London banks that invest in smuggling, or so it is said. But they use intermediaries, negociants and local merchants, so that payments cannot be traced to them.'

'East Weald and Ashford probably does the same, wouldn't you say? They have a partnership with a smuggling gang. The bank provides the money to an intermediary. He in turn contacts professionals such as . . . our neighbours, who do the actual smuggling. The goods are sold on the London markets and the bank receives its percentage, all under the table. That explains why Joshua couldn't find anyone who had heard of

Munro. The bank is using go-betweens, so no one can connect the partners to the smugglers.'

The rector thought about this for a long time. 'Who might the go-between be?' he asked. 'It would need to be someone who is not part of the bank, so the Preventives could not trace them and make a link. There are plenty of possible candidates in these parts; merchants and traders who already deal with the smugglers, lawyers . . .' He paused. 'Lawyers,' he repeated. 'The day before he departed, Munro spent an hour with his solicitor, Cranthorpe. And Cranthorpe is also Maudsley's solicitor. He's well established in these parts, been here for many years, knows everyone. I wonder.'

'But if Cranthorpe is the go-between,' said Mrs Chaytor, 'then why, after meeting Cranthorpe, did Mr Munro come to Romney Marsh?'

'Something had gone wrong,' the rector said. 'Perhaps he thought Cranthorpe – or whoever the go-between may be – had let him down, and decided to talk directly to the smugglers. Quite a brave thing to do, in the circumstances.'

'Foolhardy, as it turned out,' said Mrs Chaytor. 'I have to say I find your theory quite compelling. Finding evidence to prove it will be another matter.'

'I agree,' said Hardcastle. 'Cranthorpe is a figure of some importance, and I can hardly go accusing him without something firm to go on. We must wait and see. Stemp has a theory as to who the smugglers are, and has gone off to investigate. If he can find out for certain which gang the bank is using, he may be able to follow them back to the go-between.'

'I am still pursuing my own theory about Grebell Faversham; I shall endeavour to find out what, if anything, he might know. And I might take up the invitation of the fascinating Mrs Redcliffe too. She likes me, and if I talk to her she might open up a little more.'

'And I shall write some letters, beginning with one to Lord Clavertye,' said the rector. 'Whether they are smuggling or not, something is wrong at the East Weald and Ashford Bank. I intend to find out what.'

The Rectory, St Mary in the Marsh, Kent
22nd of August, 1797

My lord,

My constable has traced the final movements of the late Mr Hector Munro up to the time of his death. It seems highly likely that Mr Munro came to Romney Marsh to meet a gang of smugglers with whom he was working. Although all have denied it, it seems likely also that at least some of the other partners in the bank were aware of his journey and its purpose.

The prosecution of the crime of smuggling is of course a matter for the Customs Service, and I should by rights pass my suspicions on to the local supervisor of Customs. My concern, however, is that Customs will investigate the matter in their usual heavy-handed way, and the bank's involvement in smuggling will become public knowledge. This could not only damage the bank's reputation, but also seriously hamper my own investigation. I trust your lordship will agree, and will approve my keeping this matter quiet for the moment.

Yr very obedient servant

HARDCASTLE

THE RECTORY, ST MARY IN THE MARSH, KENT
22nd of August, 1797

My dear Mr Ricardo,

You may recall that we met earlier this month at the home of Mr Maudsley. I trust you enjoyed the occasion as much as I, and that you and Mrs Ricardo had a safe return to London.

I wish to avail myself of your advice on a particular detail. I have been informed by several partners of the East Weald and Ashford Bank that the late Mr Munro was engaged along with Mr Faversham in a deal to buy timber from the Baltic, and that this deal was facilitated by the Hamburg bank, Berenberg & Gossler. I would appreciate it if you could confirm that this deal took place, and if so, furnish me with further details.

Yr very obedient servant

REV. M. A. HARDCASTLE, JP

A moonless night in high summer, the sea calm and the sky clear, the Milky Way an arch of white fire leaping across the heavens. High overhead the white streak of a comet hung suspended among the fainter stars. Half a mile to the south, Dungeness lighthouse glowed, a pale spark in the darkness. Nearer at hand the waves rolled up on the shingle beach, hissing with foam, rattling as the receding water dragged the stones back into the sea.

Ta-whoom . . . sheeeee . . . ratta-ratta-ratta-ratta-ratta
Ta-whoom . . . sheeeee . . . ratta-ratta-ratta-ratta-ratta

Down at the water's edge a lantern was unveiled, and again, two quick flashes of light before it was covered. In response, a ship came nosing out of the eastern blackness, a dark lugger coasting along under a single sail. A quiet word of command from her deck and the sail came down; the anchor was lowered with a soft splash. A boat dropped into the water, with two men at the oars and a third at the tiller. There was a curious lumpen shape in the bow of the boat, covered by canvas. A few swift strokes brought her ashore, her keel grinding on the shingle. The man at the tiller stepped out into the shallow water and walked up onto the beach.

'That him?' whispered the Clubber to Yorkshire Tom. Both were lying on their bellies on the rear side of a ridge of shingle at the head of the beach, only their heads protruding over the top.

'Yes. That's Bertrand, all right.'

Along the beach came five more men, boots crunching on the shingle. One, a powerfully built man with a huge mastiff in attendance, dragged a wooden sledge behind him; two of the others pushed the sledge from behind. It was just possible to see that the sledge was loaded with small wooden kegs, ten of them piled together and securely lashed down. On the side of the nearest kegs was branded a broad arrowhead, the mark of the Board of Ordinance.

The two parties met. They spoke in low voices, but the eavesdroppers at the head of the beach were only a few yards away, and even over the sound of the sea they could hear every word in the calm night.

'Captain Bertrand,' said one of the men on the beach below them. He was more slightly built than the others, and had a young man's voice, a pleasant tenor. '*Bienvenue, monsieur.*'

'*Merci,*' said the French smuggler who called himself Bertrand. 'This is the latest consignment from Midas?'

'Just so,' said the young man. 'Have you the letter from Jean?'

'Here it is.'

'Bring that lantern, Fisky.' The lantern was uncovered and the watching men saw the group clearly now: Bertrand in cocked hat and sailor's jersey facing a young man with a broad-brimmed hat and a mask hiding most of his face, and behind him the other four big, burly men with powerful shoulders. Noakes was clearly visible among them, recognisable despite the kerchief tied over the lower part of his face, the mastiff straining on a short leash beside him. All had knives at their belts, and Bertrand had a pistol thrust through the sash around his waist.

'It is good,' said the young man. 'Jean arrived last night, and waits for us in Boulogne. When he certifies that the cargo has not been tampered with, you will receive your payment. All right; start getting the stuff aboard.'

The man called Fisky held the lantern while Noakes and the others carried the kegs one after another down to the boat. 'I cannot help observing that these casks look a little like powder kegs,' said Bertrand.

The young man smiled. 'Don't observe too much, *monsieur*. Curiosity killed the cat, remember?'

'Another of your strange English proverbs,' said Bertrand. 'I will never understand you people.'

Up at the head of the beach, Joshua Stemp pulled his own mask over his face and turned his head. 'Right. Let's find out what the hell is going on.'

The men by the water turned sharply as Stemp, the Clubber and four more men came down the steep face of the shingle bank. Bertrand's pistol was in his hand in a moment, and the blades of knives flashed in the lantern light. The same light also shone on the weapons of Stemp's party. They too had knives, and two had fowling pieces; Stemp had a pistol of his own.

'Bon jewer, Bertie,' said Stemp to Bertrand. 'Don't go pointing that popgun at anyone, will you? You wouldn't want it to go off by accident.'

Reluctantly, Bertrand lowered his weapon. 'Yorkshire Tom,' he said sullenly. 'You have come for your money.'

'I don't want the money. I want to know what you're doing.' He rounded on the young man. 'Smuggling gunpowder to the French? That's treason. They won't just hang you, they'll rip your guts out first and burn them in front of you.'

'Gunpowder?' said the young man, masked face still in shadow under the brim of his hat. 'Whatever do you mean?'

Stemp gestured. 'Drop your weapons and move back. We're going to have a look at those kegs.'

Noakes snarled and took a step forward. Quick as thought, Stemp covered him with his pistol. The mastiff growled, straining at the leash wrapped in his master's hairy fist, its eyes fixed on Stemp. Beyond Noakes, the young man leaped lightly into the boat, pulled the canvas away from the shape in the bow and crouched down swiftly behind it. Everyone else stopped still.

Long and gleaming in the lantern's light, the steel barrel of a gun snarled at them. The black muzzle gaped, hungry. At the breech they saw a round cylinder with a crank, the handle gripped firmly in the young man's hand.

'This is a Puckle gun,' said the man. 'When I turn this crank, it'll fire eleven shots in a row so fast you can't think, and each slug big enough to blow your head off. Now, back away and get out of here.'

Noakes rounded on the young man, glaring, the pupils of his eyes dark pinpoints in the torchlight. 'Don't let 'em go, you fool!' he roared. 'Kill 'em!'

'Yeh,' said the man called Fisky, still holding the lantern in one hand and a long knife in the other. He had a deep, booming voice. 'Slit their throats.'

In response, the Clubber and his men raised their weapons. There was a click of hammers drawn back, firing pan covers sliding way. Guns shone dull in the wavering light; knife blades flickered and gleamed. The mastiff growled, hackles up, quivering. They were seconds away from carnage.

Stemp held up a hand. 'I know you,' he said to the young man behind the gun.

'You've never seen me before in your life,' came the response. Eyes gleamed through holes in his mask. 'You've ten seconds, Yorkshire Tom, to back away. Then I start shooting.'

Stemp said nothing. In a voice soft and hissing with menace, the other man said, 'You might get one or two of us. But I'll gun down the lot of you. And Noakes will cut the balls off any of you still living and feed them to his dog.'

The mastiff growled again. 'I'll see you again,' Stemp said to Noakes.

'Fuck you, pig,' said Noakes.

Stemp looked at Bertrand. 'I can't congratulate you on the company you keep, Bertie. A bien-toe.'

He turned and strode back up the beach, the Clubber and the others covering him until they were out of the lantern's light. Impotent, they watched the smugglers load the last of the gunpowder aboard, taking the sledge with them too; presumably they would use it again on the other side. The dark sails of the lugger were hoisted, and she turned to catch the wind and was soon lost in the night.

'God damn,' said Stemp.

'Did they know we were coming?' asked the Clubber.

'They were prepared for a fight, that's for certain. But was it us they were expecting? Or the Preventives? Or someone else altogether?'

There were no answers. Dawn came pale in the east, silhouetting the cliffs of France against the light. Boots rasping on the shingle, they turned in the cold glow of the comet and began to walk home.

10

The Angry Man from Scotland

Miss Godfrey and Miss Roper lived in a crumbling cottage near the south end of the village. Ivy crawled up the walls and hung in thick green clumps around the door, and the thatched roof was pocked with holes where birds had bored into it. The rector frowned, wondering whether the thatch would still be thick enough to shed the rains this autumn.

The ladies welcomed him in, Miss Godfrey directing him to a chair that wobbled when he sat, Miss Roper twittering a little. Hardcastle watched them carefully as tea was brought and served. Both, he thought, were thin as scarecrows. Well, they were in their sixties, and sometimes older people did shed weight. Miss Godfrey still seemed fit enough, but he noticed for the first time a tremor in Miss Roper's fingers as she picked up the sugar tongs. There will come a time, he thought, when we shall have to care for them both.

They poured him tea, laced heavily with brandy, and he bid a silent farewell to his regimen. Miss Godrey announced with pride that they had tried today for the first time a new receipt for cinnamon cake, and begged him to have a piece. The rector braced himself. The cake was burnt on one side and a half-cooked mess on the other, and they had forgotten to include the cinnamon. Courtesy forced him to consume a second portion while Miss Godfrey added more brandy to the teapot.

'This poor man who was found in the boat,' said Miss Godfrey. 'Have you found out who killed him yet, reverend?'

'Not yet, I fear,' said the rector, brushing crumbs from his waistcoat. 'That is, as you may have surmised, the business which took me away from the village last week.'

'And was your journey fruitful?' asked Miss Godfrey.

'Yes and no,' said the rector. 'I have learned a number of interesting details, even if the full truth has yet to emerge. You will pardon me, ladies, if I do not discuss those details with you. The entire matter is of course *sub judice*.'

He could trust the two ladies, but the same could not be said of their maidservant, Kate. Gossip flowed from Kate like water from a drain. 'I do hope this has nothing to do with our village,' said Miss Godfrey firmly. Passing strangers were welcome to murder each other, was the inference, so long as they left St Mary alone. Miss Roper looked up wide-eyed at this.

'Do you think there is any danger, reverend? Are we safe?'

'I think, ladies, that we are all quite safe,' said the rector. 'There is nothing whatever to connect St Mary in the Marsh to Mr Munro's death. You may enjoy your tranquillity undisturbed.'

'Tranquillity,' snorted Miss Godfrey. 'With the French across the water waiting to invade us, and the millworkers in the Midlands all rioting, and this ghastly paper money Mr Pitt says we must now use? There's precious little tranquillity, I should say.'

That was the opening the rector was looking for. 'Speaking of money, Miss Roper; Mrs Chaytor tells me you have had a letter from your niece in London.'

Miss Roper opened her eyes wide. 'Why, yes! Oh, and such news too! I've never heard the like! The East Weald and Ashford Bank is in the most dreadful trouble, reverend, and is likely to fail at any moment! And it will take all of our money with it!'

The rector looked at her in alarm. 'Is that so? Mrs Chaytor said only that there was some rumour concerning country banks.'

'Clara, my dear, you are exaggerating,' said Miss Godfrey, looking sternly at her friend. 'I think you should show the letter to Reverend Hardcastle, and let him judge for himself.'

It took Miss Roper a couple of minutes and several false starts to locate the letter, but eventually she found it and handed it over, indicating the relevant paragraphs with a bony finger.

And now, dear aunt, there is something most important I must tell you. According to Jasper—

'Jasper?' asked the rector.

'Jasper Hobbes, my niece's husband,' said Miss Roper. 'He is from Bedfordshire; or is it Lincolnshire? Oh, I'm not at all certain now. He has been with the East India Company for many years, and is very well thought of there. There is talk that he—'

'Clara, dear,' said Miss Godfrey gently, 'allow Reverend Hardcastle to finish reading.'

According to Jasper, the Restriction Act is likely to have a most *serious* effect on the prosperity of our dear country. Now that banknotes can no longer be redeemed for gold, it seems that gold may cease to be used as common currency, and this might have an effect on the price of gold itself. The East India Company clearly believes this *will* happen, and is selling off some of its gold reserves. Jasper himself arranged a very large sale, over 3,000 ounces, just a few weeks ago.

If the price of gold does fall, Jasper said, many of our country banks will be in quite *desperate* straits. Many are very badly found, he says, and devaluation of their gold reserves could lead to loss of confidence in their paper currency. If that happens, then some of the smaller banks could fail entirely.

I asked Jasper at once if he knew which banks might be most in *danger*, and he replied that he had absolutely no idea, but certainly a large number were at *risk*. I then asked what would happen if a bank failed, and whether the depositors would get their money back, and he looked at me across the table and said he doubted it very much, and then went out to walk the poodle.

Upon hearing this news, I confess I felt deeply concerned for you, dear aunt, for I know that you are with a country bank. I felt I should pass this news on to you as soon as possible. It may be that your bank is in absolutely no danger *at all*, in which case I do hope that I have not alarmed you!! On the other hand, if your bank does face danger, then I only hope that I have been able to give you timely warning.

The rector laid down the letter. 'What can it mean?' asked Miss Godfrey. 'I confess I do not like this talk of danger and risk. At our age, we are no longer interested in taking risks.'

The rector considered while she refilled his teacup. His first thought was that Mrs Hobbes deserved a strong kick up the backside for alarming two elderly spinsters. But he remembered, too, the words of Martha Redcliffe. Were there cracks in the edifice of the East Weald and Ashford Bank?

'These are difficult times,' he said, choosing his words with care. 'But it seems that, as Mr Hobbes said, the banks most at risk are those that are small and badly found. The East Weald and Ashford is one of the largest country banks in England, and has a record of solidity and probity. I do not think, ladies, that you have much to fear. But if you *are* concerned, then I recommend you move your money to another bank.'

'But where, reverend?' asked Miss Godfrey. 'All the nearby banks, even so far away as Canterbury, are owned by the East Weald and Ashford. We should have to go as far away as Maidstone to find a different bank; and who is to say that it might not be at risk of failing also, perhaps even more than our own bank?'

'You could try one of the London banks,' said the rector, but his voice was doubtful. The aristocratic banks of the capital – Coutts, Hoares, Drummonds, Childs – would not be interested in holding an account for two provincial spinsters of no great means. He himself had no special connections in London that would help them.

'I fear we shall have to make do,' said Miss Godfrey. 'We have little choice but to leave our money with the East Weald and Ashford and hope for the best.' Miss Roper watched her, eyes bright with concern. The rector pushed Mrs Redcliffe's words firmly into the back of his mind and nodded his agreement.

'I think that is the right course of action,' he said firmly. 'Mr Hobbes is right, and the banks are facing a spell of bad weather. But if any bank can come through safely, it is surely the East Weald and Ashford. Your money is as safe there as it can possibly be. And, dear Miss Godfrey, dear Miss Roper: if you have further concern about the bank, or you need assistance, please come to me. I am always at your service.'

He departed an hour later, leaving the two of them reassured, or so he hoped. Sunset still glowed in the western sky; near at hand, the village was wrapped in twilight. Lamps shone brightly in the windows of the Star, and the rector thought suddenly of beer. It would be something to take away the taste of the cake, he told himself.

In the common room, Jack Hoad the fisherman greeted him. 'What'll you have, reverend?'

'A mug of strong, please, Jack.' Tim Luckhurst the landlord served him and poured one for himself, and they stood and talked about money; Luckhurst was another who did not like the new £1 banknotes. 'Suppose there's a fire, now?' he said.

'There goes your money, up in smoke. Or what happens if they get wet? No, sir, they can keep their paper. Give me good, honest gold and silver any day.'

'Bloody banks,' said Jack Hoad, who tended to speak plainly. 'Don't trust 'em. Never have.'

The rector thought again about Miss Godfrey and Miss Roper. Luckhurst too banked with the East Weald and Ashford. 'Where do you keep your money, Jack?' he asked the fisherman.

'Hole in the ground,' said Hoad.

The rector heard a knock at the front door, and raised his eyes briefly to the heavens. The last few days had been busy, leaving him with little time to think. Three of his parishioners were down with marsh fever, one a child who was very ill indeed; news had come that a young man from the village, a sailor on the *Culloden*, had been killed in battle at Tenerife earlier in the summer, and his family were in need of consolation; and he had had a blazing argument with his sister, who wanted to repaint the hall of the rectory in a particularly vile shade of yellow. Yesterday he had sat on the bench during a long and trying court of petty sessions in New Romney, listening to Elsie Warren attempt to prove paternity of her child against Tom Shanks. She, in the rector's view, was a simpering nitwit, while he was a scrawny youth who barely looked capable of fathering progeny on anyone. Mostly, Hardcastle felt sorry for the child.

Now he was tired, and wanted a drink. He looked up as Mrs Kemp entered the study. 'An angry man from Scotland to see you, reverend,' she said, the corners of her mouth more down-turned than ever. 'Shall I send him away?'

Mrs Kemp disapproved strongly of the Scots, along with the French, the Irish, Londoners, vagrants, Methodists, travelling salesmen, people from the colonies and women who plucked their eyebrows. The rector took the visiting card from the salver. It was plain in design, with the visitor's name written in simple script: *Mr Alexander Munro*.

The rector sighed. He had been expecting a letter from Hector Munro's family, but not a visit in person. He wondered what had brought Munro rushing south in such haste, and had an uneasy feeling that he already knew the answer.

'Show him in, Mrs Kemp,' he said.

Physically, Alexander Munro was very like his brother: big, strongly built, with the same brown hair and eyes. But whereas Hector Munro's face had been pleasant, his brother's at the moment was set hard, his brows frowning and his mouth a grim line.

'Thank you for receiving me,' he said. 'No, I'll have no refreshment. I shall get down to business straight away. Have you discovered yet who murdered my brother?'

Hardcastle watched him for a moment, gauging his mood. Mrs Kemp was right; he was certainly angry. 'Not yet,' the rector said. 'I now know with a fair degree of certainty where and how your brother was killed. I don't yet know by whom, or why.'

'Not yet? For God's sake, man, you've had two weeks to discover this!'

'The case has proved to be a complex one,' the rector said calmly.

'Complex? Complex, sir? It's nothing of the sort! It's as plain as the nose on your face what happened. Those two fishermen killed my brother. And they did so on the orders of Hector's father-in-law, that thieving old bastard Maudsley!'

'That is a very serious accusation,' said Hardcastle. 'Why might Mr Maudsley have wanted to kill your brother?'

'Theft,' said Munro. 'Theft of his grandson's inheritance, plain and simple. That's why he had himself named guardian of the child, along with his daughter; so they could help themselves to Hector's money and plunder the child's inheritance.'

The will, thought the rector. *He has found out about the will.*

Fists clenched in his lap, Munro leaned forward. 'Either myself or one of my brothers should have been named as co-guardian along with the daughter, to protect the child's interests. But according to Maudsley, we've been set aside. Well, I do not believe it. Hector would never cut his own family out of his will.'

'Do I take it you have seen Mr Maudsley?'

'I went straight to his house from London. He practically showed me the door! And I wasn't even allowed to speak to the daughter. Aye, she's in on it too, I have no doubt. They're a family of thieves.'

'Mrs Munro is grieving,' said the rector, 'and is still recovering from the rigours of childbirth. It is not surprising that Mr Maudsley should be protective of her, given that your family have not always been kind about the marriage. I understand that when Mr Munro first proposed to Miss Maudsley, as she then was, your family objected. Is that not correct?'

'Aye, we did at first,' said Munro. 'We were suspicious of her, of all of them. Hector was a wealthy man. We were sure there was some plot by the Maudsleys to get their hooks into Hector's money. But the couple seemed happy, according to his letters; and we are not unkind people. In time, we were reconciled and gave them our blessing.' Munro shook his head. 'How wrong we were.'

'Mr Munro, I can understand your disappointment in the matter of the will,' said Hardcastle. 'But I understand its provisions were spelled out very clearly. You can of course attempt to challenge the will, but you will need to return to London and apply to the courts there.'

'That will is a blasted forgery! Maudsley wrote it himself, and passed it off as Hector's. And he paid that snivelling solicitor in Ashford to back him up; oh, I saw him, too, and he insisted the will was genuine. They're all in it together. Lawyers, thieves, the whole rotten cabal.'

The rector frowned. 'You are accusing Mr Maudsley of murder, forgery and fraud. I hope, sir, that you have some very good evidence to back up your case. Mr Maudsley is a well-respected man, a justice of the peace. You cannot simply go around accusing him willy-nilly.'

'Fraud? I'll tell you who's a fraud, sir! Maudsley, that's who! He's a criminal! Man, he's a smuggler! And don't tell me you didn't know that.'

'Yes, I know it.'

'And you also are an officer of the law, and you do nothing about it?'

'Mr Munro, if you wish to lay a complaint of smuggling, I advise you to contact either the Customs Service or the Excise. Smuggling is not my department.'

Munro stared at him in disbelief.

'These two fishermen whom you say killed your brother,' Hardcastle continued. 'Do you mean the Tydde brothers?'

'Aye, that's them.'

'What makes you suspect them?'

'They're part of the same smuggling racket as Maudsley, aren't they? They told me so themselves. Smuggling and murder; they're just two different forms of criminality. People like these will easily turn from one to the other.'

Oh, dear God. The rector sat silent for a moment. He had been growing tired of Munro's ranting accusations, and was about to show the man the door. But if this was true – and a sinking feeling in his stomach told him it probably was – and there was indeed a connection between the Tyddes and Maudsley, then Munro's allegations began to take on form and substance. This was serious.

'How do you know this?' Hardcastle asked.

'I spoke to their mad crank of a mother, who seemed to think I was some sort of ghost of my brother. And I interviewed her half-witted sons. To be frank, I wasn't sure at first if either of them had the intelligence or the imagination to carry out a murder. But I expect that if someone told them very clearly what to do, and paid them enough, they'd find a way to manage it. It's plain enough what happened. Maudsley found some pretext to lure Hector to New Romney, to the home of the Tydde family. He stayed there the night before he was killed; the mother confessed as much to me. They probably killed him in the house, then waited until nightfall and took his body out to sea and left him in the boat. Oh, my God, Hector . . .'

Suddenly, Munro buried his face in his hands. When he raised his head again, his eyes were wet. Behind the accusations, behind the anger, there was a deep well of grief and mourning. That Munro had loved his brother was beyond doubt.

'When will you arrest them?' he asked.

'I will interview the Tydde family first, and ask them to account for themselves.' Hardcastle felt suddenly sick. Stemp had interviewed the Tydde brothers, and he himself had watched them give evidence at the inquest; he could have sworn they were both straight. *Could I have been wrong?* he wondered. Could they have deceived us all? It was possible.

And Maudsley. I cannot believe it of him. But better men than him have committed worse crimes.

'I shall summon them to a formal interview in New Romney tomorrow,' the rector said.

Munro wiped his eyes. 'I insist on being present when you do so.'

'As a courtesy, given that you are Mr Munro's next of kin, I will permit it. Where are you staying?'

'In New Romney. I have taken a room at the Ship. I'll be close by while you do your work. Mark my words, reverend; I intend to hold your feet to the fire. I want justice for my brother, and I'll not leave until it is done.'

'My goodness!' said Calpurnia, coming into the study after Munro had gone. 'Can he really think that the Tyddes, of all people, have committed murder?'

Eavesdropping, along with not knocking at doors, was one of Calpurnia's many annoying habits. 'I am still not speaking to you,' said the rector.

'Fiddle-faddle, you are doing so right now. What is more, chartreuse is a perfectly admirable colour, *and* you know it. Marcus, what Mr Munro said is perfect nonsense. My friend Mrs Tydde could not possibly have killed anyone.'

Startled, the rector looked at his sister. 'Your friend?'

'I know Mrs Tydde intimately. She is a dear friend, and a great admirer of my books.'

He thought of several sarcastic things to say, but bit them back. Instead, he sighed. 'All the same, Munro's claims must be investigated. I have agreed to interview the Tydde family tomorrow.'

'Really? Oh, Marcus! Ruth Tydde is the gentlest soul on this earth. She would not hurt a fly. And Eb and Flo are delightful boys, but they can barely summon the energy to catch a fish. Killing a man would be far beyond them. Murder? It is too astonishing.'

'What? Eb and Flo?'

'Ebenezer and Florian, of course. Her sons.'

Despite himself, the rector started to laugh. 'Did she do that deliberately? Name her two sons so they would be known as Eb and Flo Tydde?'

'I asked her once,' said Calpurnia, starting to giggle too. 'She affected not to know what I was talking about. In the early days of her marriage, when her husband was still a poor fisherman, she was much taken up with religion, and named her first son Ebenezer because she thought it was a godly name. Then she discovered that glorious realm of imagination and romance that is the Gothic novel, and so her second son was called Florian, after the hero of one of her favourite works.'

'Isn't there a daughter as well?'

'Yes. Rather disappointingly, she is called Mary. You know her; she is married to Juggins, the town councillor in New Romney. Mary is the apple of her mother's eye, for she has made her way in society just as the Tyddes always hoped the children would do, once their father's business prospered. Sadly, the two boys have not followed suit. They are quite . . .' Calpurnia paused to choose her word. 'Unambitious,' she said.

'Well, as it happens, I agree with you. I do not think the Tyddes are murderers. But they do have a connection with Maudsley, which I am duty bound to investigate.'

Calpurnia gazed at him seriously. 'Marcus; Ruth Tydde is a dear woman, but her nerves are not of the strongest. She will find being interviewed by you very trying. I should very much like to be present when you do so. I think she will answer your questions more readily if I am there to reassure her.'

Hardcastle considered this, and nodded slowly. If Munro had already accused the Tyddes of murder – and it was highly possible that he had, for the man had the subtlety of a sledgehammer – then

Ruth Tydde was likely to be in a nervous state. He recalled Stemp's description of her: *dancing with the fairies.* An advocate might reassure her and help concentrate her mind. 'Very well. Thank you, Calpurnia. And . . . you may have your chartreuse.'

His sister beamed at him. 'There. I knew you would see sense.'

11

A Pitiful Conspiracy

For once, Calpurnia was up early the next morning, joining Hardcastle at breakfast and tucking into ham and eggs with a hearty appetite. 'I shall squeeze into the dog cart with you, Marcus. My gig is still not mended.'

'Have you sent for the wheelwright?'

'I shall do so tomorrow.' It was the same answer she gave every time the subject came up. She sat and chattered to him about the book she was writing. He barely listened, drinking coffee with his food almost untouched before him. The sick feeling from yesterday would not go away. Could Maudsley, his friend, really have murdered his own son-in-law and widowed his daughter, all for financial gain?

Of course he could. The love of money is indeed the root of all evil.

After breakfast they drove to New Romney through a bright morning, the sky full of piled white clouds. Calpurnia hurried off to the Tydde house, while the rector went into the town hall, which also contained the courthouse. He had decided to interview the Tyddes here rather than at their home because of its formal setting; he wanted Ebenezer and Florian, in particular, to realise the gravity of the situation, and he also wanted to show Munro that justice was being properly done.

He spoke to the town clerk. The Tyddes had responded to the summons and would attend voluntarily. Munro entered the courtroom and bowed a little stiffly. His face was heavy, and he looked as if he had not slept.

'The family have been sent for, Mr Munro. They will attend on us shortly.'

'Thank you, sir,' said Munro, rather gruffly.

'I understand you are in business in Edinburgh,' said Hardcastle, his tone conversational.

'Aye. Shipping and importation. We are importers of jute in particular.'

'I see. A family firm?'

'It was founded by our grandfather, yes. My brothers and I are the partners now.'

'Did Hector retain his partnership when he went south?'

'Oh, yes. That's another bone of contention. Through this spurious will, those thieves the Maudsleys now have a stake in our firm.'

The rector ignored this. 'Did you ever have business dealings in the Netherlands?' he asked.

'Before the war, yes. We traded a little with Amsterdam.'

'And since we went to war with the Netherlands? Has there been any further trade in that direction?'

Munro stared at him, his eyes cold under their heavy lids. 'What are you insinuating, sir?'

'Nothing at all. Some British firms, in special circumstances, continue to trade legitimately with the Netherlands. I wondered if yours might be one of them.'

'It most certainly is not.'

At that moment, the town clerk nodded and entered the chamber, ushering in Mrs Tydde arm in arm with Calpurnia. Ruth Tydde was a matronly woman in her fifties with black hair turning grey, in a sombre gown and bonnet. She gave her evidence in a low voice, turning often to look at Calpurnia for reassurance.

She had offered lodging to a stranger, not thinking there would be any harm in doing so. Yes, she had thought it odd that he kept to his room and asked to take his meals there, but he was a guest in her house; he was welcome to do as he pleased. No, he had no callers, nor did he go out. None of her family had laid eyes on Munro, or even knew of his existence. Her husband was now entirely infirm and seldom left his bed. Her two sons had been out all day on Wednesday, the day Munro arrived; on Thursday they had risen late and gone out again.

Hardcastle watched her closely. 'Let us be quite clear about this. Mr Munro did not see either Ebenezer or Florian while he stayed with you?'

'No, reverend. Apart from myself, the only person who saw him was our maidservant, who took him his meals and emptied the . . . the necessary box.'

'When did you realise that the man your sons had found was in fact your lodger?'

'As soon as they told me, reverend. I recognised the coat they said he was wearing. I could not believe my ears. He seemed such a nice gentleman, and I could not fathom why anyone would wish to do him harm. But then I grew terrified that we would be blamed for his death. People might say we lured him into the house and killed him for his money.'

'Yes,' said Munro heavily. 'They might well say that.'

Mrs Tydde quailed. Calpurnia whispered to her; she nodded, and then spoke up again in a stronger voice. 'My boys don't need money, reverend. My husband and I give them everything they need. There's no need for them to steal.'

The rector silenced Munro with a look and then turned back to the woman. 'As it happens, Mrs Tydde, his money had not been stolen, so your fears were baseless. Had you informed me of what had transpired at the time of the murder, we could have cleared up the matter at once and set your mind at ease. The law does not exist solely to punish you, Mrs Tydde. It is also there to protect you.'

Mrs Tydde nodded, mute. 'One more question,' said Hardcastle. 'You are a lady of means; you do not need to take in lodgers. Why did you on this occasion?'

'He looked tired,' said Mrs Tydde simply. 'I spoke to him, and he said he was a stranger who had travelled far and was weary. I offered him simple charity, reverend, as the Lord himself bade us do. I did not ask for money, but he said he had means and insisted on paying for his keep.'

The rector nodded. 'Thank you for answering my questions,' he said.

He listened carefully while Ebenezer and Florian recounted their actions during the hours before the murder, ending with their discovery of the body. Once again, the story was unchanged from its first telling. He asked the same question he had asked the morning Munro was found. 'While you were at sea, did you see any other boat, or ship?'

'No, reverend. Like we told Mr Stemp before, the other fishermen were all down south,' said Ebenezer. 'We were up north, fishing for bass. We were all alone.'

'At some point in the night, two ships passed through the waters near here. One was the revenue cruiser, the *Stag*. The other was a Dutch lugger, broad-beamed and of shallow draft. Did you see either of them?'

'No, reverend.'

'Have you ever before seen a Dutch ship in these waters?'

They thought for a while. Munro stared at the rector, clearly wondering where this line of questioning was going. 'Can't say we have, reverend,' said Ebenezer finally.

'Very well. We are also looking for a man from Hythe, a young man, slender of build, dressed in workmen's clothes but well spoken. Did you see anyone like this the day before the murder?'

'What is this?' demanded Munro. 'Who are you talking about?'

'He is wanted for questioning in connection with the murder of your brother, Mr Munro. Well?' he asked the Tyddes. 'This is the man who hired Jem Clay's boat, and who may well be responsible for the murder. Have you seen him?'

'We'd really like to be helpful, reverend,' said Florian earnestly, 'but I don't recall anyone looking like what you say.'

'Nor me,' said Ebenezer. 'Permit me to ask, reverend; why would a man from Hythe be down here hiring a boat?'

That indeed was the question to be answered, thought the rector. He turned to the clerk. 'Thank you. We have no more need of your services.'

The clerk departed, looking puzzled. Hardcastle turned back to the Tyddes. 'Do you know Mr Frederick Maudsley, the justice of the peace from Shadoxhurst? Answer me truthfully now.'

The two men looked at each other. 'Yes, reverend,' said Florian with resignation.

'You met him while you were engaged together in the free trade. Am I correct?'

Mrs Tydde gasped and clutched at Calpurnia for support. 'You have nothing to fear,' said Hardcastle. 'I have no intention of informing the Preventive services.'

'We've run some cargoes up to Magpie Court,' said Ebenezer after a time. 'Brandy and bolts of cloth, mostly. I reckon he was keeping some of it, and selling the rest on. He treated us proper, paid us well, helped us store the stuff in his barns, even gave us a meal in his kitchen. He's a gentleman.'

'And while you were at Magpie Court, did you ever meet or see Mr Hector Munro, the deceased?'

Again the brothers looked at each other, and again he saw the weary resignation in their eyes. 'Just the once, reverend,' said Ebenezer.

Hardcastle saw Munro's eyes light up in triumph. 'Tell me,' he commanded.

'It was one of them times when he gave us a meal. We were sitting in the kitchen when Mr Munro came in to speak to the cook. We didn't know who he was; we asked cook after, and she told us.'

'You did not speak to him? You have never seen him since?'

'No, reverend. You see, we didn't know it was him in the boat, cuz of what the birds had done to his face. We only found out when we heard you tell Dr Mackay.'

'And why did you not inform myself or Mr Stemp that you had previously met Mr Munro?'

'We didn't want to draw attention to the fact that we knew Mr Maudsley,' said Ebenezer, a little miserably. 'It wouldn't have looked right.'

'No,' said the rector. 'It does not look right. You run goods for Mr Maudsley; you have been to his house; you have met Mr Munro. Then Mr Munro comes to New Romney and stays in your mother's house. A day and a half later, you are the ones who find him dead. That doesn't look right at all, does it?'

'It must be a . . . what's the thing? What's the word I'm looking for, Eb?' Florian asked his brother.

'Coincidence,' said Ebenezer, nodding. 'That's what it'll be. I swear, reverend, we didn't know Mr Munro at all. We just saw him the once.'

Munro sucked his teeth. The rector nodded.

'Did Mr Maudsley ever give you any additional commissions? Did he ask you to undertake any venture for him unconnected with smuggling?'

The two men looked perplexed. 'Don't rightly know what you mean, reverend,' said Florian. 'What kind of commissions would you be talking about?'

Did he hire you to murder his son-in-law? Of course he didn't. If Maudsley had wanted to hire a killer, he would have gone to Hythe and contacted men like Noakes and Fisk, not these two yokels.

And perhaps that was exactly what he had done.

He sent the Tyddes home, the mother still in the care of Calpurnia, then thanked the clerk and walked out of the town hall. Munro came after him, face dark with anger.

'Hardcastle! You're not letting them go?'

'Yes. They are innocent of any crime.'

'What? They've as good as confessed, man! You described the chain of evidence yourself! It's exactly as I said last night. Maudsley and the Tyddes planned the whole thing between them.'

Hardcastle halted and faced the other man. 'There is not a shred of actual evidence against the Tyddes. And if you were any kind of student of human character, Mr Munro, you would realise that they are incapable of doing such harm. A good woman with a kind heart; two simple men who dabble in smuggling for the fun of it but otherwise live their lives in peace: that is what we have here. No more.'

'Then what was my brother doing at their house?'

'It's not so much of a coincidence as you might think. You've seen the Tydde house; it is one of the largest in New Romney. Your brother was trying to stay out of sight, in case he was being followed or observed. He eschewed the Ship and the rooming houses for that reason. He hoped that in a big private house like that of the Tyddes, he could simply disappear until it came time for him to make his rendezvous.'

'Rendezvous with whom?'

'That is what I am endeavouring to find out, Mr Munro. That is why I asked the questions I did, about the Dutch ship and the man from Hythe. Unfortunately I was not able to learn anything further.'

Munro was still furiously angry. 'So what now? You'll drop the whole case, I imagine. Maudsley is a friend of yours, isn't he? Aye, you'll stick by him, and that's all we shall ever hear about who killed poor Hector. English justice!' he spat. 'I should have expected nothing less.'

'You are grieving, sir,' said the rector quietly, 'and you are exhausted from your journey. Therefore I shall forgive your words. Go back to the Ship and wait. I will attend on you when there is news.'

A little later Hardcastle delivered Calpurnia back to New Romney, and then drove the dog cart up the high road towards Appledore before turning north to Ashford, climbing the hill out of the Marsh and picking up the turnpike at Ham Street. His mood was one of dull, bitter gloom.

Munro's rage was born partly from grief; as such, he found it excusable. He had come down to Romney Marsh, certain that his brother had been murdered by Maudsley or his agents, and begun asking questions. Someone had pointed out the Tyddes as the men who found the body, and he had bullied them and their mother, taking their hesitation and that tenuous connection with Maudsley as proof that they were concealing something. He had put two and two together, and made five.

Like Calpurnia, he had never really believed the Tyddes were capable of murder. It was Maudsley who worried him. Munro was convinced that Maudsley had forged Hector's will, with the connivance of the solicitor. It was probable that he was wrong; his judgement clouded by sorrow and anger, he had refused to accept his brother's will as genuine. But why *had* Hector Munro cut his family out of his will? Something was not right here. Mrs Chaytor had thought so too.

And then there was Cranthorpe, with whom Munro had spent an hour, talking privately before going away to meet his death. What role had Cranthorpe played in those events?

Arriving in Ashford early in the afternoon, Hardcastle dismounted stiffly and walked into Cranthorpe's offices. The same clerk greeted him. Yes, Mr Cranthorpe was fully recovered and had returned to work. He would see if Mr Cranthorpe was free. The clerk disappeared into the inner office, and Hardcastle heard a long, murmured conversation through the door. Finally the clerk returned and showed him in.

'Reverend Hardcastle, welcome,' the solicitor said, bowing and smiling. 'Good to see you again. We didn't have much chance to talk at Magpie Court. Are you enjoying your mission among the heathen?'

'I beg your pardon?'

'Romney Marsh.' Cranthorpe winked. 'They eat their babies down there, don't they? Do sit down, sir. Will you take refreshment?'

'Thank you, no. Mr Cranthorpe, I am here in my capacity as justice of the peace. I have a number of questions concerning the murder of your late client, Mr Hector Munro.'

Cranthorpe at once grew solemn. 'Ask away, sir. I am entirely at your disposal.'

'For how long had you been handling Mr Munro's affairs?'

'Not long. He appointed me to act for him shortly before his wedding to Miss Maudsley.'

'Among other things, you drew up his last will and testament.'

Cranthorpe lost some of his affability. 'Have you been talking to that insufferable Scotchman?'

'The brother of the murdered man, yes.'

'Well, I'll tell you what I told him. I cannot and will not discuss the affairs of any of my clients, living or dead.'

'Mr Alexander Munro has made a very serious allegation,' said Hardcastle. 'Your full cooperation will enable me to get to the bottom of the matter swiftly and promptly. On the other hand, if you demur, I will be forced to conclude that you are involved in some sort of deception yourself.'

His voice hardened. 'As a legal man, you will know about the law of joint enterprise. If a crime has been committed without your participation but with your knowledge, you may still be convicted.'

Cranthorpe wiped his forehead with his handkerchief. It was not particularly warm in the office. 'What do you want to know?'

'When did you draw up Mr Munro's will?'

'About a month before his marriage.'

'In broad terms, what were the provisions of the will?'

'Apart from the usual bequests, the whole of his estate passed to his wife, with the proviso that if she were to have a legitimate child, the estate should then pass to the child and be held in trust until that child reached its majority. In which case, Mrs Munro and Mr Maudsley would jointly be guardians. There is nothing unusual about this.'

'No? It sounds as though, by the terms of this will, Mr Munro effectively cut himself off from his own family. That, surely, *is* unusual.'

'Not so much as you might think,' said Cranthorpe. He had recovered a little. 'Mr Munro had a falling-out with his family. They disapproved of his marriage, and I gather there were strong words on both sides.'

'He told you as much?'

'Yes.'

'But the estrangement did not last for long. Mr Munro was soon corresponding with his brothers once again. He spoke of going north with his wife to visit them.'

'It could be,' said the solicitor tersely. 'I know nothing of that.'

Hardcastle looked at him, his suspicions growing. 'Also, you said *if* she were to have a child, indicating a possibility only. Surely, once it became known that Mrs Munro was *definitely* with child, the will should have been amended to reflect this. Was this not done?'

'Mr Munro was a very busy man. I'm sure it must have slipped his mind.'

'Oh, come, come, Cranthorpe. It was your duty to give Mr Munro legal advice. You should have informed him that he needed to amend his will. Did you do so?'

Cranthorpe was perspiring again. He spread his hands. 'I . . . I may have done so, yes.'

'Did you, or did you not?'

'Yes. I did.'

'When?'

'In March, and again in June. He prevaricated. He said he needed more time to think about the terms of the guardianship.'

The rector paused, letting this sink in. 'You mean, he had been reconciled to his brothers, and was considering whether to name one of them as guardian. Is that what he finally did, Mr Cranthorpe? Is that perhaps why he came to see you on Tuesday the 8th of August, three days before he was killed?

Did he change the terms of his bequest? Did you draw up a new will on his behalf?'

Cornered, the solicitor looked down at his desk, refusing to meet Hardcastle's eye. A bead of sweat rolled down his nose and dropped onto his waistcoat.

'I require an answer, Mr Cranthorpe,' the rector said.

A stronger man would have damned Hardcastle's eyes and challenged him to prove his case. Cranthorpe simply sat and sweated.

'Yes,' he said.

'And what were the new terms?'

'Mr Maudsley was no longer to be a guardian. That duty was transferred to Mr Alexander Munro of Edinburgh.'

'You wrote out this will, and Mr Hector Munro signed it.'

'Yes.'

'What happened then?'

'He took the will with him and returned to Shadoxhurst. That was the last I saw of him.'

'But you retain your own copy of the will. Send for it, if you please.'

Cranthorpe called for his clerk, who brought the will. The rector broke the seal and read it through swiftly. The terms were as the solicitor had said.

'One last question, Mr Cranthorpe, and you must answer this honestly or it will go very ill with you. Why, when Mr Alexander Munro called on you, did you not inform him of the existence of this document? Why did you insist that the earlier will was still valid?'

When Cranthorpe did not answer, the rector rose to his feet and stood looking down at him. 'Did Frederick Maudsley ask you to deny the existence of the later will? And did you agree?'

'Yes,' whispered Cranthorpe.

*

'Reverend Hardcastle. How very good to see you.'

Two weeks had brought colour back into Cecilia Munro's cheeks, even if the shadows still lay dark under her eyes. 'It is good to see you too, my dear,' he said quietly, taking her hands. 'How are you?'

'I am beginning slowly to return to the land of the living. Father and my sisters have been so very kind and tender, and I never knew I had so many friends. Charlotte Faversham has come to stay with me for as long as I need her. She has been truly wonderful.'

Charlotte Faversham, in the rector's brief experience of her, was a flibbertigibbet, but she was also a cheerful soul. He could see how she might be a tonic to her grieving young friend.

'Mrs Chaytor called again last week, and Mrs Redcliffe has visited no fewer than three times,' said Cecilia. Her eyes searched the rector's face. 'I still think of him every hour, every minute.'

'That is good,' said the rector. 'He was a fine man, and it is right that you should mourn him. You will remember him all your life, as will all who knew him. Be his memorial, my dear, but remember too that you have your own life, waiting to be lived. Remember him, but also make him proud of you.'

'I shall try to do so.' Tears glistened in the corners of her eyes, but she was strong. 'But I think perhaps you did not come to see me? Father is out by the stables.'

'Then I shall go to him. He will return in a little while. When he does, be kind to him.'

He found Maudsley in the field beyond the stables, leaning on a wooden fence and watching horses graze in the middle distance. He turned at the rector's approach and came forward, smiling. 'Hardcastle. I heard a carriage arrive, but didn't realise it was you. Forgive me for not being on hand to welcome you.'

'That's quite all right. I saw Mrs Munro, and was glad to see her looking much improved. Maudsley, we must talk.' He looked at the grooms working around the stable and said, 'Privately.'

They walked along the line of the fence until they were out of earshot of the stables. 'You've seen the brother,' said Maudsley.

'I have. I have also seen your solicitor in Ashford.'

Maudsley stopped dead, the colour slowly leaving his face. 'I see.'

'You found copies of both wills when going through Hector's papers after he died. What did you do with the new will? Burn it?'

Maudsley nodded, unable to speak. 'So you maintained the fiction that you and Cecilia were still the guardians of her son,' said Hardcastle. 'You also involved Cranthorpe in the deception. Did you pay him? Or was it a favour?'

'I asked him to do it. I've known him for years. He handles my affairs, too, of course.'

'Of course. Why do something so wrong and illegal? Did you need the money so very badly?'

'The bank,' said Maudsley. 'It is failing. We are running out of capital.'

'Why? Bad debts?'

'Yes, and losses in other areas. Faversham came up with a scheme that he said was bound to make money; we could recoup all our losses and have a profit left over. But then that started to go wrong too. The money isn't flowing in as it should. We're in real trouble now.' He looked helplessly at the rector. 'When I saw the two wills, I realised there was a chance I could get some more money to put into the bank, perhaps prop it up a little longer. I was wrong, Hardcastle. I knew it then; I know it now. But God help me, I did it anyway.'

He looked at Hardcastle. 'What will you do now?'

'That depends on how you answer my remaining questions,' said Hardcastle. 'Did you kill Munro to get his money? Or did you order someone else to do it?'

Maudsley flinched. 'I loved Hector like a son,' he said, his voice quiet. 'As you know, my own son is crippled and ill and in pain; poor boy, he will not live many years longer. I love him also, believe me. But I wanted someone who could run this estate when I am older, take over from me and become head of the family. Hector was that man, the son who would follow in my footsteps. Upon my word of honour, Hardcastle, I did not kill him.'

'Your word of honour is not the guarantee it once was,' Hardcastle said brutally. 'Do you know of a man named Noakes? Or one called Fisk?'

Maudsley shook his head. 'No.'

'Come, Maudsley. They are smugglers from Hythe, where you often do business. You must know of them.'

'I haven't dealt with anyone from Hythe for many years. They're a secretive bunch, and I don't trust them. I work only with the Dymchurch lot now. I recall hearing the name Noakes, but nothing more.'

'And Dymchurch is where you met Ebenezer and Florian Tydde?'

'Yes,' said Maudsley, looking surprised. 'They're from New Romney, but they sometimes join the Dymchurch crew; they're well known. I asked them to carry goods for me a few times. Why do you ask about them?'

Hardcastle ignored the question. 'When Munro left on the 9th, he was not going to London, was he? There was no timber deal, was there?'

Maudsley's pallor grew. 'No.'

'Then where was he going?'

'France,' said Maudsley.

Hardcastle nodded slowly, letting the pieces fall into place. That explained why someone had hired the boat. Munro intended to row out into the Channel where he would be picked up by a larger ship, very probably the lugger Captain Haddock had seen.

'That explains why you thought he was going into danger,' the rector said.

'I begged him not to go, for Cecilia's sake if not his own. But he would not listen. Once Hector made up his mind, nothing could shake him.'

'Did you introduce him into the free trade?'

'No. Faversham cooked up the idea, last year. As I said, he reckoned we could recover all our losses and come out with a profit on top. He found out somehow about my own contacts, and asked if I would help. I refused. I thought the idea was cracked; if we were found out, it could bring down the bank. But Faversham found his own people somewhere, and went ahead. And he persuaded Hector to join him.'

'Presumably Faversham and Munro did not deal directly with the smugglers. They must have had an intermediary.'

'I would think so. But if you are asking me who the intermediary is, I don't know.'

'What are they smuggling? The usual trade, gin and vanities?'

'I assume so. Hector never confided the details to me. He said it was best that way. If something went wrong, then Cecilia and I would be protected. So all I knew was that Hector and Faversham had a smuggling gang working for them.'

'But something went wrong.'

'Yes. Hector went to see Faversham in Rye the Saturday before the birthday party. He was absolutely seething when he returned. Faversham had made a mess of things, he told me. They had staked everything on this venture; the whole future of the bank depended on its making large profits. But according to the figures Faversham had shown him, they were now actually making a loss. Something had gone wrong, he said, and he would have to go secretly across to France to sort out the matter.

'And so he went.' There were tears in Maudsley's eyes. 'Find out who killed him, Hardcastle, I beg you. I'll not sleep easy until I know what happened, and why.'

'Why did you not tell me all this when we spoke after the funeral?'

'I was afraid of what would happen. If all this got out; well, as I said, it could bring down the bank and ruin us all. Faversham said as much to me, before the funeral. "You have to think of the wider interest, Maudsley," he said. "You have to keep this quiet."'

Hardcastle watched him for a while, hardening his heart. 'You say you loved him like a son. And yet you put the interests of the bank, and your own interests, ahead of finding his killer.'

Maudsley said nothing. He stood, leaning on the fence and staring at the ground. The rector could see him shivering a little as he fought to control his emotions.

'I will find the man who killed Hector Munro,' said Hardcastle. 'No matter who he might be, or where, I will bring him to justice. As for you, you have engaged in a most pitiful conspiracy to pervert the course of justice for financial gain. You deceived myself, an officer of the law in the course of his duties, and withheld information from me. You have attempted to commit fraud upon the Munro family, and upon your own grandson.'

'And I have betrayed our friendship,' said Maudsley softly.

'That is the least of your offences, though I admit it is the one that gives me the most personal pain. I have enough evidence to commit you to prison.'

Maudsley looked up at this. His eyes were still weeping but his voice was steady. 'I understand,' he said. 'I ask only that you spare Cecilia from knowing the full truth; for her sake, not mine. She has suffered enough already.'

'I agree. And imprisoning you would devastate Cecilia still further. Stay here and be a father to her, and your other children too. But you will resign immediately your position as justice of the peace, and you will never again enter public life. Your children, your family, this estate: they are now everything you have. Serve them humbly and well, and pray every day for forgiveness. Farewell, Maudsley. I shall miss your friendship; but this is the end.'

Hardcastle returned to New Romney in the evening light, the white streak of the comet beginning to glow in the darkening sky. He found Munro in his room at the Ship, reading. The rector drew the valid will out of his coat pocket and laid it on the desk.

'You may instruct your solicitor to contact Mr Maudsley and Cranthorpe. You will find them both compliant now.'

Munro glared up at him, offering no word of thanks. 'And the murderer?' he asked.

'Neither Maudsley nor the Tydde family have any case to answer.' More gently, the rector said, 'Go back to Edinburgh, Mr Munro. Don't stay down here, eating your heart out. Go back to those who need you.'

'I told you. I'll not leave until I have justice for my brother.'

Hardcastle tapped the will. 'This is justice, right here in this document. It is up to you now to see that your brother's wishes are carried out. As for finding his killer, let the law take its course. I know you have no high opinion of me, or of English justice. But I have sworn to find the man who killed him, and I will.'

Munro said nothing. His eyes were dark and heavy with renewed grief, once more on the edge of tears. 'Mourn for your brother, Mr Munro,' said the rector quietly. 'It is I who will avenge him.'

He closed the door and stood outside it for a moment. Inside the room, the other man had begun to sob.

Back in St Mary, Hardcastle stood in the hall of the rectory, taking off his gloves and listening to his sister play the fortepiano in the drawing room. She was singing; off-key as usual. He stood listening, his mind still sick from Maudsley's betrayal. Biddy the maidservant came out from the kitchen. 'Ask Mrs Kemp to fetch me a bottle of port from the cellar,' he said.

> *Abroad as I was waaalking*
> *Down by some greenwood siiide*
> *I heard a young girl siiinging*
> *'I wish I were a Bri-i-i-DE!'*

'Make it two bottles,' said the rector.

12

Matters of Life and Death

SIXPENNY COURT, CHANGE ALLEY, LONDON
25th of August, 1797

Reverend Hardcastle, sir,

I am in receipt of your letter of 22nd inst. I can assure you that there has been no investment by the East Weald and Ashford Bank in Baltic timber in recent weeks. I know this, because I have it on good authority that there have been no investments of *any* kind in timber, by any bank or other investor at all. Since the negotiations with France began, and in particular since Lord Malmesbury's latest report expressing high hopes for peace within the next few months, the Admiralty has pulled in its horns. The price of timber for shipbuilding has plummeted, and there is no longer any interest in this commodity.

From your letter, I infer that you are investigating the death of Mr Hector Munro. It would appear that you are also looking into the bank's affairs. I feel I should like to discuss the matter with you more fully, and I feel too that it would be best if we did not commit our words to paper.

I am away shortly to Birmingham; it will be some days before I am back in London. May I call upon you on Thursday week, the 7th of September? You should expect me at about midday.

Yr very obedient servant

DAVID RICARDO

Aboard the Stag, Cruiser
26th of August, 1797

Reverend Hardcastle, sir,

I trust you will forgive the long delay in my writing to you. My ship has been at sea for the past week, and we have only just made port again, giving me an opportunity to dispatch this letter.

When we met in Rye, you enquired as to the time we spotted the Dutch vessel off Romney Marsh. I have checked the log, and am pleased to confirm that she was spotted at fourteen minutes past two of the clock on the morning of 4th of August.

I have also made enquiries among my crew as to whether any of them saw another vessel or any other unusual occurrence. The gaze of most of my crew was concentrated on the Dutchman, as indeed was my own. But Able Seaman Mossman related that he thought he had seen a smaller boat, a coastal fishing boat, adrift on the sea beyond the Dutchman.

When questioned further, he testified that he could see no one at the oars, and concluded that the boat was deserted; probably she had come loose from her moorings and drifted out to sea. Thereafter, the chase of the Dutchman being accounted the more important matter, he dismissed the boat from his mind.

I enclose a copy of Able Seaman Mossman's statement. I shall continue to keep an eye out for this Dutchman, and should I spot him again, I shall be sure to inform you soonest.

Yr very obedient servant

J. Haddock, Capt.

*

On a fine Monday morning in the last week of August, Joshua Stemp called at the rectory. He looked tired, like a man who had not been getting much sleep. He found the rector heavy-eyed and weary, too, but for a different reason.

'I had another run-in with Noakes last week, reverend. My apologies for not coming to you sooner, but I was away on business of my own 'til late Friday, and then you were away Saturday.'

Business of his own, of course, meant smuggling; it had been the new moon last week.

'Never mind,' said the rector. 'What happened?'

'He had company this time, four others. I recognised one of them, a man called Fisk. He's even more of a villain than Noakes. He's the kind that'll stab a man just for the fun of seeing the light go out in his eyes.'

'What were they doing?'

'They were on a run, but they weren't bringing goods in. They were sending them out. When I saw them, they were loading a ship bound for France. It looked like they were loading powder kegs.'

'Gunpowder!' The rector stared.

'That's what it looked like, reverend. The kegs had the Board of Ordinance mark and everything.'

'How many kegs were there?'

'I counted ten in all.'

'So few?' The rector rubbed his aching temples, trying to think. The Maudsley affair had been a distraction, and now he was having trouble picking up the pieces of the investigation again. Last night had not helped either.

'This makes no sense,' Hardcastle said eventually. 'When I buy powder at the start of shooting season, I pay about sixpence a pound. A twenty-pound keg of powder will be worth about ten shillings. That entire cargo you saw isn't worth above £5, £6 at the utmost. There cannot be a profit in smuggling that.'

He shook his head. 'I am sorry, Joshua, but I fear this rather knocks on the head your theory that Noakes and his gang were working for the bank. Faversham and Munro were expecting a profit of thousands of pounds, perhaps tens of thousands. They won't get that from a few kegs of gunpowder.'

'There's something more, reverend,' said Stemp. 'I mentioned two of the party, Noakes and Fisk; I reckon two of the others were sailors. The fifth was a young fellow, slender, with an educated voice. Do you see what I mean?'

'The man who hired the boat in New Romney.'

'And the fellow who met Mr Munro in Hythe,' said Stemp. 'It could be they're one and the same.'

The rector rubbed his forehead again. 'Then we must find this man. I'm afraid you'll need to go up to Hythe again. But not alone, not with this gang around. Tell Jack Hoad, Murton and Luckhurst that I want to see them. I'll swear them in as special constables and they will accompany you to Hythe.'

'Thank you, reverend.' Stemp hesitated. 'There's another thing, if I may.'

'Go on.'

'It's about the bank,' said Stemp. 'There's a story doing the rounds that they might be in trouble. I wondered if you had heard anything.'

It was Hardcastle's turn to hesitate. Stemp had given him his full loyalty; he deserved the truth in return. 'I've heard the rumours too,' he said. 'I don't know if they are true or not. Do you by chance have money deposited with the East Weald and Ashford?'

'I've a good bit put by there, yes. Me and Maisie, we don't need much; we're content as we are. But I'm thinking of my girls, see. When they grow up, they won't be fishermen's daughters. I intend for them to be proper young ladies, respected, with dowries so they can marry well. I don't want to see my grandchildren still fishing for a living.'

'If you are concerned, you could withdraw your money.'

'I've thought of that. But Tim Luckhurst says the bank has stopped paying out gold and silver. Because of the Restriction, see. You can withdraw money, he says, but they'll only give you paper. I'm uneasy about that, reverend, truly I am. I'm not fond of paper money, it don't seem real to me. You know where you are with gold and silver.'

'I understand,' said the rector. 'I am sorry, Joshua. I do not know what else to suggest.'

Stemp shrugged. 'I'll just have to hope for the best,' he said. 'Even if the bank is having difficulties, that doesn't mean it's about to fail. Perhaps things'll turn out right in the end.'

'I hope so,' said the rector. But he remembered Martha Redcliffe's opinion of Faversham's competence, and was uneasy.

*

THE SHIP INN, NEW ROMNEY
29th of August, 1797

Reverend Hardcastle,

Since your last visit to me on Saturday eve, I have given considerable thought to the events surrounding my brother's murder. I have seen both Maudsley and the solicitor Cranthorpe, and my brother's affairs have now been arranged in a matter that I would consider to be satisfactory. I have also seen my brother's widow, and I am forced to conclude that she is a sensible woman, with only the best of intentions towards her son. I find I can bear her no ill will.

Accordingly, there would seem no purpose in my remaining here any longer, and my own affairs now call me home to Edinburgh. I write to you therefore to take my leave. I shall continue to follow the progress of the investigation, and ask that you provide me with news as often as possible.

May I also take this opportunity to thank you for your patience and understanding during this time of great trial.

Yr very obedient servant

ALEXANDER MUNRO

Laying down the letter, the rector closed his eyes and uttered a short prayer. Some wounds, at least, were on their way to healing.

That same morning, Amelia Chaytor drove her gig through one of the ancient gates of Rye. A little heat haze hung over the wastelands of the southern Marsh, stretching east from beneath the town's ramparts. She turned in at the George, where she left her groom to look after the horse and rig, then walked down the street towards the imposing frontage of the East Weald and Ashford Bank.

The bank servants received her with deference and she was shown into the office of Mr Grebell Faversham, the manager, and brought coffee. The office was small but comfortably furnished; the furniture was fine and the writing set on the desk was of black Chinese lacquerware with silver mountings. *Hmm*, she thought, *he appears to have better taste in furniture than in clothing . . .*

The door opened and her host hurried in, stopping and making a sweeping bow. He was dressed slightly more soberly today, in grey breeches and a plum coat; he had not known she was coming.

'Mrs Chaytor! What a pleasure it is to welcome you.' He was a little flushed, his red hair slightly tousled. She thought he looked rather innocent.

'The pleasure is mine entirely,' she said in her light drawl. 'I was passing the bank, and it occurred to me that this was an excellent opportunity to return your calls. I trust I am not disturbing your work?'

'No, no, not at all.' He fussed, asking if her coffee was hot enough, if she had enough sugar, if there was any other comfort she desired. She shook her head. 'Your staff have looked after me admirably. Mr Faversham, I confess this is not entirely a social call. I am contemplating opening an account with your bank. Do you think that would be possible?'

Mr Faversham gaped at her. The thought of this fashionable lady, who doubtless banked at one of the great houses of London, offering to transfer her business here was too much to comprehend. 'Ma'am . . . are you certain?'

'A small account only. It would be useful to me during my visits to Rye.'

'It would be an honour to serve you, ma'am.'

'I do have a question for you, though.' She dropped her voice a little. 'Are we quite alone, Mr Faversham? There is no one who can overhear us?'

Grebell blushed again, to his own evident annoyance and confusion. 'We are quite secure, ma'am, I assure you. You may speak freely to me.'

'Well. I have heard a whisper, nothing more, that your bank may be in difficulties. There is some talk of debts. So I hope you can reassure me that all is well, before we proceed.'

'Debts?' His face still red, Grebell looked perplexed at the very notion. 'Ma'am, nothing could be further from the truth. The bank has never been in better health. Why, we are even thinking of expanding again. I have heard Father talk of opening branches in Maidstone, even Tunbridge Wells.' The young man smiled what he probably thought was a reassuring smile. 'You may take it for granted that this bank is absolutely solid and well found. I assure you of that, on my word of honour.'

'Thank you. I knew I could rely on you for an honest and informed account.' She smiled back at him. 'So this rumour about your Canterbury branch is just that? A rumour?'

'Oh, nothing is wrong with the Canterbury branch. Why, it is one of the most profitable branches in the bank. Cotton is a very good banker, very capable. I've overheard Father refer to him as Midas. You know; whatever he touches turns to gold.'

Mrs Chaytor smiled again. 'And this peculiar tale that the bank may be involved with the free trade; that too is only a rumour?'

Grebell stared at her in consternation. 'Ma'am, where on earth did you hear that? Begging your pardon, but that really *is* fustian. Why would a large and respected bank like ours risk its reputation by stooping to smuggling? The idea is preposterous. I say, whoever is spreading this story really should know better.'

She paused for a moment, considering. *Either he knows nothing whatever, or he is an actor of astonishing ability, and the London stage is lost without him.*

'Very well,' she said, 'I am wholly reassured. Shall we proceed?'

She waited, answering his questions as he took down her details. Part way through, she said artlessly, 'Have you seen your friend Mrs Munro recently?'

Grebell looked up. 'No, I'm afraid I have not. Charlotte, my sister, has gone to stay with her. I should call, I know, but . . . To be honest, ma'am, I am not certain what I would say to her.'

'It's quite easy, Mr Faversham. Just talk to her as you would a friend.' Mrs Chaytor paused. 'I am sure she would appreciate a call from you. She is less grief-stricken, but I think she is lonely.' When he failed to take the hint, she said, 'A visit from you might help to console her.'

Grebell nodded. 'You're right, of course, ma'am. I'll call on her as soon as I can.'

Mrs Chaytor lost patience. 'Come, Mr Faversham. You are fond of Cecilia, you said so yourself, and I am sure she is equally fond of you. She is alone in the world, bereft. And the partnership in the bank held by her husband is now vacant. There is a door open for you, should you choose to walk through it.'

'Yes, I suppose so,' said Grebell. He gazed out the window for a moment, and then back at her with his slightly bulging eyes. 'But I have been thinking about life, and death, and all manner of things since Munro died.' He dropped his eyes then, staring down at the writing set. 'I have come to the conclusion that there is more to life than banking,' he said.

Then he collected himself. 'Please forgive me, Mrs Chaytor,' he said a little anxiously. 'You did not come here to listen to me wittering on about myself. To come back to the matter of your account. How much do you wish to deposit?'

Mrs Chaytor reached into her reticule and pulled out a banknote, which she began to unfold. 'Shall we say, twenty pounds?' she asked.

Stemp and his three newly minted special constables walked to Dymchurch, where they cadged a ride on a brickmaker's dray up to Hythe. 'What do you reckon?' asked Luckhurst as they rode along, the green hills and white cliffs to the north drawing slowly closer. 'Have we any chance of finding this fellow?'

'Needle in a haystack,' said Jack Hoad.

'That's pretty much it,' agreed Stemp. 'The only person who's seen him is Jem Clay, and he didn't get a good look at him, or says he didn't.'

'We should have brought Jem along,' said Murton, who was also the blacksmith in St Mary. 'He might recognise this fellow if he saw him again.'

'I thought of that. I went back to Jem yesterday evening and begged him for help. When that didn't work, I tried threats. Nothing doing either way. He says his leg is still sore, and in any case, the fellow had his hat pulled down over his face and Jem couldn't see much. I wish we'd got a better look at him the other night on the beach.'

Hythe lay sleeping beside its muddy harbour under the shoulder of the hills. The streets were dirty and the gutters stank. They came to the Swan on the high street, seeing a post-coach waiting for its team in the yard. The common room was dark except where sunlight poured in through the windows and pooled on the floor.

Manningham the landlord looked up as the four of them entered the room. A balding man of indeterminate middle age, he wore a white shirt, none too clean, with an even dirtier apron over top. Beside him, a tall man in the blue coat and white breeches of a Royal Navy officer stood leaning against the counter drinking gin and water, his cocked hat on the bar beside him.

'Stempy,' said Manningham. 'A second visit in such a short time. To what do I owe the pleasure?'

'Same business as last time, Manny. We're trying to find out what happened to the man killed down by St Mary.'

'That business still?' asked the navy man with interest. 'You don't yet know who shot him?'

'Not yet, Mr Stark. We're making progress, though.'

Manningham made a Gallic noise of disapproval. He spoke slightly French-accented English; when on the other side of the Channel, he spoke slightly English-accented French. His real name was Meninghem, and he came from a hamlet of that name not far from Boulogne, but he had family on both coasts of the narrow sea. There were many others like him, part-French and part-English in blood and language, at home on both sides but owing allegiance to neither. To them, the war between France and England was an occasional inconvenience, but also a useful source of profit. Needless to say, they were embedded deep in the smuggling trade.

'Why do you bother?' Manningham asked, pouring mugs of small beer from the tap. 'He was a stranger. What difference does it make who killed him?'

'He left a wife,' said Stemp, 'and a nipper born just after he died. It'll be a comfort for them, to know what happened.'

Manningham snorted again. 'The world is full of misery. Comfort is an illusion behind which we hide, hoping that life will somehow become bearable. It never does.'

'Manny, you are a gloomy old bastard,' said Stark, the navy officer. 'So what brings you up here, Stemp?'

'We're looking for a man who might be able to help us. Manny, you told me Mr Munro met someone here.'

'I did. And now, you will ask me again to describe him. But, as I told you before, I did not see his face clearly. Also, it was quite dark.' Manningham gestured around the common room.

'If you ever paid for some lamp oil, Manny, you could light this place up,' said Luckhurst. 'Then you might be able to see what was going on in your own house.'

'Believe me,' said Manningham, 'in Hythe there are many advantages in *not* knowing.'

'Come along, Manny,' said Stemp. 'You must remember something.'

Manningham sighed. 'He was as tall as you, Stempy, or perhaps a little more, but not so run to fat as you. His hair was covered by a hat. He wore breeches and half-boots, which were dusty as if from walking. More, I cannot say.'

'You ever hear of anyone from Hythe going down to New Romney to hire a boat?'

Manningham looked at him incredulously. The navy officer watched the byplay with interest. 'This is a genuine question?' asked the landlord. 'You wish to know about men renting boats in New Romney? Why not ask in New Romney?'

'I have. No one knows anything.'

'No one in New Romney knows anything? That comes as no surprise.'

Stemp ignored this. 'We're also looking for a man who calls himself Jean, who goes back and forth as a courier to France. He might work with Noakes's crew. You ever hear of him?'

'Jean? Such an unusual name. I feel sure I would remember if I had heard it before. Is that all? Or do you wish to interrogate me further?'

'Sarcastic bastard. No, not for the moment. We're going to ask around town.' Stemp looked thoughtfully at the navy officer. 'I've just had an idea, Mr Stark. When you've been out on patrol these past few weeks, have you by chance caught sight of a Dutch ship? Two-masted lugger, but broad in the beam and rigged Rotterdam fashion.'

'Can't say I have,' said Stark. 'Who is she?'

'We don't know. But we wouldn't mind finding out. She's been spotted on two different occasions in these waters. Look out for her, Mr Stark, if you will.'

Stark raised his glass. 'I'll do more than that. My *Black Joke* can outrun any ship on the sea. If I spot her, I'll take her.' His face became glum. 'Assuming peace doesn't break out before I get the chance.'

Manningham raised his hands again. 'Ah, these accursed peace negotiations. Let them fail, let them fail!'

'Peace,' said Stark. 'Half the Royal Navy decommissioned, most of its officers on the beach on half pay and no chance of promotion or prize money for those that are left.'

'And the government'll crack down on the free trade again,' said Luckhurst, 'just like they did after the last war.'

'To the devil with peace,' said Stark, raising his tankard. 'By the way, Manny, you still owe me for that brandy I ran for you last month. A Royal Navy lieutenant's pay doesn't last forever, you know.'

The door of the common room opened with a crash. Stemp swung round, reaching at once for the hilt of his knife. Through the door came Noakes and his mastiff, followed by Fisk and two more big men armed with knives and wooden clubs; and as they did so, in one swift, smooth reflex action Manningham reached under the counter and pulled out a bell-mouthed blunderbuss, cocking the hammer and aiming it at the newcomers. They halted.

Stemp and his companions had knives in their hands too. 'Now, you fellows,' said Lieutenant Stark in a quarterdeck voice. 'There'll be no trouble here, do you hear me?'

'Yes, your lordship,' sneered Noakes, tugging at his greasy forelock. His eyes were narrow, his pupils dark, dangerous points within them. 'Thank you, Your Worship. We won't give no trouble, Your Honour.'

He turned to Stemp. 'Now who have we here? Is it Yorkshire Tom, the brave smuggler? No, boys, this ain't him at all. This here is Joshua Stemp, the pig.'

'And look,' said Fisk in his deep voice. 'He's got three more little piglets with him. Oink! Oink!'

'What do you want?' Stemp asked.

'What I want is to find out what you're doing in my town,' Noakes said.

'Your town?' asked Manningham, the blunderbuss rock steady in his pudgy hands. 'Have you been elected mayor, Noakes? Perhaps I missed the town council meeting where this was decided, no?'

'I want to talk to that fellow who was with you on the beach the other night,' said Stemp to Noakes. 'The one with that god-damned Puckle gun.'

'Why do you want to talk to him?' said Fisk in his booming voice.

'It's about a murder,' said Stemp.

Noakes laughed. The mastiff, perhaps not recognising the sound, began to bark noisily. 'Murder,' he said. 'Forget it, Stemp. You'll never find him.'

'Why not?'

'Because he don't exist,' said Noakes.

In her house on the hill above Hythe, Martha Redcliffe gestured to the big footman with the tattooed hands to pour the tea. 'Yes, I call on Mrs Munro as often as I am able,' she said. 'She seems to appreciate the company. She is recovering from her grief remarkably quickly.'

'More so than you or I,' said Amelia Chaytor wryly.

'Perhaps she is stronger than either of us. Or perhaps it is the child that helps. Certainly she is younger; she was not married for so long, and therefore has lost less.' Mrs Redcliffe's skin, dry and sallow against her dark gown, seemed to have no life in it. Beyond the windows the air was full of the heat of late summer, the sea rippling blue to the horizon. This room is like a shadow of the world outside, Amelia thought.

'Isn't that a little heartless?' she asked. 'Grief is grief, surely.'

'Mrs Munro was married for little more than a year. One has fewer memories from a year than one does from ten, or fifteen. There are not so many sources of pain.'

'Yes. I see what you mean.'

Mrs Redcliffe watched her closely. 'Of course you do. You have many memories, I think. Which ones pain you most?'

Amelia paused, considering. 'The things we did together, I think. He taught me how to drive, and shoot, and fish. I taught him to play music. Those were precious times. And then, our years with the embassies in Paris, and Rome. They were full of wonder and excitement, and I shall never forget them.'

'You have travelled,' said Mrs Redcliffe. 'I envy that. Perhaps, when all of this is finished, I will go travelling too. You must tell me about Rome.'

When all of what is finished? Amelia wondered. Obligingly she talked of Rome, describing its grandeur and its stinks, its beauty and vendettas. The other woman listened intently.

'But I think you have had a marvellous life too,' Amelia said finally.

'Oh?' said Mrs Redcliffe. 'What makes you say so?'

'In an age when most women are the property of their father or their husband, you have forged a life for yourself. You run a shipping business; a very successful one, I gather. You are a partner in the bank. You are a woman of substance. That is very rare.'

'It has not been easy,' said Martha Redcliffe.

'I did not for one moment imagine it would be. How do you do it?'

'Do what?'

'Persuade men to serve you. You have men in your household staff; you employ captains, sailors, warehousemen. As a woman, how do you make them listen to you?'

'I pay them well,' said Mrs Redcliffe. 'Those closest to me obey me out of loyalty. Many served my husband, and now serve me in memory of him. The rest know that I can be very unpleasant indeed when I am crossed.' She smiled. 'I can be quite an evil bitch, when I choose.'

Amelia blinked, then laughed out loud. 'Perhaps I should come and take lessons from you,' she said.

'Perhaps you should. Better still, come into partnership with me, and I will teach you what I know. I think we would work well together.'

'You are kind,' said Amelia, still smiling.

'Or perhaps it is Reverend Hardcastle with whom you would prefer to form a partnership? You are still young and comely. And he has qualities that mark him out from other men. It would be a good alliance.'

'Oh, please don't. His sister is utterly determined that we should marry.'

'But you do not wish it?'

'I had one perfect marriage. I have no intention of looking for another. Reverend Hardcastle is a friend; I talk to him when I am troubled, and he does the same to me. There is no more, and there will never be any more.'

After a reflective moment, Martha Redcliffe said, 'Perhaps you are wise to keep it that way. You are fortunate to have what you have.'

'Yes. I suppose I am.'

Silence settled over the dark room. Outside the sea gleamed vivid blue. A magpie flitted past the window, settling in a tree in the nearby churchyard.

'May I ask a question about the bank?' Amelia asked.

'Of course, but there is no guarantee I will be able to answer it.'

'Rumours are beginning to circulate that the bank may not be safe. I should like to know if they are true. I ask on behalf of two elderly friends who have nearly all their money in the bank. If it were to go down, they would be destitute.'

Mrs Redcliffe looked grave. 'I will give you the same answer I gave Reverend Hardcastle. The bank is overextended. Charles Faversham has borrowed recklessly, and invested even more recklessly. I am sorry for your friends. You should advise them to withdraw their money.'

Amelia watched the other woman. 'But if they withdraw, someone else might hear of it, and think they should remove *their* money too; and then more people would notice, and more. That is how runs on banks begin, is it not?'

'Indeed. But you need to think of your friends, and their safety.'

'How likely is it, really, that the bank will fail?'

'I don't know.' Mrs Redcliffe smiled a little. 'Only Charles Faversham knows the answer to that question.'

'I have heard another rumour,' said Amelia. 'In an attempt to recover some of the bank's losses and recruit its fortunes, Faversham has turned to smuggling.'

'I have heard the same rumour. It may well be true; it is the sort of thing Faversham would do, if he saw advantage in it. In theory, the idea is not a bad one. In practice, it will fail because Faversham knows absolutely nothing about smuggling, and he will be taken advantage of by ruthless people who do.'

'You could advise him,' Amelia pointed out. 'You could help him avoid the traps that will be set for him.'

Martha Redcliffe smiled again. 'Charles Faversham does not listen to women, Mrs Chaytor. We have, he says, *no head for finance*. My words would be a waste of breath.'

'But you cannot simply sit on the sidelines and watch as he drags the bank down. What about your own investment?'

'If necessary, I am resigned to losing it,' said Mrs Redcliffe. 'Even more than your friends, I should not remove my money, and for the same reasons. Such an action by me might well seal the bank's fate.

'The bank would collapse, and the depositors would be ruined.'

'Just so. I do not want that on my conscience. But of course, Mrs Chaytor, we speak only of rumours and not of facts. Charles Faversham continues to insist that the bank is sound. Perhaps he is right.'

'Suppose the bank *were* to fail? Could you still carry on?'

'I could, of course. I am engaged in another venture, Mrs Chaytor, one that is rather more important to me than the bank.'

'Oh? How intriguing.'

The older woman smiled again. 'Have you ever desired to make history, Mrs Chaytor?'

'I can honestly say that I have not.'

'In his will, Mr Redcliffe left me a fleet of four coasting ships. I have since built up that fleet to eleven vessels. I have fought against French privateers, Channel gales and the prejudice of my male competitors and customers, and I have defied them all. Now I am creating a monument to the work of my husband and myself. I am building a venture for which the world will remember us.'

'And I am sure you will succeed. May I ask an entirely impertinent question? For whom are you doing all this? Who will inherit this venture, when you are gone?'

'I have heirs, never fear.'

'Then may I ask a still more impertinent question? How much laudanum do you take?'

Mrs Redcliffe smiled. 'You are observant. I drink the equivalent of half a pint per day.'

Amelia drew breath. 'That amount would kill most men.'

'Which proves what I have always believed,' said Mrs Redcliffe. 'That I am stronger than most men.'

'Yes. But for how long can you sustain this?'

'Long enough. Do not fear; I know what I am doing. And when my time comes to an end, others will follow me. My story will live long after I am gone.'

'I do not understand,' said Mrs Chaytor several hours later. 'How could this man not exist when Joshua saw him with his own eyes?'

It was late in the day. Stemp and Mrs Chaytor had returned separately from their journeys to Hythe, and both had come to call on the rector.

'Noakes was trying to gull us,' said Stemp. 'He had a smug look about him, like a man who knew something we didn't. He was right too. We still don't know where this fellow is. I reckon once Noakes learned we were there, he sent the other cull into hiding. Begging your pardon, reverend, despite what you said the other day, I still think it's Noakes's gang that are working for the bank.'

'Have you any evidence?' asked Hardcastle.

'No, reverend. But something about what they're doing doesn't smell right, in the same way that there's something about the bank that doesn't smell right. I reckon we're looking at two parts of the same story.'

'Very well. Keep an eye on Noakes and his activities, but be careful. And keep searching for the other man.'

'Yes, reverend. I'm looking out for the courier, too, this man called Jean. Bertrand had a letter from him, and gave it to the young fellow on the beach. I reckon he must be the one who carries the manifests.'

'You will need to explain, Joshua,' said Mrs Chaytor.

'What happens in the free trade, ma'am, is that one party places an order. The other party gathers the goods and then sends across a manifest, itemising the cargoes that are being shipped and the price. A downpayment is usually made by the first party, and then the cargo is brought across. The goods landed are checked against the manifest to make sure all is fair and square. From the conversation I heard on the beach, I reckon Jean carries the manifest and receives the downpayment. He then gives a letter to Bertrand to carry back to Noakes and his gang, and once they see the letter they load the cargo. It'll all be checked against the manifest once they reach the other side. If all is well, the rest of the money will then be paid over.'

'Very businesslike,' she commented.

'They've been doing it for hundreds of years, ma'am, they've got it all worked out. Oh, and one more thing. I've got someone else watching out for that Dutch lugger.'

'Who?' asked the rector.

'Lieutenant Stark, from the navy. He's master of the *Black Joke*. He patrols around here, hunting for French privateers. I told him about the Dutchman, and he said he'd look out for her.'

'What was an officer of the Royal Navy doing in a smuggler's den in Hythe?' asked Mrs Chaytor. 'But no, how silly of me. Surely the question answers itself.'

'He does have a sideline in the free trade, ma'am,' said Stemp, his face immobile.

'And the go-between?' asked Mrs Chaytor. 'Are we any closer to finding him?' She looked at the rector. 'You had a theory it might be Cranthorpe.'

'I think we can dispose of that notion. If I can break him down in one short interview, he surely hasn't the nerve or disposition to be the lynchpin of a major smuggling operation. Forget Cranthorpe. What of Grebell Faversham?'

'I too was entirely wrong. He is quite moonstruck, and lacks the enterprise to murder anyone. He is hopelessly ignorant of the state of the bank, and of banking generally. He also seems to have no interest in the clear opportunity staring him in the face, to marry Cecilia Munro and take her late husband's place at the partnership table. "There is more to life than banking", he said to me.' Mrs Chaytor made a dismissive gesture. 'I have wasted my time.'

'Did he know anything about smuggling?'

Mrs Chaytor rolled her eyes.

'And Mrs Redcliffe? Did you learn anything from her?'

'Very little that we did not already know. She was quite matter-of-fact about her own involvment in the free trade. But when I suggested Faversham might also be involved, she was quite scathing. If Faversham turned to smuggling, she said, he would fail, because the smugglers would take advantage of him.'

Hardcastle rubbed his eyes. 'What do you know about Mrs Redcliffe, Joshua? She told me she is in the carrying trade.'

Stemp nodded. 'The big London negociants sometimes pay her to bring cargoes across from France. It's not a regular thing. Most of the time her ships are engaged in the legit trade, along the coast and up the river to London. But if times are slack, she'll let it be known that her captains are willing to make a run.'

'So she knows the trade well enough. We have been wondering who might be the intermediary between the bank and the smugglers. We assumed that this intermediary would be someone with no connection with the bank. But must that necessarily be the case? What if it is Mrs Redcliffe?'

'An intriguing notion,' said Mrs Chaytor. 'But on balance, I think it unlikely. Her opinion of Charles Faversham could not be lower. Would she be willing to trust and work with a man she clearly regards as incompetent?'

'But if we are correct in our assumptions, and the smuggling operation has gone wrong, then the bank's situation could be worse than before,' said Hardcastle. 'Will she stand by and let it go down?'

'She claims that even if she offered advice, Faversham would not listen to her. That is entirely possible. I have another idea. Instead of stepping in to help Faversham, she is waiting for him to tip over the edge. When he does, she will step in, buy out Faversham and the other partners, pay off the debts with money from her shipping business and become sole owner. She will save the bank and become a heroine. What do you think?'

'I think that idea sounds entirely fanciful,' said the rector.

'Yes. So do I, now that I come to examine it more closely. Ideas are like children; delightful when they first arrive, but increasingly disappointing as they grow older.'

'However, I take your point about her dislike of Faversham,' said the rector. 'Like you, I cannot see the two of them working easily together. And I recall Mrs Redcliffe saying that she doesn't take orders, she gives them.'

'Suppose the intermediary does then have an association with the bank. Who else might it be?' asked Mrs Chaytor. 'What about Mr Maudsley, with his connections?'

'We can rule out Maudsley,' the rector said heavily. 'He dabbled in smuggling, the same way the Tydde brothers do. And I believe he has not the heart or the stomach of a murderer.'

'Then what of the remaining partner, Mr Cotton? Or Munro's clerk, Mr Batist?'

'Batist is everyone's idea of the perfect bank servant: polite, conscientious, industrious, owing his entire loyalty to his employer . . . But it might be worth taking another look at him and his antecedents. He has connections with France; he might even have been born there. Batist may not be part of the free trade, but he may well have family or friends who are.'

Stemp nodded. 'I'll ask around,' he said.

'As for Cotton, he seems even more unlikely than Mrs Redcliffe. Everyone I have spoken to has been dismissive of him; a provincial dullard, someone called him. My own impression, I am sorry to say, confirmed this.'

'Charles Faversham might disagree,' said Mrs Chaytor. 'According to Grebell, Faversham thinks he has excellent judgement. He has the Midas touch.'

The rector frowned. 'That is curious. He told *me* that Cotton was a good provincial banker, but lacked breadth.'

Stemp intervened. 'Your pardon, ma'am. But what did you just say?'

'According to Grebell, Charles Faversham refers to Cotton as Midas.'

'Blind me,' said Stemp. 'You pardon, ma'am. But last week, when we ran into Noakes and his crew down by Dungeness, I heard Bertrand use that name. "The latest consignment from Midas", he said.'

'And Cotton makes gunpowder,' said the rector sharply. 'By God, there may be a connection after all. Well done, Joshua. I shall have another word with our Quaker powder-maker. And this time, I shall see to it that he tells me the truth.'

Stemp departed a little later, the recipient of a shilling from the rector's discretionary fund to buy gin for himself and his fellow special constables at the Star. Mrs Chaytor sat for a moment, looking at the rector. His face sagged heavily over the bones beneath, and there were shadows under his eyes.

'I was right about Mrs Redcliffe,' she said. 'She is a laudanum user, and a heavy one. Her daily dose would kill an ordinary man.'

'How, then, does she survive?'

'Over time, as the opium takes hold, the body demands more and more. Only a large dose will feed the craving. The longer one is addicted, the more opium the body needs and the more it is able to tolerate.'

'But in the end, surely, it will kill her,' said Hardcastle.

'Yes. Her body is like a spring being wound very tightly; eventually it will break. And I think she knows it. That explains the disinterest in things not directly connected to her, the single-minded focus on her own business ... Except that she is very sympathetic to Cecilia Munro. She calls on her often, a couple of times a week. So she still has a heart, it would seem.'

'What a tragedy,' he said quietly. 'She has spirit and courage, too, and I formed the impression of high intellect. How sad to see it going to waste.'

'Indeed. And speaking of killing doses, my dear; how much did you drink last night?'

He regarded her for a moment before answering. 'Two bottles of port, and the better part of a bottle of brandy.'

'Is this because of Maudsley?'

'I suppose that started it. I felt, and feel, betrayed by him. To think that a man I regarded as a friend could have behaved in such a cowardly way sickens me. And it makes me question my own judgement. If I was wrong about him all along, what else have I been wrong about?'

He sat back in his chair. 'What other mistakes have I made? Who else have I failed?'

'Whoever you might have failed, you cannot help them if you go back to the bottle,' she said abruptly. 'Marcus, these people need you. They need your judgement, they need your intellect. The finest mind in the Church of England, someone once called you, did they not? But your mind is of no use to anyone if you choose to destroy it.'

Hardcastle was silent for a moment. There was no mistaking the anger in her fine blue eyes. Against his will, his own temper rose.

'You sound like my sister,' he said shortly. 'I do not need lectures from her, or you, or anyone else.'

She rose to her feet with grace. 'Maudsley betrayed you,' she said. 'Don't pay him back by betraying us in turn. I'll see myself out.'

He waited perhaps five minutes after she left, then opened the mahogany cabinet and took out a brandy bottle and a glass. He filled the glass to the brim, noticing as he did so that his hand was shaking. He stared at the glass for a long time, thinking about the past, the disappointed hopes, the shipwrecked career, the lost dreams. When he was a young man, people had talked of him as a future Archbishop of Canterbury. Now the archbishop was a nonentity, a butcher's son, and Hardcastle was here in Romney Marsh.

He rose to his feet and walked over to the fireplace, holding up the glass to the light. The little flames glowed amber through the brandy, teasing him. He imagined the warmth of it running down his throat, the fumes rising to his brain, the oblivion that would come.

'*For the love of Christ!*' he said, and hurled the glass into the fire, smashing it. The brandy caught light at once. Tongues of blue flame flared up briefly, dancing across the coal, and then subsided and died.

13

Cotton

My dear Hardcastle

Thank you for your most recent letter, and I apologise for my tardy reply. Matters are coming to a head here in London. If the peace talks in Lille succeed, as it now seems certain they will, then there may well be a reshuffle in the ranks of government. It is no secret between us that I have my eye on the post of attorney-general, and to that end I have been much involved in discussions with various interested parties.

As for the East Weald and Ashford Bank, I ought to say that your news astonishes me, but it does not. I have never held a high opinion of Charles Faversham; he reminds me of those men who sell broken-down horses of dubious provenance on the outskirts of country fairs.

I see no need to involve the Customs at this juncture. Continue to investigate the murder, and let the Customs get on with whatever it is they do.

Once again, continue to keep me informed of events.

Yr very obedient servant

CLAVERTYE

Lord Clavertye as attorney-general, Hardcastle thought. Well, the country could do worse. He had known Clavertye for many years, since they were at Cambridge together; for a time, the legal scholar and the divinity student had been good friends. Those days had passed, but there was still a lingering respect.

And perhaps once his lordship is in post, he will remember his promise that my appointment as JP is a temporary one, and find a permanent replacement. Then I can go back to being a simple country clergyman; hopefully, before I alienate any more of my friends. I don't have so many that I can afford to lose them.

That reminded him, bleakly, of yesterday evening's scene. Finishing his eggs and draining his coffee cup, the rector rose and went out into the yard where the dog cart waited, Amos the groom holding the horse. Hardcastle stepped into the driving seat and flicked the reins to stir the horse into motion. At the rectory gates he hesitated for a moment and then turned the horse left, down towards Sandy House.

Lucy showed him into the drawing room where Mrs Chaytor sat at her harpsichord, studying a sheet of music. She looked up as he entered, noting his clear eyes, and smiled.

'Am I forgiven?' she asked.

'I was about to ask the same thing.'

'Then I think we are both answered,' she said. No more was said; no more was needed. 'Are you on your way to Canterbury?'

He groaned. 'I have travelled more in the past few weeks than I did in the previous year. My bones are rattling against each other. I have had another thought. Are you seeing Grebell again in the near future?'

'He comes to visit me on the slightest pretext, at least once week. I imagine it will not be long before he calls again.'

'When he next does so, can you endeavour to learn more about relations between his father and Munro? Did Faversham hold Munro in regard, or were there disagreements between them? Were they in any way rivals? And there is another thing. Munro went to see Faversham on the Saturday before Cecilia's birthday. Find out if Grebell knows what they talked about.'

'I will do what I can.' Her eyes had gone a particularly vivid shade of blue, as they often did when she was curious. 'What are you thinking?'

'Do you recall the non-existent investment in Baltic timber? Maudsley told me he was positive Hector was on his way to London to negotiate the deal; that turned out to be a lie. Batist, on the other hand, said that *might* have been where Munro was going but he wasn't sure; while Faversham claimed that he himself had already concluded the deal and Munro's journey must have been a private matter.'

'That was shockingly incompetent of them,' she said. 'One of the first rules of spying, John used to say, is to make sure everyone agrees on the cover story, and then sticks to it.'

'Your husband was a professional,' said the rector. 'These people are amateurs. Last night, in a period of *sober* reflection, I began to think again about Faversham. The timber deal, as you say, was their agreed cover story; but Faversham chose quite deliberately to depart from it. Instead he spun me a yarn about Munro, encouraging me to think of him as a devious, secretive character who went behind his partners' backs. Why?'

'He wanted to deflect your attention towards Munro, and away from the bank.'

'Agreed, but I think there may be more to it. Maudsley says Munro was furious when he returned from meeting Faversham in Rye. I wonder if they quarrelled. I wonder, indeed, if Faversham gave orders for Munro to be intercepted on his journey to France, and killed.'

Mrs Chaytor frowned a little. 'Why might he do so?'

'Anger and humiliation at having his own incompetence discovered; jealousy of Munro's superior ability; fear of being exposed as a smuggler, and a clumsy one at that; simple choler, the kind of rage which leads men to do unforgivable things. Any or all of these emotions could have been in Faversham's heart.'

She nodded. 'I shall learn what I can.'

'Thank you, as ever. I shall take my leave, and go to see Cotton.'

'Don't let him spin you a yarn,' she said, smiling. All was well once more.

It was the last day of August. Still the sun was warm but the days were growing shorter now, and autumn lurked in the dust haze on the horizon.

Arriving at the premises of the East Weald and Ashford Bank in Canterbury, the rector was told that Sylvester Cotton was not in. The rector said he would wait. Three-quarters of an hour passed before the chief clerk came downstairs once more.

'Mr Cotton has now arrived, sir. If you would follow me?'

'He has arrived?' said the rector. 'How interesting. I have had a clear view of the front door this entire time, and I did not see him enter.'

'He used the tradesmen's entrance, sir.'

'Ah. Is there someone he is anxious to avoid meeting? Or has he, by any chance, been here all the time, hoping that I would go away?'

No answer came. In the office Cotton, sandy-haired, pink-faced, blue-eyed, greeted him coolly. There was no offer of refreshment.

'I will come to the point,' said the rector. 'Are you missing any powder kegs from your stores?'

Cotton stared at him. 'What are you talking about?'

'A group of smugglers was seen last week on the beach near Dungeness, loading powder kegs onto a lugger destined for France. I wondered if they perhaps came from you.'

'I really have no idea.' Cotton had recovered his wits rapidly. 'I keep only a small number of kegs to hand. They aren't made on the premises, I buy them in from coopers; or the Admiralty sends back the empties and I refill them.'

'And are you missing any gunpowder from your mills or warehouses?'

'Absolutely not. If that were so, I would know of it at once. We keep all the powder under close guard, and make frequent inventories.'

'Have any gunpowder consignments been stolen during shipment?'

'To my certain knowledge, no. All our shipments are checked at the armouries and depots as soon as they arrive. Any discrepancy would be reported at once. None has been. May I ask the purpose of these questions?'

'Does the name Midas mean anything to you?'

Cotton covered the involuntary start well, reaching up to scratch his ear in an apparently irritable fashion. 'The ancient king of Crete? Like any educated man, I have heard of him. You still haven't answered my question.'

'The smugglers referred to "a consignment from Midas". Might you be Midas? Might they have been loading gunpowder made in your mills?'

'Do you dare to suggest that I am selling gunpowder to the enemy? That is treason!'

'I am glad you realise it,' said the rector.

'I tell you, I know nothing about any smugglers. And I find your behaviour intolerable. I challenge your right to interrogate me in this fashion. You said before that you have a warrant. I want to see it.'

The rector handed over the warrant from Lord Clavertye. His bluff called, Cotton read it and handed it back. His pink skin had started to flush red.

'When we spoke previously,' said the rector, 'I asked if you had any knowledge of Munro's connections with smuggling. You denied it, declaring that as a God-fearing man you would have nothing to do with . . . how did you put it? "Anything so heinous." But that was a lie, wasn't it?'

Cotton stared at him, mouth open. 'I know it was a lie,' the rector said before the other man could recover, 'because every other partner of the bank is also engaged in smuggling, in one way or another, and if you didn't know about it, you would be the biggest born fool under the sun. And you're not a fool, are you, Cotton? You *know* what is happening at the bank. You *know* it is heavily in debt. You *know* that Faversham turned to smuggling as a way of bringing in quick money, abetted by Munro.

'There is a joint enterprise between the partners, and you are part of it. At the very least, you will be prosecuted for smuggling. And if it turns out that you are supplying the French with gunpowder, you will also be charged with treason.' Hardcastle paused to let that sink in. 'You can avoid this fate, but *only* if you tell me, right now, everything you know.'

'I cannot do that,' said Cotton. His voice had a strangled quality. His face was now bright red.

'Why not, Midas?'

'I cannot tell you that either. I—' Cotton stopped, realising what he had done. 'What we were doing was harmless,' he said. 'My God, yes, everyone on the coast is involved in smuggling, from lords and ladies to shepherds and fishermen. I suppose we are technically breaking the law, but—'

'You are committing a crime punishable by transportation or death,' said the rector, his eyes boring into Cotton's face. 'What will happen to your family when you are gone, and they are alone and impoverished, objects of scorn in their own community? Who will look after them when you are swinging from a gallows on Penenden Heath, or manacled in the hold of a convict ship on its way to Botany Bay?'

Cotton raised his damaged hand. 'Stop. Stop.'

Hardcastle waited. 'Faversham made the decision to invest in smuggling,' Cotton said. 'Munro and I were against it at first, but it promised high returns quickly, and we needed the money. We allowed Faversham to convince us. And to be fair, all went well at first. But then something happened. The returns on investment began to decline. The margins fell steadily. We realised that if things went on as they were, we should soon be in real trouble.'

'When did you learn of this?'

'Not until early August. Faversham kept the accounts for this investment himself, so that none of the clerks should learn of it. But Munro got suspicious. He went to Faversham and demanded to see the accounts. He saw at once that we were losing money. He wrote to me immediately afterwards, saying he intended to get to the bottom of this. Faversham, he declared, was a fool; he hadn't a clue that anything was wrong.'

'Do you still have the letter?'

'Good God, no! I burned it immediately.'

'How many other people knew about this?'

'I don't know. I'm not sure anyone did. Munro wrote to me because he said I needed to know what was happening. Faversham had kept too many secrets, he said, for too long. It was time the truth came out.'

'What commodities was the bank smuggling, and where? By what routes?'

'Upon my soul, I do not know.' Cotton's face was redder than ever.

'With whom were they dealing in the smuggling trade?'

'I do not know that either.'

'The more you lie to me, the more the blood rushes to your face,' said the rector. 'I should be careful if I were you, Mr Cotton. You might bring on an apoplexy.'

The other man said nothing. He was trapped, and he knew it. 'I could send for the magistrate of Canterbury and have you arrested here and now, on capital charges,' said Hardcastle. This was bluff; he did not yet have enough evidence, but Cotton would not know that. 'But I shall give you one more chance. Think it over, Mr Cotton. Reflect on what I have said. If you assist me, I can ensure that you receive a light sentence, or even a pardon. There might still be a future for you and your family.'

The rector rose to his feet. 'Think it over,' he repeated. 'But don't take too long. I am not the most patient of men.'

On the afternoon of the 1st of September, as the rector drove wearily back from Canterbury, a little gig with blue wheels pulled into the drive at Sandy House in St Mary in the Marsh, and Grebell Faversham stepped down and knocked at the door. Lucy ushered him into the drawing room where Amelia Chaytor, clad in a simple white gown without adornment, received him. Tea was brought, and they talked briefly of the weather. The air was still warm but clouds were building up on the horizon, and they agreed it would rain soon. 'The last few weeks have been quite fine, on the whole,' said Mrs Chaytor. 'It makes up somewhat for the rains in June and July. That will have helped the harvest upcountry.'

'Yes,' said Grebell. 'We used to have a business in corn-broking, but we sold that some years ago. Pity; we'd be doing quite well about now.'

He broke off suddenly. 'I am rambling,' he said. 'I am certain you do not want to hear me talk about the bank, or corn-broking.'

She stirred sugar into her tea, wondering what he *did* want to talk about. At Magpie Court he had been gallant in a clumsy way, but with each succeeding meeting he seemed to become more tongue-tied and awkward. To break the ice, she began to talk about music once more. He asked her again, rather timidly, to play. She refused graciously. 'I play so badly, Mr Faversham. No one should be asked to endure listening to me. I feel sorry for my servants, who have no choice.'

There was a soft knock at the drawing room door and Lucy entered, curtsying. 'Miss Roper to see you, ma'am. She says it is urgent.' More quietly, Lucy said, 'She seems unwell.'

'Excuse me,' said Mrs Chaytor to Grebell, and she rose and hurried out into the hall. Miss Roper stood in the middle of the parquet floor, her face pale except for two red spots on her cheeks. Mrs Chaytor seized her hands quickly. 'My dear, what is it?'

'Oh, Mrs Chaytor. I am so sorry to disturb you, but the rector said I should call on him if ever I had a concern, and I went to the rectory but he is not there, and I felt I simply had to talk to someone. I am so sorry,' Miss Roper repeated. She gazed at Mrs Chaytor, and tried to collect herself. 'Oh, but you have a guest, I am sure. I . . . I am interrupting you. Dear Mrs Chaytor, do please pardon me, and I shall take my leave now.'

'No, you shall not,' said Mrs Chaytor, raising her hands to the other woman's shoulders. She steered Miss Roper gently but firmly into the morning room, feeling the other woman shivering. She pulled out two chairs, sat Miss Roper in one of them, took the other herself and resumed holding Miss Roper's hands. 'Now, my dear. Tell me.'

'I do not know what to make of it. It is so confusing, and my mind is all in a muddle. I overheard Mr Luckhurst talking to the man driving the coal dray, and he was saying that the owner of the coal yard has told his clerks not to accept notes drawn on the East Weald and Ashford; it must be coin or Bank of England notes only. And Mr Luckhurst said he'd always been certain the bank was up to something, and I became so frightened I had to stop listening and come away. Oh, Mrs Chaytor, I so much fear there is something dreadfully wrong, and Rosannah and I will be reduced to poverty, and we'll have to let Kate and Jed go, and we are too old to look after the house ourselves, and we'll have no fuel to keep out the cold when winter comes—'

'Hush,' said Amelia softly. 'My dear, you are distressing yourself without need. All will be well. Tomorrow I will drive you and Miss Godfrey to Rye, and we will withdraw all your money from the bank. Then you need no longer worry.'

'Oh, but Mrs Chaytor, what would we do with the money then? We cannot keep it at home, we should at once be robbed and left destitute! Oh, I am at my wits' end to know what to do.'

'I can help you,' said Amelia. She had been thinking about this ever since her talk with Mrs Redcliffe. 'I shall ask my own banker to open an account for you, in London.' Normally Thomas Coutts would not be interested in the affairs of two provincial spinsters, but as a favour to a friend of Lord Grenville, he would make an exception. 'It will take a week or so to arrange, but once it is done, your money will be as safe as the Bank of England itself.'

'Dear Mrs Chaytor. You are such a good friend to a foolish old woman. Thank you, thank you so very much.'

'You must not mention it. It is what friends are for. Now, shall we go to Rye tomorrow? We can put the money into my strongbox while we wait for Mr Coutts to complete the arrangements.'

'No, no, you are already too kind to us. We shall wait until your banker responds. I am sure that is best. It may all come to nothing anyway. I am probably just being foolish. I usually am.'

Already Miss Roper was calmer; assurance that some action was being taken had lifted her spirits. Amelia watched her face. 'I don't think we should take the risk,' she said. 'Let me convey you tomorrow to Rye.'

'Oh, no, Mrs Chaytor, please, we must not impose on you. That would be quite wrong.' She was as adamant now as she had been terrified earlier, and nothing Mrs Chaytor could say would move her.

'Very well,' said Amelia finally. 'But if you hear any further news, or change your mind for any reason whatever, you must let me know at once.'

She watched Miss Roper depart, walking a little more steadily, before returning to the drawing room. 'I am sorry,' she said to Grebell Faversham. 'One of my elderly neighbours has heard a rather unfortunate rumour.' She related what had happened. 'When I called on you in Rye, you assured me on your word of honour that all was well at the bank. Was that true?'

He had gone a little pale. His bulging eyes were troubled. 'It is quite true,' he said. 'My dear Mrs Chaytor, I would never lie to you.'

'I am sure you would not, Mr Faversham. But I think you need to acquaint yourself with the possibility that all is *not* well, and that the bank may be in a good deal of trouble without your knowing of it. I wish you to do a favour for me.'

'Of course, ma'am. Anything, anything at all.'

'I have advised my friends to transfer their money to my own bank. When I hear from London, I shall bring them to you in Rye. Their names are Rosannah Godfrey and Clara Roper. Please arrange for them to withdraw all the money in their accounts. The withdrawal should take the form of bills of exchange payable to Thomas Coutts & Co. in London. I will arrange for the bills to be forwarded to Coutts.'

'Ma'am, we can do that for you. We can send the bills directly to London.'

'I think the ladies will be more reassured if they see me do this myself. They trust me, you see. Will you make the arrangements?'

'Of course,' he said again, bowing. 'All will be done as you ask, I give you my word on that.'

She studied him. He was desperately anxious to please her. 'This is very important to me,' she said. 'I must ask you to see to this personally. Will you do so?'

'Mrs Chaytor,' he said, 'I would never fail you, or your friends. You have my word on that.'

He stood before her, clearly expecting she would dismiss him, and hoping she would not. She sighed, recalling her purpose. 'Do sit,' she said. 'There is still tea in the pot.'

They sat, Grebell looking both worried and relieved. 'Mr Faversham,' she said directly, 'do you remember Mr Munro coming to see your father? It would have been a couple of days before the birthday party.'

'Yes, I recall he came to the bank. He and Father were closeted for about two hours.'

'Do you know what he discussed with your father?'

'No, I don't, ma'am. Father rarely discussed partnership affairs with me.'

'Did you see Mr Munro yourself?'

'I saw him in the clerks' room as he was leaving. I remember he had a face like thunder. He was not happy about something, that's for certain. And when I went into Father's office, he was furious. But he wouldn't tell me what it was about.'

'Before that time, did your father and Mr Munro get along? Were they friendly?'

Grebell frowned. 'They were at first. Father thought highly of Mr Munro.' He flushed. More highly than of himself, was the inference. 'They got along well, right up until last month. But hard words must have passed between them at that meeting. Father was angry with Munro, no doubt about it. They still hadn't patched things up when Munro was killed.'

'Do you think your father regrets that?'

'I fear I have no idea, ma'am. I'm sorry.' Grebell was still anxious and embarrassed. 'Will you excuse me? I fear it is coming on to rain, and I really should return to Rye.' He stood up, looking at her, and he reminded her suddenly of a lost boy. 'I am so sorry for the distress of your friends. If there is anything else I can do to help, anything at all, will you be sure to let me know?'

'I certainly shall. And, Mr Faversham; thank you.'

Hardcastle had been expecting to hear from Cotton, but the letter came sooner than expected, in the last post of the day from New Romney. He read it quickly.

STOURBRIDGE MILLS, CANTERBURY
1st of September, 1797

Reverend Hardcastle,

I have considered further the matter we discussed. I find upon reflection that there are some other, highly pertinent facts which I would like to lay before you. In return, I expect the clemency you spoke of will be forthcoming. If this is still the case, then I think I can answer your questions to your satisfaction.

If it is convenient for you, I shall call upon you on Monday morning, the 4th inst.

Yr very obedient servant

SYL. COTTON, ESQ.

*

A gloomy Sunday evening, the Marsh shrouded with drizzle and low cloud. The tollbooth keeper at Ham Street woke from his doze to the sound of an approaching carriage. He looked out to see a small gig with a single horse approaching, driven by a cloaked figure hunched against the rain. The gig drew up at the barrier.

'Don't see many travellers on a Sunday,' the keeper commented as the driver fumbled in his pocket for coins. 'Specially not on a wet day like this.'

The driver said nothing, handing over the toll. One of his driving gloves dangled limply, as if the man was missing some of his fingers. The keeper weighed the coins in his hand. 'Going anywhere in particular?' he asked.

'Mind your own business,' snapped the driver.

The keeper shrugged and went back inside. The driver whipped up and the horse trotted forward down the high road towards Snave. Just beyond that village, however, the driver pulled up and halted. He looked around carefully, checking to see if he had been followed. Around him the Marsh lay open and empty, dull green-grey in the rain.

The driver knew the Marsh a little, and realised he had a choice. He could follow the high road to Brenzett and then turn east, keeping to the main road to New Romney. Or he could cut across country, following the green lanes and tracks through the heart of the Marsh; roads seldom travelled, where the likelihood of encountering a stranger on a wet Sunday evening was very small. If he could get to New Romney without being seen, then he could make his rendezvous the next morning. Once he had told Hardcastle what he knew, and provided the evidence he had brought with him, he would be safe. The law would protect him. Hardcastle had promised it would be so.

Sylvester Cotton shook the reins again and turned the horse off the high road and down the grassy track towards Ivychurch, driving carefully in the slippery grass and mud. The rain increased and he hunched forward still further, pulling the hood of his cloak over his face.

'Halt there! Stand and deliver, I say!'

Cotton sat up straight, staring in disbelief and then pulling hard on the reins. The horse and gig halted. Two men stood a few yards away, one on each side of the track, both holding pistols. 'Get down,' said one of the men.

'I have very little of value,' gasped Cotton.

'We'll be the judge of that,' said the other man. He had a deep, booming voice. 'Keep your hands where we can see them, bucky.'

'I'm a Quaker,' said Cotton. 'I'm not armed. Look, I've a little money. You can have that. Take the horse and the rig too. Just let me go.'

The first man walked up to him. He had a rough, lined face and gapped yellow teeth. His eyes were unearthly, deep-set, with the pupils mere dark points on either side of a badly broken nose. Looking into those eyes, Cotton saw nothing but grim intent. He knew he was facing death; he knew he ought to run, but those pitiless eyes bored into his soul and left him rooted to the spot.

He saw the other man raise his arm, the pistol coming up and pointing straight at his face. Cotton looked down the black, yawning barrel. 'Please,' he said, his voice soft with desperation. 'Please.'

'Fuck you,' said the other man, and he pulled the trigger.

14

Ricardo's Revelation

Half a mile beyond Ivychurch, a gig stood empty and abandoned by the side of the track. There was no sign of a horse. A huddled shape lay on the ground beyond the gig. Two men stood guard over it, looking wet and unhappy. One turned and touched the brim of his dripping hat as Hardcastle pulled the dog cart to a halt. His name was Honeychild, and he was the parish constable in Ivychurch.

'Who found him?' Hardcastle asked.

'One of the boys from the village,' said Honeychild. 'He went out early to go shrimping in the sewer.' The little freshwater shrimp that lived in the drains in this part of the Marsh were a staple of the local diet. 'He found the body and came running straight home. This here's Caleb Atkins, the boy's father.'

Hardcastle looked at the other man. 'Did your son see anyone? Hear anything?'

'Nothing, reverend,' said Atkins. 'This fellow's been stiff and cold for some time, I'd say.'

It was Monday morning; Hardcastle had been about to sit down to breakfast when a runner from Ivychurch brought Honeychild's message. The rector dismounted and walked across the wet grass to the body.

The dead man lay on his back, arms outstretched. His clothes were dark and soaked with water; as Atkins had said, he had clearly been lying there in the rain for some time. He had been shot in the face at point-blank range. The dark entry wound of the ball was surrounded by burnt skin and the black stains of powder residue, making him almost unrecognisable. But Hardcastle did not need the face to tell him who this was. One look at the left hand, with two fingers missing and a third curled and bent, was enough to confirm that this was Sylvester Cotton.

Oh, dear God. Not again.

Cotton had a wife and two children. Before the day was over there would be more tears, more misery, more loss and loneliness and emptiness. As if there was not already enough grief in the world.

He straightened and looked at the constable. 'Send to New Romney for Dr Mackay, if you please. Where is the horse?'

Honeychild nodded to Atkins, who hurried off through the rain towards New Romney three miles away. 'I reckon they took the horse, reverend. See here; there's tracks going up the road towards Snave. I'm thinking they both rode off on it together, trying to get away quickly before someone heard the shot and got curious.'

The rector squinted at the hoofprints in the mud, already filled with rainwater. 'You think there were only two men?'

'Looks like it. At least, I've only found two sets of footprints.' Honeychild frowned. 'It's strange, reverend. If this was a robbery, why did they only take the horse? The gig is worth a lot more than the beast.'

'This was no robbery,' said the rector. He knelt down on the wet grass and opened Cotton's saturated coat. Once again, his watch was still there. The notecase in his inside pocket had not been touched either. Yet ... someone had gone through his clothes, quite thoroughly. One pocket was turned inside out, and the seam at the hem of the coat had been cut and the lining partly torn away. The killers had thought Cotton might have something sewn into the lining of his coat. Perhaps he had, and they had taken it away with them.

Standing up, the rector walked over to the gig. Honeychild was right; it was an expensive little carriage, well made and well sprung. He examined the seat and the hood behind it, looking for blood or signs of damage, but saw none. Cotton must have dismounted before he was shot. That made sense; confronted by highwaymen, demanding his valuables or his life, a sensible man would step down and hand over everything, without hesitation.

But these were not highwaymen. These were executioners.

Hardcastle turned to the constable. 'See if you can track the horse. Whoever took it will be long gone, I am sure, but try at least to find out where they went. Also, find out if anyone saw this man in the hours before he was killed. The gig will be recognisable, and some people might remember the disfigured hand.'

'That'll take some time, reverend.'

'Send a runner to St Mary and fetch Joshua Stemp. He will assist you. This man was coming from Canterbury, so he probably drove down the Ashford turnpike. Start with the tollbooth at Ham Street.'

'Yes, sir.'

'Carry on. I'll wait for the doctor.'

He waited two hours in the drizzle, the day growing no brighter, the wind hissing around him. The corpse lay silent, its ruined face staring up at the sombre sky.

Hardcastle heard the sound of rattling wheels and turned as Dr Mackay drove up the lane. 'What have we this time?' the doctor asked.

'Sylvester Cotton,' said the rector.

'Cotton!' The doctor looked shocked. He knew Cotton, of course; they had met at the birthday party at Magpie Court, if not before.

'Man, that's bad.' Mackay stepped down from the driver's seat and tethered his horse, then collected his medical bag. 'What the devil was he doing out here?'

'He was coming to see me,' said Hardcastle.

Mackay glanced at him sharply and then knelt down beside the body. Hardcastle watched bleakly. *He was coming to see me. Someone learned of it, and sent men to waylay him.*

If I had not bullied him and threatened him, he would not have come to make his confession. And he would still be alive.

'What do you think?' he asked Mackay after a while.

'Shot dead, as you can see. As to the time of death, I'd hazard it was some time yesterday evening. Certainly before midnight, and probably well before.'

Cotton would have driven down yesterday, then, intending to stay somewhere overnight and then, as his letter had said, call at the rectory this morning. They could ask at the Bell in Ivychurch or the Ship in New Romney, or even the Star, to see if he had written ahead to ask for a room. And Honeychild's search should allow them to be more precise about the time; the tollbooth keeper at Ham Street was bound to remember, if no one else did. Not many gigs would have come through on a wet Sunday afternoon.

None of this would help them identify the killers.

'Someone's gone through his clothing pretty thoroughly,' commented Mackay.

'Yes. When you do the autopsy, check again. They may have missed something.'

'Of course.' Mackay stood up. 'I'll take him away now, so I can finish my work in the dry. Help me load him into the cart, will you?'

Lifting Cotton's remains into the cart was unpleasant; the corpse was stiff with rigor mortis, and the ball that killed him had passed clean through his skull, meaning there was not much left of the back of his head. Mackay wiped his hands on the grass when they were finished. 'Right, I'm off. My report will be ready by the morning.'

Hardcastle smiled suddenly. 'You'll drive it out to deliver it yourself, I suppose.'

'I might.' The doctor reddened a little as he understood Hardcastle's meaning. 'Do you object?'

'Not in the least.'

Mackay drove away. The rector, too, leaned down to clean his hands on the wet grass. As he did so, he glanced up at the gig. He paused, and looked again. From this angle, close to the ground, he could see the underside of the driving seat. There was a little compartment beneath the seat, really no more than a flap of leather like a wallet, where a traveller might put valuables or papers that he wished to keep dry. He could see now what he could not see before: that there was something in the wallet.

Rising, he walked over to the gig and reached inside, pulling out a folded paper sealed like a letter. This he tucked inside his coat, out of the rain. There was nothing else in the wallet.

Back at the rectory, he ordered Amos to dry the horse and give him some oats, but keep him in harness; the gig would be needed again soon. Inside, Hardcastle changed into dry clothes before packing a small valise and taking it downstairs. Here he ordered coffee from Biddy and then took the letter into his study. When the maidservant brought the coffee a few minutes later she found him frowning over a single sheet of paper. 'Whatever is it, reverend?'

'I'm blessed if I know.'

On the page were columns of numbers, written in a plain, workmanlike hand.

			Rmt fm Gh
1st of 11th	120	23rd of 11th	672.5.0
30th of 11th	258	27th of 12th	1,431.11.6
29th of 12th	310	25th of 1st	1,705.10.11
30th of 1st	355	24th of 2nd	1,917.8.2
26th of 2nd	620	20th of 3rd	3,162.17.4¼
29th of 3rd	4,327	20th of 4th	20,769.12.1
28th of 4th	1,290	23rd of 5th	6,063.5.10
27th of 5th	2,566	16th of 6th	11,547.12.7½
25th of 6th	4,014	15th of 7th	17,661.13.8
22nd of 7th	4,418	16th of 8th	19,218.7.6
23rd of 8th	3,100		
18th of 9th	5,720		

The rector scratched his head. The heading over the right-hand column was meaningless to him. The first and third columns might be dates, but he could detect no sequence to them, apart from the fact that they were roughly a month apart; sometimes less, sometimes slightly more. What the link between those two columns might be, he could not fathom. The right-hand column might be sums of money, written in pounds, shillings and pence, but it was impossible to know what this money was or who it belonged to. He could make no sense of the second column from the left at all.

And yet, Cotton had driven from Canterbury to the lonely fields of Romney Marsh to bring him these numbers. This was what the killers had been looking for when they searched the body. This was why Cotton had died.

Hardcastle made a careful copy of the figures and then pulled out the top-left drawer of his desk and reached inside. His fingers found the spring catch and released it, opening the door to the secret compartment at the back of the desk. He put the copy inside, closed the compartment and replaced the drawer. There were times in the past that this room had been searched, and there was a fair chance it might be again. He knew, now, exactly how ruthless the men he was searching for could be.

He collected his valise and walked into the drawing room without bothering to knock. Calpurnia sat at her writing desk with sheets of paper spread before her, tickling the end of her nose with her quill while gazing out at the rain. There were not many words on the pages.

'I am away until tomorrow afternoon. Dr Mackay may call tomorrow morning with a report for me.'

Her eyes widened a little. 'But wherever are you going in this terrible weather?'

'Canterbury.' He gave her the details; he might as well do so now, for Mackay would doubtless do so when he called in the morning. 'I am going to break the news to the poor woman and her children.'

'Oh, Marcus. It is such a long way.' Her brown eyes showed an unusual sympathy. She understands, he thought with surprise. She knows why I feel responsible, and why I must go myself. 'Go carefully, my dear,' she said.

'I shall.' Heavily, his shoulders bowed a little, he turned towards the door.

The weather was wet and the roads were bad, and it was late on Tuesday before the rector returned to St Mary. Daylight was already ebbing away under the clouds. The autopsy report was on his desk; it did not tell him anything new. Mackay's search of the banker's clothing had revealed nothing. There was no word from Stemp, who would still be out making enquiries with Honeychild. He greeted his sister absent-mindedly, changed into dry clothes and went to see Mrs Chaytor.

'It was every bit as dreadful as I expected it would be,' he said, sitting in her drawing room. 'Thanks to Cotton's gunpowder works, the family have been shunned by the Quaker community in Canterbury. One woman went out of her way to tell me that Cotton had got what was coming to him.'

'That wasn't very Christian of her,' Mrs Chaytor observed.

'Precisely my words to her. The widow is rather younger than Cotton; the two sons are still mere children. All are utterly bereft and do not know what to do. To them, Cotton was a kind husband and adored father. They can make no sense of what has happened.'

'Will they be looked after? I would go up myself, only I am loath to travel too far from Miss Godfrey and Miss Roper, in case there is another crisis.'

'I learned of kinfolk in Rochester and wrote to them, telling them Mrs Cotton needed their help. I also spoke to that insufferable Oxonian prig, the archdeacon, and asked if the Church might lend assistance. His response was that as Cotton had made a fortune in powder and another in banking, the family should not lack for much. I then pointed out that as the family of a patriotic Christian who supplied munitions for the defence of our country, the widow and her children deserved our support. He promised to see what he could do.' The rector sighed. 'At moments like this, I question my faith.'

'Why? Because of the archdeacon?'

'Ten minutes in the company of the archdeacon would cause St Peter himself to rip off his halo and reach for the gin bottle. No, because of the sheer ghastliness of it all. A man pecked to pieces by birds; another shot in the face; the ugliness of death, the pain and grief of the living. Seeing all this, it is hard to believe in a kind and benevolent God.'

'And yet you do believe,' she said gently.

'Yes, I do; but at the moment, only just. How did you once describe yourself? A self-doubting agnostic? I think I must be a self-doubting Christian.'

'What I actually said was that I am a non-practising agnostic. I don't know if there is a God, and I don't care enough to find out.'

He managed a smile. 'And, of course, you will tell me there is nothing wrong with doubt.'

'Everyone doubts,' she said. 'Only fools and fanatics have certainty, and we should admit neither group to our company.'

'No. We choose them as members of parliament instead. I have a puzzle for you to solve.'

He handed over the sheet of paper he had found in Cotton's gig. She read it for a long while, her eyebrows coming together in a frown. 'The first and third columns are dates,' she said. 'The dates in the third column are all about three weeks later, more or less, than the dates in the first. So this could be a sort of ledger. On the left side of the page, something is going out; on the right side, something is coming in. Or the other way around.'

It was his turn to frown. 'Why are two dates missing from the right-hand column?'

'If this *is* a ledger, the transactions are not yet completed. The 23rd of the 8th is the 23rd of August. Today is the 5th of September, so that is only thirteen days ago. The other half of the transaction might not take place for another week, or more.'

'And that would mean the 18th of September is a proposed transaction, yet to take place,' said the rector. 'Good. All we need now is to know what the second column represents.'

'There, I fear I am as much in the dark as you. As for *Rmt fm Gh*, it might mean remittance from someone whose name begins with Gh; or perhaps from Ghent. But that does not get us very far.' She looked up. 'Do you think Cotton was killed by the same person who killed Hector Munro?'

'Whether it was the same man who pulled the trigger, I do not know,' said Hardcastle. 'But I am certain the same person ordered both murders. And what is more, I think now that I know who it is.'

She watched his face, her eyes blue and intense again. 'Who?' she asked softly.

'Think about it, my dear. Who has most to lose in this game? Who is desperate to keep the bank afloat, so desperate that he will turn to crime? Who convinced Munro and Cotton that smuggling was the bank's only hope of salvation? Who already risks the gallows, and might be prepared to kill in order to protect himself? You will find, I think, that only one name comes to mind.'

'Charles Faversham,' she said.

'The bank is everything to Faversham,' the rector said. 'He built it up, and his pride and reputation depend on its success. But the bank is failing. Realising this, Faversham turned to smuggling to bring in money. But when this venture – like so many others he has planned – began to fail as well, Faversham concealed the news from his active partners, Munro and Cotton. Or perhaps Maudsley was right, and Faversham did not even notice the problem until Munro pointed it out.

'The argument between them in Rye may have persuaded Faversham that he could no longer trust Munro. At all events, he gave orders for Munro's death. And Cotton must have known this. Cotton was terrified; so terrified that at first he would not speak to me. I believe Faversham has threatened him; if you breathe a word, what happened to Munro will happen to you. When I arrived in Canterbury, Cotton realised he was caught between the devil and the deep sea. He decided in the end to defy Faversham rather than me, and that cost him his life.'

'But defying you would have also cost him his life,' she said quietly. 'He chose the possibility of Faversham's vengeance against the certainty of the gallows or transportation.'

'Like a good banker, he weighed the risks and chose what he believed to be the safest option. Only this time, he was wrong.' The rector picked up the paper again. 'I want to know what the figures in that second column mean. The moment I do, I shall confront Charles Faversham and demand the truth.'

'But will Faversham give you a hearing?' asked Mrs Chaytor. 'He is in Sussex, and your authority is valid only for Kent. He agreed to talk to you last time because he believed he could gull you. He will not be so cooperative again. He will tell you instead that you have no jurisdiction in Rye, and throw you out.'

'You are likely to be right, of course. I shall have to ask Lord Clavertye to intervene again. Assuming he can be distracted from his pursuit of high office long enough to pay attention.'

THE RECTORY, ST MARY IN THE MARSH, KENT
6th of September, 1797

By express

My lord,

I write to you once more in connection with the Munro case. A second partner in the East Weald and Ashford Bank, Mr Sylvester Cotton of Canterbury, has been shot dead, this time near Ivychurch. He was driving to see me when he was waylaid and killed.

I am convinced that Charles Faversham has a connection with both this murder and that of Hector Munro. However, I have no jurisdiction in Sussex, and therefore cannot formally arrest or interrogate him. I write therefore to ask you to intervene with the attorney-general, request him to grant me access to Mr Faversham.

I await your response,

Yr very obedient servant

HARDCASTLE

THE EAST WEALD AND ASHFORD BANK, HIGH STREET, RYE
6th of September, 1797

Reverend Hardcastle, sir,

I have just heard the tragic news about my poor colleague,
Mr Cotton. Coming so soon after the death of Mr Munro,
this is a terrible blow to us all.

Word has it that you are investigating the circumstances
surrounding the death of Mr Cotton. I hope that you will
be able to bring the affair to a speedy conclusion, and please
do inform me of any result.

Yrs faithfully

CHARLES FAVERSHAM, ESQ

Please do inform me of any result, thought the rector. A decent
man would have offered help; provided information about Cotton to assist the investigation; put himself forward to be interviewed again. Faversham merely asked to be kept informed, with
all the emotion of someone enquiring after a lost handkerchief.

The two constables, Stemp and Honeychild, traced Cotton's last movements without difficulty. The tollbooth keeper
remembered Cotton driving down the Ashford turnpike in the
evening. A quick visit to the Ship in New Romney confirmed
that Cotton had written ahead to request a room there.

No one had seen two men riding a horse, but Honeychild had
followed the tracks as far as Ham Street. The animal itself was
found there next morning, abandoned in a field. The murderers
had disappeared without a trace.

The inquest into the death of Sylvester Cotton was held on Wednesday morning in the common room of the Bell in Ivychurch, with Dr Stackpole the coroner presiding. The evidence was simple; the inquest lasted for less than an hour and the verdict of unlawful killing was delivered within minutes. The rector refused the landlord's offer of a drink, and drove back to St Mary in bitter silence.

He waited, with little patience, for Clavertye's response. For distraction as much as anything, he turned to his parochial work. He called on the more elderly of his parishioners to see if they were well; some were short of money, one had a leaky roof that needed mending, many were simply glad of the company. Miss Godfrey and Miss Roper were among those he visited, and he saw to his quiet distress that the palsy in Miss Roper's hands had increased.

'Ladies, Mrs Chaytor has offered to help you withdraw your money. If you need a safe place, you may avail yourself of my strongbox until arrangements are completed in London.'

'No, no, no, that would not be right. We cannot impose upon you any further, reverend. You do so much for us already.' Nothing he could say would sway them; they would wait until they could transfer their money directly to London.

'Mr Ricardo, reverend,' said Biddy, curtseying in the doorway to the study.

The rector rose to his feet and bowed. 'Mr Ricardo. It was good of you to come all this way, sir. Did you have a fair journey?'

'Well enough, thank you.' Ricardo refused the offer of madeira, and the rector dispatched Biddy for coffee. The stockbroker took his seat, his normally cheerful face quite serious.

'I heard the news in Ashford. Is it known what happened to Mr Cotton?'

'He was ambushed on the road. I am very glad to see you have arrived unmolested, and I hope you will take precautions on the drive home. I can lend you a pistol, if you wish.'

Ricardo smiled then, and shook his head. 'My wife is a Quaker, sir. If she knew I had handled a firearm, I should never hear the end of it. My coachman, on the other hand, has a blunderbuss; and being Church of England, he has no compunction about using it.'

The rector nodded. 'From your letter, I inferred that you have some worries of your own about the East Weald and Ashford Bank. Am I correct?'

'You are, sir. I took on the bank as a client at the behest of Mr Munro, with whom I was formerly acquainted. I trusted him and knew I could work with him. But after Mr Munro's death, Mr Faversham the senior partner took over the correspondence. I have since begun to grow uneasy. Mr Faversham's instructions are often vague and impractical. His judgement when it comes to picking investments is highly suspect.'

The coffee arrived. Ricardo waited until Biddy had departed the room and then leaned forward a little. 'Reverend Hardcastle, I must ask you a question. Was Mr Munro's death connected in any way with the affairs of the bank?'

'I am quite certain of it,' said the rector. 'I am equally certain that Mr Cotton was shot and killed for the same reason.'

'Ah.' Ricardo sat back in his chair again. 'That explains why you urged me to take precautions. Mr Cotton was not killed by highwaymen.'

'No. He was coming to call on me, and to tell me about the bank's involvement in smuggling. It now seems quite clear that several of the partners, including Faversham, Munro and Cotton, had turned to the free trade as a way of improving the fortunes of the bank. Cotton was coming to me in order to make a confession.'

Ricardo's pleasant face was full of distaste. 'Now that I know him a little better, I can believe that Faversham might choose such a dubious course. But I would have thought Munro had more sense.'

'I suspect Munro may have begun to regret his decision, though of course sadly we shall never know. If I may ask, sir, what first aroused your own concern about the bank?'

'Shortly before your letter arrived, I met George Stone from the Grasshopper. He was in a worried state. Faversham was very angry, George said, about some bills of exchange from Germany. He as good as accused George and the Grasshopper of fraud; which of course is unthinkable.'

In a business where shady activity was commonplace, the bank of Martin, Stone and Foote had always prided itself on its reputation for honesty and probity. James Martin, the senior partner, did not tolerate dishonest dealing. 'George wouldn't give me the details, of course,' said Ricardo, 'but it seemed clear that Faversham had blundered somehow, and was trying to slough off the blame onto George. It's not a very professional thing to do. Now, of course, there is this business of smuggling. I am beginning to regret my association with the East Weald and Ashford.'

The rector gazed thoughtfully at Ricardo, wondering how far he could trust him. So far, at least, the stockbroker had given him no reason not to do so.

'May I show you something?' Hardcastle asked finally. He handed the paper he had taken from Cotton's gig across the desk to Ricardo. The stockbroker studied it.

			Rmt fm Gh
1st of 11th	120	23rd of 11th	672.5.0
30th of 11th	258	27th of 12th	1,431.11.6
29th of 12th	310	25th of 1st	1,705.10.11
30th of 1st	355	24th of 2nd	1,917.8.2
26th of 2nd	620	20th of 3rd	3,162.17.4¼
29th of 3rd	4,327	20th of 4th	20,769.12.1
28th of 4th	1,290	23rd of 5th	6,063.5.10
27th of 5th	2,566	16th of 6th	11,547.12.7½
25th of 6th	4,014	15th of 7th	17,661.13.8
22nd of 7th	4,418	16th of 8th	19,218.7.6
23rd of 8th	3,100		
18th of 9th	5,720		

'It's a ledger,' Ricardo confirmed after a moment.

'I thought as much. And the heading at the top; it occurred to me just now as you were speaking of Mr Stone. Could that possibly be shorthand for *Remittance from the Grasshopper*?'

'It easily could,' said Ricardo. 'So, the figures in the right-hand column represent sums of money – in some cases, quite considerable sums of money – paid to East Weald and Ashford by Martin, Stone and Foote. I wonder if these are the bills of exchange George mentioned.'

'Why was the Grasshopper making these payments?' the rector wondered.

'At a guess, they were dividends from some continental investment made by the East Weald and Ashford, which the Grasshopper has been handling for them.'

'And what might that investment be?'

Ricardo frowned. 'The answer presumably lies in the numbers in the second column,' he said. 'These are quantities of . . . something, but quite what, I cannot think; 120 yields a return of £672 5s; 258 yields a return of £1,431 11s 6d, and so on . . .'

The stockbroker fell silent for a moment. 'That correspondence of numbers,' he said. 'I am reminded of something, but I cannot put my finger on it.'

'What do you mean?'

'The numbers in columns two and four. Divide £672 by 120 and you get about £5 12s. Divide £1,431 by 258 and you get about £5 11s; nearly the same. The next row down, £5 11s again.' Ricardo tapped his forehead. 'What does that remind me of?'

'Is the ratio the same in every row?'

'No. Look at March, the first big investment, 4,327. The remittance is nearly £21,000, which looks good, but divide that by the amount invested and you can see the rate of return has plummeted, to about £4 16s per item invested. And by July, it has dropped to about £4 7s. That's down nearly a quarter on the original rate.'

'Yet it still seems to be a good return,' said the rector. 'If I could invest a pound and receive four pounds and seven shillings back, I would be a happy man.'

'But they're not investing money, or not in the conventional sense. Otherwise the second column would also be written in pounds, shillings and pence; money out, then money in. No, they're trading *something* . . .'

Ricardo looked up. 'The smugglers the bank employs. Is it known what they bring into the country?'

'No. In fact, there is a possibility that they are actually taking goods out of the country and sending them to France. My constable saw them loading gunpowder kegs onto a French ship. But I do not see how they could earn enough money smuggling powder to justify the risk of the venture.'

Ricardo shook his head. 'I agree. Go back to the top line again; 120 pounds of gunpowder at sixpence the pound would fetch a bit over £3. Not worth bothering with. Could it be 120 tons?'

'My constable said there were only ten kegs in the last shipment. Whatever they are smuggling, the quantities are quite small.'

Ricardo continued to stare at the paper. 'When did your constable see these men?'

The rector searched through the pages of notes on his desk. 'The 23rd of last month.'

'And here it is on the page: the 23rd of the 8th. There can be little doubt about it; smugglers took 3,100 items of *something* out of the country on that date. The bank is still waiting to be reimbursed by the Grasshopper . . .'

The stockbroker shook his head. 'The connection is staring me in the face, and I cannot see it. Reverend, may I keep this paper to study it?'

'Of course. I have made copies for safety. Where are you staying?' asked Hardcastle.

'I had thought of taking a room at your local inn.'

'My dear sir, you must do no such thing. Stay with us, by all means. You can help me to entertain my sister.'

Ricardo smiled. The rector rang for Mrs Kemp, and left the stockbroker to settle in. He sat down at his desk and took out his own copy of the paper, staring at the figures for a long time, assembling and reassembling the numbers in patterns that made less and less sense each time he did so. Eventually he gave up, and went to join his guest and his sister for dinner.

The following morning Ricardo came down to breakfast, his face a mixture of consternation and excitement. 'Sleeping on the problem has done its usual good work,' the stockbroker said. 'I have the answer.'

Hardcastle drew him into the study. 'What is it?'

'It was staring me in the face the whole time. And it most certainly isn't gunpowder they are smuggling. Reverend; I am utterly shocked. Charles Faversham and his bank have embarked upon a course of action so reckless, so utterly foolish – and so entirely against the best interests of not only the bank itself, but this entire country – that I almost cannot credit it. But the evidence is plain before me. I must believe it.'

'What is it?' asked Hardcastle again.

'They are smuggling gold,' said Ricardo.

15

Accusation and Denial

They stared at each other. 'What makes you say so?' the rector asked finally.

'It was the ratios, the correspondence of the numbers. I finally realised what they meant. Do you happen to know the price of gold on the market today?'

'Something over £4,' the rector said finally.

'In this country, yes. To be precise, in London gold sells for £4 4s 7d per fine ounce. The price has been around that level for years now. But on the Continent the price is much higher. The markets there have been starved for gold, especially since the wars began.

'And that was the clue I had been looking for. I remembered the details of some gold export deals done in Amsterdam two years ago, well before the Restriction came in. The market paid £6 per fine ounce. After deducting commissions and transport costs totalling about 9s per ounce, the sellers netted £5 11s per ounce; just as your ledger indicated. Once I recalled those deals, the numbers immediately made sense to me. But I feel a fool in front of myself. I should have remembered much sooner.'

Hardcastle gazed at him. 'You must have been involved in dozens of deals since, and heard about many more. Frankly, sir, I am quite astonished that you remembered at all.'

'I have a peculiar memory,' said Ricardo. 'It retains many things; not all of them wanted.' He seemed faintly embarrassed. 'To be absolutely certain, of course, we would need evidence that the East Weald and Ashford has been buying gold.'

'They have,' said Hardcastle. 'One of the partners, Mrs Redcliffe, told me as much. The assumption was that they were trying to shore up their reserves, to increase confidence in the bank.'

'A sound policy; in theory. I wonder who they were buying it from?'

Something clicked in Hardcastle's own memory. He ran his finger down the second column. 'See here,' he said. 'August, 3,100. In late July or early August, the East India Company sold over three thousand ounces of its gold reserves. My informant, whom I cannot name, did not say to whom. But I think we now know.'

'By God, I think we do,' said Ricardo quietly. 'Given time, I can probably ferret out the rest of their transactions.'

'And do you think this gold is being sold in Amsterdam?'

'I strongly suspect this is the case. The city has the largest gold market in Europe, and offers the best prices. And I know already that one of the Dutch banks, Staphorst, has been dealing in some very large bills of exchange. It is said that these are derived from the gold markets.'

'Forgive my asking, sir, but how do you know this?'

Ricardo smiled. 'My father comes from Amsterdam, and we still have family there. One of my cousins is an official with the Stock Exchange. We send each other news from time to time . . . through, shall we say, irregular channels.'

Hardcastle nodded. 'And how is the profit from these sales returned to the East Weald and Ashford Bank?'

'I think this is where Germany comes in. The gold is transported to Amsterdam, never mind how for the moment, and sold. The money from the sale is remitted to Staphorst, who then draw up a bill of exchange and send it on. My guess is that the bills go to Hamburg, to Berenberg & Gossler. They're the largest clearing house for bills of exchange in Northern Europe; they'll deal with thousands of bills each year, and never know or care where the money comes from. Berenberg & Gossler'll redeem that bill, and then issue a further bill in Hamburg shillings, which will be sent by packet boat to London. There, someone – and from what George Stone said, I'll lay money it is the Grass-hopper – redeems it and remits the money to the East Weald and Ashford.' Ricardo paused. 'At least, that is how I would do it if I were Faversham.'

'This sounds very complex.'

'Oh, it is. Deliberately so. It's meant to make it very difficult for any investigating magistrate, such as yourself, to follow the trail. The money passes through three countries and changes hands several times.'

Munro had called this man a financial genius; it began to look as though he had not exaggerated. 'Then I am fortunate to have your advice, sir.'

Ricardo looked embarrassed again. 'It is I who have been fortunate. I have my sources in Amsterdam, and George Stone chose to confide his troubles to me. I merely put the pieces together. Otherwise I would be guessing in the dark.'

'How long would it take for the money to find its way back to London?' Hardcastle asked.

'Three to four weeks, depending on variables: how long the dispatch riders take to cover the ground between Amsterdam and Hamburg; whether the packet boat has favourable winds, and so on.'

Hardcastle nodded. 'That explains the correspondence between the dates in the first and third columns. The first is the date the shipment is made; the other is the date the remittance is received. We have solved the puzzle.'

'Not quite. There is one more thing. Remember yesterday, when I said the ratios were declining? From £5 11s or £5 12s to about £4 7s?'

'Yes.'

'If Charles Faversham is buying gold in England to sell in Amsterdam, then presumably he is paying the English market rate, £4 4s per fine ounce or thereabouts. If he realises a return of £5 11s, that means a profit of £1 7s per ounce. But over the last two months, that margin has declined, to no more than 3s an ounce.'

'It's still a profit,' said the rector.

Ricardo shook his head. 'The earlier deals I alluded to were legitimate ones, and the money was remitted directly to the sellers. The secret money trail I described has its costs; all the banks involved will be taking their own commission. And the smugglers will charge rather more to take the gold across the Channel than would an ordinary shipper. I think their transaction costs will be much higher than before; enough to wipe out that 3s profit.'

The stockbroker paused again. 'The long and short of it is, Faversham's gold smuggling operation is likely to be losing money,' he said.

Munro and Cotton had both known this. 'What do you think has happened?' the rector asked.

'I'm afraid it looks very much like fraud. And on no small scale either. I estimate the bank has lost at least £20,000 over the last ten months, and very possibly more. And at the present rate of loss, it will lose at least another £12,000 on these next two transactions; again, perhaps more. The total loss could reach as much as £35,000.'

Very few people in England had an income of £35,000; to most, a sum of that size was incomprehensible. The rector shook his head. 'And who might be perpetrating this fraud?'

'An excellent question. Faversham clearly wants to know the answer; that's why he upbraided poor George Stone.'

'And that is what Munro wanted to know too,' said the rector. 'That must be why he came down to Romney Marsh, to follow the trail of the gold. A fraud of this size could ruin the bank.'

'I fear it has already done so.' Ricardo's face was sombre now. 'It is clear to me that Faversham has gambled everything on this venture, and lost. They have spent tens of thousands buying gold, issuing paper which can now never be redeemed. The East Weald and Ashford Bank is hollow, and its fall is only a matter of time.'

'And when it collapses, hundreds, even thousands of innocent people will be ruined.' The strings of numbers had made the rector's head ache. For the first time in days, he badly wanted a drink. 'How can I prevent that from happening?'

'I do not think you can,' said Ricardo.

THE RECTORY, ST MARY IN THE MARSH, KENT
8th of September, 1797

By express

My lord,

Information has been laid before me that suggests an organised scheme exists to smuggle gold out of the country. The date of the next shipment is set for the 18th of September, ten days from now, and it is probable that the gold will be loaded onto a ship somewhere off the coast of Romney Marsh. The shipment will be a large one, over 350 lbs deadweight, and it is possible that the gold will be concealed in gunpowder kegs.

Given the urgency of the situation, I propose now to bring in the Customs Service. This matter falls within their jurisdiction, and I do not have the resources or the men to stop the smugglers on my own. The gang involved are very dangerous, and it is likely there is a connection between them and the murders of Mr Munro and Mr Cotton.

I shall of course keep you informed of events as they develop.

Yr very obedient servant

HARDCASTLE

The Rectory, St Mary in the Marsh, Kent
8th of September, 1797

Mr Cole,

I desire to speak to you most urgently on a matter of importance to you and your service. Will you please call on me at
your earliest convenience? It might be useful also if Captain
Haddock could attend on us, should he be available.

Yr very obedient servant

Rev. M. A. Hardcastle, JP

The rector sealed the letters, wondering yet again if he was doing
the right thing. Cole was the local supervisor of the Customs
Service, and Hardcastle and Lord Clavertye had already agreed
to keep the Customs out of this investigation. But Ricardo's reve-
lation had changed Hardcastle's mind.

Noakes and the gang who smuggled the gold – for it was
obvious now, with hindsight, that the powder kegs Stemp had
seen were packed not with gunpowder but with gold – were well
armed and violent, and force would be needed to stop them.
That meant calling in the Customs Service; who were notori-
ously secretive, prickly and difficult to work with. They trusted
no one, not even their fellow Preventive officers in the Excise
Service. Last summer there had even been a pitched battle
between the two services, out on the Marsh.

Cole was relatively new in his post, and Hardcastle did not
know him well. He appeared to be honest, even if there were
some doubts about his competence, and his men were not
always of the best quality. Well, they would have to do; if Cole
and his disgruntled, underpaid crew of land waiters and coast

waiters and tidesmen and riding officers could stop the next run, they might even be able to take the smugglers themselves, and Hardcastle would have his murderers. But at the very least, they would smoke the smugglers out into the open.

Meanwhile, he also had to work out how to solve an impossible conundrum: building a case against Charles Faversham for smuggling, fraud and murder, while at the same time staving off the collapse of the bank. Ricardo had regarded the fall of the bank as inevitable; the stockbroker had returned to London already determined to sever his own connections with it. But Hardcastle thought of Miss Godfrey and Miss Roper, and Stemp and Luckhurst, and Freddie Woodford's parish funds, and refused to give up just yet.

He told Mrs Chaytor what Ricardo had said, and saw her cool blue eyes narrow as she considered the news. 'And you are convinced that Faversham himself is behind the fraud as well as the smuggling?'

'I am. Munro and Cotton were both killed because they were about to expose him.'

'Will you allow me to play devil's advocate?' she asked.

'Certainly. It is one of the reasons why I value your friendship.'

'Munro didn't know the truth, not yet. He was still in search of the truth when he set out for France.'

'And if he had reached France, he would have learned what Faversham was doing. Faversham killed him to stop him.'

'But why is Faversham doing this?' asked Mrs Chaytor. 'We agreed earlier, did we not, that Faversham has the most to lose by the collapse of the bank? His status as owner of the bank means everything to him; you said so yourself, and you were right. So why would he embezzle from it, knowing that to do so will precipitate its collapse?'

'Perhaps he knows the collapse is coming, and is feathering his nest while he can.'

'Taking £35,000 is much more than just feathering his nest. That is a deliberate act of destruction aimed at the institution his father founded, and to which he has dedicated much of his life. I can understand why Faversham might kill to protect the bank. I cannot understand why he would set out to destroy it.'

'I shall ask him,' said the rector. 'Just as soon as Lord Clavertye gives the word.'

The word came by post the following morning.

MIDDLE TEMPLE, LONDON
7th of September, 1797

By express

My dear Hardcastle

I am in receipt of your express of yesterday's date. The postal system appears to be working with remarkable celerity at the moment.

I saw Sir John Scott the *current* attorney-general this morning and explained the situation. Notwithstanding the fact that he knows I covet his position, he gave me a cordial hearing. You will find enclosed his warrant authorising you to go to Rye and interview Charles Faversham. Sir John has not consulted the Lord-Lieutenant of Sussex, so I suggest you interview Faversham quickly before his lordship intervenes. The lord-lieutenant is also Master-General of the Ordinance and thus has – both metaphorically and literally – the bigger guns, outranking Sir John in the government.

Good hunting, and let me know what transpires.

Yr very obedient servant

CLAVERTYE

*

At the bank, Charles Faversham received him with just the right blend of cordiality and concern. 'I was about to write to you, to ask for news. I take it there is none?'

'Not yet, I fear.' The rector sat down before the big desk and looked steadily at Faversham. 'I must begin by telling you that I think the deaths of Munro and Cotton are linked. It is quite possible that the same man, or men, killed them both.'

'Ah.' Faversham looked steadily at the rector, his bonhomie quite gone. 'I wondered if that was so. Are the rest of the partners safe, do you think, or does this murderer intend to kill us all?'

The rector looked him sharply. 'Why should he wish to do that?'

'How should I know? None of this makes any sense to me, not Munro's death, not Cotton's, nothing. Perhaps some madman has a grudge against the bank, and is stalking us.'

'I fear the matter is rather more complex than that,' the rector said. 'Sylvester Cotton was on his way to me when he was killed. Cotton knew the bank was involved in smuggling, and was ready to confess to me. He was killed before he could do so.'

'Cotton, a smuggler!' Faversham stared at him. 'I am sorry, reverend, but I simply cannot believe it. Cotton was a Quaker and a God-fearing man. He would never stoop to criminality.'

Hardcastle watched him, his eyes narrowing a little. 'Stoop to criminality,' he repeated. 'Yes. A good performance, Mr Faversham. But not absolutely of the best, I fear. A trifle too much melodrama, which gives you away.'

'I think you had better explain yourself, Hardcastle.'

'I am about to do exactly that. You have been lying to me all along, Faversham. You lied about Munro's character and competence; you lied about the Baltic timber deal; and you lied when you said you did not know what Munro was doing before he died. You hoped to throw me off the scent. You wanted me to assume that Munro – secretive, untrustworthy Munro – became involved in the free trade and was then killed by smugglers. Your own role would never be revealed. But you were wrong.

'The time for lies has now passed. From this moment onward, you and I shall deal solely in the truth. You knew that the East Weald and Ashford Bank had turned to smuggling, because you gave the order that it should do so. You, Munro, Cotton; how many others in the bank knew?'

Faversham stared at him. 'What the devil are you talking about?'

'It is true also that you are no ordinary smugglers,' the rector went on. 'Your commodity is gold, taken out of England in defiance of the law and sold abroad, the money coming back to you by devious channels through the European money markets, so that payments cannot be traced.'

'Gold? European money markets?' Faversham shook his head. 'I have no knowledge of any smuggling, of gold or otherwise. This is ludicrous.'

'That's better. You were almost convincing there. But I know all the details, you see. Four thousand, four hundred and eighteen ounces went out on of the 22nd of July; three thousand one hundred ounces, purchased from the East India Company, on the 23rd of August; need I go on? I can also furnish details of the remittances, too, and the dates you received them. Faversham, you have gone rather pale.'

'Get out of my office, and out of my bank. At once, do you hear me?'

'I have not finished.'

'If you do not leave, my servants will throw you out.' Faversham's hand moved towards the silver bell on his desk.

'Summon your staff, by all means,' said Hardcastle. 'Then they can listen, while I accuse you further of defrauding your own bank and your partners, and deliberately plotting the ruin of your deposit holders. And your employees, too, of course, who will lose their livelihood when the bank fails. I don't imagine any of them will see a penny of the £35,000 you have taken, or will shortly take.'

Faversham's hand had halted. He sat motionless now, staring at the rector, his once-handsome face showing fear in every line and pore. 'What did you say?' he asked, his voice barely more than a whisper.

'Why, Faversham? Why wreck your own bank? Yes, it is in trouble, but surely it could have been saved. More partners could have been found to bail you out. Now look at it.' The rector gestured around the room. 'All of this is about to fall. The bank is doomed, and you are the man who has ruined it.'

'I am no such thing, damn your eyes!'

'I do not believe you. I ask again: why? Is money all that matters to you? Is it more important even than the lives of your own partners? And who did you hire to kill them, Faversham? I don't imagine for one moment you have the courage to pull the trigger yourself; and in any case, that is not how you work. You're the planner behind the scenes, the man who brokers the deals and pulls the strings. Whom did you pay to kill Munro and Cotton?'

'You must be mad to imagine such things.' Faversham rose to his feet, sweating, and walked across to the sideboard. He unstoppered the decanter of madeira and poured a glass full, then drank it in a single draught. After a moment some of the colour came back into his cheeks, and he wheeled around to confront Hardcastle.

'You have no jurisdiction here. I am not required to answer your questions.'

.'Indeed you are.' Hardcastle reached into his pocket, pulled out the attorney-general's warrant and handed it over. Faversham read it, his face guarded, then handed it back.

'I will say this much to you, Hardcastle. I did not kill Munro or Cotton. I had no reason to. And I have never taken a penny from this bank that was not my lawful share. Yes, someone is defrauding us. Munro found out about it, tried to investigate against my advice and was killed. Cotton discovered something, I don't know what, and was murdered before he could talk to you. But I am not the embezzler, and I have killed no one.

'And as for your allegation of smuggling: prove it. Find a single piece of evidence that links us with gold smuggling, or any kind of smuggling at all. You cannot, can you?'

'I have a ledger detailing dates and amounts of transactions.'

'Can it be proven that this ledger comes from the East Weald and Ashford Bank? It cannot. Does it say that the numbers refer to gold? It does not. Does it indicate that any gold belonging to anyone was moved unlawfully out of the country? It does not.'

'So, you know the document to which I refer. You have seen it? Did Munro write it out, perhaps from figures you gave him?'

'You can prove nothing.'

'I will find the evidence, never fear,' said the rector. 'You claim you are not the embezzler. Very well; tell me who it is, or who you think it might be. If I can apprehend them, you may still save your bank.'

'Tell *you*!' Faversham gave a kind of strangled laugh. 'Thank you, no. I have no desire to share the fate of Munro and Cotton. I have told you all I will ever tell you. Now, get out.'

'I can charge you here and now with smuggling and murder. Sir John Scott's warrant gives me the authority to arrest you and hold you in close confinement.'

'And when the Duke of Richmond, the Lord-Lieutenant of Sussex and my patron, hears you have no evidence, he will first compel my release, and then devote himself to breaking you.' Faversham smiled an unpleasant smile. 'I've called your bluff, Hardcastle. What will you do?'

Hardcastle watched the other man for perhaps half a minute, until Faversham began to stir nervously. 'I shall take my leave,' the rector said finally. 'But I give you fair warning. I shall return. Good day, Faversham. Don't trouble your servants; I know the way to the door.'

16

Grebell's Confession

Monday, of the 11th of September; a month to the day since Hector Munro had died.

Rising early, as ever, the rector walked Rodolpho down to the sea at St Mary's Bay, the sky dim under scudding clouds. Here he slipped the wolfhound's lead and watched the dog race away down the strand and fling himself into the waves, barking happily. Beyond lay the rolling sea, slate grey and flecked with foam.

Hardcastle's mood was as bleak as the morning. In challenging him to produce evidence, Faversham had tacitly admitted to his part in the gold smuggling. But he had insisted he was not responsible for the fraud and the murders; and the rector believed him. Despite his bravado at the end, there was no mistaking the desperation and fear in the man's face and voice. He knew full well that the bank was being systematically defrauded and destroyed.

That said, Faversham was largely responsible for his own predicament. The smuggling had surely been his idea in the first place. Part spider and part fly, he was now trapped in the web that he himself had spun, and the more he struggled to fight free, the more deeply ensnared he became.

And it was entirely possible that Faversham's own life was in danger. There had been three active partners in the bank, three who had plotted to smuggle gold, and now two of them were dead. It was not fanciful of Faversham to think that he might be next.

After leaving the bank, Hardcastle had called on Dobbs, the magistrate in Rye, where he produced Sir John Scott's warrant and gave him a heavily edited account of his investigation, leaving out all mention of gold and embezzlement but warning that Faversham might be in danger. Dobbs had grumbled about Hardcastle interviewing people on his turf without informing him, but had promised to be vigilant. They both knew that with just three constables to police a town of two thousand, there was a limit to the protection Dobbs could provide. Faversham would be advised to hire guards of his own, to protect himself and his family.

Worryingly, too, Dobbs had heard rumours about the stability of the bank. Two of its partners had died by violence; what was really going on behind that handsome brick facade on the high street? Dobbs was contemplating whether to withdraw his own money; but like so many others, he had no idea where to put his savings if he did. The East Weald and Ashford was the only bank in the area.

Hardcastle thought again about Miss Godfrey and Miss Roper, and Stemp and Luckhurst and all the others he knew who would be ruined if the bank collapsed, and felt a cold depression settling over him. He whistled to Rodolpho, put the sodden dog on the lead and walked home.

After breakfast he settled in his study and attempted to work, but could not concentrate. He heard his sister rise; some time later, the sound of her singing came from the drawing room. Does she *ever* do any work on that blasted book, he wondered. But Calpurnia was not responsible for his dark mood. His own inability to halt the coming calamity was surely the source of that.

Just before midday, Joshua Stemp knocked at the door of the rectory and was ushered into the study. 'Reverend, I was hoping to see you. There's someone here would like to meet you.'

The man with Stemp was in his mid-twenties, tall and dapper in a blue uniform coat and white breeches. 'Lieutenant Newton

Stark, master of His Majesty's ship *Black Joke*,' said Stemp, a little self-consciously. 'The Reverend Hardcastle.'

Stark bowed. 'How can I assist you, sir?' the rector asked.

'First allow me to apologise for the imposition,' the navy man said. 'I ran across Mr Stemp in Hythe this morning, and knowing he worked for you, I asked if I might meet you. I'd like to put a question to you, sir, if I may.'

The rector gestured both men to seats. 'How may I help you?' he asked.

'It's about the bank, sir. The East Weald and Ashford. I've a fair amount of gelt there, prize money, and profits from some other ventures. I'd always believed it a good, sound bank. But yesterday I heard a hark-ye that they might be in trouble. I spoke to Mr Stemp, as I know he uses the same bank, and he said I should ask you.'

'I warned Mr Stark you might not be able to tell him much,' said Stemp. 'With the investigation going on and all.'

'I understand entirely,' said Stark. 'But I'd be grateful for reassurance, Reverend, if there is any to give. I've just been ordered north for a few weeks, and we sail with the tide tomorrow morning, so I have to go straight back to Dover. There's no time for me to nip over to the bank and pull out my money, so I'll have to leave it there and hope for the best. But if there is anything you can tell me . . .'

Hardcastle nodded. 'I am afraid the rumour you heard was true, Mr Stark,' he said. 'The bank is indeed experiencing difficulties at the moment.'

'Ah. Bad news. Is it likely to go smash, do you think?'

The rector opened his mouth to say that there was a distinct possibility. An image of Miss Godfrey and Miss Roper formed itself in his mind.

'No,' he said, and his voice was firm and definite. 'The bank will not fail, and your money will be safe. You have my word on that.'

Relief was plain in the pleasant young face. 'That's good to hear. Thank you, reverend. You are quite positive that all will be well?'

'I am,' said the rector. 'And you may say the same to anyone else who asks you.' He wished Stemp would stop staring at him. 'What takes you north, lieutenant?'

'There's word the Dutch fleet is making ready to put to sea. Admiral Duncan wants the services of the fastest ship afloat, so he sent for *Black Joke*.' The young man grinned, his natural good cheer restored by the rector's assurances. *Was I ever that young*, Hardcastle wondered, *and that full of confidence?*

'Will Duncan's fleet fight?' he asked. 'It's not four months since half the navy mutinied.'

'We'll know soon enough,' said Stark. 'But *Black Joke*'ll fight, and that's probably all that'll be needed. It's only the Dutch. Well, reverend, I've taken enough of your time. Thank you again. You've quite bucked me up.'

They rose, just as Biddy knocked and came in, curtseying. 'Mrs Chaytor to see you, reverend.'

The young man perked up even further as Amelia Chaytor entered the room, and his eyes brightened. 'Mrs Chaytor; Mr Stark,' the rector said.

'Lieutenant Maurice Adolph Newton de Stark, Royal Navy, at your undoubted service,' said the officer, bowing with a sweeping motion of his arm. 'It is both an honour and a pleasure to meet you, ma'am. And yet, I am perplexed. I have served in these waters for many months; how is it that we have never met?'

'Maurice Adolph Newton de Stark,' repeated Mrs Chaytor, ignoring the question. 'Goodness; such a lot of names for so young a man. Will you grow into them with time, do you think?'

He grinned at her. 'Father's Austrian. He wanted to give me seven or eight forenames, like himself, but mother chiselled him down to three. The old girl drives a hard bargain.'

'Your mother sounds a most tenacious lady.'

'Very much so. And fortunately, she has passed that quality on to me,' said the young man happily. 'Is there a Mr Chaytor lurking in the wings, or are you happily unattached? Or even, unhappily attached?'

'Suppose there is a Mr Chaytor,' she said. 'Would that put you off?'

'It would depend on how big he is. My friends call me Newton.'

'Do they? My condolences. Perhaps you could go back to your father, and ask him for another name from the family storehouse.'

His grin increased. 'What name would you recommend? Choose one for me, ma'am, I beg you. Not just an ordinary name; any word in the lexicon, so long as it sums up my character in full.'

Mrs Chaytor looked him up and down. 'Trouble,' she said.

Stark clutched theatrically at his chest. 'Skewered. A simple jack tar like myself is no match for the wit of a clever lady. Reverend, thank you once again, and farewell. I shall return when my ship is next in these waters.' He grinned again at Mrs Chaytor. 'And whether that is a promise or a threat, I leave you to decide.'

Stemp was red in the face. 'I'm so sorry, ma'am,' he said after Stark had departed. 'He's a good lad, really. He's harmless; unless you're a French privateer, that is.'

'I am certain of it. He reminds me of Rodolpho,' said Mrs Chaytor, smiling. 'How are you, Joshua? Has your hunt met with any success?'

'Still no sign of the man who hired the boat. And Noakes and Fisk have both gone to ground. No one has seen them for at least a week.'

'Cotton was killed just over a week ago,' said Mrs Chaytor suddenly.

'That's right, ma'am. They vanished the day before the murder.'

The rector nodded. 'Noakes and Fisk killed Cotton, and are lying low in case anyone connects them with the murder and comes looking for them.' He thought for a moment. 'You were right, Joshua. Noakes and his gang are working for the bank, and also for the embezzler. But where is the link? How do we prove it? We'll get nothing more out of Faversham; if I press him further, or even visit him again, I will only put him in more danger.'

'We need to find the go-between,' said Mrs Chaytor.

'Him, or that courier, Jean, or the man who hired the boat. If we can get to one of those three and break them, we can learn the rest of the operation and bring all the various pieces of the puzzle together.'

'Easier said than done,' observed Mrs Chaytor. 'Joshua and his friends have been searching diligently, but this gang has covered their tracks exceedingly well.'

'That's the truth, ma'am,' said Stemp.

'But they cannot hide forever,' said Hardcastle. 'The next gold run is a week from today. Noakes and Fisk and their friends will have to come out of hiding, and when they do, hopefully Mr Cole and his officers will be able to lay them by the heels. You need not look so sceptical, Joshua. Like yourself, I am quite aware of the limitations of the Customs. But Cole knows when the gold will be run, and he knows what to look for. Even he should be able to pull this off.'

Stemp's look of scepticism did not alter. 'I remember that you were also going to ask some questions about Charles Batist,' the rector said. 'Have you learned anything?'

Stemp nodded. 'Like your friend said, reverend, Batist senior came over from France with his wife and son just after the last war. They lived in Hythe for a while before going up to Ashford. But they weren't the first of the family to come to England. There's been Batists settled in and around Hythe for thirty or forty years.'

'Did you learn anything about them?' the rector asked.

'They're honest, decent folk; which ain't at all usual for Hythe, I can tell you. There's a cousin who has done well for himself as a brickmaker, and another who's a clerk, and there's a baker whose two sons both work with him. There's one who works as a sailmaker, but beyond that there's no connection with the sea, no sailors or boatmen. I asked Mr Sawbridge, the magistrate, and he couldn't recall any of the family being in trouble with the law.'

'So there's no one who can be connected with smuggling?'

'Seems not, reverend. At least, no one I could find.'

'Well, it was always a long shot,' said Hardcastle. 'Carry on watching in Hythe, and let me know the moment any of the gang reappear.'

Humphrey Cole, supervisor of Customs, arrived at the rectory early the following afternoon. With him were one of his subordinates, a riding officer named Petchey, and Captain John Haddock of the *Stag*, white-haired and resplendent in blue uniform.

'My apologies, reverend,' said Cole as soon as they were seated. 'I was away in Deal, in conference with the Collector of Customs there, and only received your letter yesterday. I sent at once for Captain Haddock, and I have also invited Mr Petchey, my senior riding officer, to join us.'

'Thank you, gentlemen, for coming.' Swiftly, Hardcastle described what he knew about the gold-smuggling operation, carefully making no mention of the bank. 'The gang appears to be based out of Hythe. We are certain that Henry Noakes and John Fisk, both boatmen of Hythe, are involved. We are searching for a third gang member, a young man of slender build who is well spoken; beyond this we have no further description of him. Also, gentlemen, you should be aware that this gang are in possession of a weapon called a Puckle gun, a repeating firearm of considerable power. Be careful in your approach to them.'

'I'll put all of my officers onto this,' said Cole, 'and I'll send to Dover and Deal to ask for reinforcements. I'll have forty men on the Marsh by the end of the day. And I'll order the arrest of Noakes and Fisk, wherever they may be found.'

'That may be difficult,' the rector said. 'My own information is that both men have gone into hiding.'

'Never mind,' said Cole confidently. 'We know their haunts, and we'll track them down. Petchey will be in charge of watching the roads and tracks coming down from upcountry. He'll search every wagon and cart and beast of burden. Captain Haddock and the *Stag* will patrol the inshore waters looking for the smugglers' ship, and I'll have watchers along the coast as well. One way or another, we'll find this gang and take them.' Cole rubbed his hands. 'Twenty thousand pounds in gold! This could be the biggest seizure by the Customs for a century, perhaps of all time.'

'Who is behind this, reverend?' asked Petchey curiously. 'Noakes and Fisk don't have the brains to organise something this big, let alone the money.'

'We think it may be a syndicate in the City,' said the rector. The longer he could keep the role of the East Weald and Ashford Bank secret, the better. An idea was taking shape in his mind, but he needed time to think about it.

'Once you have arrested these men, I wish to interrogate them,' the rector continued. 'I am certain that at least one of them will be able to give me information about the murders of Hector Munro and Sylvester Cotton.'

'Of course,' said Cole. 'I'll be happy to help you, reverend. Ah, this is going to be a great day for the Customs Service.'

Already, in Cole's mind, this was to be a Customs coup; everyone else was forgotten. He departed with Petchey and Haddock soon after, still gloating. The rector did not mind; Cole was welcome to whatever credit there was. He himself was interested in two things only: finding the murderers, and saving the bank.

Gazing out the window, he pondered again on the latter. He recalled what Ricardo had said, that the money received from the sale of the smuggled gold passed through the hands of the Grasshopper on the final stage of its journey back to England. It was possible – indeed, likely – that Stone and the other partners at the Grasshopper did not know the origin of the money they handled, and from which they took a percentage for their own profit. What had Munro said? *If the Grasshopper finds out what we're up to, there will be hell to pay.*

So, I know something the Grasshopper does not, Hardcastle thought. Now I must find a way to turn that to my advantage.

Ten days had passed since Amelia Chaytor had first written to Thomas Coutts, the London banker, requesting that accounts be opened for Miss Godfrey and Miss Roper. No response had come, and she was beginning to fret.

Accompanied by Joseph, her groom, she drove to Shadoxhurst to see Cecilia Munro. Arriving, she was shown into the nursery, where she found Cecilia and Charlotte Faversham cooing over the baby. Just over a month old, Master Munro lay on his back and grinned up at the two friendly ladies. Then he caught sight of Mrs Chaytor and stared at her with round, questioning eyes.

'Good morning, sir,' said Mrs Chaytor solemnly. 'I trust my friends are keeping you suitably entertained? If they fail to do so, you must scold them. You are the man of the house, so be sure to assert yourself.'

'Young Master Munro has no hesitation on that score,' said Charlotte Faversham, laughing. 'He has a fine pair of lungs, and is not shy of using them.'

'He's a bonny boy,' said Mrs Chaytor, reaching down to chuck the baby softly under the chin and then kissing Cecilia. 'How are you, my dear?'

Her young friend was recovering well; the lines of grief and sorrow were still plain around her eyes, and might stay there forever, but her spirit was strong and resilient. 'I am well,' said Cecilia softly. 'Mrs Redcliffe called again yesterday, and my dear Charlotte is always by my side. I am cared for and loved by my friends; I could ask for no more.'

'You have a very dear friend in Miss Faversham,' said Mrs Chaytor. 'It is good of her family to let her stay with you for so long.'

'Oh, they don't notice my absence,' said Charlotte airily. 'Father is in the office day and night, attending to problems at the bank, and Grebell does nothing but mope and write bad poetry. He's lost all interest in everything else.'

'Why is Grebell moping?' asked Cecilia.

'He got in the way of Cupid's arrow. He's in *love*,' said Charlotte. 'Or at least, he thinks he is. Some silly little mort in Rye, I expect.'

Perhaps then he will stop calling on me, thought Mrs Chaytor. She took her leave an hour later, and Charlotte walked her out to the stable yard, chattering happily as always. Mrs Chaytor cut across the flow with a sudden question. 'Is your brother unhappy?'

'Of course,' said Charlotte, with the callousness of a sister. 'It's good for him. Suffering builds character.'

'And your father? Do you know what is wrong?'

'Not entirely. But I know things are very bad, and we could lose the bank. Father is worried and frightened, and so is Mother.' Her eyes searched Mrs Chaytor's face. 'Do you know what is happening, ma'am?'

It dawned on her that Charlotte was not as empty-headed as she appeared. 'I know something of it,' she said. 'I believe it is possible that your father will indeed lose the bank.'

Charlotte nodded. She was much like her brother, with red hair and slightly protruding eyes and a mouth full of rather prominent teeth; unlike Grebell, she had the confidence to carry off her looks, and a vitality that made her sparkle even when, as now, she was being serious. 'I feared as much,' she said. 'That's what Hector said to Father when he came to call on us in Rye. You know. The week before he went away.'

'You heard him say this?'

'I was in the music room, next door to Father's office, and the wall is a thin one. I could not help but hear their conversation. Someone in France or Holland was defrauding them, but they did not know how it was being done. Hector was going over to find out.'

'Do you know where he was going? Was it to France?'

'Yes, to Boulogne. He wanted to see someone called Vandamme. If Vandamme was not responsible, he said, he would bribe someone for passports and travel to Amsterdam, where he would call on another man called Staphorst. If it wasn't Vandamme, it had to be Staphorst, he said. It sounded rather exciting, and not a little dangerous . . . Which, of course, it was,' she finished soberly.

How stupid we have been, thought Mrs Chaytor. *The hours we have wasted, trying to persuade Faversham to confess, and prying into Grebell's mind; and all the time, this girl has known what we needed to know.*

She was back in St Mary in the Marsh by late afternoon, and drove straight to the rectory. Hardcastle and Calpurnia were about to sit down to dinner, but the rector came out into the hall to greet her. 'I shall not stay long,' said Amelia. She related what Charlotte had said. The rector nodded. 'I'll write to Ricardo at once about Staphorst.'

'We can trust him?'

'He unravelled the ledger, and explained the fraud, when he did not need to do either of those things. Indeed, had he said nothing at all, we would be none the wiser. I think he is on the side of the angels.'

'And this man Vandamme? Could Joshua contact some of his friends and ask around?'

'I have a better idea,' said the rector. 'We know someone who goes in and out of France all the time. Remember?'

'Peter. But will he talk to you?'

Peter was the leader of a shadowy group of men known as the Twelve Apostles, confidential agents in government service whose secretive work often led them into France. The rector had met Peter just three times, and on two of those occasions Peter had been pointing a pistol at him.

'He will,' said Hardcastle. 'He owes me a debt. Now I am calling it in.'

THE RECTORY, ST MARY IN THE MARSH, KENT
13th of September, 1797

My dear Mr Ricardo,

I am writing to you in haste concerning the matter we discussed last week. I recall your theory that the Staphorst bank in Amsterdam was likely to be involved. This has now been confirmed by a witness.

Might I avail myself of your good offices once again, and prevail upon you to use your contact in Amsterdam to investigate Staphorst? I wish to know whether they have a connection with someone called Vandamme in Boulogne, and also whether there is any opportunity for someone at Staphorst to have committed the fraud.

I am once again extremely grateful for any assistance you should choose to give.

Yr very obedient servant

Rev. M. A. Hardcastle, JP

After dinner, the rector walked down through the village to the Star. The common room was quiet that afternoon, empty save for a group of fishermen smoking and drinking gin in one corner. Bessie Luckhurst stood behind the counter, watching them. She brightened when she saw Hardcastle. 'What'll you have, reverend?'

'Small beer, my dear.' When she had brought the beer, he motioned her close and said quietly, 'Do you know where Peter might be?'

Her eyes were bright. 'I am sure I have no idea what you're talking about, reverend.'

'Of course you don't. You're a careful lass, Bessie, which is why he employs you. Tell Peter I need to see him, please. Without delay.'

Amelia Chaytor's late husband had once said that he could always tell his wife's mood by the music she played. When contemplative or thoughtful, she played Bach; when happy, she turned to Handel; Telemann was her choice when her mood became darker; and when strained or angry, she turned to

Vivaldi. She was playing Vivaldi now, fast and furiously, music flowing from her fingers like a rip tide, while outside storm clouds gathered over Romney Marsh.

She looked up as Lucy entered the drawing room, curtseying. 'Mr Grebell Faversham to see you, ma'am.'

'He is here? At this hour?'

'Yes, ma'am. Shall I say you are not at home?'

She took a deep breath. Both her body and mind were taut with tension. She was worried for Miss Godfrey and Miss Roper, whom she saw every day and who still stubbornly refused to let her help them draw out their money; *we must not be a bother to you* was their constant refrain. She had written twice now to Coutts, and still not received a reply. And she was also full of premonitions. Something was coming, something momentous and shattering, after which life would never be quite the same.

And now in the midst of everything else, here was Grebell Faversham, graceless and unconfident as ever, no doubt come to make inconsequential talk and waste another half hour of her life. She drew in another deep breath. Until the affairs of the two ladies were settled, she still needed Grebell's goodwill.

'No,' she said glumly. 'Show him in.'

Slowly, almost hesitantly, Grebell entered the room and bowed. He had lost weight, she saw at once; his face looked thinner, and his blue brocade coat sagged a little at the shoulders. 'Mr Faversham,' she said, curving her lips into a smile. 'What a pleasant surprise. Do sit down. Lucy will bring us some tea in a moment.'

'Thank you, ma'am. I will not stay for long, for the weather looks certain to turn.' The young man sat down nervously, twisting his hands. 'Mrs Chaytor, I called because there is something very important that I must say to you. But, I . . . It is difficult. I-I-I am not certain where to begin.'

'Begin at the beginning,' she said, still smiling a little. 'That is the traditional way.'

The young man swallowed. 'Mrs Chaytor . . . you must have noticed by now that I am your very fervent admirer. Your deportment and manner, your grace and wit, your musical voice, your face, your eyes . . . I admire everything about you. You have all the virtues that I do not, and, and, I-I-I . . .'

She sat frozen. He swallowed, mastering his traitorous tongue. 'I love you,' he said finally, and with that declaration his nerves passed and his voice softened. Now the words came clean and simple, straight from his tormented heart. 'I have loved you from the moment I first saw you, at Magpie Court. I do not venture to hope that you could ever love me in return. I know am too poor a specimen of manhood, too weak and too foolish ever to live up to you. But that will not prevent me from adoring you, until the end of my days. And I . . . I had to tell you. For better or worse.'

She sat still for a long time, hands clenched tightly, feeling faintly sick. Charlotte had been wrong; there was no silly little girl in Rye.

She could cope with men like Lieutenant Stark. They were good-natured and thick-skinned, and one could rebuff them quickly and move on. But Grebell Faversham's skin was almost painfully thin. He had a bright facade, good clothes, a handsome carriage; and almost nothing in the way of self-esteem.

She could cut him cold, wound him, send him crawling away never to return; but that would be wanton cruelty. She chose her words with care.

'I am honoured by your declaration,' she said finally. 'And I fear you are right to think that your love is not returned; but Mr Faversham, that is not because of any fault in yourself.

'I loved once, with an intensity of feeling that consumed me. When my husband died, it nearly broke me. I will never fall in love again, partly because the memories of the love I lost are too strong, and partly because I do not think I can endure that kind of suffering a second time.

'You are kind to tell me of your feelings, and I applaud your honesty. But your cause is a hopeless one. Find a woman who is worthy of you, and who can love you as you should be loved.'

Outside, the wind was rising. The first raindrops thudded against the windowpanes. She could see the agony in his eyes as he rose to his feet. 'I understand,' he said. 'I had no expectation that you could return my feelings. And it is kind of you to wish me well, but . . . you said it yourself. Lightning does not strike twice.'

He smiled a little. 'For once in my life, I have found something that I can stick to,' he said. 'My heart is fixed, Mrs Chaytor. If I must live the rest of my life in solitude, then so be it. My one remaining hope is that you will take comfort in knowing that, somewhere in the world, there is someone who loves you without reservation.'

'I am sorry.'

'Do not be, I beg of you. To have known you at all is a privilege. To love you is an honour, and with that honour I am content. Farewell, Mrs Chaytor. Unless you expressly wish it, I shall not see you again.'

17

Matthew

It was mid-September, and the nights were longer and cooler now. The comet had passed on, its cold light vanished into the blackness. A waning sickle moon shone above the faded sunset. Joshua Stemp rubbed his hands together and blew on them to keep them warm as he walked down the road from Dymchurch to New Romney.

He had spent the day in Hythe, watching patiently for any sign of the gang, seeing nothing. Now, his other life called to him. The new moon was coming, and he, Jack Hoad, Murton, Luckhurst and some of the New Romney men were gathering that night at the Ship to talk over their next smuggling run. Hoad had met Finny Jack three days ago and settled on the 17th as the date; the meeting tonight was to plan the transport and storage of the cargoes once they were ashore.

There were two men on the road up ahead, one of them pushing a handcart. The wheel of the cart squeaked a little. In the falling twilight the men were little more than shadows, but something about their size and the way they walked rang a bell in Stemp's mind. *I've seen these two before*, he thought. The cautious instincts of a lifetime of crime asserted themselves; he dropped back a little, staring at the two shadows and racking his memory.

He wondered at first if they too were heading for the Ship, but before they reached New Romney they turned off the high road and followed a dark track that led north and then west of the town, past the abandoned church at Hope. West of Hope they picked up another track heading south into the dark, deserted reaches of the southern Marsh. Silent as a spider, Stemp followed them.

The stars glowed. Lamps showed yellow in New Romney to the north-east, and more distantly in the windows of Lydd three miles away, little flecks of gold in the night. On the horizon shone the beacon of Dungeness lighthouse. Directly ahead, all was blackness. But the men with the handcart clearly knew their way; they pressed on over the fields, the squeak of the rusty wheel carrying faintly to Stemp's ears as he followed. Once they came to a sewer, a steep-sided drain crossed by a footbridge, the men ahead of him carried the handcart over the bridge and moved on.

Suddenly the noise of the wheel stopped. A black silhouette lifted out of the ground ahead, jagged like a row of broken teeth; the wall of what had once been a church, abandoned and ruined in the wilderness of the Marsh. This was Midley. Centuries ago, Midley had been a thriving village full of life; but plague, poverty and marsh fever had long since driven its people away, and now only ghosts lived here.

Cautiously, Stemp moved forward. He heard a murmur of voices, and saw the glimmer of a lantern. Touching the handle of his knife for reassurance, he crept on noiseless feet up to the base of the ruined wall, then slowly inched along it to the end. Crouching down, he peered into the interior of the church.

The lantern stood on the ground. Its dim radiance showed him the two men with their backs bent, using iron bars to heave up flagstones from the floor of the ancient nave. Now he could see them clearly, he recognised them at once; they were two of the men who had been with Noakes and Fisk that night on the beach. Both were sailors, with blue tattoos on their hands and faces.

'That's good enough,' said one of them. 'Let's start getting those boxes out.'

'How many are we taking tonight?' asked the second man. He had a soft, slurred accent from somewhere on the North Sea; German, perhaps, or Dutch.

'Twelve, they said.' The first man's accent was pure Kent.

'We'll have to make three trips to the wagon, then. Them boxes are god-damned heavy.'

The flagstones, cast aside, revealed a stair leading down to the crypt. The two men went down the stair and disappeared. Stemp sat thinking for a moment. He knew all about the Midley crypt – every smuggler did – but it was rarely used. The room was damp, and perishable goods like silk and lace in particular suffered if kept there for very long. He wondered what these men might have stored in this inhospitable place.

He did not have to wait long to find out. Puffing, the two sailors climbed out of the crypt again, carrying between them a long wooden box. Stemp stiffened; the box was identical to the coffin he had seen in Noakes's boat two months before. The sailors loaded the box onto the handcart, then went below and returned with a second; then a third, and a fourth.

'That's enough for this load,' said the Englishman, picking up the lantern. 'Come on.'

Stemp sat in darkness, listening to the squeaking of the wheel fading slowly away. The crescent moon glowed yellow in the deep blue starlight. That the men would return was certain; what was not clear was how long they would be gone. He guessed they were using the handcart to ferry the boxes to a wagon waiting nearby, probably on the road that led from Lydd up to Old Romney. If that was where the wagon was parked, then he had only a few minutes before the two sailors returned for their second load.

Quickly, he rose from his hiding place behind the wall and trotted across the nave to the stair. The smell of damp earth and stone rose from the dark hole in the church floor. Carefully, Stemp descended into the blackness of the crypt. He reached out and touched stone walls oozing water. Once his hand brushed across a row of hard, curved bars; the ribcage of a skeleton, embedded in the wall.

The toe of his boot struck something hard. He bent and groped in the blackness and found another of the long wooden coffins. Another beyond it, and another; God, there was no end of them. He counted twenty at least, and stopped in horror, the hair rising on the back of his neck. What if they *were* coffins? What if all these boxes contained the victims of some nameless massacre?

Gasping a little, Stemp stooped over the nearest box and pulled out his knife. Wedging it between the coffin lid and the box, he forced the blade upward. Nothing happened; the lid remained firmly nailed down. Clenching his teeth, Stemp tried again. This time the nails shifted a little. Straining, sweat breaking out on his forehead, Stemp continued to heave, and finally the nails yielded with a screech of protesting metal, the lid of the box springing up so suddenly that he nearly lost his footing.

A reeking stench rose from the box in the darkness, sickly and sweet, heady and clogging his nostrils and throat so that he nearly gagged. It was not, thankfully, the smell of a decomposing body. Covering his mouth and nose, Stemp bent over the box. It was lined with lead to keep out damp and corruption, and was filled with cloth bags containing small lumpy objects. Stemp slit one of the bags open and drew out something flat and solid covered in a leafy wrapping. The stink in his nostrils increased, and his head swam a little.

'Opium,' he said aloud.

Thin and ominous, the squeak of the handcart wheel came to his ears.

Instantly, he slammed down the lid of the coffin and then stamped on it hard to drive the nails back into the wood. He could do no more; he had to hope that the theft would not be discovered until daybreak. Back past the skeleton he ran, up the stairs to the surface of the nave and then the shelter of the wall. Here he slid down onto the grass, trying to control his breathing. Lantern light glowed in the nave once more, and the squeaking stopped.

'Pah!' said the Englishman. 'Smell that? The place stinks of poppy.'

'How did that happen?' asked the other.

Stemp held his breath.

'Maybe one of the boxes got damaged and the lid came loose. Hope we didn't do it when we handled them, or the chief will have our guts. Come on, Willy, let's not hang about. We need to get that wagon loaded sharp, if we're to be away by midnight.'

Silent under the waning moon, Joshua Stemp slipped away over the empty Marsh towards St Mary, and home.

Reverend,

He'll meet you at St Mary's Bay this evening, at sunset. Best you go alone.

B.

The drawing room door was open. He could hear Calpurnia's voice, declaiming passages from her book to the wolfhound.

'I defy you, Cardinal Principio! I defy you, I say! You will not lay one hand on me, or on my family's jewels!'

'Think you so? You are alone in my palace, surrounded by my minions. I have but to speak one word, and they will drag you down to my dungeons, where, aided by the thumb-screw and the rack, you will quickly divulge all that you know. I shall have your jewels in my hand, soon enough!'

'Hah! Hah, I say! Do you not know that I am the finest swordsman in all of Burgundy? Your minions will fall before my sword like ripe corn before the sickle's blade. Bring them on, Cardinal; if you dare!'

The rector rang the bell on his desk. 'Biddy,' he said to the maidservant when she appeared, 'will you please ask Mrs Vane if you may close the door to her room? I fear her deathless prose is playing havoc with my concentration. How Rodolpho endures it all is a mystery greater than anything to be found in her stories.'

'I shall, reverend,' said Biddy, smiling. 'Also, Mr Stemp is here to see you.'

'Ah, Joshua,' said the rector as Stemp entered the room. 'Any progress to report?'

'Not yet, reverend. But I had a rather strange adventure last night.' He related his travels in the dark, and then pulled out the opium cake wrapped in its leaves and laid it on the desk. 'I reckon all the coffins are full of these. Noakes and that gang are taking gold out of the country, and bringing opium in.'

The rector frowned. 'You are certain it's the same gang?'

'I'm positive those two were with Noakes on the beach, reverend.'

'Of course, they might be working for two different people,' said Hardcastle. 'Taking out gold for one paymaster, bringing in opium for another.' He turned the cake over in his hand. 'Opium is a curious thing to smuggle, though. Have you heard of this before?'

Stemp shook his head. 'Could be Noakes is also running opium on his own. Manningham at the Swan says someone is selling the stuff; raw cake, like this, not laudanum. And the last few times I've seen Noakes, I'd swear he'd been taking something himself. He didn't look natural, not even for Noakes.'

The rector frowned. His head was still full of Bessie's message, and the forthcoming meeting with Peter. 'Very well,' he said, handing the cake back to Stemp. 'Keep your eyes peeled for those two sailors, and tell your friends to look out for them also. If you spot them again, follow them. They might lead us to Noakes.'

'Turkish,' observed Mrs Chaytor, looking at the cake lying on her drawing room table. She unwrapped the brown leaves carefully, exposing a flat oval cake with a hard, dark grey crust. 'I suspect this is of rather fine quality. May I keep it, Joshua?'

'I'd be grateful if you would, ma'am. I'm not happy about having it at home, where my girls might find it.'

'Quite right too. There is enough opium here to kill quite a number of people, if ingested freely.' She too was frowning. 'What does this mean?'

'I don't know, ma'am. But I'm not at all sure I like it.'

'What is wrong, Yorkshire Tom? Would you not run opium yourself?'

''Course I would, ma'am, without a second's thought, if there was profit in it. It's Noakes and his gang that concern me. I don't like anything those men touch.' Stemp repeated what Manningham had told him. 'There's something wicked behind all this, I'm sure of it.'

'And why did you bring it to me?'

'Reverend Hardcastle didn't think much of it. He's concentrating on the gold.' Stemp tapped the opium cake. 'But the same men are handling both the gold and the opium. What if they are connected in some way?'

'What indeed,' said Mrs Chaytor. 'As you said before, Joshua, these might be two parts of the same story.'

When Stemp had gone, she wrapped the opium cake in its leaves once more and then called for her gig and her groom.

*

A few minutes later she was away, driving fast through the windy morning to New Romney. It was market day, the town's long street busy with people, and she slowed Asia and proceeded at a more sedate pace to Dr Mackay's house. Here she stepped down, handing the reins over to the groom, and knocked at the door. A servant showed her at once into the doctor's office.

'It is a pleasure to welcome you, ma'am,' said Mackay. 'How may I serve you?'

'I need your professional opinion on this,' said Mrs Chaytor.

She placed the opium cake on the doctor's desk and began to unwrap it. 'I believe this comes from Smyrna,' she said.

'Pardon me, ma'am, but how do you know?'

'By the colour, and the size of the cakes. Constantinople opium is more red in colour. Perhaps we should test this, to be certain.'

Mackay went to his instrument table and returned with a scalpel. Carefully, he cut away one side of the cake. Beneath the grey outer crust the opium was deep black and glistening, the consistency of pitch. The smell in the room was very strong.

'Certainly Smyrna,' said Mrs Chaytor.

'Very fine quality,' said the doctor. 'This should fetch a premium price when it reaches London.'

'Oh? How much, do you think?'

'The average price is thirty shillings per pound weight; including customs duty, of course. But the price varies according to quality.'

Mrs Chaytor nodded. 'I am always surprised to find how expensive opium is. I understand it is quite easy to produce, in the right climate.'

'But it is much in demand, ma'am, and that pushes up the price. Personally, I wish it were more expensive still. I am of the belief that opium is already too widely available. Some in my profession prescribe laudanum and other opiates for virtually any illness, regardless of whether it will be efficacious or not. If the drug were more costly, they might think again.'

'You once prescribed laudanum for me,' Mrs Chaytor pointed out. 'For headaches.'

'Indeed I did. For headaches, back pain, toothache and disorders of the bowel, laudanum is a sovereign remedy. But I might point out that I gave you a very weak solution only; and had you returned the next week and asked for more, I might well have refused you. As I am sure you know, Mrs Chaytor, opium is very effective at quelling pain, but it is also powerfully addictive. Once it gets its hooks into you, it is very, very hard to throw it off. I have seen many cases where the patient is cured of the initial ailment, but is then left with something far worse: a lifetime of dependence on the drug.'

'Yes,' said Mrs Chaytor. 'I have seen such cases too. We may have another problem on our hands. According to Mr Stemp, someone is selling opium, just like this, here on the Marsh.'

'Raw opium?' Mackay stared at her in horror. 'Ma'am, opium is a very powerful drug, which should only be handled by those qualified in the medical profession. Raw opium is poison.'

'So people who try to make their own pills or potions, and are ignorant of opium's properties, will be putting themselves in danger.'

'Very much so. We will see deaths from this. I am quite certain of it.'

'And deaths from more than one cause, I suspect. Mr Stemp also thinks some of the criminal gangs may be using opium themselves, and if that is so then we are *all* in danger. I have seen in Rome what happens when opium unbalances the criminal mind.'

They looked at each other for a few moments. 'Very well,' said Mrs Chaytor finally. 'We have established the nature of the threat. But why might anyone want to smuggle the drug?'

'For the same reason they would smuggle anything: to avoid paying taxes. The import duty on opium is 45 per cent.'

'And is there enough demand to make smuggling the drug worthwhile?'

'I know that more and more doctors are using it, yes. Beyond that, I fear I know very little about the trade itself.'

'I have a friend who imports opium. He should be able to tell us more. Keep this cake safe and secure, doctor, if you will. I may well call on you again. There is something very wrong about this affair, and I intend to find out what it is.'

SANDY HOUSE, ST MARY IN THE MARSH, KENT
16th of September, 1797

My dear Willie,

I trust this letter finds you well, and Anne also. I hear many rumours about a forthcoming peace with France, and I venture to hope that they are true. I long for the day when both nations can at last lay down their arms and resume their former amity. And when that day comes, then you, my friend, will be deserving of the highest honour and praise. I know full well how hard you have worked to bring this peace about.

I am writing to you now, though, not as Foreign Secretary but in your other role as a director of the Levant Company. It would appear that someone among our local free traders has begun smuggling opium into the country. But I am puzzled as to why. Can the trade possibly be lucrative enough to make smuggling worthwhile? Or is there some ulterior motive at work here, something that I cannot fathom?

The opium comes from Smyrna, and is brought into the country in large wooden boxes rather like coffins; beyond that, we know nothing. If there is anything you can tell me about the opium trade that would help me to understand further, then I would be most grateful.

Please convey my fond affection to Anne, and I remain your most faithful friend,

AMELIA

Orange in the haze, the sun sank down over the distant hills of Kent. On Romney Marsh, the light flowed level over the fields, lighting the grass-covered dunes that fringed the sea and glistening off the incoming tide. Far away to the east, the cliffs of the French coast shone a rusty orange, reflecting the sunset glow.

A man waited in the shadow of the dunes, a stocky, muscular man in a dark, nondescript coat and breeches and heavy boots. When he heard footsteps on the sand, his hand moved to the pistol at his belt, but he relaxed a little when he saw the rector coming towards him.

'Good evening, Matthew,' said the rector. 'Where is Peter?'

'Over there.' The man who called himself Matthew motioned with his hand in the direction of France. 'I got the message and came instead. This had better be good. There's a storm of shit falling on us already, and we don't have time to run errands for some damn' fool clergyman.'

His leader, Peter, liked and respected Hardcastle. Matthew himself, the rector knew, was more ambivalent. 'Then I shall detain you as briefly as possible,' he said. 'Do you know of a man called Vandamme, in Boulogne?'

'Yes.'

'What does he do?'

'Bit of everything. He's a banker, but he's also a broker for pretty much any commodity you care to name.'

'Does he work with the smugglers?'

'Oh, yes.'

'And does he ever handle gold?'

'Sometimes,' said Matthew after a moment. 'Why do you ask about Vandamme?'

'Do you know of a courier named Jean who crosses over to France from time to time?'

The other man shifted a little. His blunt-featured face hardened. 'What do you know about Jean?'

'He smuggles gold into France. Did you know that?'

Matthew shifted again. 'Jean works for us,' he said. 'Some of the time, anyway. We use him as an occasional courier, for routine messages only; the important stuff we carry ourselves, of course. He lets us know when he's going to France, and if we have messages to deliver, he carries them. Yes, he's probably also a smuggler, and we know he takes a few guineas with him on each trip and sells them illegally to Vandamme. We look the other way. It's not going to break the Bank of England, and Jean is useful to us.'

'Jean does not carry the gold,' said the rector. 'He crosses the Channel before each run and negotiates the deal. Then he sends word back to England, and the rest of the gang bring the gold over. And it is not a few guineas. During the past ten months, this gang have shipped more than £90,000 worth of gold to France. And they are planning to send still more.'

There was a moment of silence. 'Bloody hell,' said Matthew.

'Quite,' said Hardcastle. 'We think they then send the gold to Amsterdam, where they sell it. The profit from the sale makes its way back to England by devious routes.'

Matthew shook his head. 'No,' he said. 'That gold never goes to Amsterdam.'

'Oh? Then where?'

'It goes straight to the French national treasury in Paris. Your smugglers are running gold directly to the enemy.'

'How do you know this?'

'Among other things, Vandamme is also a government-appointed agent. Buying gold from smugglers is one of the things he does. He sends the gold to Paris, and gets a reward for doing so. Up until now it's been individual smugglers running a few guineas here and there, whatever they can carry in their pockets. But £90,000 . . . Jesus, that would keep an army in the field for months. No wonder we're losing the bloody war.'

'Tell me more about Vandamme,' said the rector.

'What do you want to know?'

'Someone is stealing from the smugglers, taking profits from the sale of the gold. Could Vandamme be that man?'

There was a thoughtful pause. 'It could, of course,' said Matthew. 'Anything is possible in this foul and treacherous world. But I'm doubtful. Smuggling is a business built on trust. You don't do business with people you can't trust absolutely.'

The rector remembered Stemp making exactly this point, after Munro was killed. 'If it became known that Vandamme was embezzling from a client,' Matthew went on, 'then other people will start to wonder about him. Some might find out they had been defrauded, too, or imagine they had, and Vandamme would be found floating face down in Boulogne harbour.'

'Two men have already been shot dead in connection with this business,' said Hardcastle.

'Then you see what I mean. If Vandamme wants to live a long and healthy life, he'll be a good boy and play by the rules. That's not to say he might not get greedy. Ninety thousand pounds is a lot of temptation. But I'm guessing if he does, he won't live for much longer.'

The rector nodded. 'The courier, Jean. What do you know about him?'

'We don't gossip in our world, reverend. Jean has family on both sides of the Channel; he knows how to travel discreetly, and where to hide; and he can be trusted to deliver a message. That's all I know, or thought I ever needed to know.'

'When does he next go to France?'

'He's in Boulogne now.' Matthew touched the butt of his pistol. 'But I'll be waiting for the little bastard when he comes back.'

'No,' said the rector. 'Let him live.'

'He's a traitor, reverend.'

'They all are. But Jean might be able to lead us to the man, or men, who employ the gang. They're the ones we really need to take. Jean is small beer.'

Matthew nodded, reluctantly.

'When is he due to return from France?' Hardcastle asked. 'And where will he land?'

'A week today, the 23rd. He'll come back through Hythe, as usual. He has connections there.' Matthew looked out over the sea in the fading light. 'But if he gets word you're after him, he'll stay in France. You'll never touch him.'

'Perhaps not now. But once the peace treaty is signed and relations between our countries resume, I shall ask for the help of the French authorities.'

'*Peace treaty*.' Matthew glared at him. 'There'll be no treaty, reverend, not now. The French have broken off negotiations. Lord Malmesbury has been ordered to leave the country. He's already on his way home.'

The rector stood astonished. 'What has happened?'

'Two weeks ago, the royalists launched an insurrection in Paris. The government crushed them. That's where Peter is now, trying to salvage something from the wreck. The Directory claims Britain supported the coup; that's why Malmesbury has been told to pack his bags. The Dutch fleet is about to put to sea, and the French and Spanish ones will follow. And they're raising new armies to send against us; paid for, this time, with smuggled British gold.'

'Dear God,' said the rector quietly.

'You'd better pray hard to Him, reverend, and hope He listens. This country is in peril as never before. And another thing. The Directory is wreaking vengeance on its enemies. They're arresting everyone, not just royalists but dissenting politicians, priests, writers and intellectuals, anyone who has ever breathed a word of opposition. The prisons are full and the guillotine will be back in action soon. Anyone who can get out of Paris is fleeing for England, and sanctuary.'

'It is the Terror all over again,' said Hardcastle.

'Yes. And so, you've got refugees coming. Hundreds of them, maybe thousands. They'll be crossing over in the next few days. Be ready for them.'

'Of course. Thank you for the warning, and we'll do our best for them.'

'Don't mention it.' Grudgingly, Matthew said, 'You're a good man, reverend. I hope you find your killer.'

The sun set. Shadows fell deep and cold across land and sea. The rector stood silent, listening to the faint crunch of Matthew's boots on the sand as he walked away.

18

The Refugees

For the moment, the East Weald and Ashford Bank would have to wait.

Sunday and Monday passed in a rush of preparation all across the Marsh. Immediately after his meeting with Matthew, the rector had sent out messages to the other magistrates and clergymen of Romney Marsh, and the mayors of New Romney and Hythe and Lydd, warning of the impending arrival of the refugees and asking them to pass the word further along the coast. He wrote also to Cole, warning that boats would be coming across the Channel and asking that his officers and the *Stag* should let them pass freely. He then went around his own parish and began knocking on doors, asking for help.

Unsurprisingly, he called first at Sandy House. Mrs Chaytor listened, her clear blue eyes wide as he told her the news. 'The shipwreck of our hopes,' she said. 'Poor Willie. He worked so hard for peace. He will feel this badly.' Then, dismissing the Foreign Secretary from her mind, she said briskly, 'What do you need from me?'

'The people coming to us will be cold, probably wet from the sea crossing, exhausted and hungry,' Hardcastle said. 'Some of them may also be injured. Our task is to look after them when they land, and help them through the first hours and days.'

'Then we need to begin collecting dry clothing and blankets. I'll ask Miss Godfrey and Miss Roper to help me; it will be good for them to have something to do. We will need to feed them too; we can use the Star's kitchen, but we'll feed them at the church, there's more room there. And we'll need billets where they can sleep.'

'I will look after the billets, if you go to the church.'

The church was the largest building in the parish; it made sense to establish their headquarters there. Within the hour, the nave of the church was vibrant with activity. Blankets and bundles of clothing brought in by every household were stacked around the walls. Bread, cheese, mutton hams and pots of soup were sent over to the Star and carried into the larder under the efficient supervision of Bessie Luckhurst. Around the village, lofts and sheds were cleared out and mattresses of straw or grass or bulrushes made ready. The larger houses cleared out rooms and put down mattresses in these too. Early on, the rector looked up to find someone at his elbow carrying pen and ink and paper. 'What are you doing?' he asked his sister.

'Making a list of who has volunteered rooms, and how many beds they have,' said Calpurnia. 'Someone must, don't you think? You'll never remember all this.'

She was entirely right. 'Thank you,' he said simply. 'How many can we take at the rectory, do you think?'

'Ten in the house, if we clear out the morning room and put beds there, and six in the stables and two in the tack room. I've already given instructions to Mrs Kemp. She took the news with surprising calm.'

'Did she really?'

'No.' Calpurnia giggled. 'But I managed her. Depending on how many people come, we might have to billet some in the church itself. But I think we should try to put as many into houses as possible. They will be warmer and drier there.' All through that evening and the following day she was at his side, and her calm competence astonished him. He saw in those hours a side to his sister that he did not know existed.

By Monday more blankets and food and bedding were arriving, this time from some of the inland villages, Ivychurch and Newchurch, Brenzett and Snave, and there were offers of beds there too, should St Mary and New Romney and Dymchurch be overwhelmed. In the middle of the morning Joshua Stemp came into the church.

'We've had a message from the other side, reverend,' he said. 'They're coming tonight. Finny says we can expect about two thousand all along the coast. Maybe a couple of hundred here in St Mary.' The run the smugglers had arranged for the previous day had already been cancelled.

'Dear Lord,' said the rector. 'All at once?'

'Has to be. The government sent troops to round people up and stop them from escaping. There's been fighting on the roads already. Now the troops are closing in on Boolong. If the refugees don't get out tonight, they won't get out at all. We could have wounded folk, along with the rest.'

'Dr Mackay has been alerted, and more doctors are coming down from Tenterden and Ashford.'

Stemp nodded. 'Jack Hoad and the Tydde boys and some others are going across this afternoon, to lend a hand. Have the Customs been told?'

'Cole's men are out hunting for Noakes, but they'll keep clear,' said the rector. 'The *Stag* will offer assistance if needed.' He turned to look around the crowded church and drew a deep breath. 'Two thousand people,' he said. 'May the Lord watch over them, and us.'

Late in the day on Monday, as the evening gloom began to fall over the Marsh, a big wagon with a team of four Belgian horses made its way down the turnpike from Ashford to Ham Street and then out onto the levels beyond. Two men sat on the driving bench, one holding the reins and the other carrying a musket, and the wagon was preceded by two outriders on horseback, both armed with cavalry carbines. The wagon's cargo was securely tied down and covered with canvas.

A little north of Snave the wagon came to Stock Bridge, a broad span over the big sewer that drained away south towards Fairfield. A patrol of Customs officers stationed at one end of the bridge looked up as the wagon approached. Petchey, their leader, held up a hand. 'Where're you bound for?'

'Rye,' said the driver, bringing the wagon to a creaking halt. 'We're making a delivery to the battery down there.'

'What's your cargo?'

'Gunpowder. Fifteen barrels of it.'

The Customs men gave each other significant looks. Petchey strode to the rear of the wagon and climbed up. Unfastening some of the securing ropes, he drew back the tarpaulin. There were indeed fifteen kegs of gunpowder, branded with the name of Stourbridge Mills and the broad arrow of the Board of Ordinance.

'Not much of a cargo for a wagon this size,' he said to the driver.

The driver shrugged. 'I only do what I'm told. Hey! What are you doing? You can't touch that, it's government property!'

Ignoring the other man, Petchey turned one of the kegs upright and prised open the lid with his knife. All he could see at first was burlap sacking. God, he thought, don't tell me this is a dummy . . . He pulled the sacking aside; and then he saw what he was hoping for, the dull gleam of gold.

'Take them!' he snapped. In a moment, his men had dragged the driver and his mate from their seats and pinioned them; pistols covered the two outriders, who slid down off their horses with their hands in the air. Protesting bitterly, the four men were dragged together and manacled, their hands behind their backs.

'Now,' said Petchey, 'let's try again. Where were you taking this load?'

A mixture of persuasion and threat soon broke the men down. They had collected the wagon and cargo, already loaded, from a yard in Ashford. Their orders were to drive the wagon down the track towards Midley and then abandon it not far from the ruined church. They did not know what would happen after that; they were paid not to ask questions. All four swore blind that they thought the cargo was gunpowder.

'Put them in the wagon,' said Petchey. He paused for a moment, thinking what to do next. He could take the gold down to Rye, but New Romney was closer. There was a lock-up there for the prisoners, and the town hall had a vault where he could store the gold. Most important of all, Cole would be somewhere near New Romney, and Petchey could find his chief and boast of his success. This night's work would be the making of him. Visions of promotion to supervisor, perhaps even collector, filled his head. Also, might there be a reward for the recovery of the gold? Dazzled by his own success, Petchey gave his orders; two of his men climbed into the wagon to guard the prisoners, another sat down on the driver's bench and took the reins, and he and the remaining man mounted the two horses and took up position as outriders.

Night was falling now. Mist rose in spectral skeins from the ground. Petchey and the other outrider rode a little ahead of the wagon to check the road. They rode watchfully, hands on the butts of their carbines, but in the night and fog it was impossible to see more than a short distance ahead. They were completely unprepared when, two miles short of New Romney, a lantern shone out of the fog. Petchey pulled his carbine from its scabbard, fumbling with the lock.

'Is that you, Petchey?' a muffled voice asked.

The riding officer breathed a sigh of relief. 'Yes, it's me. Who's that?'

'Morris, from Dover. Cole sent me to look for you. Did you find the gold?'

'I did,' said Petchey. 'I have it here.'

'Huzza! Well done, man! Aren't you the rum fellow? You'll be the toast of the entire service, when this gets out. Come on, we'll help you into New Romney.'

Petchey rode forward, the wagon rumbling behind, and then stopped. Two more lanterns were suddenly uncovered, one on each flank, showing shivering curtains of fog all around them. In the light they saw a half-circle of dark silhouettes, masked men with pistols in their hands, all pointed at the Customs men. They saw too the long, vicious shape of the Puckle gun, its black muzzle trained on the wagon.

'Drop your weapons,' said the man who had called himself Morris, crouched behind the Puckle gun. 'Or I'll send all of you straight to hell.'

Raging at himself for being taken in, Petchey dismounted. He had just time to observe that 'Morris' was small and slightly built, and well spoken for a smuggler, and then someone hit him over the head with a club. Lights flashed briefly before his eyes, and then all went black.

At the edge of the sea a wind was blowing, holding back the mist that cloaked the Marsh further inland. Torches burned, fluttering at the foot of the dunes, lighting the beach and flickering off the waves that rolled inshore. A bonfire crackled on the crest of the dunes, sending its light out to sea. The tide was nearly full.

A crowd of people stood on the edge of the beach, men and some women, too, from St Mary and the inland villages, looking out into the inky blackness of the night. Watching them in the torchlight, the rector saw the same expression on every face: quiet, tense, waiting. Beyond them to the south were more lights, at the entrance to Romney Haven, and to the north at Dymchurch, another beacon burned. There would be crowds waiting there, too, he knew.

Out at sea, a lantern shone twice. 'Here they come,' said someone softly.

They came, boat after boat, luggers and cutters and hoys and fishing boats, gliding out of the night into the orange glow of torchlight and grounding in the shallow water. Men jumped down into the water and began helping others over the side. The rector and Stemp and others waded out into the cold sea to the boats, extending their hands to the people crammed aboard, helping them down.

There were old men and women, shivering and soaked with sea spray, coughing and weak. There were children, wide-eyed and shocked by the events of the past few days; infants screaming in helpless, uncomprehending panic. There were people staggering with illness and seasickness, and there were others with raw wounds to their arms and faces and heads, shot or sabred by the gendarmes and dragoons who had pursued them. Hardcastle took the good hand of a black-robed priest, his other arm bandaged and his cassock stained with blood that had streamed from a cut to his scalp. '*Venez avec moi, monsieur. Prenez mon bras.*'

Slowly they waded through the surf, more boats piling in, more people stumbling down into the cold water and wading towards safety. Already there were hundreds of them, struggling up onto dry land and then collapsing from cold and exhaustion. The rector helped the priest to sit and then knelt for a moment beside him. '*Reposez-vous, monsieur,*' he said softly. '*Maintenant, vous êtes en sécurité.*'

'*Dieu vous bénisse, monsieur. Vous êtes un sauveur.* Thank you.'

Out in the boats the smugglers worked together, Jack Hoad from St Mary and the Tydde brothers from New Romney, Finny Jack from Ambleteuse and the big man they called Le Passeur – the Ferryman – and many more. Another big, dark lugger grounded on the sand and Joshua Stemp, waist-deep in the sea, looked up to see Bertrand staring over the side. 'I still don't have your money,' the Frenchman said.

'Don't be bloody silly, Bertie. There's a time and place to talk about money.'

There was a rush of movement in the water around him, more men coming to assist the refugees over the side. Some of the people in Bertrand's boat were sobbing with relief; others were blankly silent, stunned by the terror they had just escaped. Two frail women were carried by hand; a pregnant girl was lifted into the powerful arms of Murton the blacksmith. A child, a girl of about three, tripped on the bulwark of the lugger and screamed as she fell towards the dark sea. Stemp caught her with strong arms before she reached the water and swung her up, still sobbing, holding her against his chest. 'Hush, my bonny,' he soothed her, kissing her hair as he did his own daughters'. 'This is England. You're safe now.' And over and over the word ran along the beach, soft reassurance cutting through the bitterness of fear and exhaustion. 'You're in England now. You are safe. You are safe.'

Up on the beach, the refugees were given a few moments to rest, but they could not stay there for long; the night wind was sharp, and many of them were soaked through. The able-bodied were directed towards the village; bonfires in the fields lit the way, and some of the younger boys where there to act as guides. For those who could not walk, there were wagons and litters and handcarts. Hardcastle remained on the beach until most of the refugees had gone; then, signalling to Stemp to take over, he gave his arm once again to the wounded priest and walked him slowly through the firelight to St Mary. The other man did not speak; he was so weak from exhaustion and loss of blood that he could barely stand.

At the church, Bessie Luckhurst and Lucy the housekeeper from Sandy House dished out hot food while Mrs Chaytor directed the distribution of blankets and dry clothing. Calpurnia Vane, fizzing with good cheer and bad French, sent people away to their billets; the two Stemp girls had appointed themselves as her aides and ran back and forth with earnest expressions on their small faces, guiding people to their beds. Slowly, the miasma of fear and shock began to subside, and fatigue took over. People slumped down over their bowls of soup, falling asleep as they sat. 'The poor things,' said Mrs Vane softly. 'What will happen to them?'

'Many will want to go to London, I expect, once they recover,' said Mrs Chaytor. 'Or Canterbury, or some of the other provincial towns. Some may already have kin here.' Thousands of French émigrés had already settled in England since the start of the Revolution eight years ago. 'They will have a hard life, but at least they will be alive.'

'Yes. We are fortunate, are we not? We have never been turned out of our own homes, pursued, beaten, robbed of all we own. We are so lucky, to be allowed to live our own lives in tranquillity.'

'Long may we continue to do so,' said Amelia, but she thought about the menace now gathering its power on the far side of the Channel, and wondered how long that tranquillity could last.

Down on the beach the last boats emptied, the French crews hastening back across the Channel before daylight exposed them to British patrol vessels or their own coastal batteries.

Stemp clapped Bertrand on the shoulder. 'Go safely.' A thought struck him. 'Are you still working with Noakes and his crew?'

'No. I have, what is it you say? Called it quits, after the last run. They paid well, but I do not like them. Also, that horrible dog. It pissed in my cabin, do you believe it? I cannot get rid of the smell.'

Stemp laughed. 'With luck, dog and master won't be around for much longer.' If Cole and his men had done their jobs, Noakes might already be in custody. It was a pleasant thought. 'I'm glad you gave it up, Bertie. You're an honest man.'

'There is no need to insult me,' said the Frenchman.

'Forgive me. I forgot for a moment who I was talking to. The leader of that gang, the fellow with the Puckle gun. Do you know anything about him?'

Bertrand shrugged. 'He has authority, that is certain. The others, even Noakes, do what he wants with no questions. But he is not the chief. There is another, whose name they never mention. It is he who gives this man his orders.'

'This other man. Is he French, do you think?'

'I do not believe so. All that gang are English, or Dutch.'

'Dutch,' said Stemp, thinking of the sailor at Midley. 'Bertie, do you know anything about a Dutch lugger that's been seen around these parts? Two masts, broad beam, Rotterdam rig?'

'Ah, you mean the *Hoorn*. She sails out of Flushing. Her skipper is a man called Sloterdyke. Sometimes he is a privateer, sometimes a smuggler.'

Stemp raised his eyebrows. 'Armed, then.'

'Four sixes and a long nine, I am told.'

'That's a lot of metal. What does she run?'

Bertrand spread his hands. 'Who can say? The other Dutch ships carry gin and lace; I imagine she does the same. Tom, the tide is turning. I must go.'

Stemp clapped him on the shoulder. 'Go safely,' he said again. 'You did a good night's work tonight.'

'It is so. Tomorrow, we go back to the wicked life,' said Bertrand. He grinned at Stemp in the light of the dying torches, and turned to call orders to his crew.

Dawn broke pale over St Mary in the Marsh. The village lay silent, sleeping after the long night.

In his bedroom the rector stirred, hearing someone knocking hard and urgently at the door. He cursed whoever was doing it and hoped they would go away. The knock was repeated, and he pulled a pillow over his head.

Another knock: this time Mrs Kemp rapping on the bedroom door. 'It's Mr Cole to see you, reverend.'

'Who?'

'Mr Cole! From the Customs!'

'Oh, for God's sake. Tell him I'll be down directly.' Muttering, the rector pulled on a heavy quilted dressing gown over his nightshirt and went downstairs. His shoulders and back ached, and the chill of the sea seemed to have settled in his bones.

Cole was waiting in the hall. 'What is it?' the rector asked.

'The gold,' said Cole. His face was pale with fatigue and anger. 'It's gone.'

19

The Run

The story was quickly told. Petchey and his men had been found, fettered with their own manacles and dumped by the roadside beyond Old Romney. The wagon that had carried the gold was tracked down soon after, abandoned along with its team near Midley church. Tracks showed that the kegs of gold had been loaded onto handcarts and taken away east across the shingle banks to the sea.

'You had men patrolling the coast,' said the rector sharply. 'Did they see nothing?'

Cole's shoulders slumped. 'They clubbed two of my watchers, too, before they could give the alarm. None of the rest saw anything. They were distracted by the lights and fires when the refugees came ashore.'

'And did no one see them? Or the ship?'

'No,' said Cole miserably. 'In all the confusion on the beaches . . . they could have been anywhere. I am sorry, reverend.'

Serendipity had favoured the smugglers. They could not have foreseen the arrival of the refugees when they set the date for this run weeks ago, but they had used the situation very expertly to their advantage. The refugees were perfect cover. Who would notice one more ship, or a group of men around her? Who had the time to stop and see what they were doing? Doubtless, too, once the cargo was loaded, they had mingled with the departing flotilla and escaped unnoticed.

'And your men? Are they hurt?'

'They all have sore heads. Petchey is in a bad way. I've asked Dr Mackay to have a look at him as soon as he can. My God,

Hardcastle. My career in the Customs is finished. My reputation is entirely ruined.'

'Self-pity won't bring it back,' Hardcastle said sharply. 'Get hold of yourself, man. Get some men out to trace the movements of that wagon, and find out where it came from. I assume the driver and guards escaped?' Cole nodded. 'Search for them. And contact the *Stag* and see if Captain Haddock saw anything.'

'Yes. Yes, I'll do that.' The Customs man still looked utterly defeated. 'I'm sorry, reverend. I have let you down.'

'You have failed for the moment, yes. But there is still time to make good, if you act promptly.'

Cole departed, and the rector walked stiffly into his study and rang for coffee. He had tried to encourage Cole in order to stiffen his backbone, but in truth this was a disaster. Another £25,000 worth of gold had gone across the water, to swell the coffers of a French Republic hell-bent on the destruction of England.

Biddy knocked and entered with the coffee. 'How are our guests?' the rector asked.

'All still sleeping, reverend.'

'Good,' said the rector. 'Let them rest. I am going to dress. Ask Amos to go round to Mr Stemp's house, present my apologies and say I need to see him as soon as is convenient.'

Stemp arrived at the rectory half an hour later. His eyes were red and his pocked cheeks were a little hollow. The rector took one look at him, unlocked the mahogany cabinet, took out a bottle of brandy and added a stiff tot to Stemp's coffee. Almost as an afterthought, he did the same to his own.

'Cole has failed,' he said.

He told the story briefly, Stemp listening intently. 'I can't say as I'm surprised, reverend,' the constable said at the end. He himself had outwitted Cole many times out on the Marsh; he knew how easy it was to do.

'Sadly, neither am I.' Hardcastle spread his hands. 'However, what's done is done. As soon as you have rested, I need you back in Hythe. Call up your special constables and take them with you. I want a watch set on the port, night and day. Assuming Noakes and Fisk joined the gold run, and assuming they crossed the Channel with the shipment as they did before, then they should return within the next few days. I want to know the moment they return to Hythe. And we must find Jean the courier. I am reliably informed that he will return on the 23rd, four days from now. Find him, follow him, learn who he meets and where he goes and what his real identity is.'

'Yes, reverend. What do we do about Noakes and his boys, if we see them?'

'Watch them, but keep clear of them for the moment. Customs are a weak reed, and we don't have enough strength on our own to take these men. I am calling for reinforcements.'

THE RECTORY, ST MARY IN THE MARSH, KENT
19th of September, 1797

By express

My lord,

It is with deep regret that I inform you that a further shipment of gold belonging, I believe, to the East Weald and Ashford Bank was taken out of the country yesterday evening. This happened despite the efforts of Mr Cole, the supervisor of Customs, who I am afraid has let us down badly.

I intend now to track down and arrest as many of the gold-running gang as possible, and hope that by doing so I shall also identify the men who killed Hector Munro and Sylvester Cotton. As these men are dangerous and well armed, I may need to summon assistance. I humbly request your lordship's permission to approach the colonel of the East Kent Volunteers and ask that a file of men be made available.

I await your lordship's consideration,

Yr very obedient servant

HARDCASTLE

The rector sealed the letter, listening once more to the noises in the house. Most of the refugees had risen by now and were being fed in the dining room; he could hear Calpurnia's voice in the drawing room, other voices too speaking in French, a low and quiet murmur in the background. It was unusual to hear the big house so full of life, and Hardcastle had to admit to himself that the sound was not unpleasant.

He laid the letter to one side and was about to ring the bell when there came a soft knock at the door. 'Enter,' he said.

The door opened and the priest he had assisted last night entered the room, walking slowly, still looking pale and tired. His arm was freshly bandaged, and another white bandage covered the top and side of his head. In place of his blood-soaked cassock he wore one of Hardcastle's own dressing gowns. He pressed his hands together at his breast. 'Forgive me for not bowing,' he said gravely in accented English, 'but my head still gives me a little pain. I am the Abbé de Bernay.'

'And I am the Reverend Hardcastle,' said the rector. 'Do sit down, sir, please. Are you being looked after? I fear I am a poor host, but I have had pressing business this morning.'

'Your servants could not be more kind, nor your sister.' The priest smiled. 'She has been entertaining me by reading extracts from her latest book.'

'I am so sorry to hear it. I shall ask her to stop.'

Bernay smiled again. 'In fact, her work is not without merit. The Gothic is an interesting genre. It tells us a great deal about the workings of the mind, what the Germans refer to as *psychologia*. And I am delighted to see that, in *The Cardinal's Jewels*, Mrs Vane has set out to expose the corruption that lurks in the dark heart of my church.'

Hardcastle blinked. 'She has?'

'Be assured of it. She writes about abuses of power that I myself have witnessed at first hand. Sir, I came here to thank you for taking us in, you and all your people. We shall be forever in your debt.'

The rector shook his head. 'No thanks are necessary. You came to us in need and we offered you charity.'

'You are, like myself, a man of God; that is how you see the world,' said Bernay. 'But I am curious about the smugglers who brought us across the water, refusing any payment for doing so. I detected little in the way of godliness among them, yet they too offered us charity.'

'The smugglers on both sides of the sea have a passionate hatred of authority,' said Hardcastle, 'and they saw you as authority's victims. Helping you was an act of rebellion.'

'You are their priest, and also a justice, or so I understand. Do they not resent your authority?'

'I apply it with a light hand,' said the rector. 'Also, they know that I myself am no friend of authority. I have a long-standing feud with my archbishop, and my appointment to this living constitutes a form of internal exile. Yours is not the only Church with a dark heart.'

Bernay smiled. He had a pale, narrow, intelligent face with sombre dark eyes. 'You speak English very well, sir,' Hardcastle said. 'May I ask where you learned it?'

'I taught theology and science for a time at one of the Irish colleges in Paris; hence my interest in *psychologia*. It became useful to learn the language.'

'I see . . . How do you come to be here? I thought all priests fled France when the Terror began, four years ago.'

'When the Terror ended, the Directory offered assurances that freedom of religion would be tolerated. Priests were welcome once more, so long as they abided by the law and did not preach against the Republic. I returned to minister to my flock. Now the Directory claims the Church supported the royalists, and has turned against us once more. I am one of ten priests who fled north, pursued by dragoons. I am the only one who survived.'

'I am sorry,' said Hardcastle quietly.

'So, truly, am I. I ask myself why I should live when others died, and find no answer. One of the many tragedies of death is how it makes the living feel guilty, just for being alive.'

'But you *are* alive, and there are others living who now need you,' said the rector. 'You were chosen to survive for a reason, sir. I am sure of it.'

Bernay did not answer. The subject of conversation needed to be changed before the other man's bitterness overwhelmed him. On the spur of the moment, Hardcastle said, 'You are clearly a learned man, sir. You know about *psychologia*, and you are curious about the mind and the soul. Therefore, may I ask you a question? It concerns a problem I am trying to solve.'

'I will answer if I can,' said Bernay.

'What prompts a man to steal? I do not mean little thefts, taking bread to feed one's family, or even idle pilfering for the sport of it. Why would a man steal a vast sum, larger than the fortunes of many who count themselves wealthy? What would lead a man to behave in such a way?'

He saw a spark come into the priest's eyes. His instinct had been a good one; an abstract problem to discuss gave him respite for a few minutes from the tragedy he was living through. Bernay leaned forward a little. 'I would ask first: are you certain it is a man?'

Hardcastle considered this. 'It is a fair question. In the case I am thinking of, there are not many women who would have the opportunity to steal. But there are several men who might have done so.'

'I see. As to motive; well, you mentioned sport. For some, the bigger the prize, the more enjoyable the game. They steal because they can. Another explanation is that the money is only a means to an end. The thief has some design in mind, some purpose for which he intends to use the money. Given that a large sum is involved, this scheme must be quite large and complex. Stealing on this scale is not a whim. Your thief will have planned this operation carefully, and probably over some length of time.'

'He has also killed two men, in order to conceal the theft and his own identity.'

'That, for me, is conclusive. Men who steal for sport rarely kill, unless they are cornered and there is no way of escape. Your criminal has grand ambitions, and will let nothing and no one stand in his way. He may indeed feel that his ambition is a righteous one, and the cause itself justifies murder. Thus, the theft is only a part of some much larger scheme. That is what my study of *psychologia* would tell me.' The pale face regarded him. 'Do you know who the criminal might be?'

'Not yet. But I am beginning to understand who it might be,' said Hardcastle.

Thomas Coutts & Co., the Strand, London
16th of September, 1797

Mrs Chaytor,

Please forgive the delay in replying to your letter to Mr
Coutts of the 2nd inst., and your subsequent communica-
tions. I have to inform you that Mr Coutts is indisposed at
the moment, which prevents him from replying in person.
I have however taken note of the content of your letters,
and will attend to the matter as soon as my other duties
permit. This is a very busy time for the bank, so I fear it
may some while yet before we can respond to you fully. I
trust you will understand.

Yr very obedient serv't

JAMES HORNBY
SENIOR CLERK

Sandy House, St Mary in the Marsh, Kent
20th of September, 1797

By express

Mr Hornby,

I am in receipt of your letter of the 16th inst., and am
replying by return of post. Your reply is not acceptable to
me. I asked Mr Coutts to attend to this matter *urgently*.
The fact that your master is indisposed does *not* excuse
his clerks from carrying out their duties.

'No, *ma petite*. Sealing wax is not good to eat. Put it back on the desk, there's a good girl.'

> I require you to take action now. If you do not, I shall inform Mr Coutts of your failure to attend to my express wish. I shall also write to my dear friend Lord Grenville, the Foreign Secretary, who doubtless will make his own views plain to Mr Coutts.
>
> I expect a full response from you in the very near future.

Faithfully,

Mrs Amelia Chaytor

Retrieving the sealing wax, Mrs Chaytor sealed the letter and handed it to Lucy, who took it away to the waiting messenger. 'What am I to do with you?' she demanded in French of the little girl sitting on her lap. 'You are a nuisance and a pest.'

'I am not a pest,' said the girl.

'Indeed you most certainly are.' Amelia held the girl up and kissed her on the forehead. She, her parents and younger sister were one of three families billeted at Sandy House. The child had taken to Mrs Chaytor almost at once, and for the last two days had followed her around the house like a small, cheerful shadow.

'May I have a sweetie?' asked the child.

'What makes you think you deserve a sweetie?'

'I am a good girl.'

'But you are not a good girl. Indeed, we have already established that you are a pest.'

The small, serious face considered this. 'But I am a *good* pest,' the child announced.

Lucy tapped at the door. 'Reverend Hardcastle to see you, ma'am.'

'Your arrival is timely,' said Mrs Chaytor as the rector entered the room. 'I am in the process of losing a contest of rhetoric. I could do with your professional advice.'

Hardcastle looked at the child, thin and small in a baggy gown much too large for her, seated on Mrs Chaytor's lap with one thumb in her mouth. The child looked entirely content. So, to his mild surprise, did Mrs Chaytor. 'She looks a redoubtable opponent. I am unlikely to succeed where you have failed.'

'Then I shall concede defeat.' Mrs Chaytor kissed the girl on the head again. 'Run along to the kitchen, and tell Lucy I said you may have a sweet.'

The child wriggled down and trotted out of the room. Mrs Chaytor looked at the rector. 'Don't,' she said with a warning in her voice.

'Don't what?'

'Say anything.'

'About what?'

'You know perfectly well what. I never said I disliked children.'

'Neither did I.'

'Then stop smiling at me. How are the people?'

'They are recovering remarkably quickly.' The refugees had arrived on Monday night; it was now Wednesday morning. Hardcastle had spent most of yesterday going around the village, seeing that all the refugees were cared for, and that they and their hosts had all they needed. 'There are still a number who are too ill to travel, but some of the healthy ones are already thinking of moving on, to London or elsewhere. I have promised to help them with money for the journey, if they need it. Their strength of will is astonishing. I am not sure I would recover so quickly from the ordeal they have been through.'

'Their ordeal began five years ago,' said Mrs Chaytor quietly. 'To survive famine, war and the Terror, one has to be strong, I think . . . But with all that has happened, I expect you have had to put the investigation to one side.'

'Not entirely. Cole called again this morning, anxious to give me some good news. Captain Haddock, who is of rather sharper wit than Cole, assumed the smugglers' ship might try to mingle with other vessels to disguise its departure. He spotted the Dutch ship and gave chase, but the other had too long a start. She took refuge under the cover of the French coastal artillery, where *Stag* could not follow. We now know that she is called the *Hoorn*, by the way, and her captain is a man named Sloterdyke.'

'What was the Dutchman doing here, do you think?'

'According to Stemp, Captain Bertrand has ceased working with Noakes's gang. I think they have turned to the Dutchman instead. That is by the way. I also had an interesting conversation with one of my guests yesterday, a learned man who knows much more about human nature than I do. He has helped me to look inside the mind of our embezzler. Who has the vision and the power of will to carry out a huge and complex fraud such as this?'

'An excellent idea. How may I help?'

'Listen to my analysis, tell me if it might be right and demolish it if it is not. In other words, do what you always do.'

Mrs Chaytor rang the bell on her desk. 'A discussion of this intensity will require coffee. Lucy! When you have finished spoiling those children with sweetmeats, bring us some coffee, please.'

'Now,' said the rector, once coffee was poured and Lucy had gone to prepare dinner for their involuntary guests, 'let us first reconstruct how the smuggling operation works. Faversham's bank buys gold, which is then concealed inside gunpowder kegs. When a consignment is ready, Jean the courier crosses to France. He negotiates with Vandamme, tells him how much gold is coming and arranges payment.'

Mrs Chaytor nodded. 'Jean then sends word back to England that all is well and the shipment may proceed.'

'Noakes and his gang load the gold aboard ship and escort their cargo across the Channel,' said the rector, 'guarding it until the transaction is complete. They return to England; as does Jean, probably bearing a receipt for the gold from Vandamme.

'Now, Mr Ricardo thought the gold was transported to Amsterdam and sold there. Thanks to Matthew, we know that is not true. So what does happen? I assume that Vandamme, after sending the gold to Paris, draws up a bill of exchange and forwards this to Staphorst in Amsterdam. After that, the money follows the trail Mr Ricardo described: from Amsterdam to Hamburg, and finally back to the Grasshopper in London, who remit the money to the East Weald and Ashford.

'That is the original smuggling operation as Faversham established it. Now, let us turn to the fraud. According to Charlotte Faversham, Munro believed that the money was being embezzled at one of two places, Boulogne or Amsterdam.' Hardcastle paused. 'It is *possible* that either Vandamme or Staphorst are themselves responsible for the fraud.'

'But you don't really believe it,' said Mrs Chaytor.

'Matthew didn't think much of the idea of Vandamme being an embezzler,' said the rector. 'And Ricardo spoke of Staphorst as being an established and legitimate bank. Of course, there could be a corrupt official or clerk within either.'

Mrs Chaytor shook her head. 'The embezzler is also the murderer,' she said, 'or at least, the one who directed the murders. All my instincts tell me so.'

'As do mine,' said Hardcastle.

Mrs Chaytor's eyes were intense as she watched him. 'We have heard from our instincts. Now, what does your reason tell you?'

'I believe the embezzler must have four qualities. The first is the necessary intelligence and knowledge of how banking works, in order to design the fraud. The second is the opportunity to commit that fraud. This must include connections with the banks in Boulogne and Amsterdam, in order to manipulate the money trail. The third is the necessary motivation. Anyone can steal, but it takes an unusual and devious mind to contemplate, and commit, the theft of £35,000. Finally, the fourth is the will and the temperament to murder.'

'Go on.'

'Therefore, I have ruled out Noakes, Jean the courier and the other small fry. They can certainly kill, and they might have the opportunity to steal, but I doubt they have the necessary knowledge or, especially, the ambition to carry out a scheme this bold. Munro could certainly have done it; Cotton, perhaps; but both were killed by the embezzler, which rules them out of contention.'

'Unless there was a falling-out among thieves,' Mrs Chaytor said.

'Hmm, perhaps. I believe there are other, better candidates, however. We had previously considered Grebell Faversham, but I think we must rule him out too.'

'Grebell Faversham needs to grow up,' Mrs Chaytor said tartly. 'He has romantic ideas about his own nature and importance, but a scheme of this complexity is well beyond his abilities. I doubt if he could murder anyone, or be able to find people to do it for him.'

'I agree. For broadly similar reasons, I have also ruled out Maudsley. He hasn't the ambition or the skill to play a game like this. So I have therefore narrowed down my list to three candidates: Charles Faversham, Mrs Redcliffe and the clerk, Charles Batist.'

'Earlier you were prepared to discount Faversham,' she reminded him.

'I was. He seemed desperate and afraid, thinking he himself might be the next victim. But for the sake of completeness, we should consider him again. The man has, after all, deceived many people over the years about the strength and health of his bank. He is a fairly accomplished liar.'

'More than most bankers?' she asked. 'Very well. Make your case.'

'Faversham knows that the bank will fail. Perhaps he has given up on trying to save it. Perhaps he is trying to save what he can from the wreckage, extracting money from the bank while he still can. After it fails, he will rise like a phoenix from the ashes and begin a new venture elsewhere, perhaps in another country. And Munro and Cotton found out what he was doing, and he killed them to prevent his own exposure.'

'You have made this argument before,' she said. 'It is, however, even more full of holes than it was on that occasion. As I said at the time, Charles Faversham's reputation is intimately bound up with that of the bank. Its fall will be a very severe blow to him. More practically, given what we know from Mr Ricardo and others about Faversham's lack of ability, is it conceivable that he could carry out a fraud on this scale?'

'It seems unlikely,' the rector admitted.

'To be honest, I am surprised he could even put together something so complex as the gold-smuggling operation. Indeed, I think he must have had help to do that. A fraud of this sophistication is surely well beyond him. No; I think your initial response was correct. Faversham is a frightened man. He knows, or suspects, who the real embezzler is, and is terrified that he will meet the same fate as Munro and Cotton. You invited me to demolish your analysis.'

'I did. I wasn't expecting you to bury it completely and then plough the earth with salt. You're quite right, of course. We can rule out Faversham once again, definitively this time. That leaves us with two remaining suspects.' The rector looked keenly at her. 'What do you think of Mrs Redcliffe?'

'I don't believe it is her.'

'Why?' he teased her. 'Women's intuition?'

She scowled at him. 'Mrs Redcliffe has contacts with smugglers, and is certainly competent. She could organise the gold smuggling, without a doubt. But does she know the European banks well enough to organise the trail of money? Her experience is in coastal shipping, not finance.'

'A fair point.'

'And, I would question too whether she has the motivation,' said Mrs Chaytor. 'She dislikes Faversham, but she has no animus against the bank. She spoke of her sympathy with the small depositors who will suffer when the bank fails.'

'You mentioned once that she had another venture, something that she intended would be her legacy,' said Hardcastle. 'Did she say what that was?'

Mrs Chaytor frowned. 'No.' She paused for a moment, her teeth sunk into her lower lip, deep in thought. 'Whatever this venture is, she expects it to be concluded soon; within a year or two, she said. After that, she talked of going travelling, rather as if she intended to retire. But also, I don't know how much longer she can live. Half a pint of laudanum a day is a killing dose. She cannot survive that for long.'

'Your reason for omitting her, then, is that she has her own concerns and is perhaps too preoccupied with her own mortality to have much interest in the bank?'

'Yes. But do you know, upon thinking about it once more, I am no longer certain that is sufficient reason to eliminate her. She has the necessary competence and the strength of will, which most of our other suspects do not.'

The rector nodded. 'The question is, does she have the knowledge and resources to commit the fraud? It seems unlikely that she does.'

'And so, to Batist,' Mrs Chaytor said. 'What do you know of him?'

'Very little. To all appearances, he is a hard-working, selfless servant of the bank.'

'Perhaps that is what he wants you to think,' she suggested. 'Perhaps there is something else behind the facade.'

'Quiet, self-effacing bank clerk by day; murderer, smuggler and arch-villain by night? It sounds like the plot from one of my sister's ghastly novels . . . For what it is worth, Batist was genuinely fond of Hector Munro, and was distressed when Munro died.'

'Perhaps he never intended for Munro to die, and was shocked when it happened. One can be fond of people but still find them disposable in the right circumstances.'

Startled, Hardcastle looked at her. 'I think we must consider him seriously,' Mrs Chaytor continued. 'We are already agreed that as Munro's confidant, he is likely to have known about the smuggling. As a clerk of many years' experience, he must surely know how to embezzle money; well enough to fool Faversham, anyway.'

'He knows about banking in Amsterdam, too,' said Hardcastle. 'When I interviewed him, he spoke knowledgeably on the subject. Stemp has found no evidence that any of the Batist family on this side of the Channel are involved in smuggling. But Batist might still have contacts in France.'

She frowned. 'But what motivates him?' she asked. 'Why would a simple bank clerk wish to steal £35,000?'

'Perhaps there is some old injury or slight which he has never forgiven, and he intends to bring down the bank in revenge,' said Hardcastle. 'Or perhaps *he*, not Faversham, is the one planning to use the proceeds of the fraud to start a new venture elsewhere. With £35,000 he could go anywhere in the world and do anything he wished. He is still a young man. The future would hold no limits for him.'

'Mild-mannered bank clerk by day, evil arch-villain by night,' said Mrs Chaytor, smiling.

'By thunder; if Calpurnia's books start making sense, I shall have to take up serious drinking again.'

'Do you truly think it might be Batist?'

'He has the ability, he has the connections.' Hardcastle frowned. 'But could he commit murder, or order it done? Is there a ruthless streak behind that quiet face? I wonder. I shall speak to him again as soon as possible, and see what I can learn.'

'There is still one thing that bothers me,' said Mrs Chaytor. 'The opium. Where does it fit in?'

'What makes you so certain that it does?'

'Women's intuition,' she said.

THOMAS COUTTS & CO., THE STRAND, LONDON
21st of September, 1797

By express

Mrs Chaytor,

I write in haste, humbly craving your forgiveness. I have complied with your request in full, and accounts in the name of Miss Rosannah Godfrey and Miss Clara Roper have been established. I await receipt of your bills, upon which the accounts will be immediately credited with their full amount. As a gesture of goodwill to yourself, I am waiving our usual discount.

Please do forgive me for my earlier tardiness. I hope that my prompt action now meets with your pleasure and approval, and that both I and the bank may continue to enjoy your favour.

I endeavour to remain

Yr most obedient and humble serv't

JAMES HORNBY
SENIOR CLERK

Mrs Chaytor knocked at Miss Godfrey and Miss Roper's cottage and brandished the paper cheerfully as they opened the door. 'At last, the letter from Coutts has arrived. Now we can withdraw your money, and you will be safe.'

'Oh!' cried Miss Roper, clasping her thin hands together. 'Oh, Mrs Chaytor, what a relief!' Tears started suddenly in her eyes. 'Oh, my dear friend, how good of you to do all this for us. You are so kind, so kind! Oh, my dear, dear friend!'

'Hush, Clara,' said Miss Godfrey gently, laying a hand on her arm. 'What do we do next, Mrs Chaytor?'

'Next, I drive you to Rye. When do you wish to go? I can take you now, if you are free.'

They rushed to find their wraps and hats and reticules while Mrs Chaytor returned to Sandy House and ordered out the gig. Drawing on her driving gloves, she walked out and helped the two ladies up to the seat; there was just room for all three of them to sit abreast.

They drove to Rye on a dark, dreary September day, the Marsh blanketed by drizzle. They left the gig at the George and walked through the rain to the bank. A clerk showed them into

Grebell Faversham's office, seated them and offered sherry. Grebell himself entered the room a moment later, dressed in sober grey. His face was thinner and even more drawn than it had been before.

'Thank you for seeing us, Mr Faversham,' said Mrs Chaytor. 'These are the friends I have mentioned to you, Miss Godfrey and Miss Roper. They have come to draw out their money, as we have arranged.'

'Ladies,' said Grebell, bowing. 'It is my pleasure to meet you both.'

'Thank you for your assistance, sir,' said Miss Godfrey as they took their seats. She was suddenly rather embarrassed. 'Please do not feel that our desire to withdraw our money is intended as any slight on your bank. We simply feel that for the moment, it is better for us to have our money in London. I hope this does not inconvenience you.'

'I understand,' said Grebell. He looked down at his desk, and silence fell.

'Mr Faversham?' Amelia prompted. 'Perhaps we could proceed?'

Grebell looked up again. His eyes were full of weary pain. 'I fear, ma'am, that there has been an unforeseen difficulty.'

Miss Godfrey and Miss Roper sat silent. 'What sort of difficulty?' asked Mrs Chaytor.

'I . . . I am sorry to say this, but . . . I am unable to comply with your request for Miss Godfrey and Miss Roper to withdraw the entire sums in their accounts.'

'And why not?'

'As of yesterday, we have been forced to restrict the amount of money we can issue to any individual customer.'

Dear God, thought Amelia. *We are too late. That damned dithering fool Hornby. I will break him for this.*

Aloud, she said, 'I see. How much money may my friends withdraw?'

'I am entitled to authorise a withdrawal of twenty-five pounds from each account, fifty pounds in total, but only in banknotes drawn on this bank. I fear I cannot issue a bill of exchange as you ask.'

'Fifty pounds?' quavered Miss Roper. 'How shall we live on fifty pounds? Oh, Rosie! What shall we do?'

'There is a run on the bank,' said Mrs Chaytor to Grebell. 'Isn't there?'

'Yes. It began yesterday morning. By nightfall we had lost fifteen per cent of our deposits. Much more, and . . . we will not be able to pay out at all.'

It was hopeless, she knew, but she had to try. 'You gave me your word of honour,' she said to Grebell. 'You promised as a gentleman to see that my friends' money was safe. I am calling on you now to honour that promise.'

He went pale. 'I am . . . unable to do so. Words cannot express how sorry I am.'

'Come,' said Mrs Chaytor to Miss Godfrey, who helped Miss Roper to her feet. Grebell hurried to open the door for them, ushering the two older women through. Mrs Chaytor paused in the doorway and looked him hard in the face.

'Your word of honour,' she repeated. Then, straight-backed and quivering with anger, she walked after the two ladies.

20

John the Baptist

They drove the twelve long miles back through the rain to St Mary in the Marsh. Shocked and exhausted, Miss Godfrey and Miss Roper said nothing, and Mrs Chaytor could not bring herself to speak.

But as the gig stopped outside the ladies' tumbledown cottage, the full enormity of what had happened slammed home. The two frail women clung to each other. 'Oh, Rosie!' cried Miss Roper. 'What shall we do? We shall lose our lovely home; our sanctuary! We shall lose *everything*!'

Somehow, Mrs Chaytor got them inside. Kate, the housemaid, frightened and uncomprehending, stood staring at them. Miss Roper's despair turned to shame as she realised her loss of self-control. 'I am sorry,' she sobbed. 'I am so sorry. I am a foolish, witless old woman, and I am troubling you all. I am sorry, Mrs Chaytor.'

'Hush,' said Amelia, her heart breaking. To Miss Godfrey, who was white and shivering, she said, 'You must both get into some dry clothes. Have you any laudanum?'

'A little.' Miss Godfrey went to fetch it and Amelia looked at the girl. 'Kate, build up the fire. Good and hot.'

'Ma'am, whatever has happened?'

'A betrayal,' said Mrs Chaytor grimly. 'The fire, my girl. Quick, now.'

The laudanum did its work; within a few minutes Miss Roper was quiet and drowsy. They eased off her rain-sodden outer clothes and wrapped her in blankets. Miss Godfrey sat before the fire holding the other woman in her arms, kissing her grey hair from time to time. 'What shall we do?' she asked Mrs Chaytor softly.

'Wait,' said Mrs Chaytor. Sorrow was turning back into fury. 'They will *not* get away with this.'

In the grip of a magnificent rage, she stalked outside and drove her carriage up the rainy street to the rectory. Hardcastle looked up startled as she entered his study.

'There is a run on the bank,' she said.

'I know. I was in Ashford today, and heard about it there. And Bessie Luckhurst has just been to see me, in a panic.' Her father was up in Hythe with Joshua Stemp, watching for Noakes and his companions.

'I have just left Miss Godfrey and Miss Roper in utter despair. Their entire world has been shattered. What are we going to do, Marcus?' she demanded.

'Read this,' he said, and pushed a paper across the desk to her. 'I wrote it after Bessie left. I am now debating with myself whether to send it.'

THE RECTORY, ST MARY IN THE MARSH, KENT
22nd of September, 1797

By express

Mr James Martin, Sir,

I write to you in your capacity as senior partner of the esteemed bank Martin, Stone and Foote. You have for a number of years acted as the City representative of a country bank, the East Weald and Ashford. In particular, one of your junior partners, Mr George Stone, has negotiated a number of bills of exchange coming from Germany on behalf of the East Weald and Ashford, to the value of many tens of thousands of pounds. Your bank will have earned a commission on each of these bills, and you have profited from these transactions.

I have to inform you that these bills represent money dishonestly and immorally earned, through the illegal export of gold from this country. Not only is this in violation of the Restriction Act, but I also have evidence that this gold has gone straight into the coffers of the French Directory. In other words, Mr Martin, the East Weald and Ashford Bank has been helping to arm our enemies, and you have been a party to this.

Whether you were aware, whether you were a witting or unwitting party to treason, I do not care. Nor will the law. You will be deemed an accessory, and will be punished accordingly. I am told your bank sets great store by its reputation for honesty and probity. That reputation will lie in ruins – if this information is made public.

If you do not wish this to happen, then you must take action. The East Weald and Ashford is about to go bankrupt. You must intervene, and see to it that the bank survives. If you do so, then I will do my utmost to see that your reputation is protected.

There is not a great deal of time. I urge you to make up your mind quickly. I remain,

Yr very obedient servant

Rev. M. A. Hardcastle, JP

'Strewth!' said Mrs Chaytor, startled out of her anger. 'You're blackmailing the Grasshopper!'

'Do you think I should send this?'

'Certainly you should. And I apologise most sincerely for berating you.'

'Are the ladies deeply distressed?'

'They are devastated, the poor dears. They've already aged years since this crisis began. This could finish them.'

'I know.' The rector rubbed his forehead. 'They won't be the only ones who suffer either. I think of the splendid charity of our village, feeding and clothing the refugees. Soon, some will not even be able to feed themselves. Those reckless, criminal fools have condemned a generation of our people to poverty.'

'Then send the letter,' said Mrs Chaytor, and there was iron in her voice. 'And let them know St Mary in the Marsh will not go down without a fight.'

He smiled at her and reached for the sealing wax. 'I went to Ashford to see Batist,' he said as he waited for the wax to melt.

'Did you find him?'

'No.' He sealed the letter and turned to face her. 'The run had begun there, too, and people were clamouring to withdraw their money. Batist is away, and the other clerks were in a state of panic. They did not know where he went or when he would be back. I then called on Mr Batist senior, who says his son went down to Hythe a week ago. He is a worried man. I think he believes his son is in trouble because of the bank.'

'Can you ask Joshua to look for Batist in Hythe?'

'I was about to do so when Bessie called. He and Hoad and the others will have a lot on their plate, searching for Batist, hunting for Noakes and intercepting Jean . . . What is it?'

Mrs Chaytor had stiffened in her chair, her hands suddenly clenched. 'Biblical nicknames,' she said. 'The Twelve Apostles have always been fond of them. You said Jean worked for them, didn't you?'

'Yes,' said the rector. 'What do you mean?'

'Jean. Batist, which is a corruption of Baptiste. Jean-Baptiste, John the Baptist. I will wager anything you care to name that Batist the bank clerk and Jean the courier are the same person.'

'Of course! Great heaven; as a churchman, I of all people should have seen this. It makes sense. Batist knows the details of the gold shipments, and goes across to negotiate with Vandamme. And Matthew confirmed Jean has connections in France. Oh, I cannot believe how blind I have been!'

'So much for the quiet, self-effacing clerk,' said Mrs Chaytor. 'What will you do?'

'According to Matthew, Jean is due to return from France tomorrow. I shall go up to Hythe tomorrow to join Joshua, and we shall intercept him. Look after Miss Godfrey and Miss Roper while I am away, and will you also call on the refugees and see that they have all they need?'

'Of course.'

It was the 23rd of September, and the wind whistling across the Marsh carried with it the sour taste of autumn. Dusk fell early under a chilly blanket of cloud. As darkness gathered, a small rowing boat moved into the haven of Hythe, passing a row of fishing boats. The boat eased up onto the beach and the man inside stepped out, easing limbs cramped by a long row from the ship that had dropped him off out at sea. Still a little stiff, he walked through the narrow, cobbled streets of Hythe.

He came to the Swan, where lamplight gleamed through greasy windows, shedding little pools of light into the street. The man, quiet-faced and slender, watched the street for a while; then, satisfied he was not being followed, he pushed open the door of the Swan and went inside.

The only people in the common room were Manningham the landlord, and another, smaller man with a smallpox-marked face, drinking gin and water. As the door closed, this man turned and drew a pistol from his belt. 'Jean,' he said. 'Welcome home, *mon ami.*'

The bank clerk was fast on his feet. He turned while Stemp was still speaking and pulled the door open again. A shadow filled the doorway; another man, this one squarely built with a heavy stick in his hand. Before the first man could move, the stick came up like a striking snake and pointed at his throat, the ferrule resting just under his chin.

'Mr Batist,' said Hardcastle. 'I must speak with you.'

Slowly Batist edged backwards and Hardcastle walked into the room, pulling the door shut behind him. Stemp was behind Batist now, still holding the pistol. 'Let us speak privately,' said Hardcastle. 'Mr Manningham, may we use your parlour room?'

Manningham gestured to a door. The three of them moved into the parlour, Hardcastle picking up a candlestick and then closing the door behind them. 'Sit down,' he said to Batist.

Batist sat. Stemp came to stand beside him, a heavy hand on his shoulder keeping him pinned in the chair, the pistol still levelled at his head. 'You know who we are, and why we are here,' said Hardcastle.

'I have no notion what you are talking about,' said Batist. His face was completely still, but his eyes flickered from one man to the other, around the small room and back again.

'If I were to search you now,' said Hardcastle, 'I would find two things. First, a receipt from Monsieur Vandamme of Boulogne for 5,720 ounces of gold sold to him by the East Weald and Ashford Bank and delivered four days ago, the 19th of September. Second, a message in code which I suspect comes from Peter, the leader of the Twelve Apostles, to be delivered to Matthew, his lieutenant in this country.'

Batist's composure cracked. He stared, panic suffusing his face. 'How in the name of all that is holy do you know about that?'

'Matthew now knows about the gold smuggling,' the rector continued. 'He knows too that you have been selling gold to our enemies. He regards you as a traitor. If he finds you, he will kill you. No arrest, no formality of a trial, just a pistol ball in the head or a knife in the back. You are a dead man, Batist, unless you cooperate with me. I can restrain Matthew, but in return, you must answer my questions.'

Batist's eyes flickered round the room again. There was only one window, small and high, and Hardcastle was between him and the door. 'What do you want to know?'

'What happened to Hector Munro? Who killed him, and why?'

'I don't know. I swear to God I don't.'

Hardcastle studied Batist for a moment. 'Mediumheight, slender, well spoken. What do you think, Joshua?'

'Could be, reverend.'

'Mr Batist, on the afternoon of the 10th tenth of August, did you go to New Romney and hire a boat from a man named Jem Clay?'

'No,' said Batist.

Hardcastle nodded. 'So if we brought Mr Clay into the room now, he would not identify you as the man who rented his boat?'

Batist's shoulders slumped. 'Very well,' he said finally. 'Yes.'

'And did you also come here to the Swan and meet Mr Munro?'

'Yes. It was I who suggested this as a meeting place. I knew Manningham would be discreet.'

'You know Manningham?' Stemp demanded. 'He claimed he didn't recognise you.'

Batist spread his hands. 'Like I said, Manningham is discreet.'

Hardcastle was still staring at Batist, his eyes boring into the clerk's face. 'Tell me what happened.'

Batist swallowed. 'At the beginning of August, Mr Munro came back from a meeting with Mr Faversham. He was angry about something to do with the gold. He said he had to go across to France and fix things, and asked me to help him. We arranged that I would travel down separately and hire a boat for him. A ship would be waiting for him; I don't know how he arranged that. I was to row him out to the ship, and bring the boat back as if nothing had happened.'

'But the plan changed. Why?'

'I don't know. At the last minute, he said he would row himself out to the ship. He'd let the boat drift, he said, and someone was bound to find it and take it back to its owner.'

Batist's hands twisted in his lap. 'I should have insisted. Had I gone with him, I might have been able to save him.'

'Save him?' said Hardcastle, eyes unblinking. 'From whom?'

'From the men who killed him. I might have been able to intervene.'

'So you know who killed him.'

Batist did not trust himself to speak. He nodded, his eyes miserable.

'Why was Munro going to France? To see Vandamme? Was this in connection with the fraud?'

'Fraud?' said Batist. He looked even more desperate now. 'I've never heard of any fraud. Mr Munro didn't tell me. He just said there was a problem with the gold shipments, and he needed to go to France and see Vandamme.'

'Did he also mention the name of Staphorst?'

'He . . . he might have done. I don't remember for certain.'

'And Cotton?' asked Hardcastle. 'He was killed by the same men?'

'Yes. It was a warning to the rest of us, to keep silent.'

'A warning from whom? Faversham? Is Faversham defrauding the bank, Batist?'

'If he is, sir, I don't know a thing about it.'

'Or is it you? Are you embezzling, Batist? Are you stealing gold, or the money that comes from the gold?'

'No,' said Batist. 'I swear to God I am not.'

Hardcastle paused, staring down at the other man. Stemp's pistol moved a little, restlessly, and Batist's eyes flickered towards it.

'Who are you afraid of?' said the rector. 'You know who the embezzler is, of that I am sure. You know who ordered the murders of Munro and Cotton. Who?'

'I cannot tell you.' The fear in Batist's face was naked and open now.

The rector nodded. 'Very well. We shall let you go now. Matthew and his men are doubtless waiting for you outside. I hope for your sake the end is swift. But I know from experience that the Twelve Apostles are not fond of traitors. The last one was beaten to death by his fellows.'

'No!' Batist pleaded. 'Please don't! If I tell you the truth now, I am still a dead man. These others, they will find me and kill me. Either way, you are condemning me to death. For the love of God, reverend!'

'It would seem there is no alternative,' said Hardcastle in a voice of stone.

'No, there is, I promise you. Look, I could tell you everything now, but it would be my word against theirs. And I would never live to stand trial; they would make sure of that. Even if you lock me up in gaol, they will still find a way to get at me. Believe me, I know what these people are capable of, better than anyone.' Batist squirmed in his chair, on the edge of panic. 'Let me work for you,' he pleaded.

'Work for me? In what capacity?'

'I can bring you evidence. I know the whereabouts of papers relating to the gold exports. I can bring you proof of how the gold was shipped to Cotton's mills and packed in gunpowder casks; how it was sent down to Romney Marsh, the times and places where shipments were exported, the names of all the people involved, everything. Let me gather those papers and bring them to you.'

'How do you know all this? I thought you were merely the courier to Vandamme.'

'No. You see, the idea of smuggling gold was mine in the first place. I planned the whole thing.'

The rector stood for a moment, digesting this. 'I worked it all out,' said Batist. 'I knew gold sold for a premium on the Continent. I already knew Vandamme; my French family have connections with him, and I knew he dealt in gold. I knew too that he was trustworthy.'

'Was it you who also designed the trail the money would follow? From Boulogne to Amsterdam, then on to Hamburg and back to London?'

'Yes.' Batist blinked. 'How did you know about that?'

'Mr Batist, there is very little about this affair that I do *not* know. The only missing details are the names of the men who killed Munro and Cotton. You claim to be able to provide proof of the gold smuggling. But I also want the murderers. Who gave the orders to kill them, and who pulled the trigger? Can you tell me that?'

'Noakes killed them,' said Batist.

'Both of them?'

'Mr Munro certainly, and I think Mr Cotton.'

'On whose orders? Who pays Noakes?'

Batist shook his head. 'No,' he said. 'It's as I said. If I tell you now, I am a dead man. Let me go and I will bring you the proof; then you can arrest them immediately, and I can get away. But I want something in exchange.'

'What is it?'

'Complete immunity. No charges will be brought against me. As soon as I hand over the papers, I will disappear. You will never see me or hear from me again. I intend to get as far away as possible, so they cannot follow me.'

'We can help you do that,' said the rector.

'No. I don't want any government spies tracking me, or that bastard Matthew coming after me. I intend to vanish without a trace.'

'Of course,' said Stemp, 'if we let you go now, you might vanish anyway.'

'Look,' said Batist desperately, 'you must believe me. I want out of this whole devilish enterprise. I never dreamed of any of this when I started. My only purpose was to help the bank. I hoped that by doing the bank a service, my worth would be recognised. Mr Faversham and Mr Munro might see fit to make me a partner. That was the summit of my ambitions. Now it has all gone horribly wrong. Men are being killed, there is threat and danger everywhere. I cannot sleep at night. Every time there is a knock at the door, I think they might be coming for me. Let me work for you. It's the only way this hell will ever reach an end.'

For the first time, Hardcastle raised his eyes and looked at Stemp. 'I don't know if we can trust him,' the rector said.

'Manningham,' said Batist. 'He'll vouch for me. We're kinfolk, blood relations. He'll know you can trust me.'

Stemp hauled Batist to his feet, opened the door and marched the clerk into the common room, the pistol jammed in the small of his back. 'Manningham? You said you didn't recognise him, you lying bastard. Now tell the truth. Is he a relation of yours?'

Manningham shrugged. 'He might be. Anything is possible. Who knows what Mother gets up to, when Father is at sea?'

'Will you vouch for him?' Stemp persisted.

'Of course not. How long have you known me, Stempy, to ask such a question? I will not vouch for the truthfulness of anyone, not even myself . . . Especially not myself,' Manningham amended.

Stemp pulled Batist back into the parlour, pushed him into his chair and slammed the door shut. 'Well?' he demanded. 'Why should we believe you?'

'Because you have no choice,' said Batist. 'If you are to take your murderers and smugglers, you need proof. And there is no one but me who can give you that proof. I am your best chance, whether you like it or not.'

The rector made up his mind. 'Very well,' he said to Batist. 'We have a bargain. You have three days to return to Ashford, find these papers and bring them to me. After that, I shall inform Matthew. I believe he will have little trouble in tracking you down, no matter where you choose to hide.'

Batist nodded dumbly. Hardcastle turned and walked out into the common room. 'Mr Manningham,' he said to the landlord, 'you will not breathe a word of this evening's events to a living soul. If I find you have done so, I will have you arrested and charged with smuggling and murder under the law of joint enterprise. Am I clear?'

'Your Worship is the embodiment of clarity,' said Manningham. 'Have no fear. I have forgotten every conversation that has ever taken place in my inn. Experience teaches that a short memory is the key to a long life.'

Back in St Mary on Sunday, Hardcastle conducted the church service as usual. To his surprise and pleasure, the little congregation was inflated by the arrival of some of the refugees. He was less pleased to see the state of Miss Godfrey and Miss Roper, the latter in particular looking very pale and thinner than ever. She trembled when the rector took her hand after the service. 'You must not worry,' he said gently. 'All will be well. We shall look after you.'

'Oh, reverend. I do not want so much, truly I do not. All I ever wanted was to live in my own little cottage with my dear Rosie until it was time to go to my rest.'

'We shall look after you,' he repeated. 'We in this parish, we are your family, my dear.' He watched her walk away, shuffling, stoop-shouldered, and thought Mrs Chaytor was right; she had aged five years in just a few days.

That afternoon he and Calpurnia dined with the priest and some of the older refugees, the younger ones preferring the kitchen where they could enjoy the company of Biddy. His mind was largely absent, and he escaped into his study as soon as he decently could.

Calpurnia followed him in, looking worried. 'Marcus? You barely touched your dinner. Are you unwell?'

'I am deeply worried about our poor friends.'

His sister, who was as fond of the two ladies as he, looked mournful. 'Is there no one to whom an appeal can be made? No way of obtaining redress for them?'

'I have written to someone who may be able to help. There is no certainty that he will respond.' If not, the rector thought, then by God, my next letter on this subject will be to the *Morning Post*. He looked at Calpurnia. 'If he does not, then I think we should set up a charitable fund to help the people whose lives will be ruined by the crash.'

'Marcus, that is a most excellent idea. I have some experience in these matters; will you allow me to do this? I shall donate a portion of my royalties from my last novel, *The Lighthouse of Vavassal*, as an example to others.'

'Thank you. I am very grateful to you.' Voices sounded in the drawing room, talking in French; she had given up her own sanctum to the refugees, and he thought she looked a little lost. 'Come,' he said on impulse. 'Sit down.'

She stared at him in sudden delight; never before had he suggested she join him. 'Would you care for a glass of brandy?' he asked. 'Very fine Hennessy cognac, on which not a penny of duty has ever been paid.'

'Oh, Marcus! Run brandy! How exciting!' That evening they sat together for a long while and talked of small things, and for once he was happy not to be alone with his thoughts.

On Monday morning, two letters were delivered from the post office in New Romney.

MIDDLE TEMPLE, LONDON
22nd of September, 1797

My dear Hardcastle

Thank you for your most recent letter. Cole's failure is to be deeply regretted. The man is a buffoon and an ass. You have my permission to approach the colonel of the Volunteers if you feel you must. Try to sort out this mess as soon as you can, will you?

Yr very obedient servant

CLAVERTYE

That is Lord Clavertye all over, the rector thought angrily. *There has been a failure, and he is washing his hands of it*. Had Cole taken the gold, Clavertye would have been on the scene in a flash, ready to claim the credit. He broke the seal on the second letter.

MARTIN, STONE AND FOOTE, LOMBARD STREET, LONDON
23rd of September, 1797

By express

Reverend Hardcastle,

I am this moment in receipt of your letter of yesterday's date, and am responding by return. I tell you plainly, sir, that I consider your letter to be damned high-handed and offensive, and if you ever repeat in public the accusation that my bank was complicit in this affair, I will break you. I will brook no insolence from you, sir, and I will not allow you to slander myself or my bank. I trust I have made myself perfectly clear on this matter.

Attend on me at the offices of the East Weald and Ashford Bank in Rye at twelve of the clock on Tuesday, the 26th of September.

JAMES MARTIN, SENIOR PARTNER

Someone knocked at the study door. 'Enter,' Hardcastle called.

It was the priest, Abbé de Bernay, bowing. 'I have come to say farewell.'

'Oh,' said Hardcastle in surprise. 'So soon, sir?'

'Letters have come from the French community in Canterbury, inviting some of us to join them. Wagons and carriages are arriving shortly to collect us. Your hospitality has been magnificent, but we cannot impose on you forever. And we feel a need to be with our own people.'

'I understand,' said Hardcastle. 'In your position, I expect I should feel the same. Exiles need the company of others like themselves.'

'Indeed. My people are beginning now to realise that we have lost everything. We may none of us ever see our homes or our families again. So, we must find a new community, a new home; a new place in the world.'

'The French of Canterbury; are they not mostly Huguenots? Protestants?'

'No one is perfect,' said the priest, smiling. 'And these past few days have reinforced a lesson I already knew: that Protestants and Catholics can be friends. Our common humanity is far stronger than any difference of faith.'

'That is a noble sentiment,' said Hardcastle. 'God go with you, my friend.'

'And may He watch over you also. I hope He helps you to catch your murderer.'

It was not the hand of God that would bring the killers of Munro and Cotton to justice, but the remorseless efforts of man. Hardcastle wrote to the colonel of the East Kent Volunteers asking for men, and if possible for the services of one of his best officers, Captain Edward Austen of Godmersham. Then, on Tuesday morning, he set out for Rye.

The atmosphere in the town was tense. Two constables guarded the East Weald and Ashford Bank. A big black carriage stood outside the door, its team still in harness, watched by silent onlookers. They stared at Hardcastle, too, as he walked towards the door, and he heard dark whispers running through the crowd. *How many people in Rye had Charles Faversham ruined?* he wondered.

A nervous servant ushered him into Faversham's office. Faversham himself stood to one side; his place behind the desk was occupied by a big man in a black coat and breeches, square-faced and strong-jawed with bristling eyebrows and iron-grey hair pulled straight back from his face. George Stone was there, too, looking solemn and worried. Also present were Maudsley, who avoided the rector's eye, and Mrs Redcliffe, who looked up and smiled briefly. Dressed all in black today, she sat poised with gloved hands folded in her lap, her skin looking like old paper in the lamplight. A secretary sat at a side table, pen poised over his inkwell.

'Are we all here?' asked the big man. As if on cue, there came another knock at the door, and Mrs Chaytor walked briskly into the room.

'Who the devil are you?' asked the big man irritably.

'Mrs Amelia Chaytor,' came the reply. 'I represent some of the depositors of this bank, and I have come to see justice done.'

'Bravo,' said Mrs Redcliffe, before anyone else could speak. 'Well done, my dear. Come, take a seat beside me.'

The big man glared at them both, eyebrows bristling. 'Very well,' he said testily. 'Are we likely to suffer any further interruptions? Good. Then we shall begin.'

He nodded to the secretary, who began writing. 'My name is James Martin, and I am the senior partner at Martin, Stone and Foote. Certain rumours concerning the East Weald and Ashford Bank have come to my attention, rumours which Mr Faversham has now confirmed to me are true.'

Faversham nodded. He looked white and miserable. For him, this was the end.

'This is what now will happen,' said Martin. 'The Grasshopper will acquire the partnerships in the East Weald and Ashford bank held by Mr Faversham, Mr Maudsley and Mrs Redcliffe, all of whom were involved in or had knowledge of this disgraceful affair. The heirs of Mr Munro and Mr Cotton, who are innocent of any malfeasance, will continue to enjoy their shares, unless they wish to sell them to me.

'As the bank is now insolvent, each of you will be paid a notional sum of £1 in total for your partnership share. You will relinquish all rights and all control of the bank to me. Is that understood?'

Heads nodded.

'As the new proprietor of the bank, I personally will guarantee all deposits. No one who has money in this bank will lose a penny. I will temporarily retain the restriction on withdrawals to stop the run, but once the bank is restored to health that restriction will be lifted. I shall inject capital from my own bank and bring in new partners. I expect the restoration of the bank's fortunes will take no more than three or four weeks. If you know of any hardship cases who urgently require funds, inform them that they should make a request to my staff. Is that understood?'

Faversham and Maudsley nodded. 'That is very generous of you,' said Mrs Chaytor. 'You are assuming all the liabilities of the bank? Do you know how large they may be?'

'Having examined the books this morning, I have a fair idea. In any case, it does not matter. No one – *no one* – drags the good name of the Grasshopper through the mud.'

George Stone flinched. Martin glared at Hardcastle. 'Well, reverend? And you, Mrs . . . Chaytor, was it? Are you satisfied?'

'Quite satisfied,' said Hardcastle. 'I echo Mrs Chaytor's sentiments. You are very generous. What do you ask in return?'

'Your complete silence,' said Martin. 'Not a word of this arrangement leaves this room. If any of you spreads gossip or rumour about this affair, I will revoke the arrangements, let the bank crash and ruin you all. Faversham at the very least will go to prison. Once again, is that understood?'

'Perfectly,' said Mrs Chaytor calmly. Faversham looked sick.

'Then this meeting is at an end. Hardcastle: a word, if you please.'

When the room was empty but for themselves, the big banker looked at the rector. 'Why did you feel it necessary to blackmail me? Have you yourself invested in this bank?'

'Not a penny,' said Hardcastle. 'But many of my parishioners have. I wanted to protect them.'

'I see. It never occurred to you to simply write and ask for my help, freely given?'

'Had I done so, would you have complied?'

'I am quite capable of understanding what the fall of the bank might mean to your people. Not all of us in the banking profession are charlatans and thieves, reverend. A few of us, just a few, are honest.'

'If I have misestimated you, sir, then I apologise.'

'Thank you. One more thing.'

Hardcastle waited. 'I know you want to prosecute Faversham and see him put in prison,' said Martin. 'In your place, so would I. But you can't. If he goes on trial, the whole thing becomes public and our reputation is ruined. You'll have to let him go.'

'I understand,' said Hardcastle. 'The ultimate decision on whether to prosecute rests with the Lord-Lieutenant of Sussex and the Deputy Lord-Lieutenant of Kent, Lord Clavertye. But I will recommend that they do not proceed. Rightly or wrongly, the well-being of my parishioners means more to me than my desire to see Faversham face trial.'

He thought Martin looked surprised at his quick compliance; the banker had been expecting an argument. But Hardcastle had already decided not to pursue Faversham. He was guilty of smuggling, certainly. If he knew the destination of the gold then he might be guilty of treason, but it would be very hard to prove. He was not the embezzler, nor was he the killer of Munro and Cotton.

Martin was speaking. 'You're a good man, reverend. Your people are very lucky to have you looking after their interests. I hope they realise it.'

'Thank you, sir.'

'You're welcome. Now, get out of my office.'

The rector's dog cart could never match Mrs Chaytor's gig for speed, and she reached St Mary in the Marsh long before he did. When he finally arrived at the rectory she was waiting for him, her face taut and set, white lines at the corners of her mouth.

'What is it?' he asked at once. 'Miss Godfrey and Miss Roper, are they well?'

'I told them the news and they collapsed in tears, but they are well enough. News has arrived from Ashford. I saw the messenger as I drove into the village, and he told me the tidings. Charles Batist has been shot dead.'

21

A Face from the Past

Noyes, the Ashford magistrate, was as shocked as anyone. 'We've never had anything like this, not in my time as justice of the peace. Granted, the town can get a bit rough at times, but this was a cold-blooded assassination. And Batist, of all people! Everyone liked him. No one blamed him personally for the problems at the bank.'

Batist had been working late, the other clerks having gone home. At some point during the course of the evening he had opened the rear door of the bank; the door was found unlocked the next morning. Outside, his nemesis was waiting. Batist was forced to open the vault, presumably because it was a place where sound would not carry outside the building, and pushed inside. Like Cotton, he was then shot in the face at point-blank range.

Noyes took him to the scene. The vault door was still open, and the banknotes and papers stored inside were splattered with blood and brains. The lid of the cast-iron stove in the clerks' room was open, too, and its belly was full of ash; charred bits of paper lay on the floor around it. 'He was burning papers,' said Noyes. 'We don't know what. There's nothing in his desk but ordinary ledgers.'

Batist had known who killed Munro and Cotton, but was too frightened to say so until proof could be found and the kill-ers arrested. I sent him back to the bank to find that proof, the rector thought. *He went like a lamb to the slaughter . . .* But why was he burning papers, when he promised he would bring the evidence to me?

The answer was clear. When Batist promised cooperation, he was telling another lie; his last one. He was planning to defy them all, the smugglers, the law and the Twelve Apostles, and go on the run.

Hardcastle asked the usual questions of Noyes. Did anyone see or hear anything at the time of the murder? Were any suspicious persons seen around the town earlier in the day? Were any tracks found around the bank? The answers were, as he expected, in the negative. He gave Noyes descriptions of Noakes and Fisk and asked him to circulate these, but he had little hope that anything would come of this. The murderers, like the planners of the gold runs, were skilful and covered their tracks well.

Stemp and his men, still on watch in Hythe, could be called home now. There was no longer any need for their presence. Noakes and Fisk must know, now, that they were hunted. They would be unlikely to return to Hythe.

Hardcastle called on Batist's father, and found the apothecary a broken man. He had been proud of his only son, and loved him. Batist's death seemed to him a senseless and cruel waste. The rector told him that time would help to heal the wounds, but in this case he doubted it. Some griefs last a lifetime.

It was the 27th of September, the time of year when the days shorten and the air cools and the sun grows dim; when colours fade and hope dies. Romney Marsh, when he reached it, was cold and grey. It was nearly dark when he returned to St Mary. Wearily, he stepped down from the driving seat and went inside, calling for coffee. A letter stood propped on his desk.

Sixpenny Court, Change Alley, London
26th of September, 1797

My dear Reverend Hardcastle,

My apologies for the long delay in replying to your letter. Upon receipt, I wrote at once to Amsterdam, but getting letters into and out of that city has become rather difficult. The Dutch fleet is preparing to put to sea, and accordingly our own navy has tightened its blockade of the coast. This makes life rather difficult for the blockade runners who carry my correspondence.

My cousin at the Stock Exchange has, I hope, procured the information you asked for. He pretended to be investigating a fraud on the exchange, and Staphorst, concerned for their own good reputation, were happy to answer his questions. It was quickly established that the Staphorst bank has connections with Vandamme in Boulogne, and the traffic between them has included some high-value bills of exchange. My cousin checked the dates when these large bills arrived from Vandamme, and found that at about the same time, within a day or two, another bill was sent off to Berenberg & Gossler in Hamburg, just as I suspected.

Now, here is the interesting thing. On the same date that the bills arriving from Vandamme were redeemed, moneys were also paid into an account at Staphorst itself; and no small sums either, but the equivalent of thousands of pounds. When queried, Staphorst produced letters from an agent in the city, a man of affairs who insisted he was acting on the direct instructions of his own client. It remains to be added that there have also been some very large withdrawals from this account over the same period.

My cousin then asked Staphorst who held this account. The name meant nothing to him, of course, but it shocked me, as I am certain it will shock you. The client for whom this man of affairs was acting, and the account holder – who has written several times to authorise withdrawals from the account by her agents – is one and the same: Mrs Martha Redcliffe.

I enclose copies of four of these withdrawals. I believe if you check the amounts, you will find they correspond to the sums we think were embezzled from each of the last four gold shipments.

Please let me know if I may assist you any further,

Yr very obedient servant

DAVID RICARDO

'It was the priest, Abbé de Bernay, who first put the idea into my head,' he said to Mrs Chaytor in her drawing room a little later. 'He said, *are you certain it is a man*? I rejected the idea right away, but later found I could not stop thinking about it. I remembered then what Mrs Redcliffe said when I first interviewed her: Faversham knew nothing about smuggling, she said, but he could be taken advantage of by ruthless people who did.'

'On that point, at least, she was telling the truth.' Mrs Chaytor shivered. 'How cold-blooded she is! She has gone out of her way to befriend Cecilia Munro and visits her often; yet she killed that poor girl's husband. And she sat there yesterday, cool and calm, knowing that her men were on their way to Ashford to murder Batist.'

Hardcastle frowned. The visits to Cecilia worried him suddenly, but he did not know why. 'She is nerveless,' he agreed. 'I wonder if that is the result of the opium.'

Mrs Chaytor turned and took up a letter of her own from the side table. 'Speaking of opium,' she said, 'you may find this instructive.'

WOTTON HOUSE, WOTTON UNDERWOOD, BUCKINGHAM-SHIRE
26th of September, 1797

My dearest Amelia,

It was very good to receive your letter, as it always is. I hope you will accept my apologies for not replying to you at once. As you can probably imagine, these last few weeks have been very fraught indeed. Our hopes for peace, a project for which we had laboured for so long, are now entirely shattered, and conflict with our enemies is joined once more. I am, I must tell you, in a state of despair. How long we can continue to hold out against such a powerful combination of enemies, French and Spanish and Dutch, is not at all certain.

But I must not infect you with my glooms. Opium! There really is no end to your interests. And how on earth did *you* come to discover the smuggling? I have only recently learned of it myself! Never mind; I shall contain my curiosity for the moment, and endeavour to tell you what you desire to know.

The Levant Company is the primary trader in opium between this country and Turkey, although it forms only a very small part of the company's overall commerce. We import around two thousand pounds (in weight) of opium each year through the port of London. Our rivals in the trade bring in perhaps another thousand. We sell to the opium brokers in Mincing Lane, who in turn sell on to wholesalers, to manufacturers of opiate drugs such as laudanum, or sometimes directly to apothecaries. The total value of the trade amounts to not more than £6,000.

The market is not large; indeed, when one compares it to the millions of gallons of untaxed gin that flood into this country every year, it is positively tiny. Initially I found it hard to understand why anyone would take the trouble to smuggle opium.

Nonetheless, it has become clear in recent weeks that someone *is* bringing illicit opium into the country, and in very large quantities. Brokers outside the usual system are auctioning cheap opium in London almost every day, and there is talk of sales being held in Bristol and Birmingham as well. Last month alone, these brokers sold well over a ton of opium; more than we normally import in a year.

Our price is being undercut by as much as nine or ten shillings a pound, which can only mean that the opium is coming in through the free traders. My assumption is that they are bringing it from Amsterdam, which is one of the leading centres of the opium trade on the Continent.

The rector looked up. 'Amsterdam,' he said.

'I told you. Women's intuition.'

If things carry on in this way, there is a real danger that we and the other legal opium traders will be driven out of the market. Indeed, upon consideration, my view is that this is exactly what the smugglers intend: to flood the market with cheap opium and take the trade away from us. Should this happen, and should opium become as cheap and widely available as gin, then the effects upon the populace could be quite unwholesome and unpleasant.

So, your suspicion that there is an ulterior motive at work may well have foundation. When – or indeed, if – the present crisis abates I will look into this matter further. In the meantime, I hope I have satisfied your curiosity; and, should you learn anything further at your end, I would be grateful if you would inform me.

Anne sends her love,

I remain yours fondly,

WILLIE

'Martha Redcliffe has been embezzling from the bank and using the money to buy opium, which she smuggles into this country,' said the rector.

'That is her project,' said Mrs Chaytor. Her blue eyes were very bright. 'That is the legacy she will leave to her heirs. A commercial empire, built on the trade in opium. She will sell the drug to anyone who wants it – the curious, the ill, the despairing, the foolhardy – and they will become habituated and die, so that she and those who come after her may profit. And to achieve her end, she has ruined a bank and killed three men.'

'Yes. And she will kill again, unless we stop her.'

'What will you do?'

'I have Lord Clavertye's authority. Now I shall use it.'

Under no illusions about the difficulty of arresting Martha Redcliffe and bringing her to justice, Hardcastle gathered his forces. Letters went out from the rectory, to Cole of the Customs and to Mr Juddery of the Excise, asking for assistance. To the colonel of the East Kent Volunteers he wrote again, asking for haste; men were needed at once. Further letters went to the other magistrates of the Marsh and upcountry, warning them and asking them to be watchful. A final letter went to Lord Clavertye, informing him of the situation and naming Martha Redcliffe as his chief suspect.

Sunday, the first day of October, dawned cool and blustery. The wind was from the north, driving breakers inshore to pound against the Dymchurch Wall with a noise like muted thunder. The grasses and reeds of the Marsh bent before the blast. After church, he stopped to talk to Miss Godfrey and Miss Roper.

'You are our saviour,' said Miss Godfrey.

'I am no such thing,' said the rector, smiling and taking her hand. 'I merely did what a friend would do. You must get home now, and stay in out of the wind. I don't suppose you might have a cup of tea to offer an old clergyman? Perhaps on Friday?'

That same Sunday morning, Amelia Chaytor sat and listened to the church bells tolling, their notes distorted by the wind that whipped through the garden. Someone knocked at the front door, and Lucy came into the room, smiling. 'Miss Luckhurst wishes to see you, ma'am.'

'Send her in.' Bessie Luckhurst came into the room a moment later, neat and bright. Mrs Chaytor knew the young woman well and was fond of her. 'What can I do for you, my dear?'

'There's someone wants to meet you, ma'am.'

'Oh? Who?'

'I can't say. I've been told particularly not to say.'

Mrs Chaytor tilted her head to one side and studied Bessie. She knew what the girl's own father did not know, that Bessie was in the employ of the Twelve Apostles as their watcher in St Mary. 'Is this to do with Peter?' she asked.

'Oh, no, ma'am, not at all.'

'Bessie, you are being very mysterious.'

'Yes, ma'am,' said Bessie, her eyes shining with excitement. She lowered her voice a little. 'I was told to say this is about Mr Munro and the other gentlemen that were killed.'

'*What?*'

'And I'm to ask you, ma'am, to come to Blackmanstone tonight, after dark. I'm sorry, ma'am, but that's all I am allowed to say.'

'You are asking me to go alone at night to a ruined church in the middle of the Marsh? Bessie, have you been reading Mrs Vane's novels?'

'Oh, not alone, ma'am. I'll come with you.' The excitement deepened. Behind the gentle face of the landlord's daughter there lurked a soul avid for adventure. *This one will fly the nest before long*, Mrs Chaytor thought. *St Mary in the Marsh is too small for her.* She recognised, all too well, the look in Bessie's eyes. Once upon a time, in another age when life was young and sweet, it had shone in her own.

And because of that, she nodded. 'Very well,' she said. 'I will come. Meet me here at seven; it will be fully dark by then.'

She passed the rest of the day in a fret of impatience, willing the hours to pass, and not even music could soothe her. Darkness drew down across the Marsh, the wind still whistling around the eaves of the house, singing an eerie song of violence and cold. 'This is ridiculously dramatic,' she grumbled to herself, but by a quarter to seven she was waiting in the hall, gloved and booted and cloaked, with her pistol in an inside pocket loaded and primed. More drama, to be sure, she thought; but three people had died.

She heard the crunch of wheels on gravel as the gig was brought round, and a moment later there came a soft knock at the door. She opened it to find Bessie, cloaked like herself.

'What do we say if anyone sees us and asks why two women are driving across the Marsh after dark?' Mrs Chaytor demanded.

'Mrs Jury at Green Farm is unwell, and we're taking her some ointment and hot soup,' came the response.

'Did you make that up just now?'

'Yes, ma'am.'

'Well, we'll have to hope that no one asks to taste the soup. Come along.' The groom passed up a lantern which Mrs Chaytor hung beside her on the gig, and then they were off, riding smoothly up the street past the rectory and the church and out into the country beyond. The blanket of cloud was thin and the radiance of the moon, nearly full, shone through it to bathe the Marsh in a thin, uneven white light. The wind whipped at them, biting their faces with cold. The horse, Asia, did not like the wind either, and twice she shied at shadows and Mrs Chaytor had to shake the reins hard to keep her moving.

They turned onto the Newchurch road. Blackmanstone was yet another of the Marsh's abandoned churches, standing ruined in a field next to the road. Mrs Chaytor drew the gig to a halt and tethered the unhappy horse, then lifted the lantern from its hook and held it up, touching the pistol in her pocket with her free hand. 'Lead on, my dear,' she said to Bessie.

Silent amid the wind, the two women approached the church. All four walls of the nave still stood, though the roof had long since fallen in. A bat flew out of a crevice in the walls and whirled away, squeaking with annoyance. They walked through what had been the west door, and Mrs Chaytor held up the lantern to reveal an interior choked with grasses and weeds that rustled and whispered in the wind.

A young man stood a few yards away among the weeds, one hand on his hip, a cloak drawn back a little to reveal the pistol in his sash. He wore breeches and a coat and high boots, and a broad-brimmed hat shaded his face. 'Good evening, Mrs Chaytor,' he said, his voice light and pleasant.

'You have the advantage of me, sir,' she said. 'May I know your name?'

'On the Marsh I am known as the Rider,' came the response. 'A good name, don't you think? Suitably mysterious, for a smuggler.'

'Very well. Now that we have established how clever you are, why did you drag me out here? Why did you want to see me, in particular?'

'Because I know I can trust you,' came the response. 'You were good to me once, when I did not deserve it.'

'I was . . . We have met?'

In response, the other reached up and swept off the broad-brimmed hat, and then stood still, smiling. Mrs Chaytor froze.

She saw before her a face from the past. She remembered the mop of curly hair that glittered golden in the flickering light of the lantern; she knew that broad mouth, the snub nose, the laughing brown eyes. She remembered that same face from a June day last year; a woman's face, swollen and bruised from a lover's beating. The hair was shorter now, the face harder, but there was no doubting it was the same person.

'Eliza Fanscombe,' said Mrs Chaytor softly.

'In the flesh,' said the young woman.

'What are you doing here?'

'Where else would I be? The Marsh is my home,' said Eliza.

'When did you return?'

'Oh, quite some time ago. After my father was arrested last summer, and my stepmother and I crawled out of St Mary with our tails between our legs, we fetched up in Surrey. Eugénie found work as a governess. I stuck it for about fifteen minutes, then came back to the Marsh. I realised this time that it wouldn't do to be going around as a girl, so I started dressing as a man. I quite like it. You should try it yourself. You'd make a good smuggler, Mrs Chaytor.'

'For heaven's sake, be serious,' said Mrs Chaytor crossly. 'What is this about? Why are you here, and more importantly, why am *I* here?'

The lantern flickered, making the shadows around them jump. 'Oh, this is serious. Deadly serious. For the past eight months I have been in the employ of Martha Redcliffe. She uses me to carry orders to the smuggling gangs, to oversee their work and to hold them to account. I am one of her most trusted lieutenants. And I have come here tonight,' said Eliza Fanscombe, 'to betray her.'

The story was swiftly told. After returning to the Marsh, disguised as a boy, Eliza had joined a smuggling gang in Hythe. Her former habit of going out to watch the gangs on their runs had made her well known around St Mary and New Romney, but in Hythe she was a stranger and no one questioned her new identity or saw through her disguise; no one, that is, until she met Martha Redcliffe. The older woman had been amused by the deception.

'She took a shine to me,' said Eliza. 'She said I reminded her of herself, adventurous and fearless. She took me into her household and made me one of her confidantes. I was the one she entrusted to see that important things were done properly. I know her secrets, or some of them. How much does the rector know about what she's up to?'

'*We* know about the gold, and the fraud,' said Mrs Chaytor, 'and also the opium and the Dutch connection. And we are certain she ordered the killing of Munro, Cotton and Batist.'

'Oh, she did. Noakes was the man who executed them, or that is how she put it. She found out from Batist that Munro was planning to cross over to France. Batist brought Munro out to the *Hoorn* in a rowing boat.'

So Batist had lied about his involvement in the murder; like he had lied about everything else. 'You saw it happen?'

'Yes,' said the young woman. 'They came alongside and Batist climbed aboard the *Hoorn*. Munro began to follow, but Noakes drew a pistol and asked what Munro was doing there. Munro lost his temper, and started demanding we tell him what had happened to his gold. Noakes said if he wanted gold he could have some, and tossed a guinea down into the boat. Then he shot Munro. Captain Sloterdyke wanted to tip his body into the sea, but Noakes said they should leave him there so the others would know what happened to him. It would be a warning, he said, not to ask questions. They were still arguing about it when the revenue cruiser showed up and we had to make a run for it.'

'And Cotton?'

'We had watchers in Canterbury, and knew he was coming to see Hardcastle. I took the orders to Fisky and Noakes and told them the road by which Cotton was travelling. I had nothing to do with Batist.'

'Eliza,' said Mrs Chaytor softly, 'this makes you an accessory to murder. You could hang.'

'Oh, you won't hang me. I can help you hang Martha Redcliffe. And you want that much more.'

'But what you've said just now is enough,' exclaimed Bessie. 'If you testify against her, Eliza, she'll swing.'

'Smugglers don't give evidence in court against their own, Bessie, you know that. Or if they do, they don't live very long. If you find Martha, you can break her in a few hours; all you have

to do is withhold her laudanum,' said the young woman brutally, 'and she'll crack like a bowl of eggs. Same goes for Noakes,
and a couple of the others too; they all use it. But you have to
find Martha first, and you won't do that without my help. She's
clever, devilishly so. She knows old Hardcastle must be onto
her by now, and she's left her house and gone into hiding. She's
moving around the country from one haunt to another, never
in the same place twice. When she's on the drug, she's tougher
than any man, and twice as smart.'

'She is evil,' said Mrs Chaytor.

'Why do you say that? Because she orders people to be killed?
Soldiers do that all the time, so do Preventive men. The law
hangs people after every assize. Martha Redcliffe is no different
from the men around her, except she's more successful. I admire
her,' said Eliza. 'Or I did.'

'Then what changed? Why betray her?'

'*She* changed,' said Eliza. 'In the last fortnight, she has
changed greatly. She is suspicious of everyone now, and she has
begun to take unnecessary risks. Take the killings, for example.
I could see why Munro had to die.'

An image of Cecilia Munro and her baby came briefly into
Mrs Chaytor's mind. 'But killing Cotton was foolish,' Eliza continued. 'He didn't know enough to be dangerous to us; Batist
said as much. He'd seen the ledger, and thought it couldn't be
connected to the bank. Killing Cotton put Fisky and Noakes at
risk, and they had to go into hiding. And Batist; he was our loyal
friend. He would never have betrayed us.'

'He was planning to do exactly that,' said Mrs Chaytor.

'He may have claimed that,' said Eliza, 'but if he did, he was
lying to get Hardcastle off his back. I knew Batist well, and
I knew where his loyalties lay. He was part of the scheme from
the beginning. It was he who told Martha about the plans for

gold smuggling and urged that her gang should get involved, and arranged it so that Faversham and Munro would find it hard to trace the gold once it left the bank.'

'So Batist's loyalty was to Mrs Redcliffe, and not the bank, as he claimed,' said Mrs Chaytor. 'Why? What hold did she have over him?'

'She's the biggest dog in the pack,' said Eliza.

The wind fluttered the lantern's flame. The shadows whispered around them. 'You will have to explain that.'

'Batist was a very clever man, but also a weak one. He needed someone strong to follow, to look up to. He was always searching for approval. In the beginning, Munro was his leader; he'd have followed Munro anywhere. But Martha spotted his weakness. She praised him and encouraged him at every turn, and won his loyalty away from Munro. He became her creature, practically her slave. That's what I mean. He would never have betrayed Martha.'

'But he led Munro to his death.'

'He didn't know they intended kill Munro,' said Eliza. 'Neither did I.'

'Then he is not as clever as you thought he was.' Mrs Chaytor drew breath, angrily. 'Indeed, he was a fool. He lied to us in order to protect Mrs Redcliffe. By doing so, he sealed his own fate. She learned that he spoke to the rector and Mr Stemp, and assumed that he *had* betrayed her.'

'I know. And that is why I am breaking my oath to her. Batist was my friend, and she killed him needlessly. There's a code on the Marsh. You stick together, you protect your own. Martha broke that code. It's time for her to die.'

The wind moaned in the broken walls of Blackmanstone. The moon gleamed suddenly, then went dark. Mrs Chaytor stood for a moment, stilling her nerves. 'And Noakes and Fisk, and the others? How many are there?'

'There's plenty of hired hands, who do as they're told and know nothing about what goes on beneath the surface. Then there's myself, Noakes, Fisky and two English sailors, men who had worked for her and her husband for many years. There's four Dutchmen who have also been with her for years. They're very protective of her, almost like a bodyguard.'

'Dutchmen?'

'Martha's father was Dutch. He came over in the Fifties and married Martha's mother in Hythe. There's still a strong connection with Holland. I believe these men are old family retainers of some sort.'

The last piece of the puzzle fell into place. 'You spoke of loyalty, and sticking together. What about the others? If we take Mrs Redcliffe, they are likely to be arrested too. Some of them, Noakes for certain, will swing. What of your loyalty to them?'

Eliza shrugged. 'They know what Martha did is wrong; Fisky told me himself he didn't like it. If they choose to stick with her now, they must take the consequences.'

There was another long pause. *What an extraordinarily warped morality this young woman has*, Mrs Chaytor thought. *And yet, by her lights, she is sticking to her principles.*

'Very well,' she said finally. 'What do you intend to do?'

'As I said, you need my help to find her. I shall go back to her now. But I will send word of her movements and her plans when I can.'

'Eliza, it is far too dangerous. What happened to Batist could easily happen to you.'

'I know how to handle Martha. She'll never suspect a thing. Don't waste your breath trying to persuade me, Mrs Chaytor,' said Eliza, and she grinned. 'Has anyone ever persuaded me to do something I didn't want to do?'

Appalled still, Mrs Chaytor stood in silence among the wavering shadows. 'I need a go-between,' said Eliza, 'someone who can carry messages from me to Hardcastle. Not you, you're too conspicuous. Nor you, Bessie, I don't want to put you in danger. I'd rather it were a man.'

She wanted to say, *no, do not do this, this is madness*. She wanted to say, *I beg you, come away with me now. We will ensure that you are safe. Do anything but this*.

She said, 'Would you trust Joshua Stemp?'

'Yorkshire Tom? Yes. I'll meet him here at Blackmanstone, day after tomorrow at midnight. If I am prevented from coming, he should wait for me again the next night. I'll give him what news I can.'

'I will tell him.'

Eliza replaced her hat, and her face was once again lost in shadow; but they could hear the smile in her voice. '*Au revoir*, Mrs Chaytor. Journey safely, and keep that pistol under your cloak close to hand. You never know what kind of ne'er-do-wells might be lurking on the Marsh on a night like this.'

22

The Search Begins

A council of war was held at the rectory the following morning. Present were the rector himself; Cole the supervisor of Customs and Mr Juddery of the Excise Service, an intense young man who kept a distance between himself and his rival, Cole; Captain Haddock of the *Stag*, white-haired and grave; Joshua Stemp, parish constable and smuggler, who smiled amiably at Cole and Juddery; Edward Austen the Volunteer captain, who to Hardcastle's relief had finally arrived; Mrs Chaytor, Dr Mackay and, at the last minute, Calpurnia Vane, who slipped in and sat down silently behind the doctor. Hardcastle glanced at her but said nothing.

'I have called you here,' the rector said when all were settled, 'to help me plan and carry out the arrest of Mrs Martha Redcliffe, on charges of murder, conspiracy, treason and smuggling. Her guilt is now certain, and it is equally certain that we can force a confession from her once she is arrested. The task now is to find her.

'Yesterday, an informant close to Mrs Redcliffe came forward, promising to help us. We must hope she can do so; she is not, in my experience, the most reliable of young women.'

'A woman?' said Haddock, frowning. 'Who is this, reverend?'

'Her name is Eliza Fanscombe, and she is the daughter of Mr Fanscombe, my late predecessor as justice of the peace. You won't know of her, Mr Cole, nor you, Captain Austen. She had something of a reputation for wildness, and an unfortunate predilection for smugglers; she used to ride out over the Marsh and follow the gangs when they made their runs. She disappeared for a time after her father's disgrace, but returned to the Marsh and somehow made the acquaintance of Mrs Redcliffe. She claims to be one of Mrs Redcliffe's confidantes.'

'I think that is probably true,' said Mrs Chaytor. 'Miss Fanscombe is a fantasist of a high order, but she is knowledgeable about Mrs Redcliffe's affairs and was at the centre of the execution of the gold conspiracy. Miss Fanscombe has now decided to betray Mrs Redcliffe, to exact revenge for the killing of Mr Batist.'

'Pardon me, ma'am,' said Cole. 'But how do you know this?'

'I spoke to Miss Fanscombe myself last evening. She came to see an old friend in the village, who in turn arranged a meeting with myself.'

'But why did she choose you?'

'Perhaps she thinks I have an honest face,' said Mrs Chaytor tartly.

'I am not easy in my mind,' said Haddock. 'This girl is young, and gently born. To use her in such a fashion, to place her in such grave danger; no, ma'am, I am not easy at all.'

'It was her choice,' said Mrs Chaytor. 'I think she has ceased to be the Eliza Fanscombe we knew, and it may be best if we no longer think of her as a young woman, but as a smuggler. If I had begged her to come away with me and escape the danger, she would not have listened. Had I refused her offer, she would still have returned to Mrs Redcliffe; and probably tried to do something even more dangerous on her own. At least this way she has friends who can help her if things go wrong.'

No one could make an argument against this, though Haddock was clearly still uncomfortable. 'As well as Miss Fanscombe, Mrs Redcliffe has an entourage of armed and very dangerous men,' said the rector. 'Mr Cole in particular already knows how devious she, and they, can be.'

Cole flushed. Juddery did not even try to hide his smile. 'Dr Mackay,' said the rector. 'I asked you here today to hear your professional opinion. Mrs Redcliffe is very strongly addicted to laudanum. What sort of mind might we be dealing with?'

'Opiates affect people in different ways,' said the doctor. 'Many who are heavily addicted become torpid, and sink into lassitude. Clearly this is not the case with Mrs Redcliffe. Others may become unstable as the drug affects the balance of the brain. Their behaviour can seem erratic to outsiders, though the addict continues to believe that their actions and thoughts are perfectly normal. In some cases they are affected by a kind of *paranoea*, a mental derangement that can lead the addict to feel threatened by those around them. If so, they may lash out suddenly and violently. And we know now that some of her followers, including this man Noakes, also consume opium. They may be affected as well.'

'Then you gentlemen must go carefully,' said Calpurnia. 'If Mrs Redcliffe believes she is about to be arrested, she may order her men to attack first.'

Her words were clear and sober, and the men in the room nodded in understanding. 'Captain Austen,' said the rector, 'you and your volunteers will undertake the search for Mrs Redcliffe and her men. If we receive any information from Miss Fanscombe, it will be relayed promptly to you. However, I do not propose to rely solely on Miss Fanscombe, who, as Mrs Chaytor says, is a fantasist. You will begin, if you please, by helping me to search Mrs Redcliffe's house and business premises in Hythe. If there are any clues to Mrs Redcliffe's whereabouts, we must find them, and quickly. Every day that Miss Fanscombe remains in that woman's company increases her danger.'

Austen nodded. 'Seems likely these fellows won't give in without a fight,' he said.

'Your Volunteers may use lethal force to defend themselves, but if at all possible, I want these men taken alive. That applies particularly to Mrs Redcliffe.' The rector thought about Cecilia and her child, the heartbroken Cotton family and the shattered, sorrowing father in Ashford. 'There must be no easy escape for her,' he said. 'She must live to face the assize court, and the gallows.'

Austen nodded. 'I understand.'

'Mr Cole, Mr Juddery, I desire that your two services concentrate on the flow of contraband. Batist claimed there was enough gold for another run. We know now that Batist was lying about nearly everything, but I do not want to take another chance. Keep searching for the gold. We may also expect the opium shipments to continue, and in very large quantity, so I would be grateful if you would search for these also. Some of the opium has been stored at Midley, but I expect by now it will have been moved further inland, ready for transport to London. Search every barn, every sheep pen, every lookers' hut, every crypt and croft. Do not give up until you find what we are looking for.

'Captain Haddock; we need you to track down the *Hoorn*, and take her if you possibly can. We know now that she is heavily armed.'

The rector looked at Stemp for confirmation. 'Four six-pounder cannon and a long nine-pounder,' said the parish constable. 'The nine is probably a bow chaser.' He repeated what he had said to Bertrand. 'That's a lot of metal, sir.'

'We've guns of our own,' said Haddock, his face unmoving.

'Good,' said Hardcastle. 'You have your orders, gentlemen. God speed.'

*

The others departed, all but Mrs Chaytor. Calpurnia and Dr Mackay walked out into the rectory garden, talking earnestly about opium. *I wish they would get on with it*, the rector thought.

'We are taking a grave risk,' he said quietly. 'We are gambling that we can find Martha Redcliffe before she learns Eliza is betraying her. I hope I have done enough.'

'You have done all you can do,' said Mrs Chaytor, and she shivered. 'I cannot bear to think what they will do to her if they learn the truth.'

'She knows the risks,' said the rector, heavily.

'Does she? I suppose perhaps she does; which somehow makes it worse.'

'What do you mean?'

'Eliza Fanscombe is only nineteen. What happened to her, Marcus? How did she end up in the company of men like Noakes and Fisk? How did she become so callous, so brutal in thought and demeanour?'

'Do you think she is callous? From what you say, she sounds like the same romantic little fool who used to go riding out across the Marsh, shouting and cheering the smugglers on. She is still living in a world of dreams.'

'No, Marcus, she is not. She described Munro's death without flinching. And she spoke about breaking Martha Redcliffe like a bowl of eggs, without an ounce of emotion in her voice. You should have heard her. *Martha broke that code. It's time for her to die.* Cold and hard as the ring of a bell.'

Hardcastle said nothing.

'A year ago she seemed only a silly, flirtatious girl. Now she talks about violent death as an everyday matter. I'm frightened for her, and not just for her safety. Suppose she does live through this. How will she ever come back to a normal life?'

'Perhaps she does not wish to do so,' the rector said gently.

'I should have talked her out of it,' said Mrs Chaytor. 'I should have begged her, pleaded with her not to go back. I should have done everything in my power to take her to a place of safety. If she could get away from them for a while, come back to live in the real world, there might be some hope of restoring her.'

She spread her hands suddenly. 'But instead, I did nothing. I let her go.'

'Why did you do so, do you think?' asked the rector.

She sat staring at the fire. 'I don't know.'

'For once, my dear, I am wiser than you. I do know. She is nineteen and romantic and foolish, but she has also chosen her own destiny. You are repelled by the choice she has made, and are worried sick about her fate. But in another part of your mind, you understand her; and, perhaps, there is even a far, dark corner that respects her.'

'Are you saying she is like me?' Mrs Chaytor demanded.

'No one is like you. You are the most extraordinary woman I have ever encountered. But perhaps there is no one quite like Eliza Fanscombe either.'

'If this is meant to comfort me, it does not. I am sorry; I do not mean to offend you. But you blame yourself still for Cotton's death, because you put him in jeopardy. I feel the same about Eliza.'

'But you did not place Eliza in jeopardy. She did that herself. I won't tell you not to reproach yourself; that would be an insult to your intelligence. Yes, you failed to persuade her to abandon her chosen course. But her choice to continue is her responsibility.'

'That is sophistry. You see your neighbour walking into a burning house; you call out a warning, but he continues into the house. Do you then have no responsibility to rush after him and pull him out of the fire?'

'I believe I did once help you escape from a burning house,' he said gravely.

'Oh, don't sit there looking superior. You haven't won this argument, and you know it.' But she had relaxed a little. 'And Batist? Which version of the story do we believe? His own, that he was working to help save the bank, and became aware of what Mrs Redcliffe was doing but was too terrified to tell the truth? Or Eliza's, that he was working for her all along?'

'I suspect the truth lies somewhere in the middle. That he was secretly helping Mrs Redcliffe from the beginning, I do not doubt. But he was also genuinely afraid of her. He went back to Ashford, I am convinced, to destroy any papers that might connect him with Mrs Redcliffe, the gold or the opium. After that, he intended to disappear from view, perhaps by escaping back to France. We will never know.' The rector sighed. 'If only he had told me the truth, I might have been able to save him.'

'He chose instead to walk into the burning house,' she said. 'No; you *are* right. We can't save everyone, no matter how much we would wish to. Some people are simply hell-bent on destruction, and there is nothing that can be done about it. That is what my head tells me.'

'And your heart?' he asked.

Her blue eyes were wide as she stared into the fire. 'I cannot help it. If anything happens to Eliza Fanscombe, I will never forgive myself.'

Orders went out across the Marsh. The Preventive men swept in cordons over the fields, searching every barn and shed and cellar, stopping wagons and carts and lifting the covers to examine the contents. They met no opposition save for volleys of abuse from the locals, who hated the Preventives with a bitterness that was bred in the bone; neither did they find any trace of gold or opium. The crypt at Midley, oozing with water, was empty, guarded only by a lone mouldering skeleton. The other ruined churches on the Marsh were similarly bare.

Edward Austen's men walked quietly into Hythe, with cloaks over their red uniform coats and their muskets covered with blankets so as not to attract attention. Reaching Mrs Redcliffe's house on the hill above the church, they surrounded the building and moved inside, followed by the rector. All the inhabitants and servants had gone, leaving behind only an elderly caretaker and his wife; the furniture was covered in dust sheets, and everything of value had been removed. The lady of the house had left nothing behind that would hint at her plans, or her present whereabouts.

Yes, Mrs Redcliffe had gone away, the frightened caretaker confirmed; no, he did not know where, or for how long. It was clear that he knew nothing.

Captain Austen went on to raid the warehouse belonging to Mrs Redcliffe's shipping business, and found it empty and echoing, its cargoes long since carried away. Two small coasters moored in the haven were searched as well. Nothing was found. By now word had got out that there were redcoats in town, and the streets of Hythe were turning hostile. Austen withdrew his men, pursued by barking dogs and a shower of bottles flung from the upper windows of houses.

'There's no sign at the warehouse that she departed in haste,' said Austen, reporting to the rector. 'Everything is clean and orderly. I'd say she's been preparing for some time.'

'She's been at least one step ahead of us all the way,' said the rector. 'Very well. She needs to keep in touch with Sloterdyke and the *Hoorn*, so she won't go very far from the coast. Beat the hills behind Saltwood and Lympne; if you find nothing, continue to work your way west.'

'That's broken country,' warned Austen. 'There could be a hundred hiding places there, and while we are searching one, she will be moving on to the next.'

'I know.'

That night Amelia Chaytor slept little, and she rose early, tingling with nerves. She made her usual breakfast on strong, sweet coffee and went out for a walk, hoping the exercise might calm her. But the day was bright and cool and windy and the sea was running high; the rush of wind and bitter taste of salt in the air only heightened her senses. She returned home and attacked her harpsichord, playing with a violence that rattled the drawing room windows and made the younger maidservant cover her ears and scurry into the kitchen.

So engrossed was she in the music that she did not hear the gig arriving outside the door. Only at Lucy's knock did she lift her fingers from the keyboard and look up.

'Yes?'

'Mr Grebell Faversham to see you, ma'am.'

Amelia slammed her fingers down onto the keyboard again with a clash of tortured strings. 'That simpering nitwit is the last person in the world I want to see.'

'I'll tell him you're not at home, ma'am,' said Lucy, starting to withdraw.

'No, wait.' Amelia held up a hand. It was possible, just possible, that Grebell had come to tell her something useful, something that might help in the search. 'Show him in, please, Lucy.'

The young man who entered her drawing room looked like death. His face was white and his eyes, normally so prominent, were sunken and red. *For God's sake*, she thought irritably, *what is he doing here? Don't tell me he has come to pour out his heart again. Did he not hear me, when last we spoke in Rye?*

'Sit down, sir,' she said. She did not offer refreshment. 'What brings you here? Are there further problems at the bank?'

'I fear I do not know. Mr Martin made it clear, the day he arrived, that my services were no longer required. He has appointed his own manager in my place.'

That was hardly the most surprising news. 'Then what is your business here, Mr Faversham?'

'I have come to beg your forgiveness. I know I broke my word to you, and it is tearing me apart. I cannot bear it that you should be angry with me. Please tell me there is some way that I can make things right, and . . . and earn your esteem once more.'

She stared at him. She saw a pathetic, tiresome young man, gazing at her with the eyes of a puppy begging for affection. A few simple words would probably be enough to reassure him and send him away. But she was already nerve-sick, and there was no room in her heart for compassion. She spoke coldly.

'You promised that you would not importune me,' she said.

'I . . . I have no wish to do so. I only desire that you should not think ill of me. Tell me that you forgive me and I promise you, I will go away and never see you again. I will leave your life forever. Only, spare me a few words of comfort.'

She stared at him, her blue eyes unforgiving. 'But I do think ill of you, Mr Faversham. You promised to help my friends, and then you abandoned them. You were the manager of the bank; the responsibility was yours. You could have overridden your father's orders and made an exception for Miss Godfrey and Miss Roper. At the very least, you could have warned us the day the run began. But no. You lacked the courage to stand up to your father and do what you promised, solemnly and faithfully, to do for me and my friends.'

She saw the despair in his eyes, but hardened her heart. 'You came to me seeking forgiveness. You do not have it. Now, please leave me alone.'

She watched him rise and walk slowly out of the room. She heard the front door close behind him.

'*Damn*,' she said, and once again slammed her hand down onto the keys with a force that jarred her fingers and sent jangling, discordant notes echoing for a long time in the room.

At midnight on the 3rd of October, Joshua Stemp walked into the ruined nave of Blackmanstone church carrying a lantern in one hand and a pistol in the other. A figure wrapped in a cloak waited for him, hat pulled down over its face.

'God damn,' said Stemp. 'I know you. You were the one with that blasted Puckle gun. Noakes claimed you didn't exist.'

The figure swept off her hat and bowed. 'That was Noakes's feeble attempt at humour. The man you were looking for was not a man. Well met, Yorkshire Tom.'

'Miss Fanscombe.'

'Let's stick to our Marsh names. I am the Rider.'

'Are you now?' Stemp surveyed her. 'Would you really have shot me?'

'You'll never know,' said the Rider cheerfully.

'All right, enough games. Where can we find your chief?'

'I can't tell you, not yet. She still changes locations every night, and she doesn't tell us where we are going until we get there. I'm trying to work out if there is a pattern.'

'Tell us some of the places you have been, and we'll set a watch in case she decides to return.'

'We've been upcountry the last couple of nights, a hut in the wood near Monks Horton and another on the hill above Postling. But we were down on the Marsh before that, at Burmarsh and then a barn near Newchurch.'

'So she is sticking close to Hythe.'

'Yes, for the moment. She may be waiting for the next opium run, but I think she is also staying in touch with her own contacts upcountry. She has yet to sell the opium from the last run.'

'And where is that opium?' asked Stemp.

'I don't know. She moved everything out of Midley, but where it went after that, she didn't tell me. I know some of the boys were out for several nights, shifting it in small batches, but that's all.'

'Come along now, Rider. You said you were her confidante.'

'I also said she is becoming more secretive. She trusts no one now, not even me. She barely sleeps, even with the laudanum. I think she is starting to break.'

'Well, your job is to help us find her before she does.'

'You don't need to tell me that,' the Rider snapped. 'I'm the one taking the risks here, remember?'

'All right, keep your wig on. Can you tell me one thing I don't understand? Back at the end of July I found Noakes bringing in a single chest of opium in a boat. But I found twenty boxes at Midley, maybe more. Surely they didn't bring it in one box at a time?'

'No. What you saw was the first run, an essay. We brought in one box to see if we could ship it to London and sell it easily. When that worked, we knew we had a system. Then Sloterdyke started running in tons of the stuff.'

Stemp nodded. 'I'm glad that's sorted,' he said. 'I don't like mysteries. When do we meet again?'

'I need time to work out what she is doing. Give me until Saturday. I'll know something more definite by then.'

*

Two more days passed. The searchers made their weary way across the hills and marsh, battered by the incessant wind. Each evening Austen and Cole and Juddery rode back to St Mary to report. Nothing.

'Be patient,' said Hardcastle. 'She cannot hide forever.' He thought that Miss Fanscombe was probably right; Martha Redcliffe could not go too far away from the Marsh, not with a full shipment of opium waiting to be sold and another on the way. *I will give Mrs Redcliffe this*, he thought, *she is bloody persistent.*

But then, so am I.

On Friday afternoon, restless and worried, the rector called on Miss Godfrey and Miss Roper. They were, they assured him, much improved, the worry and strain of the last month entirely forgotten; they were their old selves again. But Miss Roper's eyes were no longer as bright as they had been, and the tremor was still there in her hand. He realised, with some pain, that it would probably never go away.

He returned to the rectory an hour later to find Cole waiting in the hall. The Customs man's face was sharp with excitement. 'We've found the opium, reverend. In a barn on Oxney. There's at least fifty boxes there. Two tons, probably more.'

It wasn't gold; but it might be enough to restore Cole's battered reputation within his service. And two tons of opium had been removed from the market, and could do no more damage. 'Well done,' the rector said warmly.

'I intend to bring the opium to New Romney, reverend. May I have your permission to use the gaol as a storehouse? It's the most secure building in the town.'

The rector paused. Customs had a bonded warehouse in Rye, which would be more secure still; but Rye had its own Collector of Customs who, if the opium came into his jurisdiction, would probably try to claim the credit for its seizure. Cole deserved a chance to regain some credit of his own. Reluctantly, he said, 'Very well, but for a few days only. I'll swear in some special constables to help you guard the building until the East Kent Volunteers arrive.'

'My men can manage, sir.'

'Don't be a fool. When Mrs Redcliffe learns you have seized the opium, she will come after it with force. You will need all the men you can muster.'

Hardcastle set out for New Romney the following morning, but had driven only half a mile when the dog cart, battered by two months of long journeys, lurched sideways with a crack and then sagged down towards the ground. Spilled from his seat, the rector climbed to his feet and then limped around, inspecting the damage. One spring had broken, and when the bodywork crashed down it had snapped the axle as well. Muttering some very unclerical language, he unharnessed the horse and rode back to the village, gave orders for the collection and repair of the dog cart and then rode the two miles to New Romney.

It was Saturday, market day, and the long street was busy as usual. All eyes were on the column of wagons drawn up outside the gaol, and the long boxes that Cole and his men were unloading and carrying inside. Armed Customs officers were already crouching in the upper windows. The rector walked inside and found Cole directing his men as they stacked the boxes in the cells.

'We've got the lot, reverend. Fifty-two boxes, more than two tons. This is an entire shipload.'

'They must have run this in at the same time as they took away the gold,' said the rector, thinking of that chaotic night when the French refugees arrived. 'Well, we've stymied them now. And if the *Stag* can track down the *Hoorn* and end her career, we might just break up the entire operation. Well done again, Cole.'

'Thank you, reverend.' The rector walked next door to the town hall, where four reasonably reliable men were waiting. They were fishermen and smugglers, but they were also friends of Joshua Stemp; they would obey his orders, up to a point. He swore them in as constables, and told them what was wanted. 'These men are no ordinary free traders. They are violent killers, who have murdered several people already. They've also been helping to arm our country's enemies against us.'

'Are you talking about Noakes, reverend?' demanded one of the fishermen.

'I am.'

'Say no more. I hate that bastard.'

'And his dog,' said another man. The rest nodded.

'Good. Then charge your weapons and go next door. You'll take orders from Mr Cole.' He smiled at them. 'It won't be for very long, I promise.'

Out in the street Hardcastle met Ebenezer and Florian Tydde hurrying towards him, the older brother with a pistol and the younger with a heavy cudgel. Ebenezer waved towards the town hall. 'Is this to do with Mr Munro, reverend?'

It was hard to tell what rumours were flying around the town, but Hardcastle nodded. 'We'd like to help, if we may,' said Ebenezer. 'Seeing how it was us that found him. We feel responsible, like.'

'If we can help take the men who killed him, that would be a good thing,' said Florian seriously. 'Mother would sleep easier too.'

The rector swore them in, and sent them to join Cole. He watched the busy street, full of people, conscious of the staring eyes. Any one of them could be a watcher for Martha Redcliffe. Word was probably already on its way to her. And she would not take this defeat lightly. Sooner or later, probably sooner, she would make her response.

'I wish that blasted girl would get on with it,' he muttered. Stemp was due to meet Miss Fanscombe again that night. He became aware of someone at his elbow.

'Yes? What is it?'

'Begging your pardon, sir, but are you Reverend Hardcastle? From St Mary in the Marsh?'

'I am.'

'I thought I recognised you, reverend. I'm from Mr Dobbs in Rye. He sends this letter to you, urgent. I was on my way to St Mary, but then I saw you in the street.'

'Thank you.' The rector reached into his pocket for money for the messenger and then broke the seal and read. Standing in the middle of the bustling street, he felt the blood leave his face.

'Oh, dear God,' he said quietly.

'What is it?' asked Mrs Chaytor. She had risen to greet him; he saw how tense she was, and the lines at the corners of her eyes. 'Is it Eliza?'

He shook his head. 'I have had a message from Dobbs, the magistrate in Rye. Grebell Faversham was found dead yesterday evening. He had been shot.'

She stood motionless for several seconds before she found her voice. 'Tell me what happened,' she said, sinking slowly into a chair.

'One of the household grooms heard a gunshot. They found Grebell in the stables soon after. He was already unconscious, and died a few minutes later.'

Hardcastle knelt, taking her hands in his. 'Amelia, I am so sorry. This was not a murder. It seems quite clear that Grebell took his own life.'

'I see,' she said. Her face was white, her eyes a deep and vivid blue as the shock began to take hold.

'This was enclosed in Dobbs's letter,' said the rector. 'It was found in his room. It is addressed to you.'

Hardcastle handed over the single sheet of folded paper. She took it with numb hands. 'Do you wish me to remain while you read it?' he asked.

'Thank you, but no. I should quite like to be alone. Do you mind?'

He bowed and left the room, pausing for a quick word with Lucy in the hall. Mrs Chaytor waited until she heard the front door close behind him, and then broke the seal. The letter contained a single, shaky line of writing.

I have no wish to live in a world where you despise me.

23

Blackmanstone

That Saturday night, Joshua Stemp waited at Blackmanstone for more than an hour. There was no sign of the Rider.

He reported her non-appearance to the rector on Sunday morning. 'I'm worried, reverend.'

'I know. So am I.' Hardcastle had many concerns that morning; Eliza Fanscombe's non-appearance was only one of them. 'She said earlier that if she missed the first meeting, she would come instead the following night. Go again tonight, if you will, and see what transpires.'

After church, the rector walked down to Sandy House and knocked at the door. A tearful Lucy greeted him and ushered him into the hall.

'She won't see anyone, reverend. She won't take food or drink, only a little coffee this morning. She just sits there and looks out the window, with that letter beside her. I've never seen her this bad, sir, not since Mr Chaytor died.'

'Lucy; did Grebell Faversham call again last week?'

'He did, reverend, but only briefly. She was angry with him, and sent him away.'

'Ask her, please, if she will see me.'

'Yes, reverend.' He waited for a long time in the hall before Lucy returned. There were fresh tears on the young housekeeper's face as she ushered him into the drawing room.

Mrs Chaytor sat facing the window. She did not turn her head to look at him. 'I could have written when I was in a calmer state of mind,' she said before Hardcastle could speak. 'I could have sent a letter, offering him my forgiveness. That is all he wanted. To know that I did not hold him in contempt.'

Hardcastle waited. 'I was so worried about Eliza that I could think of nothing else,' she said. 'Grebell was a nuisance, a distraction. I wanted him to go away and leave me alone. And he did.'

Still he said nothing.

'I hope you have not come to offer me words of consolation,' she said. 'Because I do not want to hear them.'

'I have come to do whatever I can,' said the rector. 'If you wish to talk, I will listen. If you wish me simply to be silent, I will do that too. And I will understand if you prefer to be alone.'

'I know your intentions are kind,' she said. 'But I am not . . . I am not ready to be helped. I would esteem it a great favour if you would go.'

Hardcastle nodded and turned towards the door. 'There is just one thing,' he said. 'Eliza did not come to Blackmanstone last night, as she said she would.'

This time her head did turn, and the agony in her blue eyes shocked him to the core. 'Stemp will go again tonight,' he said. 'I will let you know what transpires.'

'Please do,' she said, and then she turned back to face the window again.

'About bloody time,' said Joshua Stemp. It was well past midnight on Sunday, and he had had begun to imagine the worst. 'Where've you been, my girl?'

The young woman was breathing hard. 'Running,' she said. 'I haven't much time. We're miles away, over beyond Appledore, and I need to be back by dawn. She knows about the opium, and where it is. She's coming after it.'

'In person?'

'No. Fisky and I are in charge, with some of the sailors. We're supposed to raid the gaol tomorrow evening. She's going off with Noakes and the Dutchmen on some other errand.'

'What errand? Where?'

'I don't know, for Christ's sake! I told you, she trusts no one now, not with her whole plan.'

'How will you get into the gaol?'

'We'll come in quietly, if we can, through the rear courtyard. If it turns out the guards are alert, then we go in full tilt instead. Either way, we knock out the guards, load as much of the opium as we can into wagons and run it down to the beach. There we'll light a blue false fire as a signal. A ship will come in and take us off. We'll land the opium somewhere else along the coast.'

'Just like that?'

'She says it will work. I think it's a damn' fool scheme, and Fisky agrees. Hardcastle isn't stupid, at least not when he's sober. He'll remember what happened to the gold, and he'll have a ring of men around the prison, waiting.'

Stemp watched her in the lantern light, dark shadows wavering and swaying all around them. 'You can throw in your hand now and come with me, if you want.'

'No,' said the young woman. 'I've sworn to help you trap her, and I will.'

'What happens after you offload the opium again? Or if you can't recover it at all?'

'I'm to go to her warehouse in Hythe on Wednesday. She'll find a way to leave a message, telling Fisky and me when and where to meet her.'

The young woman turned for a moment, glancing at the shadows behind her, and then looked back at Stemp. 'I reckon that's our best chance to take her. As soon as I have her message, I'll come again to Blackmanstone. Meet me here at dusk on Wednesday, and I'll tell you where to find her. Tell Hardcastle to have the Volunteers standing ready.'

'What about the gaol? Are you going to attack it?'

'We'll have to. Martha will get suspicious if we don't.'

'All right. But keep your head down, my girl. We need you in one piece till this is over.'

She grinned at him. 'As if Cole and those Customs louts could hit anything they aimed at. Don't you worry, Yorkshire Tom. I'll be around on the Marsh for a long time yet.'

'Yes,' said Stemp. 'Lucky us.'

He gave the news to the rector on Monday morning. 'I reckon she's come up with the goods at last, reverend.'

'So it would seem.' He looked at Stemp's face and saw how tired the constable was. 'Are you fit to carry on?'

'Don't mind me, reverend. I'm used to short nights.'

'Then go to New Romney, if you please. Give Mr Cole my compliments, warn him to expect an attack. Ask him to get word to Captain Haddock. Once the captain sees a blue light onshore, he should proceed to that spot and intercept the *Hoorn*. Let us have no mistakes this time.'

'Very good, reverend. What about Hythe and this warehouse? Should we watch it?'

Hardcastle thought for a moment, then shook his head. 'No. If our watchers are spotted, Mrs Redcliffe will change her plans. We could lose her entirely. We could also put Miss Fanscombe in greater danger. Hard though it is, we must trust that she knows what she is doing and let her carry her plan through.'

After Stemp departed, the rector went once again to Sandy House. Mrs Chaytor still sat in the drawing room facing the window. She did not seem to have moved since the day before.

'Stemp has seen Eliza, and she is safe.' He told her the news. She watched him, unblinking. 'You have decided to go ahead,' she said finally.

'God help me, I have. We are thrusting her into very real danger now, but I see no choice. I have taken the responsibility for this business onto my shoulders, and I must see it through to the end.'

He paused, looking at her strained white face. 'If something goes wrong, and she dies; well, as you said, you may not be able to forgive yourself. But I very much hope you will be able to forgive me. For I shall be in sore and desperate need of forgiveness.'

The day had been fine, but after sunset the temperature plummeted. At first the air was bright and clear, the stars brilliant in the dark dome of heaven. Dungeness lighthouse gleamed in the distance. The moon, a little past full, climbed into the sky and cast a shimmering path over the sea.

Then the cold deepened, and the fog came. Rising from both sea and land, it rolled over the flat land of the Marsh and in an instant swallowed up the stars.

The darkness was not complete. Moonlight filtered down through the fog, a dim, opaque light refracting off the vapour, swirling and shivering. In that uneven glow, the shadows of running men flickered for a moment, sliding in and out of vision. Boots thudded on cobblestones. The shod hooves of a horse clanked dully, leaving echoes behind them.

In the upper windows of New Romney gaol, they saw the shadows below and took aim. Orange flashes and flares lit up the courtyard, and the crash of pistol shots reverberated in the heavy air. The running men halted and dived for cover. 'Did you get one?' Florian Tydde asked his brother as he reloaded.

'Nah. Made him think about things, though.' Pistols fired back from the courtyard, and a ball struck the windowsill not far from Ebenezer's head; he jerked back with a curse, then thrust his own pistol out the window and fired again. More shots, now from the front of the building. They could hear Cole yelling, directing his men to stand to their posts.

'Watch out! Here they come!' Shadows darted once more in the fogbound courtyard. Ebenezer fired again and other pistols blazed, but the running men did not falter. Something hammered hard on the door below them. Ebenezer dropped his ramrod and cursed, scrabbling on the floor to find it. The hammering went on, men trying to batter the door down. Florian ran out of the room for a moment, then returned carrying a heavy object. He thrust this out of the window and held it for a moment. There came a splashing sound, then cursing and shouting from below. More pistols barked, and the hammering ceased.

'They're falling back! Well done, lads! We've held them!'

Ebenezer found his ramrod and began belatedly to reload. 'Flo,' he asked his younger brother, 'did you just do what I think you did?'

Florian grinned at him in the wan light. 'You mean, empty a pisspot over their heads?' He held up the empty chamber pot. 'Worked, didn't it?'

Swiftly the shadows faded through the fog. Silence fell once more in New Romney.

The fog that rose on the Marsh also flowed up over the hills of the Weald of Kent, and hung in tendrils in the trees outside Magpie Court. Had anyone been there to see it, the smoke rising from a corner of one of the big barns might have seemed to be part of the fog. Only later did a little orange glow of flame appear, creeping slowly up the wall.

The barn was well alight by the time one of the kitchen servants, going out for a pail of water from the well, saw the blaze. She fled back inside, shouting the alarm. Parrish the butler heard her, and roused the rest of the household. Within moments Maudsley and all the servants were outside, forming a bucket brigade from the well and throwing water onto the flames. Distracted by the fire, they did not see the four men who approached the house from the far side, quietly jemmied open one of the library windows and climbed inside.

Cecilia Munro had retired early, but woke when she heard the noise of the fire. Her room was on the opposite side of the house to the fire, and she could not see the flames. Puzzled, she went out in her nightdress to find out what was happening. From the landing outside her room, a flicker of movement caught her eye. She looked down to see a dark silent figure moving up the stair.

She did not think; she reacted. She fled noiselessly on bare feet to the nursery, where she plucked her son from his cradle and held him fast, looking around wildly for a hiding place. Inspiration came; there was a dressing chest, left over from the time when the nursery had been a bedroom. It was half-full of linen still, but there was more than enough room for a small woman and a baby to hide. She climbed inside, holding the infant, and pulled the lid down on top of her. Then she sat silently, trying to still the trip hammer beat of her heart. The child still slept; she prayed he would not wake.

The door of the nursery opened. She heard booted feet and the sound of a man's hoarse breathing. He was looking around the room. He was searching for the baby, or herself, or both. She held her breath, trying not to make even the slightest of sounds. She heard the booted feet move towards the chest. The child stirred, giving a little hiccuping sigh against her cheek.

A scream from below; the voice of one of the maidservants, discovering the intruders. Another cry from near at hand; the wet nurse, who must have come out of her own room next to the nursery, aroused too by the noise. A hoarse male voice below shouted something in a language she could not understand. The man in the nursery hesitated, then hurried out of the room. She heard his boots thundering on the stair, and then the crash of the front door being flung open as her father and his men came pounding into the house, shouting.

The Faversham family had left the scene of the tragedy in Rye and retreated to their small country house a few miles north of the town. There Charlotte joined them, rushing back from Shadoxhurst when the news came. She found her family crushed. Her father, a shadow of the elegant, flamboyant man he had once been, sat staring into space; her mother, when not in a laudanum-induced sleep, was tearful and incoherent. Grebell had been her oldest child, and her favourite. Rafe, her younger brother, was silent with shock.

They passed the evening in the drawing room, sitting by the fire. Few words were spoken; no one knew what to say. Charlotte felt as if the light and warmth had gone out of the world. She had never known anything except a cheerful, frivolous life of pleasure; she had never expected to know anything else. Her friend Sissy's widowhood had been a jolt, to be sure; but her own world, her own bubble, had remained intact.

Now she felt sick, unable to think, half-paralysed by sorrow and shock. *Why?* she asked herself over and over again. Why, why did he do it?

Grief led inevitably to exhaustion. Her mother took another dose of laudanum and retired early. By the time the clock chimed ten Charlotte's body was weak and she could no longer think at all. She kissed her father and brother and then went wearily upstairs to bed, her limbs feeling like lead. She crawled into her nightdress and lay down on the bed, feeling her heartbeat thudding, a sick taste still in her mouth. She was worn out, but she could not sleep. Dimly in the distance she heard her father come up to his room, and a little later her brother.

The house had a small central section with two short wings. Her parents and brother slept in the centre of the house, but she liked her room in the east wing because it had a window that gave a view down the hill and out over Romney Marsh to the sea. She lay there now in the silence of the night, staring at the ceiling. After a while some of the lassitude passed, and she rose and went to the window and stood looking out. She saw how fog covered the Marsh and lapped around the foot of the hill, glowing white in the moon.

From somewhere in the house came a bump, like a door shutting hard. The servants locking up, she thought. The night air was cool, and she shivered a little when she climbed back into bed. Suddenly she was very tired once more, and she closed her eyes.

When she opened them again, there was a shadow over the bed. A moment of incomprehension; then she realised the shadow was a cloaked and masked man. She opened her mouth to scream, but a gloved hand clamped over her mouth. The blade of a knife flashed in the moonlight. 'Lie still,' the man hissed.

'Here,' murmured another voice. 'Give her this.'

Strong fingers pulled her jaws open. Suddenly her mouth was full of liquid, flowery and spicy but with a foul, cloying taste beneath. She tried to spit it out but could not. Eventually, in order to breathe, she had to swallow. Almost at once she felt the torpor spreading out across her body and rising up to smother her brain. The last thing she heard was the distant sound of a dog, barking.

*

Triumphant and sleepless, Humphrey Cole knocked at the rectory door on Tuesday morning while the rector was at breakfast. 'We held them off, without loss to ourselves. I didn't pursue them, as the fog was thick and I didn't want to fall into an ambush.'

He's learning, the rector thought. 'Well done. And the ship?'

'The Dutchman might have slipped past *Stag* in the fog. But no blue lights have been reported, so I reckon the smugglers retreated without summoning the ship at all.'

'That means Mrs Redcliffe's men are still somewhere on the Marsh. I'll send the Volunteers to track them. Maintain your guard on the gaol, if you please. It is possible that they will make a second attempt.'

'If they do, we'll be waiting for them.' Cole was fiercely exultant. The humiliation of the gold was long forgotten now.

And then, the messages came.

The first was a note in Maudsley's hand, describing quickly the attack on the house. The fire in the barn was meant to lure him out while the raiders kidnapped Cecilia and her baby, and only the young woman's quick thinking had prevented them from doing so. Maudsley had called up all his able-bodied tenants, left half to guard the house and set off with the other half and a pair of bloodhounds to track the raiders. He would report, he said, if there was any news.

The rector was still digesting this when the second message arrived from Rye, full of horror. Charlotte Faversham had been taken from her bed. A note had been left on her pillow, just three words: *Punishment for traitors.*

Stemp arrived at the rectory a few minutes later, in response to the rector's urgent summons. 'What is it, reverend?'

Hardcastle showed him the messages. Stemp read them, his pocked face quiet and still. 'I don't understand,' he said at the end. 'These young women are innocent.'

'Not in Martha Redcliffe's eyes,' said the rector. 'Do you recall what Dr Mackay said about *paranoea*? She has decided that all her partners have betrayed her, even Maudsley. Two are now dead, and her intention is that Faversham and Maudsley should suffer as well.'

He thought of how Martha Redcliffe had befriended Sissy Munro, visiting her and offering comfort to the widow of the man she had killed. Had this been her real purpose, to survey the house and prepare for such an attack? He repressed a shudder.

'They may also use Charlotte Faversham as a hostage,' he said. 'If we get too close to the gang, they might threaten to kill her.'

'Then I hope they rot in hell,' said Stemp.

'They will, Joshua, because you and I shall send them there. Maudsley, thank God, has kept his head. He is on their trail, and has dogs. I shall send every man I can to join him. I want every justice of the peace, constable, Volunteer and Preventive man out searching for Charlotte Faversham. I shall ask Dobbs for help as well; damn the county boundaries, this is a Rye girl that's been taken. And I shall send to the magistrates of Ashford and Dover, too, and ask for help.'

'What about Lord Clavertye, reverend?'

'By the time our esteemed deputy lord-lieutenant stops playing politics in London and gets down to the Marsh, it will be too late. Go to New Romney and tell Cole these are my orders. He is to leave a small guard on the gaol, and get the rest out onto the Marsh. I shall go to Juddery, and Captain Austen.'

'And if the smugglers do come back, reverend?' Stemp asked. 'Suppose the kidnapping is a ruse to draw our men away while they come back and attack the gaol again?'

'I rather think it was the other way around. The attack on the gaol was never meant to succeed, whatever Eliza may think; it was a bluff, to concentrate our attention on New Romney while the gang's real purpose was elsewhere. I may be wrong, but it's a chance we have to take. Charlotte Faversham's life is more important.'

All through that bitter, fogbound day they searched, and searched in vain. Trackers from Rye picked up a trail on the Walland Marsh but then lost it in the bleak wastes south of Midley. Cole and Juddery, working together for once, set up cordons between Midley and the sea, sweeping the ground and looking for more tracks, but although they found a few footprints that might or might not belong to the kidnappers, each trail soon petered out again in the water and shingle beyond Lydd. Maudsley's bloodhounds traced the Magpie Court raiders down onto the Marsh as far as the big sewer east of Newchurch, but there the scent ended. The gang must have waded or swum down the sewer to throw off the dogs. Austen's men, alerted, combed both banks of the sewer looking for tracks where the men might have come out of the water, but they too found nothing.

The day drew to its grim end, dusk falling across the empty fields. 'By now, they're hours ahead of us,' said Edward Austen in a moment of despair. 'They could have doubled back into the hills; they could be in Hythe; they could be in hell, for all we know.'

'Can your men continue?' asked Hardcastle.

'No one is going home, sir, until that young woman is found.'

'Good. Send for torches, and carry on.'

Dawn on Wednesday found them all haggard and cold, standing on top of the dunes south of Dymchurch and looking out over a rolling grey sea. The fog had gone, and a harsh wind came sweeping out of the north. A mile away the sails of a ship could be seen, cream-white against the dark water; the *Stag*, keeping patiently on her station.

The wind roared in the air around them. The clouds on the horizon were low and dark, promising rain. 'What are your orders?' asked Maudsley. It was the first time he and Hardcastle had spoken since that painful day in late August.

'Take your men into Dymchurch, and give them some food and a few hours to rest at the inn. When they are able, start searching again. We must not give up, Maudsley.'

'I had no intention of giving up, Hardcastle.'

Exhausted and freezing, the rector rode home to St Mary a couple of miles away. There, he asked Mrs Kemp for hot water for a bath, where he soaked until he could feel warmth in his bones again. When he started to fall asleep in the hot water, he climbed out, put on a nightshirt and slept on the bed for a few hours. Then he dressed, ate some bread and beef, drank a glass of claret and went out and joined the search once more. It was raining heavily now, the wind blowing grey curtains of rain across the Marsh.

By the end of the day they were all freezing again, and soaking wet. No torch would stay lit in this wind and rain, and the rector dismissed his searchers to find billets and food and dry their clothing. They would start again in the morning, and if necessary the day after, and the day after that. They would not stop until they found Charlotte Faversham.

Living or dead, he thought. And with every day that passed, the greater the likelihood that she would be dead.

There was one remaining chance. Stemp was due to meet Eliza at Blackmanstone at dusk. If she knew where Martha Redcliffe was, then there was a good chance she would know where the kidnapped girl was too. He had to hope, and pray, that Eliza would come.

Changing into dry clothes, he slumped down in his study by the fire to wait. A little later, Calpurnia opened the door and raised her eyebrows in enquiry; he shook his head. Quietly, she closed the door again and left him to his solitude.

By the time Stemp approached Blackmanstone the rain had eased off a little, but the wind was still cold and strong. The light was the colour of slate, the distant hills already blurred into the sky; the silhouette of the church was hardly distinguishable from the air around it. He approached slowly, his boots squelching in the mud.

He stepped through the ruined doorway into the nave. Shadows descended black around him.

There was movement in the dripping undergrowth ahead. 'Rider?' he whispered. 'Is that you?'

Something grabbed his hair and jerked his head back so he was staring up at the sky. Before he could move or even think, a knife stabbed into his neck just below his right ear, slicing open the skin. He felt the blood begin to flow.

'Oink, oink, piggy,' said Noakes's voice soft in his ear.

24

The Corners of the Earth

Stemp's hat had fallen off, and rain was beating on his face and running into his eyes. He stood very still, not moving. It would take Noakes less than a second to cut his throat.

'Hold him,' said a woman's voice.

Another pair of hands seized Stemp's arms and wrenched them painfully behind his back. Noakes let go of his hair, but the knife still stayed, its point resting in the side of his neck.

Light glowed suddenly as a lantern was uncovered. Stemp saw a ring of men around him, cocked hats dripping rainwater, knives and pistols in their hands. Some of them were grinning at him. One was a woman, cloaked with a bonnet framing her face. In the lantern light he caught a flash of sallow skin and dark, glittering eyes.

'Bring her,' said the woman.

Oh, Christ, Stemp thought. He felt sick.

Out of the shadows came Fisk, shoving Eliza Fanscombe before him. She struggled, trying to fight him, but the big man had her arms pinned tightly behind her; when she attempted to kick him, Fisk wrenched her arms upward until she cried out with pain. They stopped in front of the woman. Eliza turned her head then, and saw Stemp.

'Sorry, Tom,' she said.

Martha Redcliffe slapped Eliza across the face, so hard that her head rocked back. 'My little traitoress,' she said. 'My dear, treacherous little bitch ... You have been an utter fool, you know. In time, I would have given you riches. You would have been one of my heirs. Now you've thrown it all away.'

'You killed Batist,' said Eliza.

Martha slapped her again, the sound sharp and hard. Eliza's nose began to bleed.

'I don't care why you betrayed me,' said the woman. 'It matters not a whit. Now, listen to me. Very shortly you will go to sleep. When you wake, you will find yourself in a certain house in Amsterdam. You know the sort of house I mean, I am sure; I need not furnish you with details. You will be manacled by the leg to your bed, so you cannot escape. And you will remain there until you die; which might be quite a long time from now. Through the weeks, or months, or years of suffering that remain to you, you will remember this: no one betrays me and survives.'

Heedless of the danger to himself, Stemp began to struggle. 'Leave her alone, you bitch!'

Martha Redcliffe ignored him. 'I'll tell them to put you in the same room with the Faversham chit,' she said. 'You'll both want someone to talk to. Misery loves company, they say.'

She reached into her pocket and pulled out a small bottle, removing the stopper. 'Give her this, Frank,' she said to one of the other men.

'*No!*' shouted Stemp. He struggled, blood streaming down his neck. Eliza fought too, but Fisk wrenched her arms behind her back again, crippling and immobilising her. The man called Frank forced Eliza's mouth open with his fingers. She bit him; he cursed, but did not pull away. The laudanum bottle was rammed between her teeth, tipped up and emptied down her throat. She struggled for a while longer, then slumped, swaying, her head lolling to one side.

'Take her away,' said Martha. Fisk threw the unconscious woman over his shoulders like a bag of coal and carried her out of the ruined church. Martha retrieved the empty bottle and said to the other man, 'Take the blue light down to Littlestone, and light it immediately you get there. Then come back to Hythe as quickly as you can. We'll sail as soon as the wind changes.'

'What about this one?' asked Noakes, shaking the still struggling Stemp. 'What do we do with him?'

'Whatever you like,' said Martha, her voice indifferent. She walked past Stemp and out through the ruined doorway, carrying the lantern and followed by the rest of her men. Only Noakes and the man holding Stemp from behind remained. Noakes removed his knife and walked around in front of Stemp, his ugly face grinning in the shadow.

'Two against one,' said Stemp. 'That ain't fair, Noakes.'

'Fuck you, pig,' said Noakes, and he slammed his fist into Stemp's face.

The clock in the hall chimed ten. The rector stirred and opened his eyes. Exhausted and aching, he had fallen asleep in his chair.

The fire was burning low. He rang the bell, and Biddy came in quickly. 'Has there been any word from Mr Stemp?' he asked.

'None, reverend.'

He must still be waiting for Eliza, who had doubtless failed to show up again. Damned unreliable girl, he thought irritably, and then chided himself; she was the one who was in danger. He rose stiffly and put some more coal on the fire, then sat back and watched the flames. His bones still ached, but he could no longer sleep; he was consumed with worry. He sat listening for the knock at the door that would herald the arrival of Stemp, with news.

No knock came. Eventually he dragged himself up to bed, where he uttered a brief prayer for the safety of Charlotte Faversham and then fell into a restless, exhausted sleep.

He slept only a few hours, and woke up at dawn, worrying. It was Thursday, the 12th of October. Clouds, low and grey, raced overhead, torn and tossed by the wind. He dressed and went stiffly downstairs to drink a cup of coffee in the morning room.

Someone knocked at the door. It was a Customs man, another of Cole's riding officers. 'They burned a blue light near Littlestone, reverend, around midnight. The *Stag* came downwind to search, but found no sign of the Dutchman. Mr Cole thinks the light might have been a decoy, to pull *Stag* off her station.'

'So *Hoorn* can have a clear run inshore,' said the rector. The wind was strong from the north, and *Stag* had been drawn away to the south, miles from Hythe with the wind against her. A pound to a shilling, he thought, the *Hoorn* is coming to Hythe tonight, perhaps even today.

The messenger departed. Almost at once there was another knock at the door. This time it was Maisie Stemp, sleepless and worried.

'Josh didn't come home last night, reverend. I waited up all night for him, and still he's not here.'

The rector nodded. 'Thank you, Mrs Stemp. I reckon he has found the track of the kidnappers, and is following them. I will go after him, and send you word as soon as may be. Go home and rest, my dear. All will be well.'

She departed, looking dubious. 'Biddy,' said the rector, 'tell Amos to bring the dog cart round, as quickly as he may.'

His face and the tone in his voice frightened her. 'Is all well, reverend?' asked Biddy anxiously.

'No,' said Hardcastle, his voice grim. 'Something is wrong. Quickly, girl, fetch Amos.' He hurried into his study and opened his desk, taking out his pistol and checking the priming. Biddy ran in after him, looking more alarmed than ever.

'Begging your pardon, sir, but Amos says the dog cart still isn't repaired.'

'Then I will take Mrs Vane's gig.'

'Lord love us, sir,' said Biddy helplessly, 'but it's still not mended either. She's still never sent for the wheelwright.'

The rector let out his breath. 'Very well. I shall have to find another carriage. I am going out. Inform my sister and Mrs Kemp, if you please, that I may be some time.'

Outside the wind still raced across the Marsh, bitter and cold, but the rain had stopped entirely. Little patches of blue showed here and there through breaks in the cloud as the rector hurried down the street to Sandy House. The housekeeper answered the door.

'Lucy, is your mistress up? I must speak to her urgently.'

Hearing the tension in his voice, Mrs Chaytor came out into the hall. Her face was pale, the skin stretched and drawn sharply over the bones beneath. 'What is it?'

'Joshua Stemp went to meet Eliza last night, but didn't come home. I must find him. May I borrow your gig?'

'Wait five minutes while I change. Lucy, tell Joseph to harness Asia.'

'There is no need for you to come.'

'You know what a terrible driver you are.'

In less than five minutes she was back downstairs, wrapped in a heavy black cloak. In its folds, he knew, would be her pistol. The gig was outside, waiting. He handed her up to the driving seat and took his place beside her.

The ground was soft from last night's rain, but the gig was light and the mare strong and fresh. They raced up the village street and along the grassy lane to Blackmanstone in a shower of mud and spray, the wind whipping around them. The wind had backed a little, more north-west than northerly now.

Blackmanstone's ruins were dark in the dull light. Mrs Chaytor drew the gig to a halt. The rector dismounted and then drew his pistol and walked across to the doorway.

Joshua Stemp lay sprawled on the wet grass just inside. His face was so bloodied as to be unrecognisable, one eye swollen completely shut. More blood had streamed down the side of his neck, caking in his shirt. One of his arms was bent at a terrible angle. He was not moving.

Quickly, the rector lifted Stemp's undamaged arm and pulled back the coat to expose the wrist. His fingers searched the cold skin and found nothing. He cursed and tried again. This time his own numbed fingers found the right spot. There, faint and slow, was a pulse.

He heard a hiss of breath behind him as Mrs Chaytor arrived. 'He is alive. Have you any brandy?'

She handed over a small pewter flask from the pocket of her cloak. Opening Stemp's mouth, he tipped in a few drops and then turned the other man's head so the liquid would run down into his throat. When nothing happened, he tried a little more. Stemp began to choke, and the rector quickly lifted his head and shoulders. Stemp coughed again and opened his undamaged eye.

'Reverend,' he croaked.

'Thank God. Can you stand?'

'Not sure.' A little more brandy restored circulation. Between them, he and Mrs Chaytor were able to help Stemp to his feet, and then walk him with painful slowness out to the gig. Groaning with the pain of his arm, Stemp lay back on the driving bench, Hardcastle cradling the constable's head in his lap and holding on to him. Mrs Chaytor stood precariously in front of them, bracing herself against the splashboard while she turned the gig and drove back towards the village. Stemp clutched at Hardcastle with his good hand.

'Must tell you.' His voice was a rasping whisper, barely audible.

'Wait,' said the rector. 'We'll get you to St Mary and send for Dr Mackay.'

'No. Tell you now . . . Eliza. Taken.'

Hardcastle shivered. 'Taken where, Joshua?'

'Hythe. Ship . . . Holland.'

'Did they say when?'

'Today. Wind . . . changes.'

The rector looked up sharply. The wind was backing again, almost in the west now. 'They're taking Eliza with them?'

'Both girls . . .' Stemp coughed, and then cried out with pain. There must be ribs broken, as well as the arm. Hardcastle looked up at Mrs Chaytor. 'Did you hear?'

'Yes.' She shook the reins.

In the village all was confusion, people crowding around to find out what had happened, Maisie Stemp weeping as her husband was lifted out of the gig and carried inside by Murton and Jack Hoad. Luckhurst was there in the crowd, too, and Hardcastle took his arm.

'Go to New Romney, as quickly as you can; take my horse. Find Dr Mackay and tell him to come here. Then go to Mr Cole, and tell him to signal the *Stag*. The *Hoorn* is somewhere near Hythe; Captain Haddock must pursue with all possible speed. Cole must gather his own men, and send runners to Mr Juddery and Captain Austen. They must march their men up to Hythe as fast as they can go. Quickly, Tim. There is not a moment to lose.'

Mrs Chaytor was back in the driving seat of the gig. Her eyes were pits of dark blue, almost black in her white face. 'We are going to Hythe,' she said. It was not a question.

The wind was in the west, strong and steady, perfect for a ship laying course for Holland. 'I don't know how we'll stop them. I don't know if we'll even be in time.' He climbed up beside her. 'You said this horse could fly.'

It was three miles from St Mary in the Marsh to Dymchurch. They drove it at reckless speed, the wheels of the gig slipping and sliding in the mud, the mare straining at her harness as Mrs Chaytor urged her on. Hardcastle held on to his seat, trying to wipe the spray and mud and flecks of grass from his face. He tried to pray, to ask God to help them reach Hythe in time and save the two young women, but for some reason the words of the ninety-fifth Psalm came instead to his mind.

> For the Lord is a great God,
> and a great King above all gods.
> In his hand are the corners of the earth,
> and the strength of the hills is his also.
> The sea is his, and he made it,
> and his hands prepared the dry land.

They came to the first cottages of Dymchurch, where the track met the high road running north. The rector craned his neck, looking out to sea for the *Stag*. 'Any sign of her?' called Mrs Chaytor.

'Nothing. The messenger will only just have reached New Romney; probably, they have not even made the signal yet. We're on our own.'

They turned onto the high road, running north-east as straight as an arrow along the line of the Dymchurch Wall, passing the church at the far end of the village. There were pools of water from last night's rain, but the road itself was good and hard. Mrs Chaytor shook the reins again. 'Now, Asia, my dear,' she said to the horse. 'Show us what you are made of.'

No one spoke for a while. The gig's wheels rattled and roared on the hard road, and Asia's hooves hammered a constant tattoo, her iron shoes striking sparks. The wind of their passage tugged at them. The carriage thrummed with vibration. Hardcastle watched the gloved hands of his driver on the reins, guiding the horse around potholes that might break a wheel or an axle, sweeping out to curve around slower-moving drays and packhorses and passing them as if they were standing still.

This was a race they had to win. From the little that Stemp had been able to say, they knew both Eliza and Charlotte were still alive, and that Martha Redcliffe intended to take them to the Netherlands. If they could get to Hythe in time they might, somehow, stop the *Hoorn* from sailing, or at least delay her until the *Stag* could arrive. How they would do that, Hardcastle knew not; he knew only that it had to be done.

The hills above Hythe grew closer and closer, drear and green in the cloudy light. They swept past another dray loaded with bricks. Ahead, a post-coach was about to pass a wagon coming the other way. Their own gig would have to slow to let them pass.

Mrs Chaytor's eyes narrowed and her lips compressed into a thin line. 'Hold tight,' she said.

Hardcastle gripped the seat and the frame of the gig, and uttered another prayer. Closer and closer came the other vehicles, both seemingly unaware of the onrushing gig. Mrs Chaytor's gloved hands tugged at the reins and the gig swung out to overtake the post-coach, heading straight for the oncoming wagon. They would never make it, Hardcastle thought. She will have to pull up, or there will be a crash.

She did not pull up. The gig raced on, iron-rimmed wheels chattering on the stone road, the wind rushing around them, the wagon looming ahead of them, closer and closer. Hardcastle braced himself.

The wagon driver saw them coming, and stared in disbelief. When the gig was fifty yards away he began to shout, sawing on the reins of his plodding horses. Alarmed, the driver of the post-coach turned in his seat and began to yell as well. Mrs Chaytor's eyes narrowed. Thirty yards, twenty, ten, the road ahead full of vehicles and teams, and then at full rushing speed the gig shot past the post-coach. Someone inside the coach screamed in alarm. Ahead, the wagon was almost on top of them.

Seconds before they crashed headlong into the wagon, Mrs Chaytor sawed on the reins. Asia swerved. The gig lurched as it changed direction, then raced on roaring wheels through the impossible gap between post-coach and wagon, so close that Hardcastle could have reached out and touched the lead horse of the coach. Then they were away and tearing on down the open road, the sounds of frightened horses and shouting men dim on the wind behind them. Hardcastle let out the breath he had been holding.

'One day you really will break your neck,' he said.

'Not today,' said Mrs Chaytor.

The houses of Hythe were distinct ahead of them now, the church of St Leonard bulky on the upper slope, Saltwood Castle a ruined silhouette on the skyline. 'Can you see a ship?' she asked, concentrating on the road.

Braced against the vibration of the gig, he scanned the sea. 'Nothing.' Hope rose. They were less than a mile from Hythe now. 'We may be in time.'

It struck him suddenly that they might be walking into another ambush prepared by Martha Redcliffe. But it was too late to worry about that now.

Asia was tiring. The little horse had run gallantly, but now her speed was dropping. Ahead lay the first houses, and beyond them the harbour, little more than a shallow indentation in the coast protected by a bar of sand and shingle. 'Make for the Customs post,' Hardcastle said. Mrs Chaytor nodded and drove the flagging horse down towards the harbour, turning the corner around the brick block of the Customs house and onto the waterfront.

Near at hand, a few fishing boats were drawn up onshore; further on, two coasters rode at anchor behind the protection of the bar. Beyond the bar was the sea, foaming with breakers. Among the waves beyond was a ship, a big lugger with dark red sails spread and filling in the wind, rolling as the Channel swells began to take her. A sudden burst of sunlight bathed the ship. The waves around her glinted and gleamed, and on her deck there was a glow of sunlight on brass; cannon.

It was the *Hoorn*. She had sailed not fifteen minutes ago. They had lost the race.

'We are not finished,' said Mrs Chaytor. She jumped down and tethered the horse, then strode into the Customs house with the rector behind her. A single officer, an elderly man, stood up from his seat beside an iron stove.

'Where are the other officers?' demanded Mrs Chaytor.

'Out with Mr Cole, ma'am. Searching for the missing girl.'

'The ship that sailed just now,' said the rector. 'Did you see who went aboard it?'

'Ship? What ship, reverend? My eyesight ain't so good these days . . .'

'Bribed,' said Mrs Chaytor. 'Don't waste time. You. On your feet. Is there a signal mast at this station? Take us there.'

The signal mast was on the roof. They stood on the platform in the whipping wind, looking out over a grey sea combed with white. Already the *Hoorn* was moving away fast, on a north-easterly course that would take her up the deep channel between the coast and the sandbanks of the Varne. But Mrs Chaytor was looking south. Suddenly she pointed at the horizon.

'There!'

Flecks of white among the dappled waves; the sails of the *Stag*, driving up hard from the south. Hardcastle turned on the Customs man. 'Make this signal to *Stag*: "I am sending a boat to you".'

'I'm only an old tidesman, sir. Bless you, I don't know nothing about signals.'

Hardcastle drew the pistol from his mud-splattered cloak. 'Make the signal.'

Flags soared up the signal halyard. The Customs man lowered the telescope from his eye. 'She's responded, sir. Affirmative.'

'Good. Amelia: take your gig up to the Swan, and tell Manningham to stable your horse. You,' he said to the tidesman, 'will find a boat and crew who can row us out to the *Stag*.'

The tidesman gaped. 'In this weather?'

'Find them,' said Hardcastle.

The waves caught the boat as soon as they passed the sandbar and battered at them. The boat lurched crazily over the crests and sagged down into the troughs, heaving and rolling. Within five minutes Hardcastle was sick over the side, retching painfully, and no sooner had he sat up, wiping his face and rubbing his cramped stomach, than the nausea struck again. This time when he bent to vomit the sea came up and slapped him in the face, filling his mouth and nose with salt water. He sat back in the boat in a dizzy haze, his arms and legs suddenly gone weak, trying not to look at the heaving horizon.

Something wooden bumped alongside them; the hull of the *Stag*. Hands reached over the side and helped them climb aboard. Captain Haddock, in a cape beaded with salt water, saluted them on the swaying deck. 'Reverend? Ma'am? What in thunder are you doing here? I thought they were sending out more officers.'

'Captain, Mrs Redcliffe is on that ship,' said Hardcastle, gulping. 'She has kidnapped two women and is planning either to kill them or hold them hostage in the Netherlands. At all costs, we *must* overtake them.'

The hull of the *Hoorn* was out of sight below the waves, but her big red lugsails could be seen clearly on the horizon. Haddock shouted orders to his own men and the sloop turned in pursuit. 'She's about a three-mile start on us,' the captain said. 'But we'll overhaul her, never fear. We'll follow her to the corners of the earth, if we must. Reverend, ma'am, if you wish to go below, my cabin and that of my first mate are at your disposal. Jenks here will show you the way.'

Staggering and sick, Hardcastle turned to follow the sailor. 'I would prefer to remain,' said Mrs Chaytor, her eyes on the red sails. 'Tell me where to stand so I am not in the way.'

All through the day the chase continued. For a while, the white cliffs of east Kent were visible to the west; then these passed from view and there was only the sea, endless rolling waves churned by the wind which roared at them from the west. The wind pressed the sails of the *Stag* so hard that her deck heeled over; at times, her lee rail was almost in the water. Mrs Chaytor knew a little about sailing, and she could tell that Haddock was pushing his ship to the limit, extracting every yard of speed he could find, just as she had done with Asia. The deck under her feet quivered with strain, and the taut rigging overhead screamed in the wind.

The race was not yet done.

Hours passed. The clouds were breaking, and the sun shone with mocking brilliance; the waves changed from grey to steely blue, foam crests sparkling as they raced towards the ship. The red sails were always there on the horizon, but she could not tell how close they were. Once, in the late afternoon, a sailor brought her coffee laced with rum, and she drank it gratefully; she had not realised how cold she was.

'Are we gaining?'

'A little, ma'am. Captain reckons we're a little over two miles behind now. *Hoorn*'s a faster ship when close to the wind, see, but if she comes up too far, she'll be on a course straight towards our patrols. She has to stick to this course to make Holland, and so long as she does we'll have the legs of her.'

She understood only some of this, but *two miles* stood out. They were closing.

Dusk fell. The waves came on, relentless, and the deck heaved and rolled. One of the crew brought her some food, which she did not want. Sunset was a glow of gold and red barred by clouds. She watched the red sails in the distance turn dark as the light faded, and a sudden panic struck her. She went back to the quarterdeck, slowly, clinging to the bulwark, stepping carefully around the black cast-iron cannon that squatted at intervals and feeling her boots slipping on the wet deck.

'Captain Haddock! We'll lose her in the dark!'

The white-haired captain shook his head. 'The moon'll be up soon. We'll see her clear enough then. Ma'am, I really think you should go below and rest.'

She went below. She looked into the cabin where Hardcastle lay sprawled on the bed, unconscious with seasickness. For a moment, her soul softened a little.

I was wrong to send him away. I needed his humanity, his compassion. I needed his friendship. This was not the time to lock myself away.

He cares about me, I know. He has never spoken of it, but I know too that he is sorry I do not share his belief in God. Well. Perhaps I shall try a little experiment now. A prayer, to see if it makes me feel any better.

Bracing herself against the wooden bulkhead, she closed her eyes and spoke a short prayer for the safety of Charlotte and Eliza. She opened her eyes again and looked around. Everything was the same.

'Oh, well,' she said to herself, and for a moment there was a trace of her old lightness. 'It can't have hurt.'

She went into the captain's cabin and lay down on the cot. The motion of the ship rolled her from side to side like a doll, and the room smelled of tobacco. After an hour she went back on deck, just in time to see the half-moon lift over the rolling horizon and light the sails of the Dutch ship two miles ahead. She leaned against the mast, watching.

I failed Grebell Faversham. I will not fail again.

Be brave, Eliza and Charlotte. Be strong. Whatever happens to you, cling to life. We are coming for you.

Dawn broke, glowing red and pink and gold over the heaving sea, the wind still hard from the west. She was so exhausted she could hardly think. The world around her seemed to stutter. The relentless crash of the waves, the creaking of the hull, the moaning of the rigging tore at her nerves.

'A mile and a half,' said Captain Haddock. 'Sloterdyke is no lubber. He must know we're overhauling him.'

'Think he might turn and fight, sir?'

'Wouldn't you? Pipe the hands to breakfast.'

Breakfast was a form of porridge. She forced a few spoonfuls down, shuddering with a nausea that had nothing to do with seasickness. Another cup of coffee laced with rum calmed her stomach.

Blue sky overhead, enormous columns of white cloud marching over the sea around them trailing grey sheets of rain. The wind was down a little, but still the waves rolled on, streaked with white foam. The deck of the ship heaved and swayed beneath her feet.

'Sail ho!'

'Where away?'

'Port bow, captain. It's another lugger.'

White sails, rising and falling on the horizon. The sea, rolling and rolling, without end.

'She's one of ours, captain! I think it's *Black Joke*!'

'Make the recognition signal.'

Silence, waiting.

'Weather's coming up, captain.' One of the great storm clouds was rolling towards them from the west.

'*Black Joke*'s answering, captain. She's spotted the Dutchman.'

The squall was drawing nearer. A few raindrops pattered on the already wet deck.

'*Black Joke* is turning, sir! She's running to cut the Dutchman off.'

'Watch the Dutchman, lads, watch her,' said Haddock. 'She'll wait until the squall hits and then try to run back past us. Watch her sails; sing out the moment you see her turn.'

Rain was falling heavily now. Her cloak was saturated, she realised, and she was wet through to her small clothes. Her body shivered from head to foot, but she could not turn away.

'Ma'am,' said Captain Haddock, 'I am about to send the crew to quarters. You should go below.'

She did not know what that meant. She shook her head.

A whistle blew. A drum beat. Men ran across the rolling deck. The ropes securing the black guns were removed. Charges of powder were rammed down the muzzles, round shot forced home after them.

The rain hit them in earnest, pouring out of the sky, streaming across the deck. The men around her were soaked through in an instant. The horizon vanished behind the curtain of rain.

'She's turning!' Several voices shouting at once. They had seen the Dutch lugger's sails turn just before the heavy rain blotted her from sight.

'Hard a-starboard. Now, midships. Meet her.'

'Steady as she goes, captain.'

'Gun's crews closed up and ready for action, sir.'

The rain hammered at them. A powerful gust of wind followed, kicking up the waves so that the *Stag* corkscrewed across them, diving into the troughs. Mrs Chaytor grabbed for a rope and clung on as a big wave broke across the deck, green water up to her waist for a moment, then pouring away over the side.

Waiting, watching the rain for any sign of movement.

'*There she is!*'

Great red sails stretched taut, black hull shiny with wet driving over the heaving grey seas, white foam at her bow, perhaps three hundred yards away.

'*Hard a-starboard!*'

Flashes of flame, puffs of white smoke from the Dutch lugger's deck; thuds of shot against the wooden hull, something tearing a hole in the sail overhead. Hardcastle was there beside her, white-faced. 'Amelia, what are you doing? Go below!'

She could not move; she could only shake her head.

'It's that god-damned Puckle gun! Look out, they're firing again!' *Flash. Flash. Flash* from the enemy deck, more thumps against the hull. Another puff of smoke and a cannonball tore a white leaping fountain from the face of an incoming wave.

'Midships. Meet her.'

The Dutch ship was turning, too, away to port. She could see the long barrel of the Puckle gun now, and the men around the other guns, reloading. At this distance, their faces were white featureless blobs. Another cannon fired from the Dutchman's deck, gushing smoke; this time, she heard the sharp crack of the explosion over the roar of wind and water.

Rain drumming on the deck, running down her face and into her eyes. The crash of waves under the bow, spray flying up in hissing sheets. *Flash. Flash. Flash*; the Puckle gun, firing again. Shouts from the men around her as the ship was hit.

'Stand by the guns. Fire.'

White billowing smoke, a hammering in her ears that made her want to scream, the smoke twisting away quickly on the wind. 'Did we hit her?'

'No.'

'Sponge out. Load powder.'

'She's getting away, sir! She's pulled away at least a cable's length in the last few minutes!'

The rain was increasing in power. The deck around her was ankle-deep in water. Hardcastle stood braced against the mast beside her, soaked through, staring at the Dutch ship as she began to disappear behind the curtain of falling rain.

'She's right up against the wind, sir! She's got at least a knot of speed on us! She's getting away from us, sir!'

She heard her own voice screaming on the edge of sanity, raging against the fates that had brought them so close and then denied them.

A shape ahead in the rain, a huge shadow right on the edge of vision, dark, enormous wings, menacing, hungry for the kill; resolving in a moment into great spreading sails over a narrow black and yellow hull, a ship running at full speed. And then out of the rain came *Black Joke*, and her guns spoke thunder.

She saw the white smoke billowing over the sea, tongues of fire stabbing through it. She saw the splinters fly from the Dutchman's deck; she saw one mast crack and shatter and fall, crushing the Puckle gun to broken metal as its crew scattered, dragging the great sail behind it in a confusion of broken ropes and splintered wood to crash into the sea. The Dutch ship heeled around, rolling in the troughs of the waves. *Black Joke* stooped on her like a hunting hawk.

One moment the *Hoorn* was a great distance away; then suddenly they were alongside her. She looked down to see Martha Redcliffe staring up at her, face framed by a black hood. A dog, a big mastiff tethered to the remaining mast, barked furiously, straining against its lead. *Black Joke* was on the other side, bristling with guns.

'Captain Sloterdyke! *Heb je overgeven?* Do you surrender, sir?'

'God rot you,' said a big man on her quarterdeck. 'Do I have a choice?'

Haddock said something she did not hear. On the other ship's deck, men were laying down their weapons, some reluctantly. A big gap-toothed man snarled and raised his pistol; Sloterdyke spoke and two of his men struck the weapon down, pinning the other man between them. 'Help me down,' Mrs Chaytor said to Hardcastle.

'Down?'

She pointed to the *Hoorn*'s deck. 'We've got to find them. Now.'

Two of *Stag*'s sailors lifted her down. Ignoring the rolling deck, she stalked towards the captain like an avenging fury, her face white and cold. Snarling, the mastiff hurled itself forward, throwing all its massive weight against the lead. The leather snapped with a crack. The dog raced towards her, claws scrabbling on the wet deck, jaws open and teeth bared. Behind her, men shouted in alarm. Mrs Chaytor drew her pistol and shot the dog through the head, then stepped over the twitching body to confront the captain.

'Where are the women?' she said harshly.

'*Vertel haar niets!*' snapped Martha Redcliffe.

The big man rounded on her. '*Almachtig!* Enough. I'm a smuggler, not a kidnapper.' He nodded to Mrs Chaytor. 'They are below.'

'Open the hatch.' She gestured with her pistol, which was still smoking. 'Now.'

Eliza and Charlotte lay sprawled like broken dolls on a greasy wooden grating, sea water sloshing just below them. They had been pushed down the ladder, or perhaps even thrown down unconscious from the deck. Hardcastle was down the ladder at once; she realised she had not seen him come aboard. She stood at the edge of the hatch looking down, watching him kneel over the bodies, feeling sick again.

Then he looked up, and she saw his face. She put her head back, closing her eyes. It was over. The race was won.

> *The sea is his, and he made it,*
> *and his hands prepared the dry land.*

Sailors from the *Stag*, and *Black Joke*, too, came to the hatch and with great tenderness lifted the unconscious bodies of the two young women out of the hold and carried them aboard the *Stag*. They had been drugged, heavily; they would be unconscious for hours still. Both were badly bruised, probably from their fall into the hold, but there was no obvious sign of broken bones.

Captain Haddock and Lieutenant Stark had both come aboard the *Hoorn*. The Dutch captain stood with his arms folded while the other two debated his fate. 'I think we should treat her as a prize,' the navy man said. 'If the Customs take her, then she's confiscate, and none of us will ever see a penny. But if she's a prize of war, she goes to prize court, and we all get a reward. We'll split it down the middle with you and your crew, of course.'

'I don't need the money,' said the older man, smiling.

'You obviously don't live on a Royal Navy lieutenant's salary, then. Come, sir, have we a deal?'

Martha Redcliffe, her hands bound behind her, was being escorted at swordpoint onto the deck of the *Stag*. She did not look at either Hardcastle or Mrs Chaytor. Several other prisoners followed her, under close guard. Mrs Chaytor did not know what Noakes and Fisk looked like, but she assumed they were among them. The rain had stopped; the clouds were clearing fast now, and once again there were patches of blue sky overhead.

Stark turned away from the other captains and saw her, and his jaw dropped. He hurried forward. 'Mrs Chaytor! My word, ma'am! Whatever are you doing here?'

'It is a long story,' she said, smiling. She could smile now, though her body was shivering as if with fever. 'Thank you, Mr Stark. A most timely intervention. I shall have to think of another name for you now.'

He grinned at her. The action they had just been through was all in a day's work for him. 'Hero?' he offered. 'Paladin? Paragon?'

Poor Grebell, she thought. *You so wanted to be a man like him.* She smiled and closed her eyes for a moment, leaning against the stump of the broken mast.

'Ship ahoy!' a voice shouted. 'By God! It's the fleet!'

She opened her eyes, and saw an astonishing sight. Ships were coming out of the rain: two, five, ten, a dozen big ships; magnificent line-of-battle ships, gleaming black-and-yellow-striped hulls topped with towering pyramids of canvas. Over the rolling waves they came, the very picture of power and might, the sun striking glints off the gilt of their figureheads and the black iron guns on their upper decks.

'Look!' said Stark. He was almost dancing with excitement. 'Look at 'em come!'

'What is it?' Mrs Chaytor asked.

'It's Admiral Duncan's fleet, ma'am! Two days ago they took on the Dutch navy at Camperdown, and smashed 'em! They're on their way back now, back to England, home and glory. Look at them! Oh, just look! There's the *Monmouth*, and that's *Bedford*, and *Agincourt*, and *Triumph*, and that's *Venerable*, the flagship. Oh, cheer them on, boys! Huzza! Huzza!'

The crews of *Stag* and *Black Joke* took up the cheer, roaring as the great ships drew closer. She could see now how battered they were, their hulls horribly scarred and splintered, their sails riddled with holes; but they rode the waves magnificently, and it seemed to her tired mind that she could hear, above all the tumult of wind and water, the sound of invisible drums and trumpets playing the fleet home.

The last of the ships passed by and began to dwindle into distance, the line of the horizon beckoning them. 'By God,' said Stark as the cheering finally subsided. 'Seeing them brings it all home, doesn't it? We may be outnumbered on land and sea, facing an implacable foe; but we'll fight right to the end. We'll never give up, not ever. Mrs Chaytor? Mrs Chaytor, are you all right? Why, ma'am, I do believe you are crying.'

25

The Return of the Rider

They sat opposite each other in the pretty drawing room of Sandy House, cups of tea before them. Five days had passed since the *Stag* brought them home. Rain misted the windows. Autumn was well advanced now, the trees on the distant hills turning brown.

'I must thank you once again for saving my life,' said Eliza Fanscombe. 'You and Reverend Hardcastle.'

'Don't forget Joshua,' said Mrs Chaytor. 'Another man might have died from that beating, and then lying outside all night. I am convinced he willed himself to stay alive, so he could tell us what had happened to you. Without him, we would never have found you.'

'Yorkshire Tom. I must look in on him before I go, and see how he is faring. Yes, I owe all of you a debt. The code of the Marsh says as much.'

'Is there really such a thing as the code of the Marsh? I thought they just made that up for the tourists.'

Eliza laughed. 'I think it's more honoured in the breach than in the observance, to be honest. But we do remember those who helped us. Is there any favour I can do for you in exchange? I can offer you a lifetime's supply of untaxed gin.'

'Interesting. I might try bathing in it, to see if it assists my complexion.'

Amelia looked at the fair face opposite hers, rested and already restored. How quickly the young bounce back, she thought. 'You are still resolved to go?'

'I am.'

'And to return to smuggling?'

'Yes. I know what all of you think; I am the same little idiot who used to ride out after the smugglers and dream about one day joining them. Well, that has changed. I don't dream any more. I *am* a smuggler now, Mrs Chaytor. This is the life I have chosen; this is the life I love.'

'I don't even pretend to understand you.'

'Don't you? I'm nineteen, Mrs Chaytor. What happens to most girls my age? They are married off. They pass from being controlled by their parents to being owned by their husbands. They live out their lives as chattels. Oh, there are compensations for the rich, to be sure, but even wealthy women pass their days in gilded confinement.

'But circumstances have set me free. I have no family, and I will never have a husband; who would marry the penniless daughter of a convicted felon? No one; and I say, hurrah to that. I am at liberty to live my life exactly as I wish, and I am going to seize my opportunity with both hands.'

She sipped her tea. 'And if you thought that nearly being killed would change me, you are much mistaken. I am made of harder metal than that.'

'Is that what you want to be? Made of metal? Hard, without feelings?'

'Touché. No, I shall always be a woman, and I expect – I hope – I will always be a creature of senses and emotions. But you see, that is why I am attracted to this life. It makes my blood flow faster and my skin tingle. The life I live on the Marsh is exciting. The thrill of hunting and being hunted, of laying lives on the line; the fun of matching your wits against that of another man – even if he is only a Customs officer – the wildness of the sea, the flicker of torchlight, the smell of the gunsmoke. I'm addicted to it, just as Martha was addicted to opium.'

'And like opium, it will kill you.'

'I expect so. I'm that much of a realist; I know the chances are strong that I will die a violent death by the time I am thirty. I'll take that. I will die; but before I do, I will have *lived*, and lived on my own terms. I reject the drawing room and the salon, the polite manners and conventions, the ridiculous arrangements of marriage for convenience. I want none of that. Give me my torchlight and gunsmoke.'

Eliza smiled at Mrs Chaytor. 'I've not convinced you, have I?'

'No,' said Mrs Chaytor. 'We listen to different music, you and I.'

'And the world is a better place for it. Not all women should be like me; nor should all be like you.'

'I don't think any woman should aspire to be like either of us,' said Mrs Chaytor. 'Will you promise me one thing? Send word to me, from time to time, and let me know how you fare. And also, I offered you sanctuary the night we met at Blackmanstone. That offer stands. If ever you need a place of safety, come to me.'

'Bless you. But why should you make this offer?'

'Everyone needs someone, somewhere who cares about them.' It was not exactly what Grebell Faversham had said, but it was in the same spirit.

They rose. Eliza was dressed for travelling in a man's garb: coat and waistcoat, breeches and boots. She clasped Mrs Chaytor's hand for a moment. 'Of course I will call on you,' she said. 'And when you hear rumours of the Rider – as you will from time to time – think of me.'

When Eliza had gone, Mrs Chaytor went out into the cool afternoon and walked to the rectory. She found Hardcastle dozing in his study. 'Poor you,' she said, surveying him. 'Are you still not recovered?'

His seasickness on the return voyage had been even worse than on the way out. 'Oh, I am fully myself again,' he said.

'"A man who has been through bitter experiences and travelled far, enjoys even his sufferings after a time". From the *Odyssey*, I think. No, I am merely resting from my labours before Lord Clavertye arrives next week. I am to assist him in preparing the case against the "Redcliffe Gang", as the newspapers have begun to call them.'

'It makes them sound much more romantic than they really are. Speaking of romantic; she has gone.'

'Did you try to persuade her to remain?'

'Not very hard. Irritatingly, it turns out you were right. I do respect her.'

'And Grebell? Do you wish to talk about him?'

She thought about this for a while. 'One day, yes,' she said finally. 'At the moment, everything is still too raw. I need time to make sense of what happened.'

'And yourself? You are recovered from your ordeal?' She inclined her head. 'What did you think of your first sea battle?' he asked.

She shuddered artistically. 'My dear. Far too noisy. And those ships are frightfully overcrowded. No, no more adventures for me. I intend to stay here and rusticate in the peace and quiet of Romney Marsh.'

'Yes. Peace and quiet,' said the rector thoughtfully. 'When you find some, will you be so good as to let me know?'

Afterword

We have as usual rearranged the landscape of Romney Marsh a little to suit ourselves. It is not clear how much of a harbour actually remained in Hythe by the 1790s, and the construction of the Royal Military Canal a few years later probably obliterated the last traces of it; the harbour as described in this book is our invention. Buildings like the warehouses and the Customs house are also fictitious, although the Swan did exist. Our depiction of Hythe as a dark, sinister place full of thieves and murderers and dominated by criminal gangs should in no way be taken as a reflection of Hythe and its inhabitants today.

The remains of the churches of Blackmanstone and Midley can still be seen, though they are considerably more dilapidated than they were two centuries ago; only part of one wall of Midley is still standing. These ruined churches are a feature of Romney Marsh, reminding us of a time when the Marsh was much more populous than it is today.

The so-called Redcliffe Gang received harsh justice. Henry Noakes, John Fisk and four other men were convicted of murder and smuggling at the Maidstone Assizes and were hanged at Penenden Heath near Maidstone in April 1798. Others of the gang were sentenced to long terms of transportation.

Martha Redcliffe was tried separately on a wide range of charges. She refused to testify in her own defence, and observers later recounted that she appeared entirely indifferent to the case against her, sitting for much of the time in court with her arms folded and her eyes closed. Found guilty of murder under the law of joint enterprise, she was hanged two days after her confederates.

The *Hoorn* was sold at a prize court, the proceeds divided between the officers and crew of the *Black Joke* and the *Stag*. The Dutch captain Sloterdyke and his crew were interned in the new prisoner-of-war camp at Norman Cross, near Peterborough, from which they later made a sensational escape.

Lieutenant Newton Stark went on to have a fine career as a commander of light ships in the Royal Navy, serving later in the Mediterranean and the Baltic. He so impressed the Tsar of Russia that the latter gave him a silver-plate breakfast service and a purse of 100 guineas. Captain John Haddock continued to command the *Stag* and, despite being a Customs officer, became one of the most respected elder citizens of Rye. His gravestone can still be seen in St Mary's church in the town.

James Martin of the Grasshopper was as good as his word. The fortunes of the East Weald and Ashford Bank were restored, though the Canterbury branch was later sold to a relative of the Cotton family. After consultation, the Lord-Lieutenant of Sussex and Lord Clavertye, the Deputy Lord-Lieutenant of Kent, agreed that although Charles Faversham was certainly guilty, the evidence against him was too weak to stand up in court. No charges were brought against him. Faversham retired from public life and never again showed his face in Rye.

Charlotte Faversham, her spirit unbroken by her ordeal, left what she described – a little harshly – as the 'atmosphere of perpetual misery' of the family household, and went back to Shadoxhurst to live with her friend Sissy Munro. Quite what they will do with their futures is anyone's guess, but as young women of resolution and spirit, they will doubtless find some way to make their mark on the world.

Captain Edward Austen returned to his wife and young family at Godmersham, their house near Canterbury. He writes to the rector from time to time, complaining that life upcountry is nowhere near as interesting as it is down on the Marsh.

After making a killing on the stock market, David Ricardo retired from business to take up a career as a writer. He became of one Britain's best-known political economists.

The smugglers continue their runs across the Marsh, feeding England's appetite for gin and vanities. Among those prominent in the gangs around Hythe and Dymchurch is a young man called the Rider, about whom some interesting rumours have begun to circulate. One of these rumours – widely derided as improbable – is that the Rider is actually a woman in disguise.

Eliza Fanscombe (for it is she) is living her dream among the smugglers. Readers of early drafts of this book commented on the moral ambiguity of her character, but she is in fact the stuff of Romantic legend. Goethe and Schiller and in particular Lord Byron would all understand her; she is Byron's Corsair, in female form. Her prediction about her own fate, if it comes true, will seal her Romantic legend.

Joshua Stemp made a full recovery and soon returned to his old roles of parish constable and smuggler. Ebenezer and Florian Tydde continue to smuggle a little, fish unsuccessfully and be the despair of their mother.

Calpurnia Vane's novel *The Cardinal's Jewels* (written like all her books under the nom de plume Cordelia Hartbourne) was published in early 1798. Sharp-eyed readers wondered about the book's dedication, 'To an Anonymous Caledonian Friend'.

Not among these was Dr Mackay, who failed to realise that the dedication referred to himself. His courtship of Mrs Vane continues at the same glacial pace.

The rector and Mrs Chaytor will return.

Acknowledgements

Writing is a solitary business, or can be, but at the same time, no writer is ever truly alone. As with our previous novels, a host of people have input into this book in one way or another, and we shall try to mention a few of them here.

On Romney Marsh, Liz Grant at the Romney Marsh Visitor Centre near New Romney has once again been a wonderful adviser and friend, a dispenser of cups of tea and invaluable knowledge about the Marsh. Special thanks also to the Romney Marsh Brewery for their support. We hope you enjoyed the books as much as we did the beer. And thanks too to the Romney, Hythe & Dymchurch Railway for giving us a unique look at the landscape around Dungeness.

Cherie Chapman and Head Design have given the book a splendid cover, one which really captures the atmosphere of Romney Marsh. At Bonnier Zaffre, our thanks go to Kate Parkin for editing the book and giving us so many useful ideas to think about; to Claire Johnson-Creek for seeing the book through production and putting up with our lateness and our foibles; to Jenny Page for a meticulous job of copy-editing; and to Sean Costello for his proofreading skills which enabled him to spot several egregious errors which somehow slipped past us.

Our thanks especially to Gary Beaumont, who accommodated our last-minute request for changes to the map, and to Rachel Richards at Chameleon Studios for all her work on the website.

As always, our warmest thanks go to Heather Adams and Mike Bryan at HMA Literary Agency for all your hard work, advice, support and friendship. And finally, thank you from the bottoms of our hearts to our family and friends and all those who read the first two novels and took the time and trouble to write or call and tell us what they thought about Reverend Hardcastle, Mrs Chaytor and their adventures. Without your enthusiasm and support, these books would not exist.

Read on for an extract from the first Hardcastle and Chaytor mystery, *The Body on the Doorstep*. Available in paperback and ebook now

1

Death of a Stranger

The Rectory, St Mary in the Marsh, Kent.
6th May, 1796.

To the editor of *The Morning Post*.

Sir,

For the past four years, BRITANNIA has been engaged
in a state of continuous warfare against the regicides of
the French REPUBLIC and their *blood-stained minions*.
During this time, millions in treasure and thousands
of men have been committed to expeditions to Corsica,
Toulon, Holland, the Indies; expeditions which have
resulted in *no other good* than the capture of a few small
islands. Meanwhile, the coastline of BRITANNIA itself lies
naked and open to the enemy ...

The quill began to splutter. 'Damn!' said the rector. He dipped
the pen into the silver inkwell sitting on his desk, and began
again.

... *naked and open* to the enemy, so close that an *invasion
fleet* might well reach the shores of Kent just A FEW HOURS
after setting out from French ports. Yet, *not a single shilling*
has been spent on the protection of the English coast, which
is *completely defenceless*. How long, sir, before His Majesty's
government realises the danger that we face? Must we wait

until France's *blood-stained sans-culotte hordes* are ~~marching over the fair fields of Kent~~ marching over the fair fields of BRITANNIA ~~itself~~ herself . . .

The fire popped in the grate and a little shower of sparks flew up the chimney. The rector crossed out the entire final sentence and sat back in his chair, muttering to himself. 'Damn, damn, damn. Not right, no, not right at all. Blast and damn!'

He needed inspiration. He dropped the pen, reached for the port bottle that stood beside the inkwell, and upended it. A thin trickle of muddy liquid ran into the bottom of the glass, and stopped.

A sudden rage seized the rector's clouded mind. '*Damn!*' he shouted, and he hurled the bottle into the fireplace. It smashed against the fireguard, spraying bits of broken glass onto the parquet floor. A few drops of port lay on the polished wood, glinting like blood in the firelight.

'Mrs Kemp!' the rector shouted. 'Mrs Kemp!'

Waiting a few seconds and receiving no answer, still fulminating over the injustice of the empty bottle, the rector bellowed again. There came a sound of shuffling feet in the hall, and the door of the study opened to reveal a grey-haired woman with a downturned mouth, holding a candlestick. At the sight of the rector, the corners of her mouth turned down still further.

'For heaven's sake, will you stop shouting!' the woman scolded. 'Don't you realise it is nearly midnight?' Then she saw the broken glass around the fire, and raised her hands in despair. 'Oh, Reverend!' she said, her own voice rising. 'Reverend *Hard*-castle! What have you done *now*?'

The rector stared at her. Nearly midnight? It had just gone nine in the evening when he sat down at his desk to write his latest letter to *The Morning Post*. How could three hours have passed? Then he spotted another empty port bottle, and knew a moment of unease.

He rallied quickly. 'Never mind all that,' he said brusquely. 'You can clear up in the morning. Go to the cellar, and fetch me another bottle.'

'I will do no such thing, Reverend Hardcastle! You have drunk quite enough for one evening!'

'For God's sake, woman, you are my housekeeper, not my wife! Go and fetch a bottle, and have done arguing!'

The housekeeper shuffled towards the cellar door and the rector sat behind his desk, both muttering under their breath. The clock in the hall chimed midnight, confirming the hour. The rector yawned suddenly. He considered going to bed and finishing the letter in the morning . . . but then, the housekeeper had just gone to the cellar. It would be a pity if her errand were wasted.

A thunderous noise interrupted his reverie. It took him a moment to realise that someone was knocking on the rectory's front door; knocking, and with considerable force. He opened his mouth to call Mrs Kemp to answer the door, but remembered she was down in the cellar and would not hear him. Muttering again, he rose to his feet, staggered, recovered, walked steadily to the door, turned into the hallway, over-rotated, bumped into the wall, stopped for the moment to take a deep breath and then walked in a fairly straight line down the hall to the door, weaving just once when he collided with a side table. He reached the door just as the heavy door-knocker thundered again, reverberating in his fume-filled mind like the stroke of doom.

'Wait a blasted moment!' shouted the rector, fumbling with the bolts. 'Look here, whoever you are, don't you know what time it is? It is after midnight!' In answer there came more noises, a sharp crack and almost immediately after the heavy thump of something landing hard on the doorstep. Puzzled, the rector drew the last bolt and opened the oak door.

Outside all was very dark. A brisk offshore wind was blowing, roaring in the invisible trees. He peered into the night, remembering vaguely that it was the new moon. His forehead furrowed and he opened his mouth to shout again, for he could see no sign of the man who had knocked at the door and interrupted his writing.

Then he looked down and saw the body on the doorstep, lying slumped almost at his feet. He saw too the blood, pooling darkly on the stone.

Frowning still, not yet fully comprehending what he was seeing, the rector knelt down for a closer look. That action saved his life. From the corner of his eye he saw a flash of light at the end of the garden, and in the same instant something tore the air just over his head, so close that he could almost feel it in his hair. From behind came the sound of shattering glass.

Instantly, the rector's mind was very clear. Someone had shot at him. He knew he had about thirty seconds before the invisible marksman reloaded and fired again. He seized the body by the shoulders and, with a strength that few would have guessed he possessed, dragged it into the hall, slammed the door shut and bolted it. Panting, he stood leaning against the door, listening for another shot or the sound of an intruder approaching the house. His own pistol was in the desk in his study; he wished he had had the forethought to collect it before answering the door.

The housekeeper stood at the far end of the hall, motionless, mouth wide open, holding a broken bottle. Her apron was covered in blood. No, not blood, port; the shot meant for his heart had instead smashed the bottle she was holding as she returned from the cellar. 'Reverend Hardcastle,' she whispered.

'Hush.' The rector held up a hand, still listening at the door. At first there was silence. Then another shot sounded, then two more in close succession; but these shots were fainter, more distant. The sound seemed to be coming from the east, towards the sea, and he thought at once: *smugglers*. The gunfire popped and crackled uneasily for about thirty seconds, then died away. Once again all was silent, save for the moaning wind.

Now the rector moved swiftly. He pulled the body into the middle of the hall and took down a lamp from the wall so he could see more clearly. The body was that of a man, young, not more than twenty or so. He was well dressed in a dun brown coat and breeches and darker brown waistcoat, the latter stained with the blood that still bubbled brightly from the hole in his chest.

'He breathes,' the housekeeper whispered. She had not moved from where she stood, but she could see the faint rise and fall of the shattered chest in the candlelight.

'Merciful heavens, so he does.' The rector knelt by the young man's head and saw that his eyes were open, and saw too that he was trying to speak. He bent still further, taking the man's hand in his and feeling a light fluttery pulse in his wrist.

'Lie still,' said the rector. 'We will send for help.' But even as he spoke he knew it was too late, the pulse was growing slower and fainter and the blood bubbled faster. There were smears of it on the floor where the body had lain when he first dragged it inside. He doubted if the young man even heard him. It was the latter's last moment of life, and still he strained to speak, yearning to pass a message to the stranger who leaned darkly over him.

'*Tell Peter*,' he breathed, his whispered voice only just audible. '*Tell Peter . . . mark . . . trace . . .*'

The young man exhaled once more and then lay still. His heartbeat flickered to a halt. The rector knelt for a moment longer, then very slowly and with great gentleness and compassion, lifted the man's lifeless hands and crossed them over his chest, hiding the wound that had ended his young life. Then he bowed his head, and, kneeling there on the blood-stained floor with the wind roaring outside, prayed softly for stranger's soul.

Don't miss the second Hardcastle and Chaytor mystery

THE
BODY
IN
THE ICE

**A twisting tale of murder, mystery and
eighteenth-century England**

On the frozen fields of Romney Marsh stands New Hall; silent,
lifeless, deserted. In its grounds lies an unexpected Christmas
offering: a corpse, frozen into the ice of a horse pond.

It falls to the Reverend Hardcastle, justice of the peace in
St Mary in the Marsh, to investigate. But with the victim's
identity unknown, no murder weapon and no known motive,
it seems like an impossible task. Working along with his
trusted friend, Amelia Chaytor, and new arrival Captain
Edward Austen, Hardcastle soon discovers there is more
to the mystery than there first appeared.

With the arrival of an American family torn apart by war
and desperate to reclaim their ancestral home, a French
spy returning to the scene of his crimes, ancient loyalties
and new vengeance combine to make Hardcastle and
Mrs Chaytor's attempts to discover the secret of
New Hall all the more dangerous . . .

Available in paperback and ebook now

Want to read
NEW BOOKS
before anyone else?

Like getting
FREE BOOKS?

Enjoy sharing your
OPINIONS?

Discover

**READERS
FIRST**

Read. Love. Share.

Sign up today to win your first free book:
readersfirst.co.uk